It's
Been
a
Pleasure,
Noni Blake

It's Been a Pleasure, Noni Blake

CLAIRE CHRISTIAN

mira

mira™

Recycling programs
for this product may
not exist in your area.

ISBN-13: 978-0-7783-3156-8

It's Been a Pleasure, Noni Blake

Copyright © 2021 by Claire Christian

This edition published by arrangement with Harlequin Books S.A.

For questions and comments about the quality of this book, please contact us at
CustomerService@Harlequin.com.

Mira
22 Adelaide St. West, 40th Floor
Toronto, Ontario M5H 4E3, Canada
BookClubbish.com

Printed in U.S.A.

Here's to you,
and doing whatever feels good.
Here's to you,
and all of your pleasure.

It's Been a Pleasure, Noni Blake

1

I hear the rumble of the garbage truck and my eyes jolt open. *Fuck*. I forgot to put the bins out. *Again*. Joan always put the bins out. I can count on one hand how many times I've remembered to put the bins out in the eighteen months since we broke up. When my eyes adjust to the light, I realize, however, that I have not missed bin day, because my bin day is Tuesday and it's not Tuesday morning, it's Monday morning, and I'm not in my own bed, I'm in the firefighter's bed. And I can't remember the firefighter's name. I can't remember the firefighter's name because for the past few weeks I've just called her the firefighter.

Oh my fucking god I had sex. I had sex with the firefighter. I had very good, very drunk sex with the firefighter.

The firefighter in question is sound asleep, her tousled bleach-blond hair spurting onto the pillow. I squeeze my eyes shut and clench my teeth and feel my insides squish in stunned delight. This is not how I thought yesterday would end up.

I had only agreed to go to the station's community barbecue because I wanted to drop off a carton of beer as a thank-you gift for the amazing presentations they'd done for my grade ten students. I mean, I liked the idea of seeing the firefighter. The two times I'd taken my students to the station for the car-safety presentations, I'd definitely caught myself staring at her when she wasn't looking and smiling awkwardly when she did glance my way. On the second visit, we'd spoken briefly about the unseasonably hot weather. But that was it. So I had not foreseen staying for a drink, nor that drink becoming many, many more drinks, leading to me attempting to flirt with the firefighter, trying my darndest to maintain a cool composure. Which I feel I navigated superbly right up until she asked me if I wanted to go home with her.

"Abso-fucking-lutely!" I'd said, high-pitched and way too eager.

I grab my temples, feeling a surge of embarrassment at the memory of her attempting to go down on me as I flailed about distracted by the fact that I was wearing giant beige undies.

What time is it? I need to find a clock. Or my phone. Where is my phone? I get up with such stealth and quiet precision that I pull a muscle in my neck. I wince in pain as I stalk through her apartment on my tiptoes, like a cartoon burglar stealing back my decency, as I bundle my things into my arms, trying to be as quiet as humanly possible. I look at the microwave: 5:53 a.m. *What do I do? Do I leave a note? Do I leave my number? Do I want to see the firefighter again? I don't think I do. Is that okay? Shit. I don't want to be rude.* I find a pen on her very tidy kitchen table and scrawl a note on the back of an envelope. *You're lovely*, I jot down and before I realize what I'm writing my hand autopilots: *Thank you.*

I look at it. Thank you? Thank you for having sex with me? Thank you for breaking my very long sexless over-two-year drought? Thank you for not being a weirdo? Thank you for the orgasms? Thank you in advance for reading this bizarre note and nodding in mutual agreement that this was a painless and relatively well-executed one-night stand? I sign my name, *Noni*, and add *xx* to suggest an illusion of cool about the whole thing. But I am not feeling cool. Not even a little bit. I mean, is leaving a note the correct etiquette in this day and age? I've had a few one-night stands before, but they were at the beginning of the millennium, and things have most definitely changed since then. The last time I had a one-night stand, people thought shrugs were a perfectly sound fashion choice.

A note, Noni? Really. Don't leave a note. I peer back into her bedroom to check that she's still asleep as I chuck my dress on over my head. I don't want to hurt her feelings. I don't want her to think she's been used, because that's not what last night was. *Was it?* I pick up the note and take two paces toward the door, before quickly spinning around and putting it back down.

Fuck it. I leave behind the note, along with any suspicions the firefighter may have had about my one-night-stand expertise, and begin the walk of shame. Only it's not shame I'm feeling, it's a sort of pride. This is a walk of pride. And gratitude. Gratitude for the firefighter, whom I want to thank for being a pillar of the community, both as someone whose job it is to run into flame-filled situations to ensure the safety of others, and as someone who saw fit to run into the metaphorical bushfire that was my sexless vagina. It really was the best kind of community service. The firefighter is a big deal. A big symbolic deal. First, I've discovered, contrary to my own concerns, that my vagina still works, and I do still very much have a propensity for getting laid. That this propensity also leads to getting laid by very attractive, very broad-shouldered firefighters is a very nice surprise.

★ ★ ★

Breakups are tough. Breakups from nine-year relationships, where there's a mortgage, a dog and a history, are a straight-up ferocious inferno of feelings. I've basically spent the whole of these last eighteen months putting on twenty-five pounds, dying my hair too dark, spending way too much money on therapy and vomiting all over myself in a hot yoga class. Twice. So, the firefighter is perhaps the symbol I need to confirm that I am finally ready to emerge from the microwave-meal-for-one, tracksuit-pant-clad chrysalis I've been living in, into a quasi-capable adult-looking woman who can fuck firefighters back into normalcy. *Yes!* I think as I wait for my Uber. *You've still got it, Noni!*

I call my best friend, Lindell, from the car on the way to work.

"Push one if you didn't go through with it so I don't need to enter into a conversation with you about why not, because it is Monday morning, and when I stepped out of the shower just now, Julius told me that my penis looks like a guinea pig, so I am counting on you to offer me some kind of vicarious tale that will reinvigorate my self-confidence."

I had texted Lindell multiple times last night with messages that suggested my cool and aloof approach to the unfolding events. Things like LINDELL I THINK THE FIREFIGHTER IS FLIRTING WITH ME WHAT DO I DO? and fucking shitting fuck I think I'm going to have sex and What if I can't remember how? and LINDELL IT'S HAPPENING I'M HIDING IN THE BATHROOM OKAY LINDELL I'M DOING IT GOOD GOD MY UNDIES ARE UGLY BUT SHE'S SO HOT.

I laugh loudly. "Your penis does not look like a guinea pig."

"Thank you for affirming that the taunts of the hilarious four-year-old are not true." He laughs his signature guffaw before stopping sharply. "Hang on, you didn't push one! What does that mean?"

"It means I had sex."

"Eu-bloody-reka! Was it good? Are you okay? How's your mental health? Did you cum? Do you feel good? I'm sorry, I'm a little manic this morning. I've had three coffees already and it's not even eight. How are you?"

I don't know how I feel. "I'm good. It was good. I'm okay. I feel a bit weird because I don't feel weird, you know? It was very…" I pause. "Normal."

"Did you leave your number?"

"No, but I left a note."

"What did it say?"

"Thank you."

Lindell's rapturous laugh erupts into my ear. "The reputable nature of your manners will never be in question, Noni." He breathes in deep before he asks, "Are you happy?"

"I think so," I say and I mean it. I haven't been able to distinguish any kind of feeling apart from numb for the longest time, but this feels good, this feels like an improvement.

"I am happy you think so," he says.

I feel calm, and this makes me anxious. I thought having sex for the first time since Joan would be a bigger deal. I thought the sex itself would be a bigger deal. But it wasn't, it was straightforward and good. It was good, and I was good at it. Probably too eager, if I'm honest. Once it was happening, it was like my body remembered something it had forgotten, and the need for it reverberated through me like a shook-up bottle of champagne. I don't think the firefighter minded, though. *Or did she?* It doesn't matter anyway because I'm never going to see her again. I mentally add the firefighter to my list of sexual dalliances. All ten of them. Or eleven, now.

PEOPLE NONI HAS HAD SEX WITH: A LIST

1. Jakob
2. Randall
3. Felicity
4. Noel
5. The British bartender
6. Othello
7. Debbie
8. Rachel
9. Charles
10. Joan
11. The firefighter

I lost my virginity when I was sixteen. I'm now thirty-six. I have been having sex for twenty years. If you divide my number of sexual partners by the number of years I've been having sex, it means I've had sex with an average of 0.55 people a year. There are about 7.5 billion people on the planet, and I've had sex with only eleven of them. This feels strangely depressing.

"Miss! How do you do question four?"

I have a grade eleven Maths B supervision. I look down at the worksheet and then back at the class, bleary-eyed. "I don't know," I tell them. "How about this. I have a lot of work to do on my laptop, yes?" The kids are curious. "So if it *looks* like you're working, I won't actually know that you're not working. Good?" Most kids get it and nod, pleased.

"So, do you know how to do question four or not?"

Kids groan and a water bottle gets thrown across the room. "Oh!" The kid mumbles as I tap my nose twice, just as Niko, the school principal, appears in the doorway. I am instantly flustered, not because he's a hard-ass, but rather because he has a hard ass and I find him desperately attractive. This crush is the kind that makes me incapable of basic human function while I stare intently at parts of his body when he's not looking. I stand up and walk over to him.

"Teaching math now?" he smiles. "Is there anything you can't do?" He's not wearing a tie today and a perfect tuft of gray hair is visible at the top of his unbuttoned shirt. Niko is tall, broad and a bit chubby. He has thick black hair and salt-and-pepper stubble, and he's about fifteen years older than me. He's a great boss, an excellent principal, fair, funny, committed to the kids and his staff. I am crushing hard. "I should've read the supervision sheet. I was just looking for Gary, but—"

"His kid sick." I can't even speak in full sentences. "Is sick," I add with a smile. "Apparently." *Oh, god, Noni! Shut up.*

"Right," he pauses. "Did you have a good weekend?"

"Yeah. Just…quiet. Nothing. Nothing out of the ordinary." A flash of the firefighter's tongue snaking its way up my thigh as my hand grabs at her hair smacks me in the face and I blush. "You?" I fumble.

He laughs. "Good. It was fine. Lots of paperwork."

"Ugh! Paperwork on the weekend? Bor-ing!" *What is wrong with me?!*

"Yeah. Great. Well, grade elevens, make sure you work hard for Ms. Blake, please," he offers with just the right amount of authority to make the grade elevens' butts clench and me swoon.

He leaves and I sit back down at the desk, wondering if he could tell that I'd recently had sex. Something must be different about me this morning. Like, surely I'm putting out some kind of sex pheromone, or a heightened energy or a look that reflects some newfound kind of intimacy. I must seem different. Surely. Because the most intimate relationship I've been in for the last eighteen months has been with my own loneliness. A relationship full of wishes, what-could've-beens, not doing laundry, crying randomly in the liquor store, letting my roots grow out a little too far—to the point where it was obviously not a style choice. Missing my dog and my previous life. It had been my choice for Carson, our sausage dog, to go and live with Joan—we said we'd have joint custody, but I can't deal with picking him up and dropping him off. It makes me too sad. Thinking about Joan makes the usual feelings arrive: an anxiety that starts in my toes, tidal waves in my stomach, constricts my throat and causes me to cling to the desk just so my body knows it's safe.

Beautiful Joan. I'd thought she was the love of my life. Joan and I had worked at the same school. She taught grade one, I taught senior grades. We became fast friends, but I was too scared to ask her if she was interested in women, so we hung out a lot. Just the two of us. Doing things that could very well be considered dates or, confusingly, just two really good friends hanging out. We went on for a long while like that, until one night at the staff Christmas party we both got really drunk and she kissed me. I was thrilled. Later that evening we proceeded to have really, really bad sex on her kitchen floor. The morning after she cooked me scrambled eggs and we agreed that it would be best for everyone involved if we went back to just being friends.

But very soon we fell into that strange territory of being in a pseudo-relationship with a friendship label and no sex. We'd hang out on weekends, sleep in the same bed, be each other's plus-one to events, both adamantly telling anyone who asked if we were a couple that we were very much just friends. Until one night Joan called bullshit on the whole thing.

"I am so madly in love you," she had yelled, frustrated with me, and us, and our refusal to admit what was really going on between us.

"Yeah, well, I'm madly in love with you too," I had stammered back.

Joan and I had so much sex in the next forty-eight-hour period that I had to ice my vagina.

We were together for nine years. We had sex only with each other for those nine years, and up until we broke up, I thought Joan was the only person I was going to have sex with for the rest of my life.

The week flies by so quickly that by Friday afternoon my brilliantly executed one-night stand feels like a lifetime ago, and the monotony of school and normal life has taken over.

"Have a good weekend, Miss." A tiny grade-seven kid waves at me.

"You too." I smile at kids as they walk through the school gates and jump onto buses. I see Niko in the distance and curse our school sun-safe policy because right now I'm the poster child for sun safety in the world's largest wide-brimmed hat. No teacher in the history of bus duty has ever looked cool in a wide-brimmed hat. Apart from Niko, that is, who swans down the fence line in a straw fedora looking like he's one cigar and a pair of boat shoes away from Havana. I, on the other hand, look matronly and secretive.

"Ms. Blake, happy Friday." Niko smiles as he gets to me.

"Thank you. I like your hat. It is, as the kids would say, spicy." *What the fuck are you saying, Noni?*

"Spicy?" Niko laughs. "Is that good?"

"Yes. Yes, that's very good."

A group of grade-ten boys walks past. "Spicy backpacks, gentlemen." Niko nods in their direction and the boys look confused. I laugh.

"Was that right?"

"Nailed it."

"So, big plans tonight?" he asks.

"Just dinner with friends. You?"

"Hanging out with my nephew."

"Oh, great. That'll be great."

"Yes." He smiles at me and I'm thankful for the shadow that my tentlike hat is casting over my face so he can't see my cheeks flush.

Niko waves to parents and kids as they walk past. His presence is effortless.

"Well, have a—" he stops, smiling mischievously "—spicy weekend, Noni." He dips his fedora as he walks off.

"Yeah. You too," I squeak.

2

Lindell is my person. I call him that because, as an adult woman nearing forty, saying he's my best friend feels immature, and also not nearly adequate enough to describe the impact he has on my life, nor the love I have for him.

We've been best friends since grade three. I was the new kid. I will forever be grateful that Lindell saw fit to sweep me up and look after me on that first day, when Emmanuel Smith was picking on me for being fat. Lindell saved the day then, and he's been saving my chubby ass ever since.

"Say goodnight," instructs Graham, Lindell's partner, with his hands propped on the shoulders of two children, steering them up a set of stairs with expert precision.

"Goodnight Aunty No-No!" they both squeal.

"Goodnight my darlings, I love you," I shout up to them, and they giggle the whole way up the stairs. When Audre started to talk, *no* was an easy word in her developing vocabulary, and she saw no reason to add the unnecessary *i* to the second *n* in my name, so I became Aunty Nono, and it stuck. "They're divine," I swoon.

"They are." Lindell smiles as he pops the cork on another bottle of prosecco. "I can't remember who came after Shakib and before Graham," he says as his head tips to his shoulder, lost in his own memory lane of sexual conquests. "I was post-grad." He stretches his arms above his head, deep in thought. Lindell's mum is Papua New Guinean and his dad is from four generations of Australian farming stock, making him all broad shoulders, afro hair and thick rural twang.

"Was it the double-barrel barrister?" I ask.

"Ooh! The barrister." His eyes light up as he fills my wine glass. "Yes! Mmm-hmm. Winterbottom-Smythe."

"Terrence."

"Terrence Winterbottom-Smythe," he says with a disappointed scowl. "What a wanker."

We'd been talking about the people we'd had sex with, after I'd filled him in on all the details of my encounter with the firefighter.

"Then who was it for you?" he asks.

"Europe."

"Oh, yes, all of that lush Europe boning. Except for that fuckwit bartender who straightened his hair with your hair straightener before he left."

"Marc with a *c*." I roll my eyes. "Gross."

Graham joins us again, heading to the fridge to get himself a beer.

"Are we still talking about our conquests?" he asks.

"Yes." Lindell nods. "Tell us your list."

"Mine is simple… Grace Ogilvie, some guy whose name I can't remember, Thomas, and then the love of my life."

Lindell's bottom lip puckers and he flutters his eyelashes

at me as we both wail sweetly in Graham's direction and he blushes slightly.

"What's his name?" Lindell jokes.

"Who?"

"The love of your life," Lindell and I say at the same time, laughing and shaking our heads at Graham's perpetual naivety.

"Can you please tell Graham about dehydrated Debbie?" Lindell says to me.

"Lindell," I say, rolling my eyes, but I know Lindell won't let up if I don't divulge. Graham looks at me curiously.

"I fucked a girl named Debbie on a Contiki tour and ended up in an Austrian hospital," I say quickly.

Grahams jaw flies open. "Wait! What?"

"Tell the whole story!" Lindell is laughing loudly.

"We had sex in a sauna, and I got dehydrated. Really dehydrated. On-a-drip-for-two-days dehydrated," I say, sipping from my glass. Lindell and Graham laugh as I shake my head, flashes of memory gripping me with embarrassment.

"And then things slowed down for both of us after that." Lindell looks at his own list.

"Yeah, well, you fell in love." I smile at him.

"You are welcome," says Graham, smiling too.

"I don't actually think this is the most interesting list anyway," I say.

"What do you mean?" Graham's beard is covered in the hummus that he's just plopped onto the kitchen island and smothered on a cracker.

"I think maybe there's actually a second list." I bite my lip and try to gauge their reactions. "Like, there's a companion list that sits next to this one."

"And what does this companion list capture, sweet girl?" Lindell is curious.

"The people who should be on the list, you know?" I smile.

"The missed opportunities. The ones that got away. Or maybe not even got away, just the ones that you never, but maybe would've liked to…" I search for the word. "Bone."

"A should-have-boned list?" Graham laughs.

"I love this idea." Lindell smirks and his lips purse mischievously.

"What's that face?" I ask.

"It's me diving into the archives of my past." He swills his wine around in his glass and then laughs to himself. "Do you remember Karl?"

"You loved him." I nod, excited.

"I did love him. Why didn't I ever have sex with him?"

"Because—" I stop. "I don't know. Why didn't you ever have sex with him?"

Lindell shrugs and I pour myself another glass of wine, the kind of pour where you'd be better off just drinking straight from the bottle rather than dirtying a glass.

"Who would be on your other list?" I ask Graham, and Lindell looks at him pointedly.

Graham thinks for a moment. "Malcolm Bennett is definitely on my other list." He smiles. "We were friends at uni and I was never brave enough to ask him out."

"Aw," says Lindell affectionately, picking up and kissing Graham's hand.

The three of us decide to write down our "should-have-boned" lists.

"Why is it easier for me to think of people for your could've-shagged list, Noni, than mine?" Lindell asks, looking at me.

"Because you had sex with the people you wanted to have sex with."

Lindell cackles. "I did, didn't I?"

"I, it would seem, did not." Graham looks down at his

own very long should-have-could-have-would-have list with a furrowed brow.

Lindell looks over his shoulder. "Oh, babe, that *is* a lot of names."

"I didn't realize I had such a sexually repressed past."

"I did have to make the first move."

"No, you didn't," Graham says, and Lindell raises his eyebrows at him. "Well, I made the second move," he concedes. Lindell raises his eyebrows higher. "I'm a very good cook," he adds. I laugh as Lindell wraps his arms around Graham's waist and kisses him on the cheek. I love the love they have for each other.

"Right, who have you got so far?" Graham says to me as he unwraps Lindell's hands from around his middle and turns and kisses him on the mouth, before pouring the last of the bottle into his glass.

"Okay, so there's the guy at the bottle shop, that barista girl at the café near school, my dentist, one guy from high school, a couple of people from uni…"

"Did you put Sonya on the list?"

"Who?"

"The one who was sooo in the closet it was frightening. Sandra? Sophie?"

"Celia?" I jot her name down.

"Celia." Lindell raises his glass as if he's toasting her.

"I wish I'd had sex with my high school English teacher," Graham offers nonchalantly.

"This is about realistic, possible hook-ups, not adolescent fantasies," says Lindell.

"Who said they were adolescent?" Graham raises his eyebrows.

Lindell laughs before turning back to me. "You could've shagged Ben."

"Yes." I nod. "I totally could've. I think. I think he would've?" I look questioningly at Lindell, who nods reassuringly.

"Ben?" Graham asks.

"Ben was the guy we scored pills off at uni," I say and Graham shakes his head, feigning disapproval but smiling.

"The two of them would always end up on the dance floor sharing lollipops and sucking face," says Lindell.

"Sounds romantic. And what were you doing while those two weren't having sex on the dance floor, my love?"

"Just impressing everyone with my killer moves." Lindell gets up and starts swaying his hips from side to side. "Like this."

"Be careful! These are the exact same moves that attracted me to you in the first place." Graham laughs.

I like Graham. He's the epitome of a good human: smart, considerate, polite, passionate, thoughtful and so loving. He has a complex finance-related job that I don't really understand and a penchant for football and feminist literature. He's Lindell's perfect man.

"There's Doug. I should've had sex with Doug," I say.

"My Doug?" Graham asks, and I nod. "You totally could've had sex with my Doug. Why didn't you?" He grabs my arm, serious.

"I don't know, we'd text for hours but neither of us ever quite got around to asking the other out."

"What? Why didn't I know this?" Graham is stunned. "You absolutely should've. I think he'd be great in bed."

"What are you basing that on?" Lindell says.

"Just a vibe."

"Is he single?"

"Married. Kids. Spends a ridiculous amount of time fishing," Graham says.

Lindell and I both turn our noses up in disgust. It's weird digging back through your memories and trying to actively search out the missed opportunities. It's making me feel an odd sense of nostalgia.

"Ooh, you know who else?" Lindell muses. "Jess."

"Yes. I remember Jess." Graham nods, impressed with himself. "She loved you."

"She didn't." I shake my head.

"*I think you're perfect, Noni,*" Lindell mimics Jess. "That's what she sent you that night, remember?"

"I wonder what would've happened if either of us had just gone for it. We got along so well, and we'd go on these perfect dates, and every time I'd wait for her to make a move and she never did. So, I never did." We pause for a moment, like a ten-second silence is appropriate to honor what could've been.

"There was that girl who moved to Melbourne," Lindell adds, after a moment.

"Yes." I nod.

"And there's Molly." I know he's watching my face to see how I'll react.

I bite my lip at the mention of her name. "I knew you'd bring her up."

"I knew you wouldn't bring her up." He stares at me, smiling. "What's she doing?"

"She's overseas, managing a bunch of backpacker hostels all over Europe."

"Who's Molly?" Graham asks.

"Molly is quite possibly the one that got away." Lindell sculls his wine.

"No, she's not."

"How would you describe her, then?"

"I dunno. Our timing was never quite right."

I look down at my list. Molly should technically appear after each of the names I've added so far. We grew up together, except she was two years younger than me. We both did debating, and we had expert banter. She's one of the funniest people I know. When I finished school, she wrote a vague note in my yearbook that said: *"You. Me. You and Me. If only things were different…"*

Years later, we were both at the same party and we ended up having an intensely passionate kiss. It was one of the best kisses of my life—the kind of kiss that feels like so much more than just lips pressed against each other. The kiss had history, possibility, passion and bellies full of cheap beer and abandon swirling around in it all at once. That night we went back to my place and she held my face in her hands and said, "Let's wait. Let's wait until we're sober."

"Okay," I told her.

"I really, really like you, Noni. We don't have to rush, do we?" I shook my head, and we fell asleep in each other's arms. And when we woke up the next day, it was like she'd forgotten about it all, or at least she pretended like she did, and so did I, and so life resumed as normal.

Every now and then we'd text each other these long, glorious, flirtatious exchanges and agree to meet up. But then we never did. We lived in different cities and we each had different priorities. Our lives would simply move on like nothing had happened. Each time we saw each other, we'd end up in bed, but we never had sex. This happened four times in total and every time she'd say she wanted to wait. I assumed it was because she was a virgin.

When I was in Europe, sometimes she'd text or call me at night, but it'd be my morning. She'd leave me incredibly romantic but very drunken voice mails, or I'd wake up to sweet texts.

I'll wait for you.

That's what she'd texted me. I'd stood in the middle of Marks and Spencer at 9:00 a.m., reading it over and over again, feeling amazed that there was a woman halfway around the world who wanted to wait for me.

But not long enough.

When I got home, we tried one more time to make it happen, but she got so drunk she passed out.

And then I met Joan.

3

The following day, Lindell and I wander through the park as the kids ride their scooters ahead of us. I sip my coffee and smile as three elderly women in activewear power walk past us chatting loudly.

"All three of those women had camel toes," Lindell says.

"I think they were fully aware, they just didn't give a shit." I giggle. "Why don't they tell us that that's what aging is actually about?"

"Camel toes?"

"Not caring about camel toes."

"It's 'cause the goddamned patriarchy is a—" He stops and shouts across the park, "Audre, if you take that helmet off again, I swear to god I will superglue it to your head. Do you hear me?"

Audre stops and stares at us. Lindell has now ceased parenting with his voice and instead his body does all of the parenting for him, and he means business. Audre knows this, too, because she whacks her helmet onto her head and gives us a thumbs-up with a grin. I laugh and Lindell shakes his head, smiling.

"That kid, she's wild and she does whatever she wants. As a human, I love that about her, but as her parent..." He sighs, shaking his head before he smiles. "I hope she doesn't lose that."

"She won't. Look at you."

"Yeah, but we all lose it, Nons. We have to, that's what our adolescence is for."

"And our twenties."

"And our thirties, for some of us." He looks at me pointedly and pokes my arm.

"Shut up. I've gotten better."

"You have."

"I genuinely give fewer shits now. But can you imagine what my life would've been like if I was the woman I am right now in my twenties?" I let that really sink in. "Everything would be completely different."

"Oh, god!" He laughs. "Can you imagine if I was the person I am now in my twenties? It would've been fucking disastrous." He pulls an amused face and I laugh loudly. "I think aging is actually just about getting used to yourself, you know? Getting used to the way you are, the way you work, the way you process things, the weird things that make you unique. I think we spend so much time early on figuring that out." He stops for a moment. "Or fighting against it."

We sit on a bench at the edge of the playground. The kids are already at the top of a rope pyramid, laughing at each other.

"I don't hate myself like I did back then," I tell him.

"I'm glad, because thirty-six years is an exhaustingly long time to hate something, Nons."

I smile. "And no matter how much I try, I just can't seem to get away from myself. Or you for that matter."

"Yes, you're stuck with both of us." He nudges me and I smile. We watch the kids play. Julius gets to the top of the rope pyramid and stands on the ledge, dancing for us. We cheer.

"I think the stakes lessen and we just give fewer fucks," Lindell says. "And if we feel this way now, imagine how we're going to feel in our fifties?"

What an amazing thought. "I can't wait to wear my camel toe with pride in a park with you," I tell him.

"It'll be whole sack out for me, babe, and I can't bloody wait either." Lindell laughs and I snort so loudly the kids look over at us quizzically.

I think about this conversation for the rest of the day. I think about it while I run boring life errands like getting the car washed and navigating the complicated task of trying to sustainably food-shop for one. I think about it while I sit on my couch, eating a cheese platter for lunch. I call it a cheese platter so it feels sophisticated, but it's actually just a wheel of cheese, a box of crackers and an apple I don't cut. I don't even use a plate. I think about it while watching a shitty romantic comedy instead of doing the three loads of laundry that need to be done. And as I think about it, I realize that the biggest thing that has happened to me as I've gotten older is that I've started to shut up and listen to that voice, that instinct, that knows best. It was that voice that told me repeatedly for years that Joan and I were over. It was that voice that told me to finally go to therapy instead of crying on Lindell's couch every night. It told me to own up to my mistakes and it told me to cut myself some slack. It told me to have sex with the firefighter. The voice isn't new. It's always been there. I think I've just finally started listening to it. I don't regret anything that has happened in my life, except maybe that I was a shitty listener. And I can't help but wonder what would've happened, what choices I would've made, what heartache I would've avoided, what things I would've said if I'd just listened. That same voice is now telling me to take everything that Lindell and I have discussed and at least try. It is telling me to find the people on the list.

I grab a pen and write down the names on my "should've boned" list again.

1. **Bottle-shop guy**
2. **Barista girl**
3. **Dentist**
4. **Ray from high school**
5. **Closeted Celia**
6 **Ben**
7 **Doug**

Next to Doug's name I write *married and into fishing*, as the ultimate deterrents.

8. **Jess**
9. **Melbourne girl**
10. **Molly**

I stare at it. I could have sex with these people. Some of these people. Leaving room for the statistical probability that some of them are in new relationships, or just not interested in having sex with me anymore, I could absolutely go back and right at least some of the wrongs of my past. Be the woman I wish I was then, that I think I am now. Live out some of my lavish fantasies. I could have my own mini, very structured, very safe, pseudo-time-travel sexual revolution.

I grab my laptop. *Fuck it.* There's no harm in doing some research, is there?

★ ★ ★

Within two hours my research has turned me into a Post-it-wielding, mystery-solving, tangled-in-red-wool, no-one-can-come-into-my-lounge-room, stalker-level wild woman. I know who has moved away, who is married, who has kids, who is divorced, who is living overseas. I've gone down a long and winding social-media rabbit hole reading posts by ex-partners and friends about pregnancy announcements, gastric bypass surgery and new jobs. I've become way too deeply invested in Jess's cousin's small business venture, having read twelve months' worth of posts about her "journey" and her dream to open a brownie bakery.

This all feels very out of character. I'm not someone who participates in sexual revolutions. I'm a blusher—my cheeks go bright pink at the mention of promiscuity. It took me years before I could maintain eye contact with, well, anyone. I've never been able to sleep in the nude. I get embarrassed easily, and the idea of possibly being caught out naked in the middle of the night is enough to give me anxiety. I religiously take a probiotic, and I always wee after sex because I've been told it's good for me. I don't like answering the phone. I have monthly subscriptions to things I never use because the only way you can cancel them is via a phone call. I once considered using the service that deaf and hard-of-hearing people use where someone else makes their phone calls for them, but then the fact that I was even considering that made me feel like a terrible person, and I had a panic attack and donated $200 to the Guide Dog Association. Which quickly prompted another panic attack, because I realized guide dogs have nothing to do with deafness, and I felt awful for being so insensitive to the disability community. I can easily spiral like this. I watch those documentaries about animals and sugar and empathy and the chemicals in plastics and manifesting your desires and

I get sucked in and vow that I'm going to change my life and be better, but within hours I'm sucking up caffeinated sugar-stacked beverages through a plastic straw, eating a doughnut and using all of my supposed power to manifest a car park close to the entrance of the shops because I don't want to walk too far. I am all for wild ambition but it's just not me. Not really.

I ponder all of this while in the car driving the ninety-minute round trip to buy brownies from Jess's cousin's brownie bakery because that feels like the right thing to do. I stare a little too intently at her when she asks me for my order, and after I tell her, I add, "I think you're amazing. All of this—" I look around the shop feeling quite emotional about her achievements that I feel deeply invested in now too. "It's so impressive. Inspiring, even."

Jess's cousin looks confused by my gushing and says, "Oh, thanks?" I leave immediately.

Then, when I'm back on my couch eating from the box of the four brownies having just about convinced myself the whole thing is a fucking joke that I will never, ever share with anyone, ever, I find Ben. The dance-floor drug dealer from my early twenties. Ben still lives locally, and he seems to be single and relatively normal. It looks like he travels a bit, and he's bought a really nice house that he's renovating. I wonder if his getting a message from me out of the blue is weird and I worry about what he'll think. My stomach sloshes with giddy nerves and I talk to myself as I pace around my living room.

Just message him. You have nothing to lose. What's the worst thing that could happen? He says no. You can deal with a no. Just message him, Noni. Do it.

So I do.

4

"Shit, ay, Nons. It's been years." Ben has a loud voice and giant arm muscles. He hugs me a little too hard.

"Yeah" is all I manage to get out before he starts talking over the top of me.

"Yeah, I was surprised when you messaged, like, holy shit, is this chick going to tell me I've got some ten-year-old kid or something."

"What? No." I shake my head.

"Was a joke."

"Of course."

"We never fucked," he says. "Or did we? Can't really 'member, ay? Wild fuckin' times back then, yeah?"

"We didn't, no." I shake my head. "It'd be a miracle child, that's for sure," I joke. "Like Jesus." *Fucking hell.* I finish my wine in one gulp.

"Oh, shit, you religious now? I'm not really into that stuff, ay."

"Into what?"

"The Bible and that."

"Oh." I laugh. "No, it was a joke—the kid, you said there was a kid. Don't worry."

OH MY GOD, WHAT AM I DOING?! This is painful. Maybe he's just nervous. It's been a long time. Surely we'll find a rhythm and it'll be fine. I remind myself of the plan. He's handsome. All square jaw and big shoulders, like a rugby player. He has stubble the same length as his shaved head, and I stare at the uneven outline that frames his forehead and face. *You can do this, Noni. You can have sex. No strings attached. The Plan. The List. Yes.*

"Another one?" he asks, looking at my empty glass.

I nod. "Gin."

"Ooh, fancy." He smiles and I try to smile in a way that doesn't give away my trepidation.

Ben and I awkwardly navigate our way through two more drinks, catching up on over ten years of our very separate lives. After we cover humorous memories and mutual acquaintances, he finally asks me about myself.

"So, what do you do with yourself?"

"I'm a teacher."

"Teacher. Shit. Good holidays, teaching. I thought about teaching but…I hate kids." He starts laughing hysterically.

"Mmm. What about you?" I ask.

"I'm between things at the moment. Was out on the mines for a bit, made some money and invested it into some pretty slick opportunities." He raises his eyebrows at me like I'm meant to be impressed.

How did I ever find this man attractive? Ecstasy. Ecstasy is the answer. But still. We baffle our way through another round of drinks while he tells me about trips he's taken, shows me photos of him standing with drugged-out tigers, dressed in beer-logo tees, and smiling in war memorials, and I am floored. For many reasons. Mostly because his life still resembles the one we had when we were twenty-three: pills, drinking, dancing, casual work. *Was he always like this?*

There is an awkward pause. I know I should try to fill it but I don't know what to say. I stare at Ben's stubbly chin and two thoughts collide in my brain at once:

1. At least he's handsome, the sex might not be that bad.

And…

2. We have zero chemistry.

"You're really beautiful, you know that?" he says.

"Oh, wow. Thank you," I mutter, flattered. Ben attaches himself to my neck. I grab his shoulders to stop myself falling off the chair.

"Good, huh?" He smiles sloppily.

Before I answer, his mouth collides with my mouth and I kiss him back. He's a good kisser. I remember that about him. But we don't really sync. It's like our preferred paces no longer match. It's fine, but not great. I pull away.

"Wanna come back to mine?" he asks.

Say no, Noni. Say No. "Sure," I reply.

He gets two beers out of his fridge, bumping the lids on the edge of his table. I drink mine quickly, looking around Ben's place. There's a stack of rum-and-Coke cans piled high in a pyramid in the corner of the room, a football flag pinned to the wall, and cat hair all over his carpet. Clumps of cat hair. I sit on the couch and watch him as he fiddles with his speaker and phone.

"I've made this killer fucking playlist," he says.

"Great." I smile, drinking large glugs of beer. Loud rock music blares, and he turns, smiling, and does the devil-horn hand gesture. *Leave, Noni. Just leave. You don't have to go through with this.* He sits next to me, smiling, then grabs my face in his large hand and kisses me. We struggle to find a rhythm sitting next to each other, and so I move to straddle him, thinking that will help, but his thighs are wide, and so are mine, and I can't quite get comfortable on his lap. I hold his face in my hands, trying to take control of the kiss, trying to show him what I like, and he gets the message because it starts to get better. He wraps his arms around my waist, pulling me into him, and I feel good, turned on, even.

He pulls back. "Want to go to my room?"

"Sure."

There's a pile of dirty high-vis shirts on the floor and no sheet on his bed. He lies down, patting the mattress twice to indicate for me to join him. I lie down and he kisses me, running his fingers lightly up the side of my stomach and ribs, and it feels nice. He kisses my neck. *See? This will be fine. You were just overreacting. You were nervous. This is fine. This is good.* But then Ben jumps up. "I'm going to get naked now," he says, standing at the side of the bed, and I stare at him. *Really? That's weird. What's he doing? Surely we could undress each other.* But fine. Okay. I awkwardly undress myself and stare at him as he kneels over me on the bed, naked.

"Can I go down on you?" he asks.

"Um. Sure. Yeah. Okay." At least he asked, I guess. At least he's into going down on girls. But then he attacks my entire vulva with his whole tongue and the sensation makes my eyes bulge. I grab his head, attempting to steer. But he takes this to mean he's doing a good job and begins a more targeted approach. He manages to find my clitoris and I moan. *Good. This is good. Good work, Ben. Keep doing exactly what you're doing.* But he's not there for longer than thirty seconds before he changes tack completely and starts licking quick and fast, before he shakes his head like a dog with a chew toy. I push his head back, trying not to laugh at the sensation and at his audacity. I pull him toward me, as this needs to end, immediately.

He kisses my stomach and looks at me. "Was that good?" He's so impressed with himself.

"Yes. Yeah." I nod. He kisses my mouth and then rolls onto his side, staring at his crotch.

"Oh, shit, ay, he's gone to sleep."

I stare at his flaccid penis, and then at his face. "That's okay, I mean, let's just make out and—" I can't think of what to say. "Hope for the best…" is what comes out and I'm instantly mortified.

"You could help him out," he says.

Why is he calling it a him? "Oh, really, what—what does he—what do you—like?" I ask and he grabs my hand and puts it on his dick.

"Touching. Sucking." The word *sucking* makes my vagina want to retract in on itself, but I smile.

"Sure." I straddle him, kissing his neck, his chest, biting his nipples. This is good. I like this. I like being in charge. I like making other people feel good. I like the feeling I get when he moans with pleasure. I kiss across his stomach, lightly breathing in the direction of his penis, praying he'll get hard. I kiss down his thighs, while using one hand to try to pump some fucking life into the situation. I really don't want to put my mouth anywhere near his penis. It's been a long time since I've been anywhere near a penis. I'm worried I've forgotten how. But I quickly realize it's all relatively straightforward, like riding a bike, or maybe more like pumping up a bike tire.

This thought makes me laugh, but thankfully it is covered by Ben moaning, "Oh, fuck yeah."

I hide my head in his thigh and roll my eyes. *Come on, Ben.* I use my tongue with the smallest amount of effort and keep my hand doing what it's doing. *Real life penises aren't that robust, are they?* I mean compared to the plastic, vibrating penis-shaped objects I'd enjoyed for a decade. They're far more veiny than I remember too. Ugly, really.

When he's hard, he looks at me through squinting eyes and says, "You woke him up."

"Well, I was determined," I say. *Fucking hell, Noni.* "Put a condom on," I tell him, and he does. With the enthusiastic verve of a teenage boy. I decide that I'll ride him because then at least this might be over quickly.

And it is.

"S'pose you're one of those women who like to cuddle, so here." He points at his chest and looks at me with a kind of smugness that suggests he thinks he's mastered the female species.

"No, I'm fine." I smile, laying my head back on the pillow.

He yawns and I try desperately to think of something to say, but I come up with nothing, so I point to the door and tiptoe out to the bathroom, picking up my underwear on the way.

What was that? What is this? I sit on the toilet trying to catch my breath. The plan. The stupid fucking list. The ridiculous notion that this would somehow prove that I'd changed. I'm frozen on the toilet. My mind racing. *What are you doing? Should I stay? Do I have to stay? I don't want to stay.* And then loudly and clearly the word *leave* drowns out everything else. I instantly feel anxious. My heart races. *What am I going to say to him? He'll think I'm weird.* I stand up. *It doesn't matter what he thinks of me*, the voice says. *I don't owe Ben anything.* Besides, he might prefer it if I leave. Surely. We both knew what this was, didn't we? My hands feel strange; I open and close them over and over, trying to get the blood to flow. *Should I leave? What if no one ever finds me attractive again?* And there it is. The honesty stings, but it propels me out of the bathroom, because I'd rather be real with Ben than deal with my own honesty.

"So," I say. "You're probably really tired, so, I'm gonna go." I look around the filthy floor for my clothes.

"Oh, really? You don't wanna—"

"What? I can if you want—if that's—" I mumble, but I continue to get dressed.

"Nah, yeah, go. That's cool. I hate sleeping with other people anyway, so that's good."

"Good." I get dressed and try to appear casual.

"I don't normally fuck fat chicks, but that was good, ay," he says with a thoughtful nod.

I stare at him. "What?"

He looks at me. "That was a compliment. Take it as a compliment. I'm saying that was good."

"That was—" I pause. He still has the condom on and it's dangling on his flaccid penis as he talks, which I'm finding incredibly distracting.

"We should do this again, yeah?"

I sigh loudly, the disbelief and disappointment so thick in my body that it escapes involuntarily. *What the fuck am I doing?* I'm shocked by my own stupidity, and his, too, but mostly my own. "You are—nope. This isn't gonna happen again," I say, shaking my head.

"What? Why not?" He seems genuinely surprised.

"'Cause you have a Southern Cross tattoo," I spit, and walk out the door.

"What?" I hear him mumble, but I've already grabbed my bag and am slamming his door shut. I march onto the street, weirdly electric, sad and confused. *What a fucking idiot.* I don't know whether I mean Ben or me. Maybe both of us. I walk down to the main street as a cab drives past. I hail it and jump straight in.

I have always been somewhat surprised that people like me. Like that. That people want to have sex with me, are attracted to me. I don't feel likable in that way. I have a list, a long list, of the things that I think are wrong with me, and with my body. *Why did I just do that?* Because it was nice to be wanted. Joan and I were together for so long that a lot of my insecurities got hidden away, in the comfort of a long-term relationship. I thought I'd dealt with it. Changed. Grown up. But turns out I was wrong. *Because no one is ever gonna like you again, let alone love you again? Joan was a fluke and you fucked that up. You don't get a chance like that again, Noni. It's done. You're going to be alone forever. You're too fat. Too plain. So, take it while you can get it. You should message Ben and apologize. How dare you leave? How rude. How entitled. You're lucky he wanted to fuck you. You're not exciting at all. What's so special about you? You're entirely unlikable. Unfuckable.*

I think I am unfuckable. I feel like I've been punched in the gut. I know these thoughts are stupid, and I've done enough therapy to know all about my inner critic. But fuck, it's brutal. My eyes well.

"You good, love?" the taxi driver asks, staring at me in the rearview mirror. I nod. I feel stupid for thinking I could go through with this plan. It's just not me. *What was any of this going to prove? What did I really think was going to happen?* It was just one of those Friday night wine ideas that should've been thrown in the bin along with the empty bottles. Past Noni didn't have sex with Ben because, clearly, he's an asshole. It didn't happen because it wasn't meant to happen. I feel like an idiot for thinking diving into my past would change anything about the present.

★ ★ ★

I go straight home and stand in the shower, feeling exposed and woozy from the alcohol and the revelations. I'm disappointed. When I left the house, I'd felt nervous and excited, like things could change. Like I could be different. Like I could act on whims and be a sexy woman. *But I haven't changed at all.* I sit on the floor of the shower and let the water run down my spine, my elbows on my knees and my head in my hands. *I can't believe I let that happen.*

I wrap myself in a towel and glance at my phone. There's a message from Lindell.

So? it says.

I reply quickly. He's a dickhead.
I'm a dickhead.
Plan is in the bin.
It was a dumb idea. Sorry.

Sorry?
Why are you sorry?
Are you okay?

I lie on my bed. *Am I okay?* Yeah. I feel disappointed and embarrassed and stupid. But I'm okay. Yes, I reply. I don't want to explain to Lindell what happened, not yet. I already know what he'll say. He'll tell me I'm amazing, and that I should've followed my instincts, and then he'll talk long and pointedly with linguistic flair about what a giant fucking idiot Ben is. I already know all of this, so I don't need him to tell me. I just want to wallow for a little bit.

Just disappointed.
My life is destined
to be boring and
predictable, I text.
Oh, and sexless.

It's probably true, because I'm never doing that again. I'm not going to put myself in that situation again. The three little dots appear, and then disappear, and then appear again. I wait for a long Lindell lecture.

If you're unhappy
with your boring,
predictable, sexless life,
then do something
about it is all he says.

I shake my head. I tried to do something and I fucking failed, miserably. Never again. Then there's another message:

How do you want
to feel, Noni?

I start to type a reply about four thousand times but I delete them all. *How do I want to feel?* I don't even know.

5

By Monday lunch I'm still in a daze. I'd spent the rest of Sunday tired, hiding and hungover. I'd stayed in my pajamas all day and left the house only to go to the McDonald's drive-through. The whole drive I cursed the happy families on their way to their Sunday activities, the couples looking deeply satisfied from their morning sex and coffee, people with plans and places to be. Lindell's question had been running over and over in my head all day and I kept pushing it away, unsure how to answer it. My shit mood had carried over to Monday and I'd unnecessarily made a girl in grade nine cry by being too hard on her and threatening to expel her, even though I had no intention of doing that. I felt awful.

"Did you read about that fire?" Colin asks as he forks a tin of tuna in the staff room. I try to hide my disgust, even though I'm appalled at him for eating fish in an enclosed space.

"No. What?" I say.

"It's there in the paper. Big industrial fire—something collapsed, two firefighters in the hospital and one died." My stomach lurches as I lunge for the paper and there she is on the front page. My firefighter. Dead.

"It's terrible, hey?" says Colin, still chewing unconcernedly.

I open my mouth but no sound comes out. I just look at her face staring back at me. She was thirty-six too. My age. Fuck. I don't know what to do. *My firefighter.*

"You all right, Noni?"

"I don't… I knew her. She…she was at the station with the kids on the—"

Colin looks up from his tuna. "I'm sorry. Were you close?"

I shake my head, and a flash of us in her bed, giggling, flashes into my mind. I read the article. *Ruby.*

The firefighter's name was Ruby.

A few years earlier, Joan and I had a friend, Xavier, who had a brain aneurysm and died. Just like that. He was making crumpets for his boyfriend in their kitchen one morning and he just fell down.

Dead.

Crumpets.

Fuck.

At his funeral people talked about the way Xavier had lived his life. They said that he had achieved so much, traveled so far, that he was constantly learning new things, pushing his body, challenging himself, inspiring others. That he had loved and been loved. And they said that knowing all this made this one shitty random anomaly slightly easier to comprehend— because he had lived his life well.

Joan and I were rattled. We talked about it a lot. For the next few months all of our conversations would manage to find their way back to Xavier. To what happened to him. So we booked flights to Thailand and climbed a mountain, danced on beaches, had loud sex and marveled at beautiful landscapes and we promised that we'd live our lives better in order to honor our friend.

It's so fucked up that it takes a tragedy to make us act—to put what is most important into perspective. But do you know what's shittier? That eventually monotony settles on top of the grief and you get consumed by routine and bills and all the unimportant details until that new drive you felt gets pushed down deep. It's present, but it never feels as urgent as in the immediate moment after the tragedy. You forget about the way you wanted to live your life, you push aside your good intent.

By the time I get home from supervising the school debating team, I'm completely drained and can't believe only twelve hours have passed since I left. It feels like a lifetime. I head to the fridge, knowing that the only things in there are half a bottle of Gatorade, some off milk, a soggy apple and some yogurt that has far too much sugar in it to be healthy. I grab the yogurt and sit on the couch, and I sob. I feel weird for feeling so upset because I barely knew Ruby. I know very little about her. Surely, tears should be reserved for people who know more than what she did for a living, that she was neat and she was great in bed. She died. She's dead.

I wonder what people would say about me if I just dropped down dead in my lounge room right now.

> *Noni was nice.*
> *Constant.*
> *A good friend.*
> *She did some stuff.*
> *Worked hard.*
> *Um.*
> *Which one was Noni?*

Oh, her?
Oh, I didn't really know her very well.
She was a six if she wore makeup.

This makes me cry more. This imagined summary feels devastating. I want people to say more than this.

Then I notice the hastily scrawled should've-boned list on the floor under the coffee table. I grab it, and with thoughts of aneurysms, firefighters named Ruby and my own mortality swirling wildly, I know what I have to do.

I pace around my tiny kitchen, giving myself a pep talk worthy of the climactic moment in a sports movie. *This is our moment. Our moment to defy the odds and rise above the adversity of missed opportunity. We need to take our future into our hands and be proactive. We can.*

"I can!" I holler. My voice booms weirdly in my quiet apartment.

I pick up my phone and start to type.

Hey. I delete it.

Molly! Hi. I delete it—too many exclamation marks.

So... Weird. Don't send that.

A joke maybe? But I don't know any good jokes. Or a topical reference? I could ask her about that thing that was all over the news. Closer. A personal joke. Something that will make her smile. Good. Something that lets her know that you're thinking about her. We once watched *Labyrinth* in a hungover stupor. We laughed about Bowie's impressive codpiece and said that all we could ever hope for in life was to find someone as supportive of our dreams as that codpiece.

Labyrinth is on, I lie. **And I'm once again left with a lot of feelings. Like, could I pull off a ruffled sleeve?** Funny. Reminiscent. Asking a question so she has to answer. Well, if she wants to. Good, I think this is good.

So why am I not hitting Send?

Because what if it's another complete disaster? I might make a fool of myself and end up looking like a complete idiot... again. Doing this may disrupt the very comfortable fabric of my life. And that's petrifying, because I'm very comfortable here. I know how things work. How I work. I'm happy being relatively unhappy.

The realization stuns me. *I'm happy being unhappy.* The tears quickly well. *I'm happy being unhappy.* I don't want to be happy being unhappy. I want to be happy.

"Fuuuck!" I yell as I hit Send.

6

The fluro lights are bright, which amplifies the general air of frustration emanating from the throngs of people wandering the enormous mazelike shopping center. No one looks good under fluro lights. Molly hasn't replied. She hasn't even read the message. I've checked pretty much hourly, but no change. When I'm not thinking about Molly and the fact she hasn't replied, I'm thinking about Ben and that whole stupid night, or thinking about Ruby, the firefighter. I'm thinking that I don't want to die amid the flames of my boring, predictable, sexless life and that I've got to do something about it. But what? Deep-diving into the should-have-would-have-could-haves of my past doesn't feel right anymore.

I walk past one of those shops where everything is tight and busty and vintage looking and the staff look like pinup girls. Straight-up bombshells. A skirt catches my eye and I take two steps inside before a woman swoops in on me. "Can I help you with anything?"

"Maybe a pencil skirt. But I don't know. I've never had one. I thought maybe—can I try one on? Will it even fit me? Your sizes, I mean?"

I've always, always wanted to wear a pencil skirt. Always. I don't wear anything tight. I'm too desperately insecure about my bumps and people seeing them. But maybe I can start with a skirt?

"Of course, doll. Shall I get you a few to see what you like?"

Within minutes she's back with a handful of skirts. I try the first one on and I hate it. I don't even need to go out and look in the mirror to know it's not for me. I hate when there isn't a mirror inside the change room. I know it's a bullshit sales technique, but I'm pretty sure it makes insecure women less likely to buy, not more. I try on the second skirt and it zips up with ease, but it's tight, black and simple, with a flared hem. I go out hesitantly, praying that there's no one around. But the girl is ready for me and she pounces. I like her. She's wearing bright red lipstick and her enormous boobs perch perfectly out of the top of her tight dress. We're roughly the same size, and I think she's gorgeous. But I'd never be confident enough to wear a dress like that. *Or would I?*

"Doll. Yes." She smiles wide.

"No." I look in the mirror and all I see is my stomach paunch. "What about this bit?" I say, pointing to it.

"Your stomach?" She looks at me with her eyebrows raised. "Everyone has one, doll."

"Yeah, but—"

She interrupts. "If you're not comfortable, then take it off, 'cause you're never going to wear it if you're not comfortable. But let me get you something else." She trots away and I pull the curtain closed, take off the skirt and stand in my stretched, baggy, used-to-be-lilac-but-are-now-a-weird-gray-color cotton fuller-than-full-brief undies. She hands in another skirt.

"Try that. It's got a peplum waist."

"A what?" I have no idea what she's talking about, but I try it on. It sits high on me and I discover a peplum waist is like a longish frill kind of thing that flares and sits at the top of my hips. The skirt is tight and hits above my knees with a slit at the back. I walk out and look in the mirror. And… I don't hate it.

The girl plops a pair of kitten heels at my feet. "Just stand in those—watch what happens to your legs."

I look at her, expecting some kind of magic trick, which it sort of is, because in the mirror I look longer, curvier. You can see the slide of my waist into my hip and into my leg.

Holy shit. I look like a bombshell.

"Doll, if you don't buy that skirt, you're an idiot," she says.

I laugh, "Okay."

So, I buy it. I buy it because I want it, because I felt good when I looked at myself in it in the mirror. The pencil skirt acts like a can of petrol on a tiny fire and I walk out of the shop and straight into a hairdresser.

Jools is vibrant. All full-sleeve tattoos, pink hair and a no-bullshit vibe. I like her instantly. I can tell that she doesn't care what people think, but that she cares about people. Jools is the kind of woman I want to be.

"So, what do you want to do?" She beams brightly. I have two photos of haircuts saved in my phone. I show her the first, which is a slight riff on what I already have—shoulder length, brown, with a long side-swept fringe—a haircut that hides the roundness of my jaw. Sensible.

I show Jools. "Yeah, cute," she says unenthusiastically. We get talking, and somewhere around her massaging my head at the basin, I tell her about the should've-boned list. It all kind of bubbles out of me, and I feel a certain thrill as she stands staring at me, mouth agape, eyes wild with awe.

"This is fucking excellent." She repeats every syllable. "Fuck-ing-ex-cel-lent." She cackles joyously. "We don't prioritize ourselves enough, babe—we're so worried about what other people will think. But it's such a liberation when you stop giving a flying fuck." Then she tilts her head to the side and I'm pretty sure she looks directly into my soul. "What do you actually want to do with your hair?" she says and I smile.

The second picture, which I've had saved on my phone for years, is a short blond pixie cut. I've never been brave enough to show anyone, not even Lindell, in case they affirmed my worry that it'd look dumb on me.

"Well—" I say, swallowing hard and scrolling through my pictures. I hold the phone close to my chest. "I've always wanted to, maybe, do something… I was thinking that this could…" I show her the pixie cut.

She actually leaps in the air with a squeal. "This. We're doing this. Yes? Fuck it. Right?"

Oh, god. "Yes?" I ask, but I'm nodding.

"Absolutely, this is going to look amazing."

"You don't think my face is too round?" I whimper.

Jools looks like she's going to kill me with kindness. "Do you want this hair cut?"

"Yes."

"Then that's all that matters."

"Really?"

"Yeah, babe." She bundles my hair into a ponytail and with a snip it's gone. There's no backing out now. I feel immediately lighter—physically and metaphorically. She gets to work, chopping and snipping and shaping, and as the hair flies to the floor, I sit in this weird middle space between awe and shock. I can't help it—I start to cry. I don't want to cry. I don't know why I'm crying—it's involuntary. But tears well and spill, well and spill. I wipe them from my cheeks and Jools doesn't say anything. She lets me cry.

The feelings swirl in my midsection, big and wild—disappointment, sadness, excitement, anger, freedom.

I feel free.

Which I am, as evidenced by the years' and years' worth of boring, dead hair sitting on the ground all around me. A symbol of all of the things I no longer need.

I say a silent goodbye. *Thank you for your service, old Noni. But I will no longer be needing you. It's time to let you go. I've decided to move in a new direction, try something new. I wish you all the best with your future endeavors.* And then I add a silent prayer. *Please don't look like shit. Please don't look like shit. Please don't look like shit.*

I look in the mirror. I do not look like shit. In fact, I think Jools was right. I look amazing.

7

"So, tell me again what happened?" I stare at Callum Simons, a tall, lanky, gray-skinned grade-ten kid, and do my best to not laugh in his face.

"They said if I did it, they'd give me twenty bucks."

"And you thought, hey you know what, that sounds like a great deal?"

"Yeah."

I look at his squishy, embarrassed face and a deep moment of self-reflection passes over me. *This is my job. I am getting paid to have this conversation right now.* "And so then you put the trumpet—"

"Just on my butt, Miss. On it. Not in it. All the kids are saying in it. But it wasn't that at all."

"Okay. So you put the trumpet on your bare butt and what?"

"Farted." He says this with the deepest, sincerest tone I've ever heard in my whole life. "Or I thought it was just a fart, but it wasn't."

"No, Callum, no, it was not." I take a deep breath. "Where was Ms. Connelly while this was happening?"

"She was helping the girls with their compositions in the practice room."

"Right, and then what happened?"

"I just ran out, ay. Went to the bathroom and hid there until you came and got me." Tears spring into his little beady eyes, and my heart cracks a bit, because my fucking kryptonite is an emotional teenage boy.

"As you can understand, Ms. Connelly is really upset about this," I tell him as seriously as I can.

"Yeah."

There's a knock on the door. Niko walks in and stares at Callum, who winces in such a way that if he hadn't just shit in a trumpet in front of his class, I would believe he'd just shit himself right now.

"Mr. Simons, can you step out for a minute, mate. Ms. Blake and I need to have a chat."

Callum slinks out of the room and Niko shuts the door. I start laughing and Niko does too.

"Jeez, Noni." He stops, completely caught off guard. "You look great."

"Thanks." I touch my head self-consciously and smile.

I had been completely overwhelmed by the compliments I'd received that morning. Working with teenagers means that you get an instant—and very loud—throng of comments on your appearance the second you change anything. Today the kids had whistled and smiled and said things like "Good hair, Miss," or "I like your hair, Miss." A couple of female teachers had told me they loved it, and that they themselves could never be so brave, which made me sad, because I had felt like them too. One of the receptionists, Carol, who was just a little older than me, grabbed my arm in the photocopy room and blinked her big green eyes as she said, "Good on you, Noni. I wish I could do that. I've always wanted to."

"It's just hair," I caught myself saying. But I knew it wasn't just hair. I squeezed Carol's hand and said, "If I can, then you can." She'd smiled at me, but I knew she didn't believe me.

"So, this is completely unprecedented," Niko says. "In my thirty-plus years of teaching, I've never had to deal with a kid shitting into an instrument." He is wired and smiling.

"Neither have I." I try not to laugh. "It was a dare."

"What?"

"They dared him twenty dollars to fart into the trumpet and he…" I search for the right words. "Followed through."

"Where was Miranda?"

"In one of the practice rooms. She is *pissed*."

"Yeah, I know. I've never seen a woman angrier in my whole life. And I'm Italian. She stormed into my office and yelled…" He lowers his voice and mimics Miranda's posh tone perfectly: "'What kind of shit show are you running here?' And I started laughing, which did not help the situation, Noni, let me tell you."

I giggle. "I don't know what we're meant to do."

He starts giggling, too, all raspy, through his nose. He touches my shoulder in solidarity. I'm very aware of his hand on my body. If this is what it feels like for him to touch something as safe as my shoulder, I wonder what it would feel like for him to touch other parts of me.

"Who is going to deal with the trumpet?" I ask, when we settle down.

"I called Tony. He's furious too."

"There's only a month of school left. We can't expel him." I look at Niko sincerely. "He's a good kid," I add.

"Noni, he shit in a trumpet."

"Exactly. If he comes back here next year, that's what he's going to be known as. The kid who shit in a trumpet. I hope he leaves of his own accord. For his own sake. He can't come back from this."

"I went to school with a girl, and there was a rumor that she put a Barbie inside her."

"What?"

"Yeah. In grade eight. Some girls started it because of some spat they'd had, and that's what she was known as the whole time we were at school. It even traveled across different schools."

"What? Barbie?"

"Yeah. I can't even remember her actual name."

I laugh so hard tears spring from my eyes and Niko bites his lip, trying to contain his laughter. "Okay. Okay," I say, trying to stop.

"What do we do?" Niko asks. "Give him a warning and tell him he has to replace the instrument?"

"It's his trumpet."

"Does he even play the trumpet?"

"Yeah. Apparently he's very good. Which is why Miranda is pissed off because he's going to take over from Charlotte now that she's graduating."

"Well, fuck, who is going to play 'The Last Post' if he leaves?" he asks, half serious, half kidding.

"Exactly."

Niko smiles. "Okay. I think he needs a punishment. The boys who dared him, too, for stupidity's sake. Let's give them all a week of after-school detentions. Callum has to write Miranda a letter. And we'll address it at year-level assembly, talk about maturity and making good decisions, and say that we don't want to hear one word about dares and brass instruments. Sound good?"

"Yup."

"You call his mum, okay?"

I roll my eyes. "Niko. No," I whimper sarcastically.

"I know. This will be a character-building conversation, though. For both of you. It's not every day you have to deliver, or receive, the news that your teenage son has shit himself into a brass instrument in front of several of his peers."

"Fine."

"Good." He walks toward the door and looks at me. "I really love your hair like that."

"Thanks. Thank you."

"Fucking Mondays." He rolls his eyes, gripping the handle of the door. "You ready?"

"No." I shake my head. He winks at me, then takes a deep breath in through his nose and opens the door. "Mr. Simons, in you come."

There's a missed call from Joan when I finally check my phone. My heart skips. *What's wrong? Something has happened. Fuck.* I call her back.

"Hey, you on lunch?" she says after only one ring.

"Yeah. What's wrong?"

"The apartment. It's sold, Nons." She sounds distant and my heart lunges. Not because the unit is sold, but because she called me Nons—I quickly think how weird it is that something can feel equally foreign and familiar.

"Really?" is all I can say.

"Yeah," she says. "Rachel called—the offer is higher than we thought, Nons. She was going to call you, but I told her I would do it. I wanted to tell you."

"Why?" I ask.

"I dunno. Sentimental. The last piece of the puzzle and all that." She sounds quiet. Neither of us says anything. I listen to her breathe. I become aware of my own breathing, and it sounds loud. Too loud. My heart hurts.

"How are you?" she asks.

"I'm…" *How am I?* "I'm really well. How are you?"

"I'm good. Good now. Yeah. So…"

"How's Carson?"

"He's good," she exhales. "You can come and get him anytime."

"I know."

Beautiful Carson. That doofus sausage dog makes me so sad. He reminds me of when we picked him up, when we bought the apartment, the plans we made, the things we did and the way we'd thought our lives would be. And when some of those things didn't work out how we thought they would, it knocked us over. Then we let our relationship fizz like a bottle of flat champagne sitting on the table the morning after a riotous party.

We had sex three times in our last year together, and only because we felt like we had to. We lost our passion, and as we discovered, neither of us had the energy to grab a magnifying glass and go on some kind of sleuthing trip to recover it.

We gave up. Not on each other, but on us.

"So we'll need to sign some shit at the office, but we can sort that later. Rachel will call—she's good, she's been a good agent, don't you think?"

"Yeah." *Is she fucking the real estate agent?* I mean, she's pretty. Thin. Blonde. She draws her eyebrows on and it freaks me out—they're too dark for her pale complexion and she uses a lot of brown blush. Which annoys me. When I look at her, I just want to scream YOU DON'T BLUSH BROWN, but I don't. Would Joan fuck someone who didn't know what color cheeks blushed? Maybe. I dunno.

"Then in a couple of weeks it'll all be done."

She means we will be done. Really. Nothing binding us together anymore. Nothing legal, at least. Just memories. My body remembers, remembers everything about Joan, about us. And in a couple of weeks it'll all be done.

"I don't know what to say," she tells me.

"Me either. You happy?" I ask.

"Yes. Yeah. I guess. You?"

"Bittersweet" is all I can manage. We pause.

"Bye, Nons."

"Bye, Joan."

I love Joan. I will always love Joan. I loved Joan more than I have ever loved another human being. But Joan and I were not in love. And the love, respect and admiration we had for each other was not sustainable. We both feared getting to a place where we'd be frustrated by the other. We're both kids of divorce, so we didn't want to put each other through that. The worst thing is that no matter how much glitter we threw at our relationship, it was still shit. A turd rolled in glitter.

I've grieved so much since we broke up. For my normal life with Joan, before all the shit happened. I've grieved for our weekends. For our routine. For her family, who became my family. For the stupid made-up songs Joan would sing. For our car conversations. For the way she'd tell me I looked pretty in the morning. I've grieved for my life and for what it looked like for nine whole years and for the ease with which we lived together. I think part of me will always grieve for some of these things.

The worst part of our breakup has been missing her, just the lack of this person that I knew so well. When we finally broke up, we made the agreement to go cold turkey, to not see or talk to each other unless it was completely necessary. We had to do it like that because we knew we'd very quickly fall back into old patterns, and as much as it hurt, we knew it wasn't right. We weren't right. We're not right. We'll never be right.

Don't forget, Noni.

8

"What are you going to do with the money?" Lindell asks, sipping his beer. We're in a small bar a block from the community hall where we're about to take part in a dance-in-the-dark class.

"I don't know. I haven't really thought about it," I say, and I haven't. Ever since the apartment sold, I've been feeling out of sorts. Maybe this is too much change all at once. Plus, Molly never even replied to my message.

"I think you should do something with it that continues this…" He pauses, floating both his hands around my head. "This bold-haircuts and fewer-fucks energy," he finishes. I laugh, because it sounds like a bad marketing slogan. "Seriously, Noni, do something just for you. Something that will make you happy."

"Shouldn't I be investing the money into property, or shares, or freezing my eggs or something?"

"Really?" Lindell looks stunned. "I didn't know that you were thinking about—"

"I'm not. Or I am. I don't know… Shit. I don't know what I mean."

"Try."

I take a swig from my bottle, closing my eyes, trying to put words to feelings. "I'm just scared," I mumble finally.

"Of what?"

"Of fucking up."

"We all are, my darling."

"You're not," I scoff.

"Of course I am." He grabs my arm to emphasize his point. "I'm scared of being boring. Of losing myself. Of going mad. Of loving my kids so much it kills me, because I just want to control everything in their lives to ensure they never feel anything but joy." He smiles and his eyes flash protectively.

"Not that you've thought about it." I smile.

"No. Not even a little bit." He rubs my arm, finishing his drink. "All I know is this—these last few weeks, for what seems like the first fucking time in like a decade, you've actually been thinking about yourself, and what you want, and I feel like it has caused some positive changes. And really, you haven't done anything all that drastic."

"Hello!" I point to my head.

"That's just hair."

"And fucking the guy with no sheet on his bed?"

"Sometimes we need to experience things to know they're what we don't want. I just think—" He stops himself.

"You think if this is how I feel doing small things, imagine what might happen if I do something big," I say.

"Maybe." He nods mischievously.

"I'll think about it. It's a risk, though, yeah?"

Everything external to my life has told me that by this point I should have my shit together, and I don't have anything together at all. I feel like a fuck-up.

"Do whatever will make you happy, Noni. That's all that I want."

"Because life is too short, yada yada yada. Yes. I know," I hiss, frustrated.

"What are you freaking out about?"

"What if I make a bunch of changes and it doesn't work? What if it's a waste of time and money and I don't change anything? And people think I'm ridiculous?"

"What people?" He looks at me seriously.

I shrug. "They're not real people, metaphorical people."

"Well, fuck the metaphorical people," he says, shaking his head. "They have zero input, or impact, on your choices." He stares straight into my eyes to make sure I'm really listening. "Fuck. Them."

I nod, so he knows I hear him. "We'll see," I say. The thing is, I really don't know what I want to do.

There's a huge line by the time we walk around the corner to the hall where the dance-in-the-dark session is being held. All different kinds of people are lined up and chatting excitedly. Lindell and I look at each other, raising our eyebrows. We have no idea what to expect. I heard about the class from a woman at work—apparently there's a cracking soundtrack playing and they turn off all the lights so it's pitch-black and you can just dance. The hall is dimly lit when we walk in and there are huge speakers in each corner of the room. People are happily limbering up and smiling.

"They're stretching. Should we stretch?" I ask Lindell and he shrugs, just as mystified as me. We half-heartedly stretch.

The music starts and the lights slowly fade to black. Almost immediately, Lindell begins singing at the top of his lungs and I can sense him wildly moving his body. He just dives into things. He can read a room and actively insert himself into any situation. I love that about him. I do not dive in. I casually meander along, after thinking carefully about the pros and cons. *Gosh! I'm so boring.* I awkwardly shift my weight side to side, feeling desperately self-conscious. I then spend way too long imagining that everyone else has been given night-vision goggles except me, and that this whole thing is just an elaborate, cruel and very expensive ruse to see me dance like no one's watching, when in fact everyone is. *You're being ridiculous, Noni.*

The next song begins and it's one I know, so that makes things easier. I start to sing and move a little more freely, reminding myself that no one can see me, that what I do doesn't matter. I begin to realize that I don't actually know how to dance without the additional layer of self-conscious tension that comes from the idea that people are looking at me. Ever so slowly, I stop thinking and I move. I do what feels good. Sometimes that's moving my hands, or just my shoulders in some ridiculous motion along with the music; other times all of my limbs flail wildly in some kind of buoyant jump. By four or five songs in, I'm moving with wild abandon. It makes me laugh. It's so dark that I can't see anything, really, except slight shadows. Occasionally I feel the bump of another person next to me, but it doesn't matter, because the music is so loud and no one cares what I'm doing. This isn't about anyone else. It's about me. And I learn something I don't know about myself: I'm very sexy in the dark. Like next-level, hip-swivel, hands-all-over-my-body, getting-down-low sexy. This surprises me. I like this new knowledge.

When the lights finally come up, Lindell and I are far away from each other and he smiles wide and sweaty as he pushes past people, his eyes popping with joy as he hugs me.

"Well, I bloody loved that. Did you?" he says gleefully.

"Yeah, at first it was a bit weird, but then I just did whatever felt good," I tell him and Lindell smirks. "What?" I ask.

"*I just did whatever felt good*," he mimics me exactly as I roll my eyes and push him toward the door.

Just do what feels good, I keep repeating over and over again in the shower as I think about what big and bold choices I could possibly make, and what things I might like to do. When I get out of the shower, I check my phone, and there's finally a reply from Molly. It has been two full weeks since I sent the first message.

I had checked every time my phone was in my hand to see if the little "read" icon had appeared, but it hadn't. She hadn't seen it. As more time passed, I convinced myself that she had in fact seen it pop up and had just chosen not to open it, that a message from me no longer required her attention. I figured I'd become a low priority and that she just wasn't interested anymore. I feel instant relief as I open her message.

> I think it's not
> actually about whether
> you can pull off
> a ruffled sleeve,
> but rather about
> who you're allowing
> to pull this
> ruffled sleeve off
> your body?

Sorry for late reply.
I've been up a mountain.
P.S. Perhaps consider
an easy-access ruffle?!?

I smile wide and feel the pulse of joy saturate my insides.
I text Lindell.

I know what
I'm gonna do.
I'm going to Europe.

9

I sit on an armchair outside Niko's office next to a pissed-off grade-nine girl who is in trouble for fighting.

"Are you in trouble, too, Miss?" she asks and I nod in solidarity with her.

"Noni?" Niko is at his door and he's in a dark blue shirt with a mustard tie. He looks particularly handsome in this color combination. *Who am I kidding? I always think he looks handsome.* I stand up and walk into his office and sit in the chair in front of his desk.

"Show me your hands," he says as he sits down in his large black swivel chair.

I hold my hands up. "Why?"

"Checking for an envelope. For a letter. 'Cause I would've shit in a trumpet if you were resigning," he jokes, and I laugh awkwardly.

"Well—" I begin the monologue I'd meticulously prepared, but he cuts me off.

"Oh no, Noni?"

"Not resigning. Just leave. I want to take some leave. I know it's inconvenient, but I want to take the first semester off next year. Come back after the June–July holidays."

"What are you going to do?"

"Go on a bit of an adventure," I say and wish I hadn't, because I suddenly feel like I'm thirteen again and I'm talking to a boy I like about Dungeons & Dragons, only he's an older, worldlier boy who doesn't know the difference between an orc and an elf.

"I'm intrigued."

"Travel. Feel grateful for my British passport. Read. Do whatever—" *and whomever,* I think to myself "—feels good. Just some time for me."

The second I'd got that first reply from Molly, I'd decided that I should absolutely spend the house money on a trip to Europe. An adventure. But the next few texts we'd sent back and forth confirmed the decision.

I'd agonized over my first reply for a few hours. Of course. I hadn't thought about an easy-access ruffle. I've been out of the game too long. Any tips on how to be single in your midthirties would be much appreciated. I hear the kids are using that thing on their phones? Grindr? I'd wanted to be sure she knew I was single and to see if she was too. She didn't use social media all that often and posted only one photo every six or so months, so I couldn't be sure.

She replied straightaway. I don't know how you'll go on those 'apps,' I believe they're called. You were always shit with your directions. This makes me laugh. She then sent a photo of her fingers in an L shape along with a message that said, This way means no.

In response I sent her a photo of my right hand doing a

thumbs-up, and How's Europe? because I know questions are important to kind of force a reply. Even so, she didn't reply for a whole day, which I told myself was just because of our different time zones.

It's great. Although
I've heard from
numerous sources
that it'd be
infinitely better if
you were here.

When I read this, I swooned.

Funny you should
say that actually...
I'm coming to your
side of the world
in January. My plan
is to stick around
for six months.
I'll start in London
and then see what
takes my fancy.

Meaning, I'll see if you still take my fancy. And I still take your fancy. If we fancy each other.

SHUT UP. Really?
Brilliant. If you need
a place to stay, I know
a great backpackers...
or six. Very clean.

Sexy owner.
I hear she has
a penchant for
Australian women.

SHE IS FLIRTING WITH ME. HOLY SHIT.

I can't wait to meet your co-owner, I'd joked. She replied with three crying laugh emojis and You'll like him. He has long hair. We had been texting like this on and off every few days since.

Niko smiles at me. "Well, good on you. Time away is good for teachers. More life lessons mean more valuable classroom lessons. I think we sometimes get stuck and boring, and it's easy to lose years in this profession. I don't ever want to be boring, or bored, you know?"

"Exactly. Yes." I smile and swoon. *Exactly, Niko, exactly.*

"Can I ask you something, Noni?"

"Of course."

"What are your goals here? Do you have a five-year plan, or a personal plan you're striving for? Do you want my job one day?" He smiles.

"Oh, I know I don't want your job," I say a little too quickly, with a little too much disgust in my tone, and Niko feigns offense. "But I don't know. I think this trip is partly to work that out." That feels like a natural end to the conversation, an adequate and honest answer, but my mouth keeps speaking without me. "I did have a plan. I'm a planner. I need a plan. But when everything happened with Joan, and with the— well, yeah." I stop because he's looking at me far too intently, and I need to lighten the mood. "Yeah, well, that plan kind of crumbled like a…a shart in a trumpet. A big one. A really big messy one."

Niko laughs but he continues to look at me with sweet, slightly concerned eyes. "You could absolutely say that, yes."

"And now I don't know what the new plan is in this version of my life, now that has all happened. My midthirties feels like a shit time to be working it out, though, you know? Sorry. I'll stop talking about shit."

"Don't apologize, please." He pauses. "Plans change all the time. It's my favorite thing about us."

When he says "us," I think for a brief second he means him and me, and I like the sound of him and me as an us. I wonder what he would do if I dramatically swiped everything onto the floor and we fucked right here on the desk. But my split-second vision of me sprawled across the paperwork is quickly replaced by the far more rational realization he's talking about the collective us. The human us.

"Change?" I ask.

"Yeah. That we're not fixed. That we have freewill. That we can always do, or be, something entirely different from what we thought we could. We are endless potential. Always. I mean, it's an entirely privileged perspective, but you get what I mean, yes?

I exhale loudly at this. "Yes. What's that saying? Uncertainty is the only certainty we have."

We are both silent for a moment. "And I'm sorry, too, for everything you went through. I don't think I ever told you that when it happened," Niko adds.

This startles me. "The school sent flowers," I mumble.

"Yeah, I know, but that was the school. I mean me. I never told you that I was sorry for it all."

I just smile tightly and awkwardly, because I don't know what else to say. I never know what to say when people tell me that they're sad about what happened. I feel a weird mixture of gratitude for their empathy but also a fiery rage, because it seems as if there's no way they could ever understand what happened, and so perhaps they should just fuck off with their misplaced feelings.

"Well, your job will be here for you when you come back." Niko smiles. "If you come back."

I laugh. "Oh, I'll be back. It's just six months."

"Well, take this." He opens his top drawer and hands me a business card. "If you need a reference, or to call me, it's all on there."

"Thank you." I reach for the card.

"We'll all miss you, Noni. I'll miss you," he adds and I'm sure our fingers linger together as he says this. Our eyes certainly do.

"Same" is all I manage to say as I stand up and walk out.

Fuck. Here we go.

"I'm worried you're having a quarter-life crisis." My father looks down his nose at me, concerned.

I laugh. "I think that maybe that wouldn't be such a bad thing."

"But your hair?"

"It's just hair."

"I mean, I love it." He squishes his face up. "But I read an article about what it means when your child makes dramatic changes to their appearance. Is this a warning sign, Noni? Should I be worried? You've been through a lot these last few years. I'd understand if you were feeling…" He pauses. "I dunno. Out of control."

"I'm fine, Dad."

"But Europe is so far away. And you've already done Europe."

"Not all of it, Dad. It's a big place." A waiter puts down our food, and I'm grateful for the moment of reprieve.

"Yeah. But isn't that just—"

"What?" I ask.

"Just something you do in your twenties. Not in your thirties."

"I didn't know there was age restriction on European cities," I say, biting into my burger a little more aggressively than necessary.

"Aren't you worried about your career?" He looks genuinely worried, which is a welcome change from the usual glum look permanently plastered on his face.

"It's just a semester, Dad."

I take a sip of my tea as a way to stop myself spiraling into a parent-fueled rant like a teenager. Which is precisely how my Dad makes me feel. He has good intentions, but he has never dealt with the trauma of my mum leaving him for another man when I was thirteen. Their divorce was messy and complicated. I lived with Mum—it was the practical option, since Dad worked away so much, but he got into this habit of trying to parent me extra hard when he did see me. Like he felt as though he had to make up for our time apart. It's a habit that hasn't died.

"Okay," he says, but his eyes tell me he doesn't believe me. "Just don't change too much."

I can't help it. "Why?"

"Because I like old Noni."

"But maybe that's just it, Dad. I don't think I do."

"What are you talking about?" he scoffs. "You're being silly—there's nothing wrong with you."

10

I walk into the café all too aware of the clothes on my body and the makeup on my face. The clothes and makeup that I had spent hours agonizing over, for the very specific reason that I want them to look like I had not spent hours agonizing over them.

Joan and I have agreed to meet in the coffee shop on the corner of the street near our solicitor's office. I'm nervous. Nervous because I care what Joan thinks. Because I want her to think that I look good—that I look happy, but not too happy. It's got to be the exact right balance of happy. Too happy and you're the asshole swanning about, reveling in how amazing your life is now that they're no longer in it. Not happy enough and you're the loser who clearly can't live without them.

I check my phone while I wait and there's a message from Molly. She has sent a stunning photo of a bright orange sunset.

The view from
the hot tub
in Estonia.

Looks awful, I reply.

Thought you'd
say as much.

I send her a photo of the menu:

The view from
this suburban café.

Eat some overpriced
avocado for me.

"Noni," Joan says, standing next to me.

After the pleasantries and the polite hug—which puts bodies in contact that haven't been in contact for a long time but
that know each other so well, bodies that reel with memories
of each other. We sit. We talk. We find a conversational flow.
A flow that, while still stilted by what was and what is now,
sits somewhere close to comfortable.

"Really? Head of the junior school? That's amazing," I
tell her. Joan has pined for this position, this promotion, for
a long time.

"It's fucking frightening, that's what it is." She sips from
her coffee. She looks happy. Nervous. Her hair is darker and
shorter and she's wearing clothes I don't recognize.

"So, old dickbag Denise has finally jogged on?" I muse.
We hate Denise.

"Yup. Thank god. I nearly texted you when we got the email." She pauses briefly and we eat and sip as a way of momentarily acknowledging that this news would have once caused celebratory living-room dancing and dinners out.

"It ended up coming down to me and Brian."

"And he's a lazy wanker."

"Exactly, that's what I was about to say, but he looks good on paper. I didn't know what they were going to do. I was a bit stunned when they told me."

"It's great. You're going to be great." I mean it.

"I hope so. It was time for a change. Not even a change, Nons, a new challenge, I guess. I need to use my brain in a different way."

"You know what this means, though?"

"What?"

"You're going to have to deal with kids in grade six, and they're basically teenagers. Are you going to be okay?" I smile.

She laughs. "I did think that. Gross." We never could quite understand the other's preferred age range. Joan is strictly early childhood and I am very happily fifteen-and-up. The other end is petrifying to both of us. "I don't know how you do it" was the most common phrase spoken in our house as we shared evening what-happened-at-work-today anecdotes.

"And you? What's happening with you?" Joan asks.

"Not much." I smile, unsure why I'm not being forthright about my adventure, about traveling, about Molly. I feel nervous about telling her. So many of my major decisions were previously made with Joan in mind. I don't know what I'd think if I told her and her opinion was less than positive. I think she'd still have enough sway to make me doubt my choices, and I'm barely clinging to my plan being a good idea as it is.

"I think that is a boldfaced lie." She raises her eyebrows and tilts her head to the side, searching my face for information.

"Maybe."

"Hold that thought," she tells me as she stands up. "I want to hear everything." She walks toward the bathroom and I exhale loudly. *This is good. This is okay. We're both okay.*

Her phone flashes with a message and I glance at it without thinking. The message is from someone named Que, and it says, Babe, can you get a tin of cannellini beans?

My throat tightens. *Babe. Cannellini beans.* She's seeing someone. She's living with someone. She's someone else's babe. Someone else's go-to for shopping errands. *Oh, god.*

Another message flashes up: three red love hearts. I can see her phone lock screen is a photo of a mousy woman holding Carson and smiling wide. It's like someone has flicked a rubber band at my heart. *Shit.* I look toward the bathroom to see if she's on her way back yet because I just need a minute to recalibrate. To fit this new information into my brain. Joan has moved on. Another woman is holding my dog. Another woman is making dishes with cannellini beans with *my* Joan. I don't even know how you use cannellini beans so that means she's making new recipes with this new woman. She doesn't want me anymore. She doesn't need me anymore. And I can't tell if I'm upset because she's with someone else, or upset because she's with someone else first. And then I feel fucking miserable. Miserable that I think it's the latter. Selfish that I'm sad. I want Joan to be happy. She should be happy. I couldn't make her happy.

My breath is quick and heavy in my chest as I stand up and walk outside. I hear Joan call my name as I get out of the door with a ding of the bell. I walk a few paces down the street, staring at the sky, trying to will the oxygen to fill me up but it doesn't feel close enough, like it's right within my grasp but I can't grab it. I start to panic.

"Noni? What happened?" I try to speak but nothing comes out. "Hey, hey, hey, come here. Come here. Lean here." There's pressure on my shoulders and I'm being pushed backward until my back meets a hard wall. "Breathe. Breathe. Noni, look at me. Breathe." Joan is holding my face. Her voice is slow as she rhythmically tries to catch my breath with her voice. "In." Pause. "Out." Pause. "In." Pause. "Out." I fall into her rhythm. She wipes away a tear. I squeeze my eyes shut.

Eventually I exhale loudly and peel my eyes open. Joan wipes both my cheeks quickly with her thumbs, her hands still pressed gently onto my face, eyes staring into mine. This is second nature to her. Dealing with me. This is like breathing.

"I'm sorry," I squeak.

"Don't be stupid. What happened? Selling the house, it's a lot, yeah? I'm freaking out a little too," she soothes.

I bite my lip. "Cannellini beans."

"What?"

"Someone needs you to get cannellini beans." She has no idea what I'm talking about, but I watch the recognition collect on her face as she pulls her phone out of her pocket.

"I'm sorry. I shouldn't have read it. I didn't mean to read it. I just—"

"Fuck, Nons."

"I know. I'm sorry," I rush.

"No, I mean that's shit, that's a shit way to find out. I didn't want you to find out like that."

"I'm fine. I am. I want you to get cannellini beans for someone else. That's good."

"It's new," she says, stepping away.

"It's good. I'm okay. I am. I don't even know why that

happened. I'm sorry. Let's just…" I look at my watch. "We're going to be late."

"Noni, do you want to talk about this?" Joan's eyes are squinting with concern.

"No. I'm fine. Really. I am. Just overwhelmed. This is all very overwhelming."

"Yeah. It is. But we can still talk to each other. We don't just have to be all pleasantries, you know? It's fucking weird."

"It's so weird. You feel weird?" I ask.

"Yes." She nods and softens. "I'm still me. There are parts of us that are still us. That—fuck." She sighs loudly, throwing her hands over her head, which is a very specific Joan sign that she doesn't know what to say. Right elbow over her eyes, left hand holding her elbow means she is exasperated, speechless. Two hands clutching her own face means she is angry. *Will I ever know this level of detail about someone else?*

"I know you," I mumble.

"I don't know what to say, Nons. This is just big, yeah? It all feels fucking big." She glances at me and then leans against the wall. We stand next to each other, neither of us saying anything. We are silent, but the space between us is not. It's alive with over nine years of knowing. Filled with years and years of memories, conversations, sex, love and arguments. The space between us churns with energy, but still neither of us says anything.

Finally, I look at her. "I don't know if I'm ever going to get cannellini beans for anyone else."

She looks sideways at me. "Oh, Nons, of course you are."

"No, no. I mean, I don't even know if I can, if I know how. Like, I only know how to get you cannellini beans." I smile, knowing I don't make sense, but knowing that Joan will make sense of it anyway.

She laughs. "Yeah, yeah, I know."

"But this is what I want," I say. I don't want her to think this is some kind of legume-centered plea to get her back. Because it's not that at all. "This is good. But it's—"

She cuts me off. "Weird."

I nod and we hold eye contact for a moment before both looking away. I watch the business of a Saturday morning passing us by. Couples in cafés eating breakfast. Bloody Mary drinking groups of twentysomethings. Tired mums pushing strollers. Then a little kid in a neon helmet on a scooter speeds past us, followed quickly by a dad with a baby strapped to his chest calling his name loudly. He nods at us with a "Kids, huh?" expression as he strides past. Joan and I look at each other and I feel an all-too-familiar ache in my heart. I can see she feels it too. I see it punch her guts and constrict in her throat the same way it does for me. The ache for everything that could have been. For what should've been. I want to touch her. Hold her hand. Lie and tell her that it'll be okay. Anything to take the ache away. Even though I know there's nothing that ever will.

"I really fucking miss you," she says.

The tears spring into my eyes and I try to smile through them. "I really miss you too," I mumble.

Now Joan starts crying as well and we sob and wipe tears and she wraps her arms around me and I lean into the hug fully, lean into her fully, and she leans into me. Tears and snot and feelings pour out of me like a cartoon oil leak finally springing freely from the dirt. The comfort eventually turns to embarrassment and we pull back, laughing.

"We must look fucking ridiculous," she says.

I mumble a yeah as she fixes my makeup with two swipes of her thumbs on my cheeks again and I touch my face insecurely. The vulnerability is big and raw around us.

"I don't even know what cannellini beans are," she says and

I laugh loudly. "She's a vegan," she adds, raising her eyebrows with an amused expression.

"You fucking cliché." I laugh.

"I know. She keeps telling me that Birkenstocks are the most comfortable shoe ever created."

"And you told her she is wrong, yes?"

"Yes, of course. But I have developed quite an affection for tahini."

I scrunch up my nose in disgust. "You've changed."

"Says she with the bombshell fucking pixie cut."

She holds her arm out for me to put mine through, I do, and we walk toward the solicitor's office. I exhale.

Okay. I can go now.

11

The sake is free-flowing, nineties hit after nineties hit is being murdered on the karaoke machine, and Diana, the home economics teacher, has just done an emotionally rousing version of "Black Velvet." You haven't met a group of adults who need to unwind until you've met a bunch of high school teachers at the end of the year. Shit is getting real. I'm wearing the pencil skirt. I'm drunk. Tonight is the night I'm going to make a move on Niko. I've decided. Lindell has decided. *It. Is. Happening.* I'm leaning hard into doing what feels good, and I know that Niko will feel good. And if he doesn't, I'll have six months to recover from the embarrassment.

"Thank you for another excellent year, Noni," Niko says as we stand at the bar. We have always been able to banter easily. Other staff members find him a bit abrasive, but I like that he just says what he thinks. You know where you stand with him. I wish I was able to be like that. I guess we've always flirted, but I was with Joan for so long that we just never crossed the line. That is, until tonight.

"No, thank *you*," I tell him. He passes me another shot and we clink our glasses. He makes eye contact and I grin. Niko's eyes smolder. I know they smolder, because my vagina tells me they do.

"What's that face?" he asks, staring at me.

"Just—nothing. You have nice eyes," I say. I get the bartender's attention and signal for two more shots.

"Thank you," he says. "I know I've already told you, but your hair looks great like this. I really like it."

"Thank you."

The bar is loud; Niko leans in closer. "I also really like this skirt."

When the second shot arrives, I swallow hard and swing it back. *Fuck. Here we go…*

"If you were hitting on me, you could've said something like 'It'd look better on my floor, though.'"

Niko laughs loudly and swallows his drink, not taking his eyes off my face. I think he's trying to read my intention. *BE SEXY, NONI! NOW!* I try to make my eyes smolder, but I think I just look really drunk.

"Would you like me to hit on you, Noni?" he asks and my insides squelch.

"Yes," I squeak, hoping that's the right answer.

Niko smirks. "Well, in that case, it *would* look better on my floor," he says. *It bloody worked.* I smile and squeeze his shoulder and then I immediately head to the bathroom and call Lindell. This is too much bold action for one night. I need backup. He doesn't answer. I check the time. It's after 1:00 a.m. Of course he isn't answering. *You're on your own, Noni.* I look at my phone again, then remember Niko's business card. I pull it out and stare at the number, biting my lip.

Want to play a game? I message.
Love, Noni.

                              With you? Of course,
                              he replies straightaway.

Fuck. Okay. Um.
Give me an adjective, I type.

                              Beautiful, he replies.

Tell me something…
beautiful, I text back.

                              You, he replies.

Your turn, I type.

He takes his time. I watch my phone. Two other teachers come into the bathroom and they screech when they see me. My phone dings. I don't pay attention to what they're saying.

                              Tell me something…
                              sexy, he writes.

Being kissed on the neck,
I type. *Here we fucking go!*
Tell me something…sexy,
I send.

                              You, he replies.

I flutter from the inside out. My phone dings.

Tell me something…
that turns you on,
he adds.

This, I type.

The two other teachers wrap their arms around me and drag me out of the bathroom. I type my next message as we head back into the bar.

Tell me something…
you'd like to do.

Niko is on the other side of the room in a circle of teachers with a beer in one hand and his phone in the other. He smiles at me. Then looks down at his phone; I watch him read and type. My phone dings.

You.

My smile comes from someplace that's not my face; it comes from someplace lower. It pulses joy around my body. I walk over to the table where my bag is stashed, pick up my belongings, hug a few people and head over to the group that Niko is standing with.

"I'm off," I say as I hug the others. Niko is last. I hug him, breathe him in. He smells so good.

"I'm coming with you," he whispers in my ear. This is exactly what I hoped he'd do. I nod and walk out of the bar. I stand waiting out the front and within seconds there is a hand in the small of my back that ushers me toward a taxi. The door opens and I slide in; Niko slides in next to me, gives the taxi driver an address, looks at me, grabs my face in both his hands and kisses me—he does all of this like it's one swift movement. I'm so desperately impressed.

We kiss in the back of the cab the whole way back to his house. His hand under my skirt and on my thigh—the pencil skirt is so tight his hand can't go any higher. *Oh, god, I wish it could.*

He opens the door of the taxi and takes my hand as I get out. He lives in an apartment building in a part of the city that I could never afford to live in. It requires a swipe card to do anything. Everything is clean black marble. He kisses my neck as we fly up floor after floor in the elevator and I am so turned on I can barely keep it together. He unlocks the door to his unit.

"After you."

I walk in. It's slick. Neat. It smells manly, like aftershave and wood and cleaning products. I sit at a silver stool at the kitchen counter and take my heels off, looking around. This is the kind of decor where everything has a place. There's a stack of perfectly aligned coffee-table books in the center of the coffee table. All that's on my coffee table is a pile of single socks I can't find the other halves to, a stack of unopened mail and an empty glass of wine.

"Wine?" he asks.

"Vodka?" I reply.

He opens a cupboard and looks in. "Gin?"

"Fine."

I walk toward the giant floor-to-ceiling window, the carpet plush under my feet, and glance at the lights across the river. The view is amazing. I'm glad we came back here and not to my shitty one-bedroom unit where the carpet is threadbare and I'm pretty sure the tenant before me had a cat because sometimes when it's really sunny it smells like urine. Niko walks up behind me, kisses me on the shoulder and hands me

a glass. I take a sip. I watch him walk away, flick on an expensive lamp and sit on his very square couch.

"You are a very sexy woman, Noni."

"It's the skirt," I mumble.

"It's not the skirt."

"It's the hair, then." I smile, touching the short lock clos-
est to my forehead. There is certainly no hiding in this skirt,
or this haircut.

He shakes his head. "It's you."

I don't know what to say, so I don't say anything. There's
a maroon legionnaire's cap sitting on the coffee table. I pick
it up.

"This yours?"

"Of course." He laughs. "No, it's my nephew's. He stays
here sometimes."

I laugh and put it on. "How do I look?"

"Still sexy."

"I think I'm the first person to ever receive that compliment while wearing one of these."

Niko holds out his hand; I place mine in his and he pulls
me toward him. He stays seated but his hands slide around my
hips to the back of my skirt. He unzips it and slowly slides it
down. I'm not wearing any underwear. The skirt is so tight
you could see every line, so I just didn't bother.

"Amazing." Niko smiles when he realizes. I step lightly out
of it, kicking it away as he lifts the fabric of my top and kisses
my stomach, running his hands up my legs from my ankles
to my knees, standing when he gets to my hips. He kisses my
chest up to my neck. I kiss his mouth and pull at his shirt,
which we both unbutton as quickly as we can.

He takes my hand and guides me to his bedroom. It's dark
but I can tell his bed is made. I don't know why that's sexy,
but it is. I lift my top over my head and lie down. Niko kisses

me. Every part of me. I squirm with the pleasure of it all. A moan comes from a place that is not my vocal cords. It is all desire. I run my hands over his bare chest down to the waistband of his pants, unbuttoning them. He stands to slip them off, and as he does, the blanket shifts slightly down the bed to reveal a texture I'm not quite used to. Rubbery. Actually, not rubbery. Just rubber. Niko has rubber sheets.

My brain whirs. I try to stay in my body. In the pleasure. I pull him toward me. We are both naked and he is hard and I am ready, but no matter how many signals I give him, his penis comes nowhere near my vagina. We roll over so I am on top but he rolls me back over and he lies next me, staring into my eyes. It feels all too intimate for drunk, first-time sex so I kiss him as an excellent avoidance strategy, but he pulls away.

"Noni, I'm not really into penetrative sex."

"What?"

"It's not really my thing."

"Okay."

"But we can still have a good time? Yeah?"

He kisses my neck and runs his fingers down my inner thighs, finding my clitoris, and I guess it feels good but I am way too in my own head. *The rubber sheets. No penetration.* He stops, leans over to his top drawer and pulls out a long rubber string of balls. It looks like the string of ice cubes my mum used to put in punch in the eighties.

"Have you ever used these?"

I shake my head. It's a sex toy. I don't know how I feel about someone pulling out a sex toy the first time. Is this his go-to move? How many women has he used this on? I am instantly out of my body and into my head and I feel my vagina's metaphorical arms fold and she is shaking her head in disapproval.

"No. I don't think I want—"

"It's for me."

Oh, it's for him. Well, that's okay then, I guess? "Is that—"

"They're anal beads."

He wants me to use anal beads. He pushes a switch. They vibrate. They're vibrating anal beads. This feels like some Christian Grey shit that I am completely unprepared for, and now all I can think about is the location of his sex dungeon.

"We can go slow," he says, and as he does, a surprise tube of honey has appeared and he is squirting it onto my stomach and licking it off and groaning. He puts the beads in his own butt, and with the vibrating of anal beads in my ears and Niko writhing wildly eating honey from my flesh, I stare at the ceiling and think about poo. And then I think about the fact that sometimes people just surprise you. There is no saving this situation for me sexually. No coming back from this distracted array of thoughts. No cumming for me, which is fortunate because he cums loudly, biting my stomach hard, and I squeal.

"Ow."

He looks at me soggy, sticky and satisfied. "Let's have a shower."

I nod.

It turns out when it comes to sex, I'm quite happy being described as beige. I tell Niko an inarticulate version of this sentiment in the shower. He's not embarrassed, not even a little bit. I, however, squirm my way through the whole interaction. I'm mortified. I quickly get dressed, watching as he sprays and wipes his sheets, and I kiss him on the cheek.

"I'm going to go home," I tell him. He nods.

"Have a great trip, Noni," he says.

I'm a cliché. I'm sitting on the floor of Lindell's living room while he combs nits from my scalp.

"This is love," I tell him.

"I can't believe you slept with a guy who gave you nits." Lindell giggles, stabbing my scalp with the comb.

"He didn't give me nits, his nephew gave me nits. And I didn't sleep with him."

"I still don't understand how this exchange happened."

"His nephew's stuff was in the living room, including his legionnaire's cap. I put it on and made a comment about no one looking sexy in a legionnaire's cap. It became a thing."

"Please tell me you had sex while wearing a legionnaire's cap."

"Very nearly." I seductively swing my nit-shampooed head around and peer at him, smiling.

"Please tell me the legionnaire's cap got swept off in a moment of passion, then," he mutters.

"Exactly." I raise my eyebrows and we crack up laughing.

"Did you get too drunk and pass out?" he asks.

"No. Not at all."

"Why do I feel like you're holding out on me?"

"Because I am."

"Why? What happened? Are you okay?"

"I'm fine. I'm just—" I stop. "I don't know. Embarrassed. I think I'm beige."

"What?"

"In bed. Am I boring?"

"I dunno. I doubt it. Did Niko say something? Did he call you boring? That fuckwit."

"No. No. Fuck. We didn't really have sex, or we did, but it was…not what I'd usually do."

"You need to start using your words immediately." He is clinging to my shoulders and staring at me.

"It was messy. He's into making a mess."

I watch Lindell's face process this, and his eyebrows almost fly off his forehead. "What kind of a mess?"

"He had rubber sheets."

"Shit!" He bites his lip.

"And he said it like it was no big deal, like, we're half-naked and he just, like, whips out some anal beads and told me he doesn't like penetration."

"What did you say?"

"I blathered about like an idiot and we kept going, but my mind was racing with images of cleanup, and then he poured honey all over me, and honey is so sticky—"

"Wait, what about the anal beads?"

"He used them."

"On you?"

"On himself. And so he's having a great old time and I'm just thinking about how people surprise you, yes? Then I'm thinking about messes, and then I remembered that time I babysat and Julius pooed everywhere as I was changing his nappy and that was one of the vilest things…"

Lindell is laughing so hard that tears drip onto the collar of his shirt.

"He just acted like it was no big deal."

"Well, to him it isn't." He smiles. "Has he said anything since?"

"He sent me a message the next day that said, 'We good?' and I just sent back a couple of emojis."

"Which ones?"

"The thumbs-up, a poo and a yellow love heart."

Lindell loses it laughing again, his head lolled back. "Noni!"

"I didn't know what else to say."

It takes him ages to stop laughing. Me too. "Well, you have to tell him his nephew has nits."

"No!" I put my face in my hands, shaking my head. "Nothing about this feels good, you know?"

"Oh, but it feels very, very good for me. What about Molly—any more messages?"

I hand him my phone and show him the thread of texts. We've pretty much been talking every day since she first replied. Nothing too deep. All flirtatious and funny. I watch his face as he reads, and my stomach flips with excitement thinking about Molly, about what's going to happen with Molly.

"Well, this looks promising," Lindell says, as he returns to combing nits out of my hair. "This doesn't, though." He shows me the comb. "This is fucking disgusting."

12

The month before I leave is filled with problem solving and panic attacks. Moving out of my unit and storing everything at Dad's. I didn't want to pay rent for six months, but as I sweated stacking boxes and listened to Dad tut disapprovingly, I wished I'd just taken the financial hit for ease's sake.

Christmas came and went with lunch with my Mum and my stepdad. Mum is the opposite of Dad—she doesn't vocalize her worry or concern, just faffs about with a constipated look of trepidation on her face. She bought practical gifts, like toothbrush travel cases and makeup bags with drawstrings, and said things like: "Still wear a good SPF, because those European rays can trick you into thinking they're not as dangerous as ours, Noni, but they are. Just because they're not directly under the giant hole in the sky like we are doesn't mean they're not just as violent, and you have such lovely skin. And don't forget your neck, and the backs of your hands. Every-one forgets their neck and their hands, and, well, look, they're the places that give away your age. Here, I've got some in my handbag. It's a fifty-plus one. Take it. I'll get a new one later." I know she means well.

Dad, on the other hand, mentioned my haircut only three times, my weight twice, and how I'm making a terrible mistake that I will regret forever because six months away will irrefutably make me unemployable, especially now that I no longer have a mortgage or a Joan, once, over dinner. So you know, he perked up for Christmas. *What a gift.* I usually have more patience for Mum than Dad, but their energy combined on one day amid such a big change was a lot, so I faked a migraine and was in bed by 8:00 p.m. messaging Molly.

See you soon, darlin' was how she signed off her last message when I was finally ready to sleep. She called me darling. Merry Christmas indeed.

The week between Christmas and New Year's is spent with Lindell, Graham and the kids. Which highlighted how impossible spending six months without them feels. They are family— the family I've chosen for myself. The family who get me, who back my choices, who champion my whims and tell me I can do anything. Not only that I can, but that I should, and that it'll be fantastic. And because they believe in me more than I believe in myself, I start to spiral emotionally when I consider just what the hell I am going to do with them being twelve hours ahead of me.

"What if I need you and you're asleep and so I make bad and reckless decisions that I regret for my whole life and have to clean up my own messes? Or heaven forbid, just make decisions without your counsel?" I say to Lindell, who rolls his eyes at my dramatic outburst.

"You're going to be fine, my girl," is all he says.

And then it's January, and my life here is packed up, and it's time for Lindell to drive me to the airport. It's time for my adventure to begin.

He turns the music down in the car, exhaling loudly. "I'm

your best mate, so I feel like I have to tell you this," he says, clutching the steering wheel tight. "You don't have to go if you don't want to. We can turn the car around and go home. And that will be fine. Also, you don't have to stay there for the whole time either. You can come home anytime you want. Because you are an adult. And you're capable and smart and brilliant and this isn't about anyone else, Nons. This is about you and what you want. This is your timeline. Your trip. You have zero obligations, and that's gonna be fucking rare in your life, yeah? So this is a very specific moment in time that you can just relish. And if it all goes to shit, come home. You don't have to stick anything out because of some sense of duty to a timeline you have set for yourself. But it's not going to go to shit. It's going to be great. Because you're great. Okay?"

"Okay" is all I say as we both get out of the car in the drop-off zone, because I refuse to let him pay the extortionate airport parking prices. We hug tight.

"I love you so much," I tell him.

"And I love you so much," he says. "Just have a fucking ball and do all of the things, and people, you want to do."

As he drives off, I nod, wave and smile huge as a way of showing him that I'm fine, and that it'll all be fine, and that I'm not freaking out. But as soon as his car is out of sight, I burst into tears.

I cry at check-in. I cry while drinking a coffee. I cry while going down the escalator to customs. An airport official in her fifties, with a frizzy perm and a thick accent, looks at me curiously. "You in love? Only women in love cry like that."

I shake my head and walk straight to the bathroom to try to get my shit together. I don't know why this feels so emotionally fraught. I remind myself that I'm fine. That all I'm doing is going on holiday. I think it's because it's a change, because I don't know what this next bit looks like, because I'm scared.

Scared of fucking it up. Of the unknown. Of being happy. It feels selfish. It feels indulgent. It feels like I'm a fucking idiot for being upset about going on holiday and focusing on doing what feels good. I sob quietly in the stall so as not to overwhelm the other people in the bathroom. Airports are stressful enough without having to worry about the woman crying in the cubicle next to you.

When I think I've finally contained the tears, I exhale hard and fast. *Fuck that*, I think. This is one of the best things I learned in therapy—that when you catch yourself in an anxiety spiral, or negative spin, you need to recognize the thoughts that are false, or self-sabotaging bullshit, and reprimand them. *You're not helpful*, I think, concentrating on my breath, on being mindful, on noticing what is real. The feeling of my feet in my shoes, the cotton of my dress on my skin, the pressure of the seat pressed against my legs, the whir of the air conditioner.

And then I break out the gem worth every cent of therapy dollars and time. *It's okay to feel safe, Noni*, I tell myself.

Inhale.

It's okay to feel happy.

Exhale.

It's okay to trust your instincts.

Inhale.

It's okay to make mistakes.

Exhale.

It's okay to feel safe.

Inhale. Exhale.

"It's okay to feel safe," I whisper to myself out loud, because speaking makes it real, takes it out of my head and into the world.

"It's okay to be happy," I whisper. "In fact, it is encouraged."

13

I'm standing in a pub that was built in 1667. My thirty-six-year-old body feels insignificant in a place that is close to four hundred years old. If these walls could talk, indeed. Tourists snap photos of the signs on the walls as I wait for Naz, a dear friend from university. She realized teaching wasn't for her pretty early on, when a grade-eight class was acting so wild that she called the police. When the police showed up, wondering what the hell she expected them to do with thirty wayward teenagers, they asked if she thought she was in danger. She told them that of course she fucking did. She moved to London shortly after. Now she works in some ritzy PR job and lives in a ridiculously cool studio loft in East London with her beautiful partner, an art-director-turned-yogi named Tom.

"Well, you can fuck right off now because you look STUNNING. This!" Naz squeals as she arrives, touching my hair. "I am all about this."

"Hello, darling." I laugh and we hug for a long time. "I

was just sitting here thinking of how insignificant I am in the grand scheme of world history and ancient pubs."

"All right, sad sack, enough of that. I'm getting pints and chips with gravy and you're going to tell me every fucking salacious detail of this too-early-to-be-midlife crisis you're having." Naz raises her perfectly penciled-in eyebrows and grins joyously.

I watch her standing at the bar sweet-talking the handsome barman, who laughs loudly. Naz is wearing a floral-print shirt in swirling grays and pinks, French tucked into slim-cut blue trousers, with pale pink stilettos, her full head of short dark brown hair perfectly styled. I suddenly become very conscious of my elastic waistband and trainers.

We very quickly settle into fast conversation, drinking pints and laughing so loudly that people stop and stare at us. Naz has that effect. She is wild, filthy, confident, and she brings those qualities out in me. I tell her all about the should've-boned list and my adventure.

"Fuck me, doll, this is sensational. I love this. Good on you." She holds her glass up to mine and we clink them together ceremoniously.

"How is Tom?" I ask.

"He's perfect. As always. He's got a whole bloody section in our flat now dedicated to his crystals and bloody sage and whatever. It was taking over my house, and I was like, Thomas, darling, we've got to control the amount of amethyst in here, because it's blocking the fucking telly." She pauses, emptying her glass. She looks over at the bar, making eye contact with the dishy barman from before, and holds two fingers up. This isn't a table-service pub, but the barman nods at Naz. "I do yoga now, babe. And I meditate. And I stopped smoking fags."

I gasp, feigning horror. "Who even are you?"

"Exactly. I like it, though. If it means I'm less likely to call Rachel in marketing a fucking useless asshole every two seconds, then that's a positive."

"Fucking Rachel."

"Fucking Rachel, exactly. Fucking postmillennials. I'm like, babes, no one gives a shit about your poached eggs, or that you remembered your stupid travel mug. Get off your fucking phone and get the social deliverables done."

"So work is good?"

"Work is great. You? I can't believe you're still teaching."

"I love it. But a semester off will be good."

"Good? It's going to be golden." Naz drinks before staring at me seriously. "How are we in our mid-fucking-thirties?"

"I don't actually know."

Later, when I am very happily buzzed, Naz storms back from the bar excitedly.

"Ding, ding, ding, baby, I've just had a fucking stellar idea—what are you doing Saturday night?" She smiles wide, putting a bottle in an ice bucket on the table between us.

I raise my eyebrows both at her excitement and at the bottle of wine. I am not piss-fit for a European jaunt. I should've thought of this. Europe in winter is basically shorthand for replacing your blood with booze. Who am I kidding? Summer in Europe is the same. I should've been in training before I left.

"You should come with me to this work do. Tom can't come and I was going to go solo, but come with me—the food will be delish and it's free booze. Good booze too. Hella boring, but I'll get you a room. Come."

"I can't. I'm seeing Molly."

"*Molly* Molly?" Naz looks at me suspiciously.

"She runs a whole chain of backpackers across Europe. We're gonna catch up."

"And?"

"And talk, I suppose? See if there is still—"

She cuts me off. "See if she's still a giant shit head?" I roll my eyes. Naz was never a fan.

I'd messaged Molly from Changi airport. I can't believe I'm still another thirteen-hour flight away. But at least there's a butterfly garden here, so you know.

I got her reply when I turned my phone on after landing. I can't believe we're actually in the same time zone. Good morning, gorgeous. I'm going to be in London all weekend, so, let's catch up and drink premix vodka out of a can like the good old days.

I change the subject with Naz. "Hey, I never thanked you for sending flowers when—" I start, but she cuts me off.

"You're welcome, my love. Relationships ending, especially relationships like yours and Joan's, are like a fucking death and they deserve commemoration." She drinks and breathes deep, taking a moment. "The apartment sold. That's good, babe."

"Yup. It's fully and completely done."

"Did you see her before you left?"

"Yeah, we had to sign a heap of papers. She looks good."

"Like 'I want to fuck you against the wall' good, or just 'I know you so well that I can tell that the personal changes you've made look good on you' good?"

"The latter. It's done. We're done." I look around the room at the crowd. People on dates, women clinking glasses of rosé, twentysomething boys in zipped-up tracksuits flipping coasters on their table and laughing loudly. A girl and a guy kissing. I turn to Naz. "But being single in my thirties? This was not the plan. I don't even know how to get the fucking Bluetooth speaker to work in my car—how am I going to date now? I don't know how to date."

"Do you want to date?"

"No. Yes. Fuck, I don't know. Maybe I won't have to, if the catch-up with Molly goes well."

"Just see what happens." She squeezes my arm with a cautious smile. "So, you're hanging around here for Molly."

"For the beautiful scenery."

"Yeah, babes, for the scenery of her fancy flaps in your face."

"Don't ever use the words *fancy* and *flaps* in the same sentence ever again." I laugh.

Naz clinks her glass with mine. "What else do you want to do while you're here?"

"I want to travel a little and then see what happens."

"Well, you know what I see happening? Us blowing this popsicle stand and heading over to this brilliant new bar across the way that does the best fucking martinis in the whole city. They put rosemary, or fire, or some kind of fermented wankery into them, and they're amazing."

"Don't you have to work tomorrow?"

"Babe, I've told everyone I've got meetings in the city until one o'clock, so we are fine. Get your shit. Let's go. I'm going to pay our tab and tell that bartender that I will be fantasizing about him when I fuck my husband later," she muses.

"Naz."

"What? Tom won't care. How do you think we've been together for sixteen years?" She pouts before quickly adding, "Happily."

The new bar is dimly lit, all dark wood, black leather and hints of copper glinting off the mirrored walls. It's busy. Suit-clad men who you know will smell good and elegant women in gray with plump red lips sit cross-legged staring between their martini glasses and each other. This is the kind of place where you'd wear the pencil skirt. But I'm not. I'm wearing an outfit entirely appropriate for getting shit-faced in a pub with your mate, not swanning about in some luxe bar where the gold fixtures in the bathroom cost more than my entire apartment.

If I wasn't as drunk as I already am, I'd probably care more than I do. But I pull out a dusty pink gloss from the bottom of my handbag and swipe it across my lips while Naz is in the bathroom. There is a band playing—four gorgeous musicians in versions of suits. The double-bass player has an incredible afro and dark-rimmed glasses, the saxophonist sports a dark, dark heavy beard, and the drummer is a tiny elfin girl with a sharp white-blond bob. I catch the eye of the trumpeter and smile wide, thinking of Callum Simmons and his bet, but the trumpeter thinks I'm smiling at him and he smiles back. The trumpeter is tall and square, thin but strong. He has thick fair hair that looks effortlessly swept back, but you know it actually took a lot of effort and product. He's wearing a crisp white shirt with the sleeves rolled expertly to the elbow and there's one more button undone than normally would be.

Naz plops down a cocktail with way too much foliage popping over the glass and stage-whispers, "Which one are you staring at? The drummer? I like her beret."

I whack her, gesturing for her to be quiet, but I whisper "The trumpeter is cute" into her ear and she nods approvingly.

"Mmm-hmm. The bass player, though—his ass is like a perfect bubble. And I know just the perfect place for him to sit." Naz flutters her eyelashes and holds both her hands under her chin, presenting her face sweetly. "A beautiful throne fit for a king." I laugh so loudly people turn and look at us. "Can I ask you something, darling?" she whispers.

"Of course."

"How long has it been since you had sex with a man?"

I think, sipping my tart-as-all-fuck cocktail and squishing

up my face. In this instance I'm going to say that Niko doesn't count. "It had been over ten years."

"Had been?" She leans in conspiratorially, smirking. "Spill."

I tell her about awkward sex with Ben, and the honey, anal beads, and nits with Niko, and she flails between cackling hysterically and horror.

"Fucking hell, Noni." She looks at me like I just vomited on the table. "You need to have it off with one of those beautiful young men. Now. On this table. Tonight. Go."

"They're like twelve, Naz." We fall very quickly back into conversation about politics, people we know and celebrities who annoy us. Every now and again I watch the band. Watch the trumpeter. He moves his hips with more fluidity than you think he'd have. He laughs easily, and with his whole body. I've never thought brass instruments were sexy. Cool, sure. I guess. Not sexy, though. But this guy? There's something about this guy. He catches me staring at him again and he smiles but quickly looks away. I think he's shy.

"God, I love jazz, babes. I do." Naz whoops loudly and the band all smile over at us. Another few cocktails down, they say their thank-yous with a finished set. The bar has thinned out by this point.

"Come over here now, you four, please, let my friend and I buy you drinks to say thank you. You're all delicious!" Naz bellows across the whole bar.

"I'm sorry," I mouth behind her.

"Two bottles of champagne," Naz yells over to the bartender. "Do you drink champagne? Yes. Champagne. Whatever they drink. A round. On me, yeah?" Naz is shouting, but her charm is so enamoring that she can get away with a certain amount of arrogance.

Naz follows the band to the bar and I watch as she introduces herself, shakes hands, makes them laugh. She schmoozes them hard and fast and they fall for it. Naz has glasses and a bucket with champagne in it and she's passed off another bucket to the bass player. The others are carrying beers and brown liquids in small glasses and they all head over toward me. Naz introduces me to Holly, Arnie, Akram and Jeremy, the trumpeter, who it turns out is American.

We drink past the point where the bar has closed and the bartenders have all joined us. The band pull out cards and teach us a game that I am terrible at. But it's very funny. We discover they are all studying music nearby. They're in their early twenties, which makes me feel incredibly old. Jeremy sits next to me, close, so we're almost touching. He's engaged in the conversation but seems shy, not saying much. He smiles wide and I smile back. I try to talk to him but it's awkward; we can't find a rhythm. He apologizes. I apologize. We giggle nervously and I feel grateful when the bass player, who is sitting on my other side, strikes up a conversation with me. We end up in a deep conversation about the arts and the financial reality of being a musician.

"All we ever tell kids is do what you love, follow your dreams. And this is my dream, I know what I love. But the reality is it's highly likely that I'm going to have to do something else that I'm not going to love to fund the thing I do love. And I know that's reality. But that sucks. We're kind of sold a lie, you know? It's disheartening," he says.

"I feel like I'm in my midthirties and I'm still trying to find out what I love. So you're lucky in one sense," I tell him.

"I suppose." He sips his drink. "You know, I've always wanted to go to Australia."

"You should."

"After college. That's the plan. Just see the world."

"I did something like that when I was your age. Highly

recommend. Five stars. In fact, it's kind of what I'm doing again now."

He smiles at me, a flirtatious smile, like he's trying to read my face. "So, Jeremy called dibs on you," he says finally.

"What?"

"Dibs."

"Well, that's weird, because he hasn't even spoken to me." I smile. "Dibsing people is also kind of gross, don't you think? Although I can't say I don't feel flattered by it." We both laugh.

"Yeah. Absolutely," he says, taking another sip of his drink. "It's also a deep shame."

"It is?"

"Yeah, he beat me to it."

We look at each other for a moment.

"I'm gonna head home," Jeremy announces to the group. "Nice to meet you, Noni." He shakes my hand and leans down to kiss me on the cheek, but as he gets close, he whispers, "I think you're really sexy." I am stunned. *Twenty points to the American*. He says his goodbyes, hugging his friends, and heads toward the door. I'm still sitting with my mouth agape, watching him go.

Naz plops herself down hard onto the leather booth next to me, thinking she's whispering. "Go. Do the things that feel good. With that young man. Now." She pushes me off the chair so I'm standing.

"Wait," I say out loud. Jeremy turns and looks at me as I clamber past everyone to him. "I just wanted to say, um—" *Jesus, Noni, get it together* "—Naz thought, well, that we were very much fucking with our eyes earlier. And I just wanted to see what you thought about that." *God, I am such a dork.*

Jeremy smiles. "I think Naz was correct."

"You do?" I say, trying to contain my excitement and behave in an alluring and sexy manner. "But you didn't talk to me."

"Doesn't mean I wasn't thinking about it." He grins, and I'm sure he blushes a little too.

"Well, then, er, would you like to fuck with more than just our eyes?" I say, trying to hold his gaze, but I feel like a fucking idiot. "Sorry. That's so lame," I say and he laughs.

I try to save it. "But I mean it. I think we should. I mean. Do you want to have sex with me?" I sober up just enough to read his face in case it follows with instant rejection.

"Yes, I would. Like that. Very much."

"Well, that's good, then," I giggle. "Let's go."

My mouth is stretched in the widest smile my face can possibly manage as I head back to the table to grab my coat and bag, giving Naz a secret thumbs-up. She whoops loudly. "This is fucking excellent," she squeals, announcing her approval to the whole group.

"Good night. I love you," I whisper.

"I love you," she slurs.

"Have a good time, Noni." The bass player smiles at me. And I shake my head with an exaggerated nervous face, all teeth, flexing the muscles in my neck with a throaty "holy shit" sound.

"You treat my friend good, you hear me, dude? YOU. TREAT. HER. WELL!" Naz yells over my shoulder and I look at Jeremy standing by the door with his jacket on, his trumpet in its case in one hand, and a smile on his face.

I discover two things during my evening with the fetching young American trumpet player:

I am too old to be having sex with someone who thinks having a mattress on the floor is an acceptable sleeping arrangement. I am, in fact, too old to sleep on a mattress on the floor. I am at the age where lumbar support and ensemble bases are actually not just a nice suggestion but a necessity.

When you do the math on the amount of time that brass players spend exercising their mouth muscles, you will be astounded. My clitoris is astounded. Quiet and shy Jeremy had tricks with his tongue, and fingers, that I was unprepared for. I thought I'd have to take charge, but I didn't. The second the door closed to his tiny bedroom, it was on. Or he was on me. Hands and lips and his tongue all over my body. He went down on me straightaway and I assumed I'd let the polite amount of time pass before kicking things up a notch, but once he was down there, his tongue moving and pressing and doing things I couldn't actually comprehend, I let him stay there because it was so good. I didn't want him to stop. If I'd had a computer and a printer, I would've made him a certificate because he fucking deserved it.

Welcome back to London, Noni.

14

After the eventful welcome-back-to-London shag and hang-over, I hibernate and settle into a life that looks nothing like my normal. I read a whole book in a sitting. I lay about my tiny, rented studio flat in flannelette pajamas, eating marma-lade on thick, buttery white toast, and reading. I don't talk to anyone, or go anywhere, unless it's from the couch to my bed, to the kitchen or the bathroom. There's a large floor-to-ceiling window next to the bed that I happily look out at the dreary London winter, feeling giddy whenever a black cab or double-decker bus goes past. I wear replenishing facial masks, paint my nails and binge-watch shit TV for hours at a time. It all feels so indulgent. After a couple of days I venture out and buy a new winter coat and scarf because I'm finally ready to think about beginning my life here. On the way home I crave pasta in the way that only cold weather and a deep sense of self-satisfaction can inspire. I decide to wander and see what I can find, exploring side alleys and happily getting lost. When

I see the large blue neon sign in scrawling Italian, I don't even look at the menu on the wall outside, I just walk in. Inside it's white walls, dark-wood furniture, a shining polished concrete floor and an open kitchen where staff members shout to each other with perfect musical accents that make my ears happy.

"Do you have a reservation?" the mustached maître d' asks.

"Nope. Just for one, please," I say, looking around. *Shit. This place is fancy.*

The waitstaff all have straight backs, and there are far too many men in tweed perched at tables alongside their perfectly coiffed wives, who all have giant diamonds on their fingers. The soundtrack is loud, slow, smooth jazz, all piano and snare drum. I'm shown to a seat by a handsome waiter who pulls out my chair and places a napkin on my lap in one swift movement.

"Still or sparkling water?" he purrs.

"Sparkling," I say with a smile, because this is modern-day foraging at its finest, and I am going to spoil myself. I'm not going to look at my phone, I'm going to sit here and pretend that I'm a fancy, confident woman who is absolutely unruffled by solo meals in fancy restaurants. I am going to lean into this experience and toast this whole wild ride.

I pore over the menu like there'll be a test later and I order the things that make my mouth water. Starting with something called a mojito spritz, which I drink slowly, as a personal declaration to savor every part of this meal, and every part of this trip.

Except when the handsome waiter asks, "Do you want shaved black truffle on top of that?"

I laugh and shake my head. "What? No." I'm all for spoiling myself, but a lady has got to draw a line.

After I devour a delicious entrée, I decide I can read my book for distraction, because I feel like I'm too deeply invested in the stories of the other customers around me. I've built whole narratives for each of the tables. A first date. They met online. He used old photos and now she's not as interested. He's trying to be as impressive as he can, and he's a nice guy, but she's spending the whole meal looking forward to leaving and hate-fucking her ex.

Next to them is a buttoned-up young couple who I'm convinced have been together for a long time, because every glance just looks like a plea for a proposal. She fears that everyone in their lives has stopped wondering when it will happen, and they're now curious about whether it will happen at all. She's planned their whole wedding via a secret Pinterest board, and as each of her friends' weddings come and go, her desperation climbs. She wants to be married, damn it. But will she ever say anything? Hell no. She's not one of *those* women. I laugh loudly at this thought and she glances at me, so I smile. She does not smile back.

Next to them are an elderly white-haired couple who have been married for sixty years and who sustain their relationship by reading the newspaper to each other and start drinking each night at 5:00 p.m. They look happy. And that makes me equal measures of happy and lonely at once.

I order a dessert with lavender in it, drink my third mojito spritz and finish my second book for the week. When I finally look up, the restaurant has almost entirely cleared out around me and I haven't even noticed. I breathe in deep, the kind of breath that expands with possibility. Because that's what all of this is—the last few days, this meal, this trip—it's about what is possible. And right now, what's possible is absolutely anything.

Except seeing Molly. After I pay, I look at my phone and there's a message from her. **So sorry to do this but something** has come up. I can't come to London this weekend after all. Soon, though.

I'm gutted. I was so looking forward to seeing her, to see if anything would happen, to see if she still liked me, and if I still liked her. The anticipation is a lot. I want to reply straightaway, I want to tell her I'm disappointed, that I want to see her, to ask her where she'll be and tell her that I'll come to her. But I don't. I don't want her to know any of this.

Instead I message Naz.

I'll come with you
on Saturday,
if the offer still stands.

She replies straightaway.

> Fucking Molly.
> And then again.
> You'll need a frock.
> And then again. Yes, babes!

"You look fucking delicious." Naz is smiling as wide as her face can stand and I do a spin.

I've bought a dress that made me think *If I was ballsier, I'd totally wear this* when I tried it on, as a kind of forced exposure therapy. It's an off-the-shoulder structured number, with a flamenco vibe but with more boning, in black. The night before, when I'd hung it up on the back of the door, my faked nonchalance mocked me and I felt stupid for thinking I could pull it off. But I'd persisted, and when I'd sent Molly a photo of me in the dress, she'd replied with a photo of a fire. Which made me blush.

Naz was running me through everything I might need to

know about the function we were off to. Her company had booked two tables at a fancy fundraiser in order to schmooze some of their bigger clients.

"The stakes are not that high, but if we're charming, it'll make my job easier in the coming months, you know? So just don't call anyone a cunt or talk about Brexit and we'll all be grand."

"Got it," I said. Look good. Be charming and inoffensive. Make Naz look good. This last point felt a bit moot, since Naz has enough charm for the whole fucking universe.

"Let's get sloshed," she says as we walk through double doors into a dimly lit ballroom. Instantly I know these are not my people, all branded suits and cascading jewels, Botoxed foreheads and professional blowouts. Naz introduces me to the people at our two tables with a running commentary whispered in my ear. They're mostly all old white men with varying degrees of hair on their heads.

She points at the first guy. "Big money, like personal-butler big. Martin, hi!" she says, squeezing him in a hug. The next is a man with black hair plugs. "The bill for his secret nondisclosure-agreed children would be more money than you will earn in your entire fucking lifetime." She pats him on the back as he stays seated. "Rick, great to see you, this is my friend, Noni." He kisses my hand. "Wash that immediately," she whispers to me as we get to the next couple, a broad-set woman with an eighties Diana haircut and a royal-blue pantsuit with huge shoulder pads, and a slight man with a thin Walt Disney mustache. "Rachel, Jerry, good to see you. This is Noni." We say hello and Naz keeps her hand on my waist, ushering me forward. "I'm sure she's a big lesbian. Husband is dull as fuck." I smile as Naz waves at the other table and quickly gives me the rundown on each person sitting at it. "He is sure he knows Banksy. Rumor is that they went to the ER in the same ambulance after they stabbed each other during an argument. His fourth wife is nineteen." I wave and smile politely. "His kid is on one of those reality shows about wealthy fuckwits. And their house was on *Grand Designs*."

My eyes pop wide and I stare at Naz. "Which means they've met Kevin McCloud?"

Naz laughs. "I do not understand your wide-on for Kevin McCloud." She looks at the woman. "Sheila, Noni here wants to fuck Kevin McCloud, so don't ruin him for her, okay?"

Sheila laughs. "Oh, really, Noni? Well, he's very lovely."

"I think I'd be devastated if he wasn't," I tell her, and the rest of the table pipes in with anecdotes about celebrities they've met who are lovely, or more interestingly are complete fuckwits, which is how Naz describes one of the D-grade pop singers from the early 2000s who she met in an elevator and who told her to give him a blow job.

"I did." Naz shakes her head, disgusted. "But I mean, don't be a dick about it, you know?"

I follow Naz over to a couple who are sitting next to two empty chairs, which by the look of it are ours. "She's the only one I genuinely like here. She runs a huge nonprofit and her wife is some famous art curator. How chic are they? Bonnie, Roberta, babes! Good to see you. This is Noni—she's my lush Aussie friend here on a quest to pleasure herself through Europe."

I whack her and smile. "It's not like that at all," I say.

Bonnie or Roberta, I don't know which one is which, smiles. "I wish it were true. Sounds divine." Her sharp black bob swishes as she talks.

The wine is free and good, and young waiters keep pouring it. I don't know how many glasses I've had because technically

I've had only one, as it has never been empty. We get through our entrées without a hitch and by the end of the main course Naz and I are a wisecracking comedy duo, landing jokes and witty repartee with the ease that comes with eighteen years of friendship. Naz is regaling the table with an anecdote about the time we accidentally stole someone's houseboat, when a short, fashionably stubbly guy with a nice suit and a sweet smile approaches our table. We make eye contact and he smiles, saying "Hello" just as he trips over his own feet.

There is a tightening in the air around us, and I'm sure someone gasps. He instantly looks down at his feet and then back up. "Nice entrance that was, yeah?" He is rattled and it makes me laugh too loudly. We make eye contact, he blushes, and I try to turn my smile to consolation. "I'm Billy," he says.

"Hello! Billy!" Naz bellows loudly.

"I'm a magician and I'm here—" He stops abruptly. "Sorry, I'm still stuck on the entrance." Everyone laughs politely and Billy blushes again. I think he's cute. "Right, you guys up for some magic?"

"I am so ready for some magicianing!" Naz exclaims.

"Yes!" I cry "Magish us immediately."

Billy looks at me, laughing slightly. "I've not heard that before. Magished. Good. I might get it on a T-shirt."

"Trademark that immediately, then, Noni," one of the old white men says, chortling.

"Shall I do some?" the magician offers.

Everyone agrees gleefully, boozily, and so he pulls out a pen from his pocket and a deck of cards. He makes Naz choose a card and draw something on it, without showing him. Naz draws a dick and I laugh loudly. With some sleight of hand, and good gags, he impresses us by moments later pulling the right card from the deck.

He glances at the card. "The dick of clubs. Great."

I giggle.

He does some more magicianing, cards get put away, someone else at the table is holding them, there's a whole spiel. "So what I need you to do now is put your hand in my pocket," he says to me.

"I bet you say that to all the girls," I flutter.

He's now hit a charming rhythm and has shaken off his entrance; he's very comfortable, he's very good. "It's not a trick pocket. Check." I put my hand in. "Feel around. Check that there are no secret zips or holes." I do and I shake my head; it's empty apart from a playing card. "Can you feel anything?"

"There's a card," I say.

"Just the one?"

"Yes."

"Okay, pull it out," he says. Naz and I snort and Billy blushes again. "I've been oblivious to the innuendo in this act for years now, but this table has completely undone me." We all laugh.

I pull out the card from his pocket and squeal. "It's your dick, Naz." I'm a mouth-agape giddy girl. I don't care that there's a logical explanation for all of this trickery, or that I've fallen for sleight of hand and distraction and speed. I want to believe that he made this card fly from that pack in the old man's hands across the table into his pocket and then into my hand. I want to believe so badly that this man is magic that I find myself purposely placing myself in his eyeline for the rest of the night. Making sustained eye contact. Thinking powerful, sexy thoughts so that I'm radiating "come and fuck me" energy in his direction. It works. He brings me a glass of champagne and tells me his shift is over, and I ask him if he has any other tricks he'd like to show me. He nods.

An hour later I find myself in my hotel room and my vagina is being magished...badly. In bed, the magician is a one-trick pony. One position. One speed. One move. There is no sleight of hand at all; his hands just kind of paw at my body clumsily. If I'm honest, I probably don't even need to be there; he could've just shagged a damp pillow and it would've been exactly the same. I pull a weird face, accompanied by a strange sound, when he gets naked—still visually perplexed by real-life penises and all—but I cover it up by pretending to moan, turned on. I am not. Not really. The whole thing is quick and disappointing and I watch the ceiling as he hammers in and out of me, willing him to finish. Bored. I refuse to fake it out of feminist principal, of course. And then I feel mature and grown-up, because twentysomething Noni would've absolutely faked it for him and his ego.

"How was that?" he asks, throwing the condom onto the floor next to the bed, which feels gross.

"You're a very good magician," I say, drunkenly.

I wake up to an empty bed and my phone ringing next to me. I am so hungover. I feel instantly nauseated at the tinging sound, at the light, at the weight of my own limbs, sweaty on the bed. I look at the clock—9:55 a.m. *Fuck. Shit. Fuck.* I've got five minutes till checkout. I launch myself around the room, gathering all my belongings into my bag. There is no time to shower. I wee, clean my teeth, get dressed and get in the lift in four minutes. I catch a glimpse of reflection in the mirrored glass of the elevator and audibly whimper. I look like a crumpled version of myself. Like a rough draft. Like the bit of paper you scrunch up and throw in the bin because you can do better. I rummage around my bag for a packet of wet wipes to try to get some of last night's mascara off my cheeks. Finally, I grab my phone to check who had been calling, knowing it will be a punctual Naz wondering where the fuck I am. But it wasn't Naz, it was Molly. There's a voice mail message. I hit Play immediately.

"Hi, darlin'. So, I'm shit, I know. Work is mental right now, so, as it turns out, I'm around for one night only tomorrow, if you haven't made plans and you don't hate me. I'd love to see you."

Shit. Fuck. Shit.

Tomorrow? Tomorrow is only one sleep away. Yes, I want to see her, of course. But I'm still pissed off at her for canceling. And tomorrow is so soon.

Naz is across the lobby staring at me as I exit the lift. "Did he make his dick disappear?" she says, smiling happily. She does not look like a rough draft, she looks like the good copy. The final copy. The polished copy made by a fucking world-renowned artist.

"Morning," I mutter, stealing the water bottle from her hand and glugging it violently.

"Pull an orgasm out of your hat?"

"How many more do you have?" I grumble.

"Cum you in half?"

"What?" I ask, hunting for my sunglasses in my bag.

"A riff on cut you in half. Admittedly not my best work," she says. "That's it. That's all I've got." She looks me up and down. "You look how I feel," she chuckles, putting her large gold sunglasses on.

"He disappeared."

"What?"

"No sign of him this morning or the hundred quid I had in my clutch."

"Shut up! That scumbug. Was he at least any good?"

"A one. At best."

"Oh, babes. So disappointing. Come on, I'll buy you breakfast."

★ ★ ★

We sit in a proper workman's café and order full-English fry-ups and eat for a solid ten minutes before we both say another word to each other. All I'm thinking about is Molly. And hash browns. But Molly mostly.

"Molly wants to meet up tomorrow," I say finally, when I feel full enough and the coffee has triggered function to my form.

"I thought she couldn't meet you?" Naz says.

"Well, she can now. She said work is busy and she's back for one night only."

Naz raises her eyebrows suspiciously. "Is that weird? I think that's weird."

"It's not hard to believe that backpackers would be a shit-fight to run, so I don't know. It's not weird she wants to see me, is it? We've been talking for weeks."

"Have you replied?"

"Not yet. I should do that, shouldn't I?" I pull out my phone.

"If you want to see her tomorrow, babes, then you should definitely make that plan." Naz mops up baked beans with buttered white bread off her plate and into her mouth in one move. "But…"

"But what?" I ask, pleading with my eyes that she doesn't ruin this for me.

"One night only sounds conditional. Just trust your gut, Nons," she says pointedly.

I roll my eyes, opening a new message, and then I freeze. "Naz, what do I say?"

"Say, you're lucky, I'm free. Don't overthink it, dear." She smirks at me.

Don't overthink it. Tomorrow. I'm going to see Molly tomorrow.

I can be free tomorrow, I type. Tell me when and where and I'll be there. I hit Send.

Tomorrow. Shit.

15

I swallow hard. The pulse of adrenaline hits me hard the second I see her walk into the bar. She looks exactly how I remember, but also not at all. She's older, her hair has changed—it's shorter, but still it's her signature whitish blond and still swept across her forehead diagonally. Her body is different; there are curves in different places. But her style is the same. Black jeans, black T-shirt, expensive leather jacket. She's beautiful. I am smacked by nostalgia and possibility at exactly the same time so my heart doesn't quite feel like my own anymore.

"Hello," she says as she reaches me.

"Hi." I stand and we hug, and she kisses my cheek.

"Wow! You look—" We speak over the top of each other.

"Incredible. I love your hair like that," she says, sitting down on the burgundy chesterfield.

"Oh, I don't—" I stop myself and receive the compliment. "Thank you." I smile, breathing it in. Her in. *She thinks I look incredible. I feel incredible.*

We chat easily, though it takes a little while to find a flow. But we've always been like that. Better in writing. She asks me about work and Joan and I tell her short, uncomplicated versions of both. She tells me all about the chain of backpackers around Europe she invested in.

"It's like I've never grown up."

"I wouldn't recommend it."

She still plays with her hair, pushing it out of her face with her palm, when she's nervous. I like that I make her nervous. I laugh at her jokes. She's funny. She laughs at mine. We drink wine. We catch up. It's friendly. Not really flirty. It's nice. I don't know how she feels. I can't read her. I've never really been able to read her.

With a deep breath, a swig of wine, and a mission to find out once and for all if this is meant to be, I ask, "Why didn't we ever seal the deal?"

She laughs, shocked by my directness. She smiles and I can see her trying to read my face. "I dunno. We were young."

"Yeah."

"And I was scared of you," she adds, grabbing her glass for protection.

"Of me?" I ask, surprised.

"Yeah, of your confidence," she says and I smirk, shaking my head. *She has no idea.* "Of the way you made me feel," she continues. "I'd never been in a relationship, or had a beautiful woman in my bed, or at least not a naked one who was happy for me to touch her boobs. It was too much."

"I'm sorry if I made you feel uncomfortable," I tell her, trying to receive this new insight graciously.

"Noni, you have nothing to apologize for. Believe me. I dunno. I'm sorry I was a dick." She looks at me sincerely. "A lot." She holds out her drink and we clink glasses. There is another pause. It's full of possibility.

"Are you going to tell me why you wanted to see me?" she finally asks.

"To see," I rush out.

"What?"

"To see if—" I stop. "It's a long story."

"I've got all the time in the world." She bites her lip and then looks at her watch. "Well, until one o'clock tomorrow, when I have to catch a flight to Sweden, but you know, until then." She smiles and I think she's finally flirting with me. I'm surprised by how quickly we've fallen back into this place. We're good in this place. It's the next bit we've never quite successfully navigated. I think she's so beautiful. The should've-boned list pops into mind. So I tell her.

"There's a list."

"I'm on a list?"

"Yeah."

"What is this list?"

"A list of people who I should've slept with and didn't."

She splutters a mouthful of wine onto the table. "Your bucket list is actually a fuck-it list?" She laughs loudly.

"Kind of." I feel suddenly shy, so I wait for her to speak.

"I've thought about it," she says, looking me in the eye.

"What?"

"You and me." She glances down at her glass. "A lot. Us together." She looks at me, her lips part slightly and she grins. "Fucking." I stop breathing. "I've thought about making you cum." She drinks from her glass slowly, purposefully. I take in every single detail of her hands as they move toward her face and back down to her lap. "It makes me cum."

OH. MY. GOD.

"I like that," I mutter. I'm surprised that words have even managed to escape my body. "Tell me," I ask.

"What?"

"Tell me what happens," I plead, my fingers landing on my cheeks as she starts to talk.

"We lock eyes across a party—" she says.

"What kind of party?" *WHAT THE FUCK ARE YOU DOING, NONI? IT DOESN'T MATTER WHAT KIND OF PARTY. LET THE WOMAN OF YOUR DREAMS TELL YOU ABOUT HOW YOU MAKE HER CUM IN HER MIND.*

Molly laughs. "I don't know, I've never thought about what kind of party. A good one."

"Good. I'd hate for us to be at a shit party." I giggle a little too loudly. *GET THIS TRAIN BACK ON ITS FUCKING TRACKS NOW, WOMAN.* "What happens after we lock eyes?" I ask.

"We're not with each other, but we can see each other. We make eye contact and I nod toward a hallway," she says, biting her lip gently. She moves closer to me, just a little, but it's enough. She lowers her voice. "You make your way across the party and meet me there. We go inside a room, it's a bedroom, but we don't get any farther than the door. I don't let you touch me, but I touch you all over with my mouth, my hands, my tongue."

I swallow hard. I have ceased being a person and am now instead just made up entirely of wanting. The desire pulls hard and deep and I rock my hips back in the chair for some kind of respite. "I am amazed that you're not wearing underwear..."

"What a minx," I whisper, trying desperately to shift the tension. She smiles and keeps talking, edging closer to me.

"I like that you're not. I move my hand up your thigh."

My breath is so deep that each inhalation moves my whole body. Molly hasn't touched me. I move closer to her; I want more than her voice inside me. I lean my neck closer to her mouth, willing her to kiss me. I place my hand on her thigh and she puts her hand on top of mine, and with just the tip of one finger she starts tracing single lines from my fingernail to my wrist, slowly, deliberately. The touch wakes up my whole body. I feel her touch in my chest, in my stomach, in my thighs.

"You think I'm going to touch you," she says low and quiet, "but I don't."

I swallow. "You don't?"

"No. I lie down on the floor and I ask you to straddle my face."

My eyes open wider than they ever have. Ever. And all I do is nod. She quickly flips my hand over and now draws circles on my palm, leaning into my neck to whisper into my ear, "I like the way your magnificent ass gyrates each time my tongue does something you like."

I open my mouth but no sound comes out. *SPEAK, NONI.* "You do?"

"I do."

"Do I cum?" I ask, because good god I want to.

"I don't know. Am I good enough?" She looks at me and bites her lip again, letting it slowly run through her teeth.

I stare at her, shaking my head in a swirl of disbelief and desire. "Yes," is all I manage to say. I look in her eyes.

"You are fucking stunning, Noni Blake."

"Kiss me," I tell her. I don't ask. This is a demand. And I'm so relieved that she does. All passion. One hand grabs my cheek, one hand grabs my hip, I grab her face with both my hands, lick her lip, she bites mine gently and a moan escapes my mouth that I have no control over. We are pressed hard against each other as we kiss and kiss and kiss.

I pull back, look at her and smile. There are no words. She laughs, shaking her head.

"Ask me to come home with you," she says.

★ ★ ★

The passion from the bar only increases when we get back to my flat. I flick on a lamp and sit next to Molly on the couch, but she pulls me onto her lap. Then her hands are all over my boobs and my body; she rubs her hand up my neck and looks at me with a kind of intensity that startles me. She grabs my hands and I rock my hips into her. I pull her T-shirt off and lay her head back on the couch, kissing her neck, her jaw, her beautiful collarbones. I pay particular attention to her nipples, to the way my tongue, and light grazes of my teeth, make her moan.

"God, I want you," she says, and I feel giddy. We take our time getting undressed. It's like we both acknowledge the time it's taken us to get here and now we don't want to waste it.

Molly kisses every inch of my skin, and whenever I try to take any control and kiss her back, she stops me. Everything about this feels like it's for me. Molly is all sly grins and deep moans. "I'm so fucking turned on," she whispers. She is getting so much pleasure from pleasuring me, and it's the hottest thing ever.

"Oh, god, Noni," she moans. Every time she says my name, I feel it in my chest cavity, like a water bomb hitting concrete. It fills bits of my body I didn't know I could have feeling in. She goes down on me so well, and for so long, that I can barely keep my eyes open. I pant hard and she smiles gleefully, lying on her side looking at me.

"Good?" she says.

"Better than…" I mumble, arching my back and stretching my arms out. I look at Molly, then sit up, taking her hand, leading her to the bed. As I do this, I make a promise to myself, a deep commitment to fuck this woman with every skill I possess, until she can orgasm no more.

And I do.

I roll onto my back and puff air into my lungs in sharp in-
takes.

"What a relief," I say.

"What?" Molly asks, holding her chest and smirking.

"What a relief that wasn't shit." I smile, and Molly laughs.
"How disappointing would it have been after all this time if
that was shit?"

"Horrifying," she says and we both laugh. I tickle lines
slowly over her arms, stomach, and neck, staring at her flushed
face.

"If I'd have known that's what it was going to be like, I
would've leaped right in back then," she says.

"No you wouldn't have." I smirk, poking her.

"No, I wouldn't have. But I'm not the same person I was
back then." She holds my hand in hers. "Thankfully."

"Sometimes I think I'm not, and then other times I still
feel like my fifteen-year-old self has complete say over everything, you know?"

She picks up my hand and kisses my fingers. "You are very
special to me, Noni. You always have been. You know that,
yeah?" She glances across her shoulder at me.

I blush, and she leans over and kisses me gently on my lips. I
roll onto my side and she spoons me, wrapping her hand tight
around my waist. We interlock fingers and fall asleep. Happy.

The vibrating of my phone on the bedside table wakes me
up. I peel open one eye, quickly glance at the phone, see the
capital L and know it's Lindell. It's still dark outside—we can't
have been asleep long, I think, as I sneak out of the bed, so as
not to wake Molly. I quickly maneuver into the bathroom,
wrapping a towel around my chest so Lindell doesn't have to
stare at my boobs, and hit the green button to accept the video
call. My eyes are bleary. I don't even know what time it is. I'm

still asleep. I'm still sex fuzzy. I'm still giddy from what has happened tonight, from what it means, from the bliss, from this whole trip being the entirely right decision.

"Who the fuck are you?" A woman who is mostly black fringe is staring at me.

"Lindell? What?" I ask.

"Where's Molly?" she spits.

"Where's—What? Lindell?" I ask.

"Who the fuck is Lindell?" She has a thick, maybe French, accent and she is furious. I suddenly realize this isn't my phone. This is Molly's phone. And this must be Molly's...

"Who are you?" I ask.

The door flies open and a stunned Molly looks ghostly white. I stare at her. The woman speaks French.

"Luana, babe—" Molly says, grabbing the phone out of my hand and walking back into the room.

Luana? *Fuck.* Babe? *Fuck.* Molly? *Fuck. Fuck. Fuck.* Molly is speaking in French. I didn't even know she spoke French. I feel like my feet are frozen to the bathroom floor, like my brain is telling them to move but the message to my body isn't computing. I can't take it in. Can't take in that clearly this Luana woman, Molly's "babe," is not happy about the sudden revelation that I am with her—I let the word find me—girlfriend? *Her girlfriend. Molly has a girlfriend.* Molly has a fucking girlfriend. It feels like cold water splashed onto my face and the shock propels me forward into the room.

"Molly, hang up the phone," I say, but she doesn't hear me. I try again. "Molly, hang up the phone," I yell. I yell so loudly I stun myself and Molly looks at me. She says something in French, ends the call and looks at me. "Was that your girlfriend?" I ask.

"Why did you answer my phone?" She stares at me.

"I thought it was my phone. Also, not the fucking point. Is that your girlfriend?"

"I can explain, there is an explanation—" She stops talking and stares at me.

I try to find the answer in her face, but she gives me nothing, "But you're in a—?"

"Relationship. Yes. I'm in a relationship," she sighs.

I close my eyes really tight, trying to work out what to say. Thoughts pummel me wildly. "Why the fuck wouldn't you tell me that?" I spit. *Oh my god. What? Why am I here? What is she doing?*

"I dunno. 'Cause. 'Cause I wanted to see you. I really, really wanted to see you." *This is fucked. You came here for this.* "And I didn't think there'd still be chemistry between us, but there is. It's pretty undeniable, actually. I guess I needed you to know I'm not the same as I was back then, that I could—"

You're an idiot. You're an idiot. You're an idiot. Something snaps. *No. Actually. Fuck her.* I cut her off. "Stop talking. I don't need to hear whatever you're going to say." My brain spins like a carnival ride that turns so quickly it defies gravity, and my thoughts cling upside down on the walls. Heavy. "Fuck you" is all I manage.

"I know I'm shit." She gingerly takes a step toward me. "I wanted to see you, Noni."

"Well, we could've fucking Skyped."

"I'm so sorry." She grabs my hands but I push her away. We stare at each other. She looks positively tiny framed by the big window, with the city behind her. With her big blue eyes and fluttering eyelashes she's like a deer, and I am equally torn between throwing something at her and protecting her from hunters.

"I don't care. I don't actually care what you want," I say. She opens her mouth but she doesn't say anything, so I continue.

"I don't want your bullshit. Again. Fuck. I'm a fucking idiot." I shake my head, feeling the weight of my own stupidity.

"I do want you," she says low and quiet. "Clearly. Can we just—can we talk?"

"So you can lead me on a little more?"

"I didn't think it would be like this. So much time has passed and I thought it was—"

"We've been talking for months and you didn't think to bring it up?"

"I thought it'd be different in real life. I thought—I dunno, okay. I don't know what I thought. I wanted to show you that I've changed."

"Into an epically shitty person?" I spit.

"Yeah, I guess," she says, looking quickly at me. "I don't know what to say to you, Noni." She sits on the edge of the bed.

The voice in my head starts screaming. *MAKE HER LEAVE. THIS IS A TERRIBLE IDEA.* The back-away siren inside my head whoops loudly. *DO NOT SIT DOWN.* I get goose bumps.

"Please, Noni, can we just talk?" She leans forward, grabbing my hand, and I feel the touch in every one of my millions of cells, and the alarm in my brain whoops louder. *DON'T BE A FUCKING IDIOT.* "We can sort it out."

I step toward her, breathing her in. *DON'T YOU DARE.* "No." I shake my hand free. "That is a terrible idea."

"Noni?"

"Just...no." I exhale loudly. Every inch of my skin tenses and the muscles in my throat constrict so tight that I'm surprised words are actually able to escape.

"Fine." She starts getting dressed. She's pissed off with me. *She's pissed off with me? Fuck her.*

I shake my head. "You need to fuck off right now."

She groans, pained. "Noni, you need to let me fix this. I can fix this."

"Go," I say.

She stares at me, her eyes pleading me to change my mind. I don't. She gathers the rest of her things and walks to the front door.

But before she opens it, she looks at me. "Noni?"

"Go," I say.

And she does.

16

I stare at the door for I don't know how long. What the hell just happened? I feel entirely disoriented. Used. And stupid for all of the energy and hope I poured into tonight. Into Molly and this perfect vision of what I thought was meant to be. I feel stupid for coming here. I feel stupid for thinking I could change my life. Some things are just the way they are.

My phone buzzes on the lounge. I pick it up. A text from Molly.

Noni, I'm so sorry. I don't want you to think that I was leading you on, that wasn't my intention. I'm so glad tonight happened. I want to talk to you. Talk this through. Please. When you're ready. You're incredible. Tonight was incredible.

I burst into tears. *Stupid. Stupid. Stupid.* I climb into the bed, cocooning myself in the covers. And I sob.

★ ★ ★

When I wake up, it's raining and the sky looks exactly how I feel. I check my phone. I've been asleep for hours. There's a message from Joan. The message is four words long.

Two years, my love.

At first I don't know what she means, and for a second I suspect she's sent the wrong message to the wrong person. But she hasn't, because the revelation runs into my chest like a slow-moving coal train, long, heavy, oh-so grubby, and without hope of stopping. I check the date to be sure, but I already know what she means. *Our due date.*

Today should've been her birthday.

Socially infertile. That's the medical term for same-sex couples navigating fertility treatments. I never got used to seeing the red stamp in our folder at each appointment. It made me rage. Joan thought it was ridiculous. The cracks in our relationship had already begun showing before we started trying for a baby, but we were in too deep for either of us to be able to put up a hand and say, "I'm drowning." Drowning in our life, our mortgage, our dog, in the amount of money we were spending on IVF, and sperm and medical appointments. We were drowning in the expectations of what all of these things meant, of how we should have been feeling versus how we were actually feeling. Because the alternative was too hard. Too difficult to consider.

The knowing that it wasn't right was easier to live with than the unknown of doing something about it. I was thirty-one, Joan was thirty-three, we were prime baby-having age. We had put in the work. We had done all of the right things. We would fix our shit. We would make it right. We would stay together. We would be parents. We would be great parents. We would be okay. And this feeling would go away. Eventually. We just had to keep working.

IVF is an asshole. Like a smarmy bald guy who gives you backhanded compliments, never harsh enough to be abusive, but enough to make your ears prick hot and question whether they did in fact just call you fat, but you let it slide with a wry smile because it happened so quickly. I was pumped full of hormones, and tears and extra pounds and raw heart. We did everything we were told to do, and then some. The pressure was high. Our first three cycles didn't take and it was just... hell. I know now that any kind of fertility journey is actual hell. Without the flames, but with the heat of expectation, and stress, and hope, and fury at every single person who's ever had a baby and every single person who doesn't understand what you're going through. Which feels like every single person on the entire planet.

It's a kind of mental fuckery that no one ever talks about. Deeply isolating. Confusing. Lonely. So about your body, but so in your head. There's no reprieve. I never understood that stereotype of the fanatical fertile woman craving a baby. I never thought that would be me. But it was me. It was us. There was a distinct turning point where we became consumed by it. Everything in our life was split into two-week time slots. Waiting to ovulate. Waiting to see. Waiting. Waiting. Fucking waiting. And in the meantime, it feels like every single fucking person in the whole world is pregnant except you. And you don't talk about it because it just feels so dripped in shame.

And then we were pregnant.

And everything shifted again, because the thing that had been the goal for years now had happened. We were elated, like joy that had blissed out on excitement. We were focused on nothing but our future. We had a goal. We were talking more than we had in a long while. We were showing up for each other. We were connected. It was intimate. It all seemed possible. Not that things between us were fixed, by any means, but possible that we would make it work. I believed that with my whole heart. We, the three of us, were going to be okay.

And then we weren't pregnant.

Our baby died. Our baby, who had suddenly appeared in our sphere and defibrillated our relationship, had died. She was gone. When her fifteen-week-old heartbeat stopped, so did the heartbeat of our relationship. We couldn't save it. Any of it. We spent a whole year afterward trying, but we were both too tired and sad. And so one night, when Joan came in the front door after walking Carson and saw me sitting on the stairs, she took three steps toward me, kissed my forehead and started to cry. I cried too. We stayed like that for hours, neither of us saying anything. We didn't need to. There was nothing left to say.

It was done.

We were done.

For good.

Two years. *And I forgot*. I hit the call button and it rings three times before she answers.

"Hey," she says.

"Hi."

"Where are you?" she asks.

"In an Airbnb. In London."

"In London? Why?"

"I forgot. I forgot about the date," I cry. My throat clamps as I listen to her breathe.

"I'm sorry, Noni."

"Me too."

The plain and simple truth is that our hearts broke. We broke. Smashed, even. Into smithereens. Like glass hitting tiles.

And there was no way that we'd ever have been able to put the pieces back together, because the pieces were everywhere.

Just like smashed glass, Joan's text message acts like one of those pieces that you step on months later, barefoot, and you bleed. And sob. Which I do, sitting up in bed. Joan listens.

I hear her crying too. "Are you okay?" she asks.

"I dunno. No. You?"

"Me either."

"I'm just—I'm trying to be happy and it feels like it works sometimes, and then other times it feels like such an effort, you know?"

Joan chuckles a little. "Yeah, I know."

"This isn't how things were meant to be. I don't know what this version of my life is. And I'm trying really hard. And maybe that's the thing, yeah? You shouldn't have to try." I pause. "I have no fucking idea what I'm doing."

"I think that's all of us," she says.

"Do you think about her?" I ask.

"All the time."

"Same."

"Do you talk about her?" Joan asks.

"Not really. No. It hurts."

"I don't either. And it feels awful not to, but it just fucking kills. It kills me in my body, Nons. Like, it stings so bad."

My quick intake of breath is so loud it's startling and we both make throaty pained sounds that come from deep places. "I'll be fine one moment, and then out of nowhere it just smacks me," I tell her. "I imagine it's like a plank of wood to the face, you know like those old slapstick skits? And then other times it just fucking creeps up on me."

"Baby-wearing dads," she says.

"What?"

"If I see a baby-wearing dad, I just want to kick him in the dick and steal his baby, but also howl with the ache."

I laugh at this. "Please don't steal anyone's baby."

She laughs too. "What are you doing in London?"

"Trying to be happy."

"Is it working?"

"No. Not at all. I'm a fucking idiot. I don't know. Nothing ever goes as I plan." Neither of us says anything.

"It's okay to be sad," she says eventually. "It's okay to be happy, too, Nons. It is."

"Are you happy?" I ask.

"I'm getting there."

The tears drip down my cheeks, but I'm so used to crying that I just let them. "How's cannellini-beans?"

"She's fine."

We breathe together, feeling the weight of this thing that feels so unique to us, even though it's not, even though millions of people have experienced this very same thing. Which in theory should make me feel better. But it doesn't, because it feels like it cheapens our experience. That it's somehow normal. And nothing about it, about this kind of pain and grief, is normal at all. It hurts. I have been happy. And that feels bad. Just last night I was happy. Until I wasn't. And right now what Molly did feels deserved. *I should be unhappy.* I catch that thought, knowing it's wrong. Because I want to be happy, I do. But this pain is rigid and felt all over my body. No matter where I think I hide it.

"I love you, you know that, right?" she says finally.

"Yup. I love you too."

"I know."

We say goodbye and hang up. Joan is right.

What the fuck am I doing here?

★ ★ ★

I let myself be consumed by my grief and confusion and rage, and I sob heavy and hard into the pillow. The kind of sobs that fold your body in half and hang as heavy in your throat as they do in the air.

I get up, pull the curtains closed and get back into bed. And I don't move for hours. But when I'm ready, I message Lindell.

Molly is in a
relationship, I text.
I discovered this fact
when I was naked.
And on the phone
to her girlfriend.

WHAT THE ACTUAL FUCK?!?
he replies.

Molly and I had excellent,
excellent, excellent sex last night.

Lindell's messages arrive in quick succession.

YOU DID? WHAT? NONI!

And then I answered
her phone accidentally
thinking it was my phone
and that it was you.
It was not you.
It was her French
girlfriend, Luana.

I'M DEAD,

Lindell writes back straightaway.

ACTUALLY DECEASED.

And then after a moment:

Do you want me to call?

Do I? Of course. But also not, because I know the love and concern in his voice will make me want to cry again. Yes, I reply.

The phone rings. I tell him everything, and when he feels like he is across the whole drama, he kicks into peak best-friend mode.

"I'm so sorry, my girl. Fuck. What an ordeal." He sighs, gathering his thoughts. "But you can't forget that you're a powerful fucking boss bitch and this actually has nothing to do with you. This is all *her* bullshit. Not yours." I picture his eyebrows knitting in the middle and his lips pursing with matter-of-fact precision.

"Yeah. Just—what a shitty, shitty thing to do. I feel so used," I say, feeling it in my chest and arms like it's crawling under my skin, making me itch.

"Of course you do. You were. She used you. What was she thinking?"

"She said it was because she didn't think this thing between us would be a thing anymore," I paraphrase sourly. "And then it was, and I guess it took her by surprise, and she got swept up in the moment." I punch the pillow in my lap flat.

Lindell scoffs loudly. "It's the dishonesty that fucks me off. It was so manipulative. Was there chemistry, though?"

"Yeah, of course, there's always been chemistry between us. We just get along so well."

"But is it chemistry, or is it history?" he says.

"Oh, god, I don't know." I don't know where he's going with this.

"I mean, I don't want to be shit, but you wanted this to happen, not the French girlfriend bit obviously, but the fucking, the chemistry bit, yes?"

"Of course," I tell him, pushing the flattened pillow into my lap and hugging it tight. "So?" I want him to finish this thought. He doesn't. "Did I make this up?" A pang of anxiety hits.

"You didn't make it up, babe, of course not, but did you only see the good? Was Molly giving you other signals, maybe?"

Was she? Did I miss something? "I don't think so. I think she was doing, and saying, everything I wanted her to, and now I'm like, was any of it real? Fuck, Lindell, was this just her plan? Is she that egotistical? She just wanted to make me look like an idiot?"

"You are not an idiot." I picture him shaking his head and pacing. "Fuck her," he groans. "She's got so much work to do. Shit." He goes quiet for a moment. "Thank god you know now, though, yes?"

Holy shit. "Yes. You're right. What if I hadn't picked up her phone? Then what? Oh, god. It makes me feel sick." What if I hadn't found out? Then what?

"You dodged a fucking bullet. You were meant to answer that phone, babe. Clearly. You know what you fucking deserve, Noni, and this isn't it."

"Yeah, and that's not all that happened," I say. And then, very slowly and very reluctantly, I tell him about the phone call with Joan.

"I forgot. I forgot about the date. I'm sorry, darling," he says.

"Why would you remember the date?" I say, pulling the blanket up over my shoulders and rolling onto my side.

"I want to remember everything. Fuck." He exhales loudly. "I'm not going to ask you if you're okay, because that's shit. I'm just going to tell you that I love you and I'm here, and remind you to tell me whatever you need and I'll do it," he says. I can hear his pain and worry. I start to cry. "Oh, my darling. I know. I know. Just cry. I'm here. Just cry it all out," he says, his voice twinging with sadness too.

"I'm okay. It's your voice. Your voice, just—" I tell him through sobs.

"I know."

"I feel like this whole adventure idea was only a distraction from feeling like this."

"Maybe, my love, but you're allowed distractions. All of this is very much a big, exhausting, inside job. Hang on—Julius, put the guinea pig back in its cage now. Now," he yells. "Sorry."

"You got a guinea pig?"

"Don't ask. I fucking hate the thing."

This makes me laugh a little and I rub my forehead, trying to alleviate some of the pressure in my head, on my thoughts. "I'm so sick of my own shit. You know? Like, I think I've dealt with things and then I'm smacked in the face with how fundamentally I have not dealt with things."

"Oh, darling, that's life, that's grief, that's being human. And there is a hole. There is a hole in your heart, or your life, or however you want to look at it. That baby, she is a hole, which you're never, ever gonna fill. You're just gonna get better at living with the hole," he says, far too honestly for me to bear, but I know he's right.

"Fucking hell."

"I know. It sucks. And it's all fucking inside work."

"Ugh." I sigh loudly and roll onto my back.

"I miss you, so much," he says.

"I miss you."

"Now, pop a Valium and go to bed," he says. I sigh loudly and agree, hanging up. Just as I put my phone down, it dings again with a text from Naz wanting to know how it went. I give her the short version.

> WHAT A FUCKING ASSHOLE
> SHIT CUNTING PIECE
> OF FUCKERY, she replies.

Then again.

> I just told Tom.
> He's furious too.

Then again.

> What are you doing
> this weekend?
> Cancel it.

I'm not doing anything,
I reply.

> Good. You're coming
> away with Tom and me.
> We're going to Scotland.
> I'm arranging it now.

Okay, I reply.

I don't have the energy to do anything but agree with Naz.

> Good. We're going to some
> retreat for four days. It's about
> relaxation and clearing
> your poxy fucking chakras
> or something, but there's
> facials and massages
> and spas. You're coming.

Okay, I reply again.

Getting away will be good. A change of scene and pace will be good. I have nothing keeping me in London anymore, anyway.

My phone dings again:

> Good. It'll be a right
> old laugh.
> Get out of town.

Then again.

> FUCK HER.

Then again.

> FUUUUUUCCCCKKKK HER.

I smile. I've never been to Scotland.

17

I stand next to the information desk at King's Cross station, "The one near the escalator," Naz had said. I have all of my stuff and I am feeling deeply curious about what I've agreed to. I hear Naz squeal behind me; she's wheeling an oxblood snakeskin suitcase and she has a matching tracksuit on with ridiculous gold sneakers. Tom trails behind her, rolling his eyes but smiling at me. She squeezes me tight.

"Are you fucking ready?" Naz asks and I shake my head.

"Hey, Noni." Tom hugs me hard. "It's so good to see you."

Tom is an art director in one of those fancy open-plan of-fices, but he's also a man who has the ocean in his veins and the sun in his skin, the quintessential surfer type. He says he could surf before he could talk. And Naz jokes that he prac-tically combusts if his feet don't touch sand every few weeks. She thinks his brain loves their city life, but his heart longs for a beachside life. Which she is unsure she'll ever be able to provide because she is all city, all the time. If Tom has sand in his DNA, Naz has smog. They've lived in London so long now that I think he's just gotten used to it, and he loves the capacity to jump on a plane for forty quid and be somewhere entirely new in a matter of hours. He's calm. And he completely offsets Naz's combustible energy.

Once we're on the train, and I'm sitting across from Tom and Naz, she looks at me, worried, and says, "Babes, do you want to talk about Molly or not? We weren't sure."

"We're armed and ready to talk about it if you want to," Tom adds.

"I'm okay right now, I think," I say. "I'm mostly just mad about how deceitful she was about it all. Months and months of fucking bullshit that could've so easily been avoided." I stare out the window.

"Dick moves left, right and center on her part," Naz says.

"People find it hard to speak honestly about their feelings or intentions. I know I can't speak for Molly, but I can't imagine that her intention was to hurt you," Tom offers, relaxing his hand on Naz's thigh. She doesn't react. It's like his hand belongs there.

"I don't know about that." She looks at him.

"She's not a sociopath, is she, Noni?" Tom asks, opening a pack of chips and offering them around.

"No. Just confused. She acknowledged that the thing between us was legit, that it took her by surprise and that she wasn't thinking. But she has a fucking girlfriend. So, who knows," I mumble, looking out the window as the city disappears and is replaced by flashes of green. Molly had tried to call me three times and sent me five messages over the past few days. I read them out to Naz and Tom. "Noni, can we please talk? Please." "I hate that I've hurt you. I've really fucked up. I know that." "Let me explain. Or apologize. Both. I'm so sorry. But please. Call me." "Fine. You don't want to talk.

Just know that I want to fix it, but I respect your wishes too."

"Goodbye, Noni." I ignored them all. It took every inch of self-restraint I had.

"Not your circus, not your monkeys, babe," Naz says. "She has made her bed and now she can fuck off, and you can fuck someone entirely new and exciting."

"But also, feel what you feel, Nons," Tom says.

"Yes. You're both right. I don't want to talk to her. I don't care what she has to say. I mean, what *could* she say? Nothing is going to change the outcome, is it?" I say this to myself more than to the two of them. *Should I message her back?* I catch them glancing at each other.

"Nope. She's an asshole," Naz says.

"Naz, that's not helpful, I don't think." Tom is all eyebrows and subtext, with a side-eyed glance at Naz, who shakes her head.

"Where exactly are we going?" I ask, keen to change the subject.

"It's a four-day retreat," Tom says. "Yoga, massages, spa treatments, vegetarian feasts, optional workshops… It's going to be great. It's on the side of a mountain, completely sustainable. Run by this amazing woman. I did it last year and loved it, so I wanted to bring Naz." Sheer joy is painted across his face.

"He assures me it's not all crystals and hippie bullshit, and is actually just lots of time to be quiet and recharge." Naz makes eye contact with me and pulls a face, before grabbing Tom's hand supportively.

"Center," Tom adds.

Five hours later, our train pulls into Edinburgh station and we find the car rental place.

"You're doing that drive today?" The gruff man with the thick Scottish accent asks us.

18

I walk past the tattoo shop three times before I finally go in. It smells different from how I thought it would: like cleaning products and lavender. I thought it would smell of leather and debauchery. A tiny girl with a lot of piercings smiles at me.

"G'day, lovely." She's Australian. I can understand her. My brain doesn't need to process an accent. I breathe, relieved. "How can I help?"

"I was hoping to maybe get a tattoo at some point, please, if I could."

"First time?"

"How can you tell?"

She smiles sweetly. "You pacing up and down the street mumbling to yourself was a pretty good indicator."

"Oh, good, well, now that I've suitably embarrassed myself, I'll be off." I jokingly head toward the door as a further wave of anxiety washes through my entire body. The girl laughs heartily. She's pretty. I relax.

"Have you got a picture?" she asks.

"Um. No. Do I need a picture? It's just words. Can I have just words?"

She laughs again. "It's your body, babe." I exhale, nodding. If only she knew how poignant those four words were for me right now. She grabs a piece of paper and slides me a pen. "Write down your words."

I do. "It's from a poem. A beautiful poem. A poem I've fallen in love with. I wanted something that reflected this thing that I've been doing and this feels right. I was thinking of getting it here." I point to just below my sternum. "So then only I'll see it. Or people who I want to see it will see it, you know? It's not like I'm going around with my top off. But I could, you know? What I mean is that it's for me. This tattoo is for me. It's important, yeah?" *Noni, stop talking.*

"You nervous?" She smiles wide, the diamonds in her lip glinting in the fluorescent light.

I nod. "Sorry."

"Don't apologize. Normally you'd have to book a few weeks out, but one of our artists has literally just had a cancellation, so you might be in luck. Give me a second, okay?" She leaves.

My hands are clammy. I stare at the pictures on the walls, trying to give off a calm energy, like I'm cool, like I belong in a tattoo shop in Edinburgh having conversations with pretty girls with face piercings.

"Orright?" I turn and am greeted by a giant—a very tall man with broad shoulders, long brown hair pulled back in a low-slung bun and a slight beard. He's more Viking than man. I stare and I don't speak. Only my vagina can speak on behalf of the two of us now and all she can say is "wow" and "oof" and "Jesus."

"You want to get a tattoo?" I nod and hold up the piece of paper. He takes it out of my hand and chuckles. "You want it on your sternum?" he asks and I nod again and it is at this point that I realize I have yet to say anything. My brain screams *Would one of you please speak?* at either my mouth or my vagina. At this stage I don't care which one of us it is, I just hope someone says something soon.

"I'm Noni" is all we can muster.

"Hi, Noni. That's a bit of a tough spot. Notoriously a bit higher on the pain scale. Do you mind?"

I shake my head.

"Are you nervous?"

I nod and mumble, "How can you tell?"

"Just a vibe." The Viking smiles and I ovulate. "Orright, and this is your first tattoo?"

"Yes."

"You're just going to jump in the deep end, then, yeah?" He smirks and I smile. Or at least I think I smile. I'm too busy staring. And thinking about him wielding a sword and shield. "I like that," he says, then looks down at the paper where I've written the poem fragment. "Do you want just the words, or do you want me to do something with them?"

"Like what?"

"Like flowers, or a banner, or something."

"Yes. You do you. You're an artist. Just. Yes," I stutter and the Viking laughs.

"Okay, take a seat."

I do. He leaves and I close my eyes. *Please let me get my shit together. Please let me be cool. Not even cool, just act like a normal person. Please let this be a good idea and not be shit.* I take a deep breath. *You are on a pleasure quest, Noni. You can get tattoos and be audacious and talk to attractive people. You can.* Yes. I feel calmer.

The Viking appears moments later with a piece of paper, which he hands to me. I look down at it. The words look like they're growing out of flowers. Blooming. It's perfect. I'm speechless.

"We can change anything you don't like, Noni. You've got to love it."

"I do. It's better than I had in my head. It's so—" I look at the flowers. "Is it—" I stop.

"Is it what?" he asks.

"Can these flowers be daisies instead…is that possible?"

"They your favorite?" he asks.

"Something like that."

"Easy. Give me a couple of minutes."

This is a good idea. "Thank you, thank you so much, this is just—"

"Cool. How about we tattoo it on you first, then you can thank me."

Once he's redrawn the image with the daisies, and I've gushed a little more, I follow him to the back of the shop into a rust-orange room. There are sketches on tracing paper taped all over the walls, along with photos of the Viking in various settings with beautiful women and handsome men. Always smiling.

"These are incredible," I say, meaning everything.

"Thanks." The Viking nods at my jumper. "You'll have to take that off."

Of course. *Shit.* I had not thought of that. Why hadn't I thought of that? I do a quick mental assessment of what bra I put on this morning and begin the arduous task of pulling off layers while still trying to look cool. Which, I discover, is impossible. No one looks cool pulling off a thermal long-sleeve top. No one. By the time I get to my four billionth layer, the Viking starts laughing.

"Cold, huh?"

"You have no idea." I stand there in my bra. It's a good one, a black push-up T-shirt bra. Thankfully it's not the graying one, which used to be white, that I pulled the underwire out of because it kept digging in to my side, so it literally does nothing except cover my nipples. I start shaking, both from the cold and from nerves, not to mention from how incredibly vulnerable I feel having his eyes on me. Or not on me. He looks at the floor, or the side of the room, or into my eyes, but never at my boobs. I like this. I like that I can see an air of effort in his interaction with me now. I like that he has manners; it says a lot about him. Though I also feel a slight pang that him having manners is a turn on for me, because how fucking low does the decency bar have to be for men? He hands me the sketch, which he has now cut out.

"Check that you're happy with that size in the mirror," he says.

I stand with the piece of paper at my sternum and the Viking stands behind me, staring too.

"I think that's good, yeah?" I say.

"Yeah. Happy?"

I nod.

"I'll go make the stencil, then."

He leaves and I look more closely at the sketches on the walls. The Viking's work is brilliant, lots of pretty, delicate designs that contrast directly with his size. He walks back into the room and I don't look up.

"I really like her." I point to a sketch of a naked woman, sitting cross-legged with a whole bouquet of flowers blooming out of the top of her head.

"She's new."

"She has excellent boobs." I turn and look at him and he laughs, surprised.

"She does, indeed." He bites the corner of his lip, looking me in the eye. I have to look away because an adolescent giggle escapes my mouth that I have zero control over. I feel ridiculous. I stand in front of him as he sits on a chair holding the stencil in between his fingers. "Orright, you ready?" His face is exactly at boob height and I look at the ceiling.

"Absolutely not."

He smiles. "Good."

His fingers lightly brush my skin and I flinch. "Your hands are fucking freezing," I say.

"Are they? I'm so sorry." He rubs them together quickly. I can see his bicep muscles move through the fabric of his dark green shirt. I swallow hard. "Let's try again." He puts the design on my skin and dabs a wet paper towel on it, leaving a purple outline lingering on my flesh. "Look in the mirror," he says. I look at the purple marks on my flesh. "What do you think?" I bite my lip, trying to get my brain to compute the permanence that these soft lines represent. "Noni, we can do this as many times as you like—you've got to be one hundred percent sure." He looks closely at my face. "You're not happy."

"No. No. I'm—" I twist my head from side to side in the mirror. "How can you tell?"

"Your face. What are you thinking?"

"I think it's too low. Do you think it's too low? I think it's too low." I look at him, waiting for his answer, except he doesn't answer, he just looks at me with the slightest smirk. I'm positive I see a diamond glint in the corner of his eye like a cartoon fucking prince.

"I think it's too low," I mutter once again.

"Good. Okay." He wheels his chair toward me, his thigh muscles flexing in his dark black jeans as he pushes forward. "That means you're going to have to take this off." He points to my bra.

"Oh. Yes. Um." I look around for something to cover my

nipples—I draw the line at lying in this Viking's presence without a top on. "I know," I say, and I grab my new tartan scarf out of my bag. The Viking turns around and I slip my bra off and fold it neatly on top of my things. Instinctively I hide the label so he can't see what size I am. But just as that thought rolls in, it is met with another louder thought that yells, *For fuck's sake, Noni, he can see with his two fucking eyes what size you are.*

I catch a glance of my half-naked body in the mirror. *Fuck,* I mouth to myself, I'm really going through with this. I wrap the tartan scarf around my boobs and try to convince myself that I look absolutely on trend. That is, if I were a pop singer in the nineties. I'm a choker and two buns away from being worthy of the cover of *Seventeen* magazine. The scarf barely skims my giant knockers.

The Viking turns around and he laughs. "Well, hello, Sassenach."

"What??" I ask.

"You haven't seen *Outlander*?"

"No." I shake my head. "What is that?"

He looks genuinely surprised. "Oh, just…" He trails off. "It's a book and a TV show—it's a romance—a time-travel romance." I look at him, puzzled, and he continues. "The sex scenes are—" He blushes just above his beard.

"And so?" I ask, trying to not overreact at the word *sex* coming out of his beautiful mouth.

"And so there's been this influx of women coming to Scotland to have the best sex of their lives." He grins at me.

I start laughing. "And he calls her Sassenach?"

"Yeah."

"What does it mean?"

"An English person." He nods at my chest. "Is that yours?" For a split second I think he means my boobs, before I realize he means the print on the scarf. "The tartan? Oh no. I bought it on the high street for three quid because it's so fucking freezing here."

"Oh, are you cold? You hadn't mentioned it." He laughs.

"Good, mock the petrified, half-naked woman." I'm enjoying this.

He grins wide. "Orright, let's try again." We fiddle with the stencil a few times until we're both happy. I was happy the first time, but the Viking wasn't. He put it on, washed it off, and put it on again another two times. He puts on gloves and sits back on his chair, fiddling with needles and filling tiny tubs with color. I lie on my back, staring at the ceiling. The tattoo gun buzzes loudly.

"Here we go." He starts with the smallest line. "You okay?" He stops tattooing and looks at me.

"This is entirely unpleasant," I say and he chuckles from his chest.

"That is one way to put it. Yes."

"How long have you been doing this again?" I ask clenching my teeth.

"About a month," he mutters and I look at him, startled. "I'm kidding. Nearly twenty years."

"You must love it."

He nods, concentrating. "What do you do?"

"I'm a teacher."

"What do you teach?"

"English. But now I mostly work with the kids who get in trouble."

"Cool. Hence the poem. It's Mary Oliver, yeah?" he asks and I'm shocked he knows.

"You know the poem?"

"'Starlings in Winter'—it's a great poem." He nods and

keeps working. *He knows the fucking poem. Who is this guy?* "So you want wings, Noni?"

"Yeah, I guess, and some other stuff. It's a good reminder of how to be." We're silent for a moment and he starts tattooing again. I wince from the pain.

"Ooh, yeah, ow!" He winces too. "Not that I can feel it—I just, for sympathy, yes?"

"Thank you." He's sweet, a player, clearly—no man who looks like that isn't. But sweet.

"So are there just a bunch of Scottish men going around calling foreign women Sassenach on the off chance they'll have sex with them?" I ask.

He smiles, coy. "I'm not Scottish." He keeps working.

"Where are you from?"

"I'm a Geordie."

"Like the TV show where they get pissed and vomit on each other?"

"That's it." He grins. "But my accent is a hybrid now. I've lived all over the world."

"Right." I smile. "So, has the Sassenach thing worked?" He shrugs his shoulders and I laugh. "It has?" He doesn't say anything, but he definitely blushes. My mind wanders. *He called me Sassenach. Does that mean he wants to have sex with me? No! Stop that. Pleasure is not a person, Noni.*

We don't talk for a while. I look at the ceiling, reminding myself to breathe and relax, happy for each minute that passes because it means we are a minute closer to being finished. The worst part is I can't see where he's up to, so I just have to imagine. This is excellent practice in not being in control. Which I hate.

"What brings you here?" he asks.

"To Scotland, or to get tattooed?"

"All of the above."

"Well, it's a fucking tale, I'll tell you that." *Are you a pirate? Calm down, woman.* I will never not be shocked at the way my brain quite genuinely implodes around people I'm attracted to.

"Conveniently, I'm not going anywhere." The Viking smiles.

"I came here for a girl." I give him the simple, easy version.

He stops tattooing and looks me in the eye. "I see. And?"

"And it did not go well."

"I'm sorry to hear that." He touches my hand and leaves it there for a second, squeezing it ever so lightly. It's such a simple but genuine gesture that it obliterates the dam wall to my feelings.

"It's okay. She was just one thing on a list of—" I search for the right word "—misguided challenges."

"Challenges?"

"Well, not challenges…tasks. No, dares, I guess. Dares I'd given myself. But that's changed now. Now it's—" I stop, realizing I'm rambling. "I think I'm having a bit of a quarter-life crisis, actually." He looks at me, smiling, and I peer down my body at him for a moment, but mostly I look at the ceiling.

"Tell me more."

"I just got out of a long long-term relationship. Not like recently—it's been two years—but it's taken me longer than I thought to sort out some things. And I felt really boring, really beige. People think I'm beige. I mean, I don't really do—" I stop because it hurts. "Ah, fuck, ow."

"Ooh, sorry. Yeah. That's a cartilagey bit. Sucks, yeah?" I nod. "You don't really do what?"

"This. Get tattoos. Go overseas for girls. For sex. Not just sex. For pleasure. I'm on a pleasure quest." And with that confession, the wall comes slamming down again like one of those large steel doors in a dungeon. I feel exposed. Literally.

I glance at my bare stomach and the scarf around my boobs and I just feel stupid. *So stupid.*

"Really? That sounds fucking great."

I laugh nervously. "Yeah?" I pause. *You've come this far, Noni, you may as well reveal it all.* "I've made a list. A list of all of the things that will make me, I don't know—"

"Happy?" he asks and I nod. "I really love that." He looks me in the eye and smiles wide. A real smile, all teeth and energy. The combination of his stunning green eyes, my adrenaline, and the fact that I'm topless and in pain creates a cocktail of reckless abandon that shatters the negativity tape that's been on a loop, if I'm honest, for my whole fucking life. And so we talk. Actually talk. No bullshit. No nerves. Just honesty. I tell him all about the pleasure quest, about Joan and about Molly. He's an excellent listener.

"I think what you're doing is really brave."

"Shut up," I say.

"I mean it. So many people are miserable. Aren't they? Just boxing up secret dreams and getting pissed every weekend because they think they can't do the things that'll actually make them happy. It's scary. What you're doing is fucking scary." He stops and looks at me, differently than he has before. This look is like he's searching for something in my face. "It's brilliant, Noni."

I like the way my name sounds in his mouth, on his voice. "Wow," I say, feeling deeply touched. "Thank you for saying that."

"It's true. I once tattooed this guy, in South Africa. Cool dude. An Aussie. He had a serious job, kids, mortgage, the lot, yeah? In his fifties. But he said something happened when he turned forty. That the end of his life looked closer than it ever had before and not because he had, say, forty or fifty years left—that felt like a long time—but because he realized he had only forty or fifty summers left. And that felt like a really small number to him. So he made this list. This fifty summers list. And he showed me this battered list with scribbles and words crossed out. And it was simple shit, places he wanted to surf, stuff he wanted to show his kids, camping and that. Nothing crazy, but he was just ticking shit off every year."

I breathe his words in. It's the most he's talked the whole time I've been in the shop. "What would be on your list?" I ask.

He looks a little bewildered and his eyes widen. "I dunno. But I'm going to think about this conversation for a while, I know I am."

We sit in silence and I feel the sting of vulnerability. I've bared too much, too quickly.

He squirts some liquid onto the tattoo and it drips down my side. He catches it with a piece of paper towel and he smiles at me. "And we're done."

"Really?"

He holds out his hand and I grab it with one of mine, the other holding on to my tartan boob cover. I stand up slowly and walk over to the mirror, and when I see my reflection, I inhale quickly. *It's amazing.* I can't help it, I well up. But I'm smiling. They're happy tears. I am the kind of woman who gets tattoos. Amazing tattoos. Important tattoos. A beautiful and permanent reminder of how I want to feel.

"You good?"

"Yeah. It's really good. Thank you." I look at him. "I love it." I keep staring in the mirror, checking every angle. I'm in my own world.

"No. Thank you, Noni. It's been a fucking pleasure. You sat like a champ."

"I really, really love it. Thank you," I say again. Without thinking, I walk over and hug him, forgetting about the scarf, which floats to the floor as my bare boobs smoosh directly into his chest. "Oh my god." I quickly grab the scarf off the ground and spin around, horrified.

The Viking laughs. "Like I said, it's been a pleasure."

"I'm mortified."

"It's fine, it's fine. I have to wrap you up anyway," he says.

"I'll just put on my—" I pick up my bra, willing my bright red cheeks to calm down.

"I wouldn't wear that if I were you. Nothing that'll rub."

"Of course." I put my singlet on and turn back to him. "What's the lady equivalent of free-balling?" I ask, trying to keep it light, even though nothing about this, or me, is light.

"Free-balling?"

"When men don't wear underwear."

He laughs. "I dunno what the equivalent is. Free-boobing?"

"Perfect." I smile as he wraps cling wrap around the tattoo, touching me ever so lightly as he tapes it in place.

He gives me instructions for looking after the tattoo and walks me out to the front of the shop, where the lovely Australian girl is sitting, tapping away on a computer.

"All good?"

"So good," I say, way too enthusiastically.

"Well, all the best, Noni. With everything," says the Viking, and I smile at him. This bit feels weird. Like we've crossed some kind of intimacy boundary and now we're floating in an awkward in-between space.

"Yeah, you too," I say.

He stretches out his arms for a hug. "Shall we try again?"

I pull my jacket on. "I think you'll be safe this time." I gesture to my boobs and pull a weird face, that I match with a loud throaty sound, and immediately wish I hadn't. *Pull it together, woman.* We hug again. He smells like good aftershave, floral shampoo and man things. All smells I like. We pull back and he nods, turns on his heel and walks back up the corridor, leaving me with the Aussie girl.

"Beau's a peach, isn't he?"

His name is Beau. A Viking named Beau.

"Yes. Lovely. So nice. I was a hot mess but he was—is— he's lovely." *Oh, shut your face.*

I leave the shop and am hit by the bitter cold, but I feel good. I feel different. I look up the street and like the fact that the people passing by don't know what I've just done. That I've just altered my body forever. I throw my boob scarf around my neck and beam all over. This is a moment. A marker. A change. *You can do whatever the fuck you want to do, my darling.* And for the first time in my whole life that possibility doesn't petrify me.

19

I've made two big decisions since getting my tattoo this morning:

Tonight I want to drink wine and dance.

I'm going to go back to the tattoo shop tomorrow to ask the Viking on a date.

Both decisions are equally petrifying and thrilling. I've never gone out drinking on my own, and I've never asked someone I've just met out on a date. But the list insists, and I insist on committing to it.

Even so, the idea of standing in a pub on my own makes me feel weird. *What will people think?* I catch the thought as it flashes in my mind. *Fuck it. Pleasure must lead, remember?* I figure I'll walk to the pub on the corner, drink a pint or two, and dance my guts out and then tomorrow I'll worry about the Viking.

While I'm in the shower, I drink the rest of the bottle of wine I bought earlier. *Why is drinking in the shower so deeply satisfying?* Within thirty minutes I've got a spot of red lipstick, a can-do attitude, and I'm out the door feeling pleasantly buzzed.

I walk into the dimly lit pub and it's absolutely packed with people. A cover band has just started their set. Beer sloshes onto the floor as people sway from side to side, singing and bouncing along to the music. I head to the bar and order a glass of bubbles, because this is a celebration and I am a woman on a mission. I push my way as close to the front of the makeshift dance floor as I can and I let go. Like dancing-in-the-dark let go. I dance because I want to feel the way that only dancing makes me feel—heart racing, smiley, sweaty, like there's forward momentum, movement—that I'm in control of being out of control. When dickheads try to dance with me, I push them away, thrashing my head around and cheering wildly as each song ends. I can feel the music all through my body and I wonder if maybe this is what pleasure actually looks like for me, crammed in a pub in Edinburgh, shoes sticking to the floor, its musty scent stuffed up my nose. The band finish their set with a promise to be back soon. I am sweaty, happy and thirsty, moving through the thick crowd to the bar and ordering, but as I go to give the barman my card, an arm appears over my shoulder, moving my hand out of the way, paying for my drink. I spin around to tell them to get fucked, but then I see that the arm belongs to the Viking. My smile is immediate and takes up my entire face. The perfect fusion of glee and shock. I don't say anything, I just stare at him. He says something but I can't hear—it's too noisy and he's too handsome.

"What?" I yell.

He leans down and speaks into my ear. "I said, nice dance moves." He pulls back and beams.

I blush. "Cheers." I'm grateful that it's so loud and that we can't really talk, because it means we have to be close to each other to even kind of make out what the other is saying. "I'm glad you're here," I say.

He smiles. "Why's that?"

I laugh and shake my head in astonishment, placing my hand on his bicep to check for sure that he's really real. "I was gonna ask you something." My stomach flips with my false confidence. *Who is this woman? She can stay.*

"Oh, really?"

I nod. He looks at me curiously, then shouts next to my ear, "You here with anyone?" and I can feel his words in my vagina. I shake my head, happy with the feeling. He gestures toward the other side of the room, indicating for me to follow him. I start to move through the throngs of people and he puts his hand on my waist to help usher me through the crowd. I am very aware of the exact placement of his fingers on my body. He leads me to a large circular booth in the corner and introduces me to his friends. They all seem so cool; all tattooed and pierced, with asymmetrical haircuts and bold fashion sense. These women at this table certainly wouldn't have made such a big deal about buying a pencil skirt, I can tell. I scooch in next to a guy named Adam, who has a perfect black flattop and is wearing a bright eighties tracksuit.

"I like your jacket," I tell him as I slide across the bench seat. Beau squishes in next to me.

"See!" Adam yells loudly to the group and they all laugh boisterously. "These assholes were telling me I look like the nerd brother in the *Fresh Prince*."

I laugh. "Clearly they're jealous."

"I like you, Noni, meanwhile the rest of you can fuck off." He gives them the finger.

"This is the woman I was telling you all about," Beau announces to the table, and they all look at me, nodding. He turns toward me. "I hope you don't mind, I kind of told them about your quest."

"I love it, Noni!" A girl with a thick Nordic accent and blue, blue eyes smiles at me. "What sort of things have you been doing?" They all stare at me, waiting, and I don't know what to say.

"It's only just started, really. I'm, like, eating what I want and traveling. I cut off all my hair, and, um, I had sex with a magician, oh, and my principal, but neither of those experiences worked out quite how I'd planned."

Beau quickly interjects. "Noni's a teacher."

"Oh, yeah, yeah, no, I'm not *at* school. It's not illegal. No. Two consenting adults." We all laugh. "I've read books, stayed in bed, and I went to the movies on my own, 'cause I'd never done that. Too chickenshit. In fact I've been doing lots of things that I was, um—" I correct myself. "*Am* scared to do, like getting a tattoo." I turn to Beau and smile at him, grabbing his forearm and squeezing it, before promptly freaking out about what to do with my hand next, and leaving it drooping on his arm for far too long. *Move your hand, Noni.* I do.

"So, it's about more joy, yeah?" Adam asks.

"Yeah, pleasure in everything," I say.

The others start to share their ideas for their own pleasure quests. The guy with three nose rings and good teeth says he'd cut off all communication with his family because that'd make him feel amazing. The Nordic girl wants to live in a cabin on her own. Adam wants to see all of his favorite musicians. Beau refuses to share and they all give him shit about it, but he doesn't cave and I start to relax. Rounds of drinks are bought. Pints are drunk. I feel included. Eventually Beau leans in to speak in my ear again. "How's your tattoo?"

"Let's say I'm fully aware it's there."

"That's normal." He's speaking so close to my ear I can feel his breath on my neck.

"And what do you think of Edinburgh, Noni?" Adam asks.

"I like that I feel very aware of history and Harry Potter," I say, drinking from my beer.

"What do you mean?" Beau asks.

"I dunno, it feels like an old city, which makes me feel small, or miniscule, comparative to time. I never feel that way at home. And shit is magical here, maybe."

They all laugh and Beau says something that I don't catch because the band starts back up, and then he scoots out of the booth and holds his hand out for me. "Come on. Let's dance."

We are all dancing, jumping, laughing at each other's stupid moves and singing loudly. Adam requests MC Hammer and jumps up onto the stage to sing along and we cheer wildly. I feel drunk and light. Happy. Thankful for good conversation and for people who laugh at my jokes, who think I'm a little bit impressive. That something I'm doing is impressive. I don't think I've ever done anything that other people have deemed impressive. Safe, sure. Helpful, of course. Impressive? Never.

"I *love* this song," I announce to the whole room, closing my eyes and rolling my shoulders with the joy of it all. I open my eyes and Beau is standing at the side of the dance floor with another round. I rush over and take a large swig of beer and successfully pour it all over my chin and boobs. He laughs at me.

"Hot, right?" I say, grabbing a napkin.

"You have no idea." He grins wide and I blush a little.

The song changes and Beau whoops loudly, "Tune!" He puts two hands on my shoulders, pushing me back onto the dance floor, where the others are already thrashing about wildly. He wraps one arm around my waist and takes my hand with his other hand and we shimmy from side to side. He spins me out and then back into his chest, singing at the top of his lungs. As he spins me back out a second time, a voice very loudly, and very articulately, speaks inside me with such distinct clarity that it kind of overwhelms me. This is the kind of voice that knows things. Things you don't ignore. That tells you not to walk up that street, or to lock your car doors at the intersection, or to never, ever wear white swimwear. The voice says it again, to make sure that I definitely hear it. *This human. Pay attention to this human.*

He pulls at the bun on his head and his shoulder-length hair unravels around his face as he thrashes about, laughing with his friends. My eyes bulge joyously at the sight. I dance eagerly and at the peak of the chorus Beau turns and we sing to each other, laughing, and without a single beat of hesitation I grab his face with both my hands and kiss him. Because it makes sense. Because I want to. Because I think he wants to too. He does. There're bodies pulsing up and down around us, pushing us closer together. The song ends and we don't stop kissing. The crowd goes nuts, cheering and clapping, and it feels like they're applauding me and him. His tongue is in my mouth, his hand on my waist, my hands on his neck. We kiss and we kiss and we kiss. Until finally I pull back, smiling wide. He's smiling too. My cheeks flush and I laugh with my whole body. Beau cheers loudly with the rest of the crowd, which makes me laugh more.

Pleasure may not be a person. But what if it is a Viking?

I scan his apartment. It's neat, with lots of wood, art and plants. It's on the ground floor in an old tenement building that has been renovated. I look at the framed photos on the dark wooden side table. There are only three: one of him and what I'm presuming are his mum and his grandma, an old wedding photo from the twenties, and one picture of a little boy. I kneel down to look through the impressive record collection underneath the TV when all of a sudden I'm nudged in the side of the face by something wet. It catches me off guard and I fall to my side. A big black dog stares back at me, and I squeal in absolute delight. His huge eyes look at me, longing for me to pat him. I scratch him behind his ears with both my hands, and he looks deeply satisfied. I get how he feels. If only I could master that look.

"Noni, meet Shaquille. Shaquille, meet Noni," Beau says.

I fall instantly and desperately in love with Shaquille. "This is not a dog. This is a horse." Beau smiles. "I miss my dog so bad," I tell him.

"Oh no. Where are they staying while you're here?"

"Well, my ex got him when we split. Carson. He's the actual opposite of this dog."

"That's rough."

"Tragic. Completely." I speak directly to Shaquille. "So I might just steal you and hide you in my suitcase and take you home with me, okay? Yeah?" *Home. God. I don't live here. This isn't my real life.*

"You haven't even seen his tricks yet."

"He does tricks?"

"Oi, Shaquille," Beau says and Shaquille immediately turns. He shapes his fingers like a gun, pretends to fire and Shaquille FALLS TO THE GROUND LIKE HE'S BEEN SHOT. *OH MY FREAKING GOODNESS.* I cannot withstand the cuteness and I do not care that I am a blathering, dog-slobber-covered, giggly, squealing mess, as I roll around with the giant dog on the floor for a very long time. Finally, I get up and wash my hands in the kitchen, then watch as Beau gets two beers from the fridge. His shirt lifts as he's bent over, and from what I can tell, his entire back is covered in tattoos. He bumps the lids off the bottles on the edge of the counter and hands one to me.

"Can I ask you something, Noni?"

"Of course."

"Good, because I'm a bit confused about something."

"Okay. I'm worried."

He laughs. "I fancy you."

I stop and stare at him. Just like that. He just says it. And now it just sits there in the space between us and my stomach does a loop-the-loop. I smile.

"I fancy *you*," I say.

"You do?"

I nod in disbelief. *How can he not know this?* "Yes."

He closes the gap between us and kisses me softly and sweetly before he pulls back. "Cheers," he says, holding his bottle up to mine, which I clink instantly.

"Wait, what was your question?"

"You just answered my question."

"You were confused about whether I liked you?" I look at him, all raised eyebrows and disbelief. "Have you ever looked in a mirror?"

He blushes slightly. "I don't know. I thought maybe you were—" He stops, biting his lip. "I thought maybe men weren't your thing, but then you kissed me and came home with me—"

"Oh." I smile, and then I giggle.

"Not that I presume anything is gonna—"

"Is it my haircut?" I joke.

His cheeks flush. "Fuck! Do I sound like a dickhead?"

I drink from my bottle. "Just so we're clear, I like men too." I look him in the eye.

"Got it," he says, holding my gaze. I can tell he's embarrassed.

"I mean, I like having sex with men." I say slowly, staring at him, my breath slowing down as my heart rate quickens. He takes the bottle out of my hand, places it on the counter, grabs my face with both his hands and kisses me again. Really kisses me. I moan loudly, I can't help it.

His kisses are passionate, but his hands are gentle as they glide over my body, from my lower back up over my hips, to my shoulders and down my arms. He kisses my neck. He makes frustrated, gruff moans as he tries to get to my skin amid the layers of clothes. Pulling off a cardigan, ripping open my dress and sliding it off my shoulders. He pulls the singlet over my head and throws it behind him so quickly that I inhale sharply at the speed of it, and the level of his wanting. He takes the briefest moment to look at my bare chest, and boobs billowing out of my bra, and I'm sure he looks impressed. *He wants me.* He growls into my neck, kissing me. And I can feel my eyes roll into my own head. I mean, this Viking of a man wants me. Really wants me. He puts two hands on the side of my tights and I push at his chest, breaking our connection, because rational Noni chides in louder than any other voice. "Don't rip these," I say.

"What?" He tries to come closer again but I hold him back with my hands pressed against his chest.

"Do you have any idea how hard it is to get tights that stay up and fit ladies with bodies like mine?"

He laughs hard, rolling his head back. "No, no I do not."

"It's near fucking impossible." I push him back slightly so he's an arm's length away from me. "You stand there." But he instantly steps toward me, kissing my mouth. I give over to the kiss but feel his hands on my hips again and I push him back, smiling.

"Wait there," I tease. "No touching." He stands watching me as I try to do my best to roll down my tights as sexily as I can, but I very quickly realize that no one born into a human body could ever make the action of rolling thick woolen tights off of a squidgy body sexy. It's just not. *Fact*. Looking at his face, at the very obvious bulge in his trousers, I'd say he doesn't agree with me at all.

"Quickly," he says.

"Why? You in a rush?" I smile. Faking confidence. Faking sexiness. Faking control. Faking that I'm not completely aware of standing in this kitchen in just my bra and undies while he still has all his clothes on. Although some of these feelings do feel real, I think that's the beer more than the actual feelings themselves. I start to fold the tights and he groans, taking them out of my hand and placing them gently on the counter.

He kisses my mouth quickly before moving down my neck. I pull at his shirt to try to even this clothes-to-nakedness playing field, but he spins me around so he is standing behind me, his full body pressing into my body. He kisses down my spine and his hands move up under my bra and over one nipple. I inhale sharply and push back into him. His other hand glides across my décolletage, pushing my head gently to the side so he can kiss my neck to my shoulder and back again. I lean fully into him as his hand moves to the waistband of my underwear, shifting my hips, guiding him where to go. But he knows. His finger lands gently on me and starts moving back and forward and pulses of joy pummel my body as I reach behind me and grab the back of his neck, pulling him as close as possible. My weight drops into my knees and my head moves back, resting on his shoulder as he continues to kiss my neck and move his fingers with such expert precision that I think for a moment this is a fantasy and not actually happening in real life. He exhales breathy wanting into my skin. And I think of the women he's been with before me, not in a comparative way, but in a deeply, deeply grateful way. Because this kind of teaching, this series of movements on my body right now is bliss. Whoever you are, ladies of Viking past, I am grateful for you and your role in his life. Because HOOOLLLLYYYYY SSSHHHIIIIIITTTTT.

As I get closer, I grab the edge of the countertop for support. I am so close. *Ahh! Ahhhhh! Oh. Oh. Oh. Oh. Ohhhhhhh*. But suddenly we're nudged forward and he stops and he vanishes, shouting "Shaquille!" I spin around and see that Beau has grabbed Shaquille's collar and is dragging him back into the lounge room.

I grab my face, embarrassed. When he comes back into the kitchen, he is blushing. "I am *so* sorry," he says, and I start laughing. I can't say anything, so I just pick up my beer. "Cheers," I mutter, taking a swig. He looks at me and I look at him and in one second flat he strides toward me and kisses me keenly, ushering me backward. We step together, and as we do, I pull his T-shirt up over his head and quickly glance at his chest. It's covered in tattoos too. *Good god*.

We trip and kiss and swiftly peel and tug and throw clothes recklessly, all tongues and panting, hands on bare skin, grabbing, smiling, grinding, and trying desperately to be as close as humanly possible. I land sideways on his bed with his whole body above me. I can't kiss him deep enough. Can't touch him quick enough. He doesn't say anything when he reaches to the side drawer, grabs a condom and puts it on. He's confident. He looks at me and smiles, not awkwardly but presently, sexily, and I lose my mind a little, because I've not had sex like this the first time with someone ever. This is intimate sex. This is *I know you* sex. This is *We drank just enough tequila to talk about our secret fantasies and try something new* sex. We sync in a way that is easy. Connected. I am more turned on than I've felt in a long time. I stop thinking, just writhing and rolling my hips, throwing my head back, not worrying about making the right moves, or being impressive, or angles, or expectations, or belly fat, or even Beau. Just thinking about me. About pleasure. About *ohhhhhhheeeeeeeaaaaaaaahhh ooooosssssssshhhhh aaaaaahhhhhhhhhh errrrruuuuuuuuuhhhhhhhhhh- hhhhhh.* My body shudders as rapturous waves collide into my skin, and I exhale loudly, falling into his chest. He cups my cheeks with both his hands, pulling my head up as he kisses my forehead, chuckling. I lean my chin on his chest and look at him, smiling wide.

"High five," he says.

"High five?" I ask.

"It's the first thing that came to mind." He smirks. "It was either that or 'shagging is fun,' so I went with the former."

I laugh so hard I snort, shifting my weight to lie on my side next to him as he stares at me.

"Noni, that was like—" he stops.

"Yeah." I nod, then lift my hand in the air for a high five and he quickly claps my hand with his. Sometimes there aren't words. Sometimes only your body knows what to do.

20

I'm feeling self-conscious and all kinds of hungover. Booze and vulnerability. I lie on the bed, pretending to still be asleep, which I know is dumb because Beau has seen, and touched, almost all the parts of this naked body already. I'm busting to wee. *Right, Noni, don't be a weirdo.*

I pretend to wake up, blinking my eyes like Bambi, and stretch luxuriously, feigning complete comfort, and that I'm not at all thinking about how exactly to let my natural beauty shine. *Act effortless.* Beau is still asleep. I stand up and walk on my tiptoes to the en suite, like I'm completely oblivious to the gorgeous man waking up and watching my jiggling ass as I go. I drink directly from the tap and give myself a brain freeze. *Why is the tap water here so fucking glacial?* I clean my teeth with my finger, wash the leftover makeup from my face, and do what I can with the short bits of hair spiking jaggedly all over my head. All the while my insides squirm with flashbacks from the night before. Bits of conversation.

The kiss. The kitchen counter. Beau saying "You're so fuck-ing gorgeous" as he kissed me all over. I cover my eyes with my hands and feel the fire in my cheeks.

I smile and stare at myself in the mirror. *Who are you?* I stare at my naked body, and although it's not wild praise I throw upon her, I nod in admiration at her efforts and feel some kind of weird pride. Like those sequences in movies where the master is proud of their subject but they can't let on just how much, and so they fill the space with a wry look and a dumb comment, like *You did good, kid.* I am totally Mr. Miyagi-ing my own body right now. Trying with all my might to not point out her flaws, or the bits she could improve. *Go back to bed. Don't let any of the things you feel on the inside be reflected on the outside.* I am the very essence of faking-it-till-I-make-it right now.

When I open the bathroom door, I see that Beau is spoon-ing Shaquille. "In bed with someone else already?" I say and Beau laughs.

I go to lean my shoulder on the wall next to the bed, cross-ing my legs one over the other for maximum sexiness, but my center of balance is askew and I miss the wall completely. I stumble and have to quickly take three hops forward so I don't fall flat on my face. *Look at me not being weird.*

"Good morning," Beau says looking somewhat perplexed by my morning gymnastics. Worrying about that, however, is overridden by how unbelievably hot he looks right now lying naked in the bed.

"Good morning. So, I've got a few things to do this morn-ing, so I'm going to—"

He pushes Shaquille off the bed and pats it twice, indicat-ing for me to join him again.

"What things have you got to do?"

"Just things. Important things."

"I only have one thing to do this morning before I go to work." He pats the empty spot next to him again and raises his eyebrows cheekily.

"Is it me?" I say as I slide under the blanket next to him, unable to resist. He nods, and a weird half giggle, half giddy squeal exits my mouth. It isn't even the slightest bit cool, but I don't care as I grab Beau's desperately handsome face and kiss him deep.

"Do you know that I wanted you from the first moment I saw you?" I can hear the smile in his voice. His voice is hotter in the morning. Deeper.

"What? Why?"

"Because you're beautiful." His hand is on my hip, and I roll onto my side to face him. His head is cocked to the side, his hair flowing. "You were funny. Your accent. And you owned your nerves."

"I was petrified."

"I couldn't tell." He pauses. "It was torture," he says, running his hand down my thigh. "Having to touch you, but not being able to *touch* you." I can't talk. I just watch. "First you happily stand there in your bra." His fingers slowly trace up my other leg.

"What else was I meant to do?"

He smiles. "You could've just rolled one of your tops up."

I inhale, embarrassed. "Why didn't you say that?"

"Because I was not complaining." His fingertip traces one of my nipples lightly. "Then when I turned around and you were standing there in that scarf, the bottom of your boobs peeking out, I was, like, instantly hard. Thank god for my apron."

I titter in disbelief. "Really?"

"Yes. It was sexy as hell." I roll forward into his chest, blushing. "You're sexy, Noni."

"I just, I don't—" I stop myself.

"Well, you should." He lifts my head up, looking in my eyes. "You're sexy, Noni." He kisses me. "I wanted to use the scarf to blindfold you." He kisses my eyelids, moving his own body so I roll onto my back and he's lying on top of me. "Close your eyes." I do. "I wanted to kiss your neck." He does. "And do this." He runs one hand down my side, and his tongue lands on my nipple; he sucks and licks and I make soft throaty sounds. "I wanted to take off your jeans, and spread your legs." He moves my legs and the pull in the base of my stomach is all wanting.

"Then what?"

"Then this."

I feel his breath first. Then kisses on my right knee. I open my eyes. He looks at me.

"Close your eyes. You're blindfolded, remember." He moves down my thigh, kissing the whole way. I push my hips toward him so he knows what I want, but he kisses back up my thigh all the way to my left knee. He repeats this over and over again. I clutch at his hands, pull at his hair, my hips flex toward his kisses, but he doesn't oblige. Then I feel his hands under my shoulders and he rolls me over so I am lying flat on the mattress. I inhale sharply at the quickness of it all. The ease with which he could move me.

He kisses down my spine, pulling me back onto my haunches, so I'm sitting between his legs. Finally he touches me, and the sound that escapes my lips takes me by surprise. My hips dictate the pace and I hold his hand exactly where I want him, until it's too much. I fall forward on my knees as he pushes into me. His hand is on my hips as I move to get comfortable, my cheek pressing into the bed. One hand slides around and he rubs and thrusts at the same time and all I can do is give over to it. His other hand finds mine and interlocks with my fingers, and I shudder hard, waves of pleasure of building and releasing all over. But he doesn't stop, doesn't give me a second to catch my breath; he thrusts deeper and harder and I move my hips against him quicker.

"Oh, fuck, Noni, you are—" and he cums before I can cum again, grabbing me around my waist and biting my shoulder as he groans, squeezing me tight. "Oh, good god, you are—you are fucking sublime." I start slowly circling my hips.

"Oh, fuck, Noni that's—" I don't stop. I feel him shaking but I keep circling and move his hand back to my front. He knows what to do. He mutters into my ear but I'm not listening, I am in this moment, in my body, in his bed, orgasming again.

He lies on his back next to me, and I roll onto my back, panting. I put my hand on my chest. My heart is pounding.

"You good?" he asks.

"Yes!" I rasp. "You?"

He just laughs, picks up my hand and kisses it, and we lie like that for I don't know how long. Eyes closed.

"I've got to get ready," he says, rolling over me, stopping as he straddles me, kissing my belly before getting up and walking toward the bathroom. His calves are divine. I've never thought about calves being divine before. It seems like a weird body part to invoke divinity, but the curve of his muscle, the tan of his leg, the soft throw of pale hair—it's all perfect.

I hear the pulse of the shower and I lie back on the bed and let the giddiness envelop my body, breathing it right into the pit of my stomach. I grab a pillow and squeal into it wildly, thrashing my body about before I feel self-conscious and mentally picture Beau standing in the doorway watching me. I throw down the pillow and check that I'm still alone. I am.

★ ★ ★

I find my phone and message Lindell. Do I have a
story for you, my love.

A good story or a bad story?
he replies within minutes.

An orgasmic story.

Yes! Yes! Yes! Yes!
he sends back
along with three
firework emojis.

The Viking tattoo artist
and I bumped into
each other last night.

Can I call?

No. I'm in his bed.
He's in the shower.

YOU SAUCY FUCKING MINX.

Beau appears in the doorway with just a towel wrapped
around his waist. I put the phone facedown on the bed and
stare at him.

"Want to walk me to work? We can get a coffee?"

"Yeah." My phone dings. And dings again. And again.
And again.

"Someone is popular." He moves into the room and starts
rifling through his drawers, getting dressed.

"My best mate." I flick it on silent.

"So, how'd I do?"

"What?"

"My report card." He pulls a T-shirt over his head. "The debrief with your mate." He nods toward the phone.

I smile. "It went something like, got a tattoo and bedded a Viking."

"A Viking?" He laughs. "And their response?"

I flip the phone over and smile wide. There are a throng of messages from Lindell. I laugh as I read them.

> Oh my fucking god.
> Eggplant. Eggplant. Eggplant.
> Firework. Firework. Firework.
> You bloody minx.
> This is amazing.
> I miss you.
> Brilliant.
> I'm cackling.

Then there's a photo of Lindell on the couch with a squishy laughing face. I show Beau the photo. "He's happy."

"I'm glad." Beau smiles and it pulses through me. I smile back with my whole body. I quickly shower and get dressed, and Beau laughs at me when I put all of my layers back on. "I do not remember taking that many clothes off," he says as I blush.

It's a beautiful day. Freezing, but beautiful. Still. And the sun is out. We walk down the street in silence, but it's not awkward. He takes me down to the waterfront, which is lined with large barges, where everything is gray brick, marble and stone, with black wrought iron fittings and the occasional glint of mossy green. If Edinburgh were a person, it would be a broad-shouldered old man with calloused hands, pain in his heart, but soft eyes.

We walk up a laneway to a café and order takeaway coffee and doughnuts. While we stand outside waiting, he puts his arms around my waist and I'm taken back by the relaxed intimacy.

He kisses me light and soft on the lips and smiles. "So, what are your plans, Noni?"

"Well, I'm going to Amsterdam...tomorrow."

His eyes widen. "I love Amsterdam so much. I could totally live there."

"Hookers and weed? Of course," I tease.

"Are they not your two nonnegotiables when looking for a city to live in?" he jokes, his eyes glinting.

"I guess that's the good thing about your job—you can do it anywhere."

He nods. "Definite perk. Back issues and RSI are not perks, but you know, I'm not complaining."

"Beau," the barista says and we separate from our hug to get our order and walk back along the cobbled street toward Beau's tattoo shop.

"But I can't complain. I feel very lucky to love what I do. I think I'd go nuts if I was one of those people whose passions could only simmer away on the weekends, you know?"

"Yeah, because often those people are too tired on the weekends from their week to even consider what their passion might be," I say sipping my coffee.

"Sounds like you know these people well."

"I guess. Yes. I mean I am here, aren't I?"

"You are here. I love that you're here." Beau smiles. "I want to know all about you, Noni. Tell me things."

"Like what?"

"I dunno. Important things. Like—" He thinks for a moment. "Like, who's your favorite Spice Girl?"

I laugh. "Important things? Right. Well, it's Scary. Of course."

"Ginger. Ginger caused a sexual revolution in my house."

"That honor goes to Peter Andre for me," I tell him. Beau laughs deep, and with his whole body.

"It was the middle-part and plaits, wasn't it?"

"How'd you know?"

"Because I thought for sure girls would dig my middle-part and plaits because of him."

"And they did not?" I ask.

Beau shakes his head and I laugh. We walk in silence for a little while. I try to think of something to say, of things I want to know about him, but come up blank, especially as I can now see the shop in the distance, and the only thing left to say then will be goodbye.

"What are your plans after Amsterdam?"

I shrug. "Dunno. I'm letting pleasure lead."

"Lucky pleasure." He smiles at me and I smile, too, suddenly nervous. "Well, I think we should definitely hang out again. If you want to."

"My report card was good, then?"

"All A+'s."

"Shit." I smirk.

"Will you let me know if you're around Edinburgh again? I'm in London often too," he says.

I stare at him, amazed by his honesty. "You just say what you're thinking, don't you?"

"I'm nearly forty, Noni. I've played a fuck-load of games in the past and now I'm of the opinion that it's better to say what you want."

"Yes. It is better. Just rare."

"Let me give you my number and then it'll be your call."

I hand him my phone. He puts his details in and hands it back to me. He's saved his contact as "Beau Viking." I laugh.

We get to the shop and stand facing each other out front.

"I hope I hear from you, and I hope that I see you again. That's what I want."

"Okay" is all I can manage.

"And you want?" he asks.

"To kiss you," I say. He smiles, leans forward, kissing me softly at first and then deeper, making my stomach do a flip.

"I hope you find what you're looking for, Noni," he says, kissing me on the cheek, and then heads inside the shop.

I walk back up the cobbled street feeling like I maintained an air of cool aloof energy during that whole conversation— especially since internally it was just all loud screeching.

LINDELL! ARE YOU FREE? I NEED YOUR WISE COUNSEL, I text.

Ten minutes later the phone rings and we debrief over the last twenty-four hours. He squeals with delight while cooking the kids' dinner.

"A man who says what he's thinking, praise all that is holy— are you sure you want to leave?"

"I know, right? He's too good to be true, though. Surely there's something shit about him."

"Surely. He probably irons his jocks, or doesn't clean his hair out of the sink or doesn't eat vegetables, or something equally fucked up."

I laugh loudly. "Or he just does this all the time so he's really good at it."

"Yes. Too smooth. His moves are too polished," Lindell muses.

"I don't think I'll see him again. I think it was perfect as a one-night thing."

"Whatever you think, my darling."

"I mean, I don't want to chase some guy around Europe, because that defeats the whole fucking point of the pleasure quest." I poke at the dirt around the cobbled stone pathway. "That worked out so well with Molly."

"Fuck Molly, this isn't about Molly. This is about you," he says. "Noni, this is all about doing whatever you want to do."

"Yes! You're right. And what I want to do right now is know all about you." I stop outside a cute shop, pacing up and down, as I don't want to be the obnoxious person on the phone inside.

"I am fine. We are all fine. My life is pretty much exactly the same as when you left, just not nearly as fun. Julius cut his own hair yesterday. He looks like a four-year-old Lionel Richie from the *Dancing on the Ceiling* era. Which, to be honest, I don't completely hate."

I laugh loudly and a woman walking her dog smiles at me as she walks past. "I miss you," I tell him.

"And I miss you. But if you don't wring out every last fucking drop of pleasure from this trip, I will be so disappointed in you. And so will you when you get home and everything is back to normal, and you'll be wishing you had done everything you wanted to."

"You're right. Absolutely."

"In short, go to Amsterdam and do whatever you want and if you feel like you might want to fuck the Viking again, then do that. If not, then don't," he says, matter-of-fact.

"Okay. Okay. I love you."

"I love you, my darling," he says and I hang up, giddy with the possibility of all the pleasure to come.

21

I open my eyes and immediately catch a glimpse of my reflection in the mirror. Single boob hanging out of my singlet, wild hair in a side Mohawk and pillow creases across one cheek. *Hot.*

I sigh, deeply pleased and disappointed all at once, because he's not here. The Viking. I had been dreaming of his hands on my hips and his tongue running up the back of my thigh. He made me cum and he's not even here. I look around my new room, a self-contained all-white unit with a spiral staircase up to my new loft bedroom with a big square skylight that makes it feel like I'm sleeping under the stars.

I'd arrived yesterday afternoon and checked in. The owner, a woman named Magda who I'd talked to only via the app, had left me a bottle of wine and some decadent pastries, so I ate them and drank two glasses of wine before setting off to explore. Amsterdam is beautiful. The cobbled streets feel like they vibrate with history. Beautiful children sit in baskets on the backs of bikes, being pedaled around by their equally beautiful parents. There are tiny shops with a million things in each I'd love to buy. On the canals, happy people leisurely recline on long boats, radiating maximum relaxation. It feels calm. I fell asleep last night thinking about how glad I was that I came here.

Later in a café a woman with long dreadlocks stands over me as I sit on a sofa waiting for the single space cake and iced chocolate I'd just ordered to arrive, reading my third book in a week. She offers me her joint and I decline, before remembering the pleasure quest and quickly accepting instead. *Why not.* She stares at me intently, watching me inhale deeply. We smile at each other. She has a beautiful smile. She's wearing a tie-dyed negligee under a big furry coat, and she has a leather bum bag on her hip.

"You were a healer in a past life," she says. "But they thought you were a witch."

I laugh, thinking she's joking, but she's clearly not.

"Yeah, and you had an issue with alcohol in another, maybe like the late sixteen-hundreds—and you broke someone's heart. She never forgave you."

"Oh, god, really?" I say, intrigued. I'm stoned. I'm susceptible.

"You were a soldier in England. A knight. You were in love with a fellow soldier. He died in your arms on a battlefield. You never recovered."

"Did I have any past lives that didn't end horrifically?" I ask.

"You've loved wildly and had your heart broken. This life is for—" She stops and looks intensely into my eyes, leaning her hands on my knees and standing inches from my face. "You're beautiful—why don't you think so?"

"I...um," I stutter.

"Stop it," she says.

"Okay," I say and she gets up and walks out onto the street. "This is my life for what?" I say out loud to no one in particular.

"Getting wasted," says the young waiter who has just appeared with my order, and so I do. I get deliciously and giddily stoned. I eat a giant fruit flan by the canal and giggle at myself for having the audacity to be living this life. I wander and smile at strangers and marvel at the wind on my face, the shape of leaves, the music blaring from shops, the boats on the river and the air in my lungs. I end up in the red-light district and I sit in a pub on a corner with a pint, watching the world around me. I have a perfect view of five windows with women wearing lingerie standing lazily in them. Across the canal a group of young boys, eighteen or so, ushers one of their friends inside. They wait outside, eager for his return. It doesn't take long. He stumbles onto the street, wide-eyed and biting his lip. The boys leap and holler around him, laughing and patting him on the back. I message Lindell and tell him because I know he'll think it's funny. I watch the women in the windows. I wonder what they're thinking about. I wonder what their pleasure quests might look like.

I spend the next few days mixing tourist must-dos with wandering and seeing what I find, letting pleasure lead. I buy a vibrator, or a clitoral stimulator, to be more specific. The campy bald guy in the shop wearing a dog collar tells me I'll cum in two minutes or less.

"If you don't, I'll buy you dinner." He pushes the box across the counter with an interested grin.

"Is that a promise?" I ask.

He nods. "Trust me."

So I trust him, and I cum in less than two minutes. I walk

past the same shop the next day and he raises his eyebrows at me from across the alleyway, so I nod and he gives me a thumbs-up.

By Saturday night I'm bored of my own company, and I want to have sex with someone other than myself. And then I realize I don't even know how to get laid on purpose. Every experience I've ever had had been after a long buildup or a complete accident. After Joan and I broke up, I downloaded all the dating apps and very quickly realized what a mostly impossible shit-fight they all were, and how they made me feel stressed and overwhelmed. Between guys with photos of them shooting a gun or holding a large fish, and girls being very specific about what they liked or didn't like, my insecurities were deeply triggered. I struggled with the stalemate of no one making the first move, conversations that fizzled quickly, and being asked about my position on anal sex in the third sentence of talking to someone. It all just felt like swarms of people either demanding to be impressed or being all too nonchalant. I didn't have the energy for online dating, so I avoided it. But tonight I have the energy for a straightforward one-night stand and I believe in the apps to help deliver that outcome.

I sit at a communal table in a quiet bar with a glass of champagne. I redownload an app and start to scroll. *Left, left, left, left.* Two photos of yourself and nothing in your bio apart from your height? *Left.* An amusing bio but only one abstract close-up side-profile photo? *Left.* A few handsome photos but your profile is all lowercase and reads, "Looking to eat sweet butt"? *Left.* I know I want to get laid but I also want there to be chemistry, or at least a wicked attraction, so I can calm the parts of my brain that tell me it's a terrible idea. I swipe right on a couple of people who I think will fit these categories, but no matches.

"It's a great tragedy," says a young, lanky, bright-smiling man in an Australian accent. He's sitting a few seats up from me with a beer and a notebook in front of him, and a pen in hand.

At first I don't think he's talking to me, but he's looking right at me.

"What's that?" I say.

"A beautiful woman in a bar, on her own."

"How do you know I'm on my own?" I say, eyebrows raised.

"I don't. I'm hoping you are, though." He stops himself and smiles. He has nice teeth. "Sorry. I thought I'd try a pickup line, but I think that was entirely terrible. I'm so sorry."

I start to laugh. "It was pretty bad."

"Yeah, I know. I had this idea that I could go against my very character and be super smooth, but I have proven that to be desperately incorrect. Sorry for wasting your time." He stands up as if to leave.

"It was bold, that's commendable." He stops. I add, "I thought people didn't know how to talk to each other in real life anymore, so it was refreshing."

"Oh, it was very tactical. I saw you were on Tinder before I sat down. So not bold at all, just working the odds."

"Oh, so you thought you'd prop yourself in front of me with your notebook, looking pensive and pretending you're writing a masterpiece?"

He laughs. "Exactly." He sits back down and drinks a mouthful of beer from his glass.

"Is that even your notebook?" I ask.

"The notebook is real. Yes. Everything else, a bold-faced

lie." He has curls that bounce, and a slight frame hidden by an oversized long-sleeve shirt.

"Good to know. What are you writing in your notebook?"

"Poetry."

"Bullshit." I smirk.

He laughs loudly. "I am. I'm actually a poet."

"You are not." I shake my head, sipping from my glass.

"I am." He opens the notebook, flicks to a page and slides it over to me. There are words underlined and sentences scrawled.

I read aloud. "'Her pixie cut cuts deep, beware of girls with magic in their hair.'" I smile. "Me?"

"Maybe." He shrugs with a grin, then leans over and takes the notebook back, placing a rubber band tight around its center like he's locking his thoughts away. I drink the last from my glass. "I'm Gideon," he says, looking at me through his curls.

"I'm Noni. Can I buy you a drink?" I ask and he nods.

We talk easily. He is not confident but he's self-assured, weird and sweet and he asks a lot questions. I think he must be in his midtwenties. He's been traveling for over a year. He tells me funny stories about living in London, about weird warehouse parties and Contiki tours.

"Good to know that nothing has changed since I was your age." I'm tipsy. We've been going round for round for a while now.

"You mean your friends got so wasted on space cakes and kept watching *The Matrix* on repeat so you had to leave your hostel tonight too?"

"See, that's the age difference, because there comes a point in your thirties where you don't ever need to sleep in a hostel again if you can help it."

"You mean I've got another decade of hostels to bear? Shit."

My ears prick. "A decade? How old are you?"

"Twenty," he says and I scoff loudly. "What?" He looks at me and the bizarre face I must be pulling. *Noni, he's twenty. You are not having sex with this young, young, young man.*

"I thought you were older than that," I say.

"I get that a lot," he says.

We continue to chat easily, and then I decide it's time to go, because if I drink another prosecco, I will have sex with this young, young, young man.

"I'm gonna go."

He nods. "So am I, but let me walk you home."

"Okay," I tell him.

As we stroll along the canals, I tell him about the pleasure quest, which he loves, and he tells me what he's learned being away from home. He's articulate and smart. A lovely guy, and it feels easy being with him.

"I think I'm starting to realize that the things I thought were super shit about me a couple of years ago are actually not shit at all," he says.

"I get that feeling. Only you're having it a lot earlier than I did."

"I am not solely responsible for this revelation. I have a ridiculously self-assured sister, and a great therapist. Like, I don't want to lead you astray here, Noni, this isn't all me at all."

"It doesn't matter how you've come to it. It's good that you have. You've got a full sixteen-year head start on me. Imagine what you'll be like when you're my age," I tell him.

"Oh, I'll probably be a complete megalomaniac asshole." We both laugh. "Don't worry, the world will do something to knock me down a few pegs between now and then. It always does."

"That's a depressing thought," I say.

"No, that's life," he says.

How is this young man so articulate and considerate at his age?
"How do you not have a girlfriend?" I ask.

"Oh, Noni, I ask myself that question every day." He smiles
and I laugh more. "I'm really enjoying dating. Plus, there's a
girl back home." He raises his eyebrows and nudges me with
his shoulder, his hands stuffed in his pockets.

"There always is."

"Yeah. She's meant to be coming here at some point this
year. We talk all the time. But who knows. To be completely
honest, I'm really enjoying meeting as many amazing people
as possible. It's really fucking cool."

"Yeah, I feel that way too."

"I don't know if you can tell, but I was a big dork in school."

"No," I say, sarcastic.

"I know, right? So me and girls weren't really…a thing." He
blushes a little but leans into it, showing me his rosy cheeks
like he's proud of them. He's so cute.

"And now?" I ask.

"Now, you could say, I'm making up for lost time."

I nod. "Me too." I point to the entrance of my unit, stopping and standing in front of him.

"This list of yours…"

"Yes?"

"There's a twenty-year-old poet on it, isn't there?" he says.
I think he's joking, but also testing the water. *Noni, he's twenty!*
But this feels good. It feels right.

"There wasn't." I grin.

He raises his eyebrows expectantly. "But?"

"But, there is now."

"Good, 'cause I really want to kiss you, but I don't know
if that's something that you would be—"

I kiss him. It's slow. Sweet. I grin and he chuckles slightly, then he grabs my face with both his hands and kisses me, tongue in my mouth, teeth biting my bottom lip. His hand runs up my chest and gently holds my whole neck. He looks at me for a moment, biting the corner of his bottom lip before he kisses me again, quick and clumsy, but not awkward at all. We laugh and kiss and he runs his hand slowly back down my chest, pulling back, watching his hand dip between my cleavage and running his fingertips across my nipple.

"Fuuuck" is all he says, which makes me laugh. I kiss him again, we push into each other, desperate, hot. My hand slips under his jacket and shirt at the back, until I touch skin, tracing my fingers around his belt line and running my thumb over his hip bone. "Fuuuck!" he says again, shaking his head in disbelief.

I giggle. "Do you want to come up?" I ask.

"Nah," he says, smirking. "What gave you that impression?" He kisses me, quick pecks, over and over, saying "Yes" between each one.

I unlock the door, flick on the lamp, push Play on some music and look at him sitting on the small couch, watching me. I'm curious about what he'll do next, whether he'll wait for me to make the next move or not. He doesn't. The moment I sit down, he leans over and kisses me, and we make out like teenagers. Pressing into each other, moaning in pleasure and longing, changing tempo, fast, teeth clashing, then slow and deliberate exploration. He lies on top of me and slowly, one by one, he unbuttons my shirt, then he sits back on his haunches between my legs, his hands on my knees, looking at me, taking me in.

"What?" I ask, feeling sexy and insecure all at once.

"You're fucking hot."

"Thank you." I feel it. He is totally in the moment with me, right now.

He takes his time kissing my entire torso. Slowly. Intentionally. Purposely. I reach back and unclip my own bra because I can't stand this pace any longer. He takes this as a cue to take his shirt off. I want him. I want to indulge myself in this sweet man.

"Tell me anything you want and I'll do it, Noni," he says.

So I do. I tell him exactly what I want. Exactly what I like. I've never vocalized so specifically what turns me on before, but when I do, he loves it, loves getting it right, loves pleasing me, loves watching me orgasm, and his eyes on me, grinning, proud, turn me on more. I love everything about it.

"What do you like?" I ask him, kissing his chest, lightly biting his nipple, and he moans softly.

"You know," he says in a low voice. "I've never tried doggy-style. Could we maybe do that?" I giggle loudly and kiss his chest and he blushes again, grabbing my shoulders. "What? Is that not cool? Why are you laughing?"

"Because you're fucking adorable," I say. "We can absolutely do that," I tell him and he raises his eyebrows, pleased.

In the morning I wake up and Gideon is gone. There's a ripped notebook page on the pillow. The page with the pixie cut line on it. He's added another line. "Beware of girls," he's written, but then he's crossed that out and rewritten it. "Beware of women with pleasure in their tongues, they'll lick lavish spells over your torso, changing you forever." I hold it in my hands and I laugh out loud, stretching out in the middle of the bed and smiling with my whole body.

22

I want to buy lingerie. Real lingerie. Hot lingerie. I want to be the kind of woman who owns and wears really hot lingerie.

The woman in the shop has black braided hair piled into a beautiful crown on top of her head. Red silky straps shoot across her chest in intricate patterns out of the tip of her dress, crossing at her neck. The crystals on the straps catch the light of the giant chandelier above my head and I feel entirely unsexy in my thermals and polar fleece.

"How hot do you want to feel?" she asks, her accent thick.

"Like on a scale?" I ask.

"Yes, on a scale of don't touch me to Beyoncé 'Partition' fucking in a limousine, how do you want to feel?"

"Oh, okay." I consider the scale. "Like I've just fucked in a limousine and the memory is fresh while I swan about in public all hot and bothered, flushed and sexy with a secret."

"Great. Go in there." She points to a dressing room curtained with thick purple velvet. "I've got just the thing."

I get undressed in front of the mirror and make a point of watching myself. It's something new I'm trying. My usual process would be to avoid all reflective surfaces as a way of avoiding the barrage of shit things my mind has to say about my body. But lately I'm trying to look and point out things I love. Just one new thing every day. The asshole voice doesn't go away, it's still there, but this new voice, this voice that sounds suspiciously like Lindell, is at least competing. *You have long legs. Good legs. Strong legs*, the voice tells me today.

Beaded black hangers push through the break in the curtain. They look like fancy plastic anal beads, and a flash of Niko writhing into my honey-covered stomach pummels my mind's eye. I laugh when I see what she has picked. There are straps and clasps and an entirely epic two-piece operation of black and emerald-green lace and exposed skin. I exhale. *Let's do this.* The bra is longline and covers the squidgy bits that sit under my boobs, skimming the top of my waist. The cups aren't full; rather, a single piece of black fabric runs from the bottom of the cup and stops halfway, exposing the bottom of my nipple like a sexy runway. The top of the cup is an emerald-green satin that sits high across my chest, flowing into thick straps. The colors look good on my pale skin. The underwear sits high on my stomach, like proper granny panties but in a sexy way, something I didn't think was possible. They are black on the sides, with green sheer fabric across the front, covered with intricate black lace that grows like ivy from my crotch. A triangle peephole with a glistening gold circle charm sits above my belly button, exposing it like a beautiful frame.

A hand comes through the curtain, handing me four thin clasp straps. "You can attach these to turn the bottoms into suspenders and then clasp them to these." A pair of sheer black thigh-high tights appear. I try it all on and gasp a little. I look positively vampy.

"So? How'd I do?" the shop assistant says from outside the curtain.

I can't stop staring at myself. I spin and turn, examining myself in the mirror from every angle. I look like a vixen. "This is next level," I tell her.

"How do you feel?"

"I feel like a fucking goddess."

She laughs. "Good."

"I don't care how much it costs. I want it all."

My phone buzzes and I glance down. It's Beau.

Look what I just did.

An illustration of an eighteenth-century woman's face adorned in pearls stares back at me. It's beautiful. Beau and I have been messaging on and off since I left Edinburgh. He'd sent me a photo of himself as a teenager with his Peter Andre–inspired plaits, with the text *In case Amsterdam wasn't sexy enough for you*, and it made me laugh out loud. The Viking is funny. He gets my jokes and responds with answers that make my brain swoon. Hot and smart and funny.

What are you up to? he sends.

My heart quickens. *Should I send him a photo?* I feel weird about a mirror selfie. I sit on the plush pink velvet ottoman in the change room and flip the camera. Leaning my shoulder forward, I snap a photo of one boob. *That's weird, isn't it?* No face. Just a random boob in lingerie. I take another. My face is in this one, looking down. *Maybe with a filter?* I look at the photo and just see arm rolls and double chins and lace.

You have great legs, the voice says again. So I sit my thighs together and shoot from high above, suspendered legs, a touch of lace. That's better.

I'm deciding if I should buy these,
I type and hit Send,
making a weird throaty
embarrassed noise.

"You okay?" the sales assistant asks from outside the curtain.
"Yup," I mutter.
"Just give us a yell if you need anything, all right, chick?" the girl says and I hear her heels click away on the wooden floor.
My phone buzzes. It's Beau's wide-eyed face, his mouth slightly agape, doing a thumbs-up.

She's beautiful,
by the way.
I hit Send.
The tattoo, I mean.

She IS beautiful,
he replies,
quickly followed by
a second message.
You, I mean.

I swoon hard. I quickly take a bunch of high-angled selfies, turned-away face, mostly boob in the amazing bra. Another buzz. This time it's Lil from the retreat.

Noni! I'm back
in Edinburgh

later this week.
Shall we drink?

Brilliant. A reason to go back to Scotland that isn't just sex with a Viking. *Thank you very much, Lil.* I flick through the selfies and pick the one that I like the most. I crop out even more of my face so it's just all boob and a tiny bit of neck and pouty lip and hit Send. And I know I've fucked up the second I've done it. The horror is instant. *Fuck. Fuck. Fuck.* I sent that to Lil. Not Beau. I sent the fucking famous boudoir photographer a shit selfie of me in a bra in a change room. *You idiot, Noni.*

I'll take that
as a yes?
she replies.

My fingers can't type quickly enough as I send a tirade of messages.

HOLY SHIT LIL.
I'M SO SORRY.
THAT WAS FOR SOMEONE ELSE.
I'M DOING FOUR THINGS AT ONCE.
Oh my god. I'm horrified.

She replies.

I am not.
Noni, I'm laughing.

Yes. To drinks.
Of course.
I'm so sorry, I send.

You look amazing.
I'm glad we're
catching up, I
want to hear
all about who
this was actually
meant for.

I'm in the change room
right now. I haven't
bought it yet.

Buy it. Have you sent it
to the right person yet?

I think I will. AND NO.
Just you. I don't think
I will send it to him now.
Too traumatized.

Hahahaha.
Give me two minutes,
she replies.

I get dressed. It feels weird when I see myself in my clothes
again and not in the intricate design of silk, lace and perfectly
placed strips of fabric. My phone buzzes again. Lil has taken
the photo I sent her, made it black-and-white and whacked
some filters on it. It looks amazing.

Send him this.

I do. I send it straightaway.

Then I write back to Lil.

Holy shit, Lil. I look hot.

> Let me take actual
> photos of you in it?
> Please? she sends.

I flick the curtain open and head to the counter, plopping the lingerie down. The cost-to-fabric ratio on this purchase is extortionate, but I don't care. I look at my phone. A message from Beau.

> The other artists in the
> shop are giving me shit
> for blushing.
> Thanks for that.

"Have a good time, darling." The woman behind the counter smiles at me.

"Oh, I will." I take the beautifully wrapped package as my phone buzzes again.

Can I see all of this in real life? Beau asks.

I smile wide and reply to both him and Lil.

Yes. Absolutely.

"He sounds lovely," Lil says. We are halfway through our second bottle of wine, and if you were looking at us from across the room, you would assume we had been friends our whole lives. "And he doesn't know you're back in Edinburgh yet?"

"No. I'll message him tomorrow to see if he wants to get a drink, I guess."

"Yes. Perfect." Lil laughs.

"This trip is about putting *me* first, and about what *I* want, so I'm treading carefully," I add and Lil smiles at me with kind blue eyes. We're having one of those meals—one of those conversations—that instantly cuts through all of the bullshit and gets straight to the heart of who we are and how we're feeling. I find it fascinating that some of the most honest, vulnerable, intimate conversations I've had in my life have been with near strangers. I've told Lil things tonight that I haven't told many people. Things about my baby, my guilt, my grief and the complete mind fuck that is even beginning to wonder about whether I'll have another child. Or whether I even want to. I've told her about the shame and heartache I feel when I see friends post photos of their babies growing up, or make announcements about second or third babies. How I want to scream at them for being so inconsiderate. And then I feel selfish and shit, because their news is joyous, of course. We've talked about how I cycle through variations of these feelings every single day, and that I'm not quite sure where they fit now. Lil listens and nods and she doesn't say much at all. And I'm so grateful for it.

"Go easy on yourself, though, Noni. The idea that everyone is on the same timeline and that we're all striving for perfection is absolute bullshit. There's always mess. Always. We're always having to clean up, or process, something. All we can do about it is be kind to ourselves." She sips from her wine glass. "I spent so much of my life wasting energy on people who treated me like shit. Real assholes. But the most devastating thing, once I'd done the fucking work to get rid of the assholes, was that I realized I was still left with one. Me. I was a real dick to myself for so long. Brutal. No more assholes kind of became my mantra."

"I love it," I tell her.

Lil tells me more about her past, her shit relationship with her parents, dumb boyfriends she had when she was younger, and then a traumatic relationship with her first husband, who was abusive in every sense. She survived it for fifteen years until one night her teenage son stood up to him in an attempt to protect her and she said that something snapped. Something primal. She grabbed her kid and walked out the door with just the clothes on her back and she started again.

I feel a pang of guilt as Lil tells me about her life. Guilty because my worries and insecurities seem so small compared to Lil's. My worries about the pleasure quest seem so unfounded compared to completely starting your life over again.

"You're very good, Noni," she says, as we share the most incredible baklava.

"What?"

"At hiding it." She pops another spoonful into her mouth and closes her eyes, savoring it.

"Hiding what?" I ask.

"Your pity face. This is the moment in the story where people feel desperately uncomfortable and don't know where to put their feelings, and then I end up counseling them about it."

"Oh no, I don't want to be that person." I shake my head, knowing exactly what she means. It's partly why I've gotten so good at not talking about what happened to me. My own feelings are difficult enough to deal with, let alone someone else's.

"No one does. No one does it intentionally."

"Can I be honest with you?" I ask.

"I would want nothing else."

"I was actually thinking about myself." Lil laughs loudly, and so I nod and continue. "About how me freaking out about my quest is so ridiculous. I've been so worried about my intentions, and now I don't really understand why. Or I do, but I feel stupid that it felt so scary. That simply wanting to be happier caused me so much anxiety. I feel like a fuckwit."

"You're not a fuckwit. You're human." Lil's neat manicured hand grabs mine. "You're a woman," she adds and we stare at each other.

"Also I'm feeling that life is desperately unfair and I'm sorry you had to go through any of that." I place my hand on top of hers.

"Me too," she says, we smile and clink our glasses together.

"I don't think we can compare shit. We all go through it. One person's trauma doesn't negate someone else's feelings. They're still legitimate. I just wish we'd all stop being so hard on ourselves all the time. And I mean, *all* the fucking time," Lil says.

"I'm trying really hard."

"That's all we can do. Now," she says, changing the topic. "Are you actually going to let me take your photo?" She smiles brazenly.

"Yes. Yes, I am."

"Well, my love, that's great fucking news. Can I ask you something else?"

"Of course."

"Do you want a job? With me?"

"What? Really?"

"Yeah. I thought of you instantly. I need someone to help out on a project I'm doing about bodies and taking up space, and pleasure. Being naked in nature. It's gorgeous."

"Lil, that sound amazing."

"It would be an assisting gig. Bits and bobs. Running errands, answering emails, helping on shoots, reminding me to breathe. A couple of weeks. I didn't know if you had a plan or you were moving on, but I thought I'd ask."

"I'm very, very interested," I tell her, and I am. I want to be around Lil, I want to hear her speak more, I want to hear her stories and take in as much of her wisdom as possible. Something in me says *Say yes.* So I do. "I'd love to work with you. Absolutely."

"Brilliant." She beams. "I think we're gonna have a lot of fun."

23

We decide the best way to solidify our newfound intimacy and celebrate our new working relationship is to drink. Tequila. In a backpacker pub. Lil has accosted a group of three Swedish tourists and is making them speak Swedish for us. When they do, we obnoxiously repeat what they've said and laugh loudly.

The music is loud, the air is smoky, and I am flirting and drunk and being outrageous and I feel happy. Horny. One of the boys is flirting with me. A lovely, chubby, bearded man who keeps trying to dance with me but he has no sense of rhythm. He's cute. I can't remember his name. I know I could have sex with this man if I wanted to, and that knowledge is making me feel a kind of wild power. Plus I'm wearing the fucking lingerie, which is also fueling this powerful energy. I feel sexy. I don't want this Swedish man, though; I want the Viking. I pull out my phone.

Hey, I text and I wait. *Smooth, Noni. Smooth.* Within seconds my phone lights up.

Did you really just "hey" me? he replies.

I call. Beau answers straightaway. "Well, hello," he says.

"It's one in the morning—isn't that what you're meant to do? I thought it was a thing. To *hey*," I bluster. I am drunk.

He laughs. "What are you doing?"

"I'm at a pub with a group of Swedish backpackers."

"Oh, really. How's that?"

"It's fine. What are you doing?"

"Are you trying to booty call me, Noni?"

"That depends."

"On what?"

"Do you want to be booty called? 'Cause I'm in Edinburgh. So…" I say. And I'm sure I can hear Beau smile on the phone.

"Do you want to come over?"

"Yes," I tell him. I hang up the phone, kiss Lil on the cheek, grab my jacket and walk through the double doors of the pub and into a cab. I'm walking up to Beau's apartment and pushing the buzzer all in about, oh, ten minutes.

Beau's voice crackles through the intercom. "That was quick."

"I come quickly." *NONI! I mean, really.* He pushes the buzzer and I walk inside. I take a minute to catch my breath before I let myself in. And there he is, hair out and wearing a dressing gown, his face beaming.

"I like your dressing gown."

"You're drunk."

"Very," I say and he laughs.

"How was your trip?"

"It was great. Pleasure-filled," I say. He's smiling at me from across the room, watching me as I take my coat off and drop it on the floor.

"And what brings you back to Edinburgh?"

"A job, actually."

"Really?" he sounds pleased.

"So, how does this work?" I ask.

"What?"

"I've never booty-called anyone before."

"I think you're meant to seduce me."

"Take your dressing gown off," I say and he does. He's naked. I feel my chest and cheeks flush.

"Take your dress off." He smiles.

I do. And I praise the pleasure quest and the braided beauty at the lingerie shop for her impeccable suggestions when I see Beau's face as my dress falls to the floor.

"You look—"

"This old thing." *Noni, don't be a fuckhead.* "Now what?" I ask.

"You called me. What do *you* want to do?"

"I want to know what you want to do."

"That's not how this—"

I cut him off. "Tell me a fantasy. Tell me what you want to do to me." His eyes are locked on me. On my body with all of its new strappy lace fixings.

"I want to fuck you," he says, his eyes narrowing.

"Where?" I ask.

"Over the back of the couch."

I smile, trying to be sexy, even though I know I'm swaying a little. I kick my boots off and keep reminding myself to not stand awkwardly, to look like a woman who is used to wearing lingerie. To act like a fucking sex goddess.

"What do *you* want, Noni?"

"I don't—" I stop myself. I was about to say *I don't know* even though I do know. Even though my body is telling me exactly what it wants. I think about Amsterdam. I'm only going to say exactly what I want from now on.

"I want you to go down on me." I walk to the wall and lean my back against it. "Here."

Beau strides across the room and stands so close to me, looking me in the eye, I think he's going to kiss me, but he doesn't. He looks at me and I become very aware of my breath and my chest moving up and down. Up and down. Keeping his eyes on mine, he kneels down, running his hands down the sides of my legs. He starts kissing my stomach, right under my belly button, and now I understand why that frame is there. He lifts one leg over his shoulder. I clutch the wall. He doesn't take my knickers off; he just pulls them to the side and starts licking. Slowly. *JESUS*. The moment a self-conscious thought creeps in, I tell it to fuck right off, and instead I give over to the pleasure. Beau is enjoying himself. A lot. He's making low, soft, sexy sounds, and I am feeling more sensual than I ever have. His hands grab at my ass, and I rock my hips into him, my own hands running over my body. His tongue and fingers are all entirely focused on me. My thighs quiver, I moan loudly, over and over again, until I want more. More of him.

I grab his hair and pull his head back to look up at me.

He kisses my stomach, across my boobs, and up my chest to my neck and lands at my ear, whispering, "What do you want, Noni?"

It's the sexiest thing anyone has ever said to me, ever. I push him back over to the couch so he's sitting. I want to kiss, and lick, and bite every inch of his body. I want his skin to feel as alive as mine does. I start at his collar bones, licking up to his ear, nibbling his ear lobe.

"What do you want, Beau?" I mimic him.

"You," he says, grabbing at me, but I pull away. I kiss down his chest, and run my nails down his body and thighs. I kiss his hip, scrape my teeth lightly against his skin. He squirms. I like the sounds he's making.

I like teasing him. I like learning him. Learning where he likes my tongue, my fingers. What makes him feel good. What makes him moan.

"If you keep doing that I'm gonna—" he sighs.

I look up at him, moving my tongue deliberately while our eyes are locked. He moans again, moving his hips away, as his hands grab at my shoulders, pulling me up towards his face. He kisses me hard.

Then he quickly dashes to his bedroom. Undoes a condom packet as he walks back into the room, sits back down exactly where he was, and puts it on.

"Stand up," he says.

I do. He then takes my hand, guiding me to stand between his legs, taking in every part of me. Grabbing either side of my undies, he slides them down. I straddle him. Rocking my hips. His arms wrap around my waist tightly. Our bodies press against each other. Our mouths, tongues and teeth clash passionately.

"Fuck, Noni." I like it when he says my name. This feels incredible. My body knows exactly what it wants, and my hips move deliberately.

"Slow down," he says, closing his eyes. "I'm going to—I just need a—this outfit is—" I don't slow down. I keep going. I want him. I want him to lose himself. I want to be responsible for his pleasure.

"Noni—" he gasps, his hands squeezing my hips tightly as he pushes into me and I lean into his neck, biting softly. He groans and shudders. And then smiles drowsily, kissing me.

"You're beautiful, woman," he mumbles and I laugh, folding into him.

An alarm buzzes me awake, and I feel Beau's arm slide over my waist to the bedside table to turn it off.

"Good morning." He spoons me, nuzzling into my neck, and I stretch out and into him so our bodies lie flush together. I feel small, wrapped up in him and his blanket.

"What time is it?" I ask.

"It's ten. I have to be at work in an hour," he says. He doesn't move, though, and I hug his hand and kiss his knuckles. His finger starts tracing circles on my stomach and my legs, sliding between my thighs. I bite my lip and push my hips back into him, signaling my desire, for him, for this gesture, for his hand on my body and his breath on my neck. Moments of pleasure pass but my wanting gets too big for just his fingers. I want him. All of him. On top of me. In me.

I roll to my back and pull him onto me. The craving is immense. He reads my need and thrusts deep and I moan loudly. It feels so good.

"Fuck me," I say, and there's a far-off distant thought that nods, impressed.

He buries his face into my neck and pushes one leg up farther with his bicep. I startle myself with my own flexibility as I grab at his back, his ass, clutching him as closely as I possibly can.

"Good morning," I say with a smile, kissing his face all over once we're finished. He rolls over to lie on his back and I settle in the nook of his arm.

"I love all of these," I say, tracing the tattoos on his chest. His tattoos are mostly old-school designs in primary colors. A mix of big and small pieces. This is the first time I've really looked at them. "Do they all mean things?" I ask.

"Mostly," he says. "Designs I liked, artists I thought were cool. Moments in time. Being young and stupid." He points to a skateboard on his hip with the words *ride or die* and chuckles. "Eighteen. I thought I was well hard."

I laugh, taking them all in. There are pin-up ladies with

bright flowers in their flowing hair, a dagger surrounded by blooms, a thick-lined blue eye, a crab, a treasure chest and ship, an hourglass with the sand evenly balanced. There's an anatomical heart bursting with flowers like a vase in the center of his chest. The words *don't fret* are tattooed on his knuckles.

"These?" I ask, pointing to three intricate butterflies that take up his whole bicep.

"My mum, my nan, my sister." He turns around to show me the inside of his arm with a chrysalis surrounded by flowers. "My kid."

He has a kid. Shit. "How old?"

"Zeppelin. He's sixteen," Beau says, smiling. "He's awesome." He glances at the clock. "Fuck. I've gotta get ready." He smirks mischievously at me as he gets up and walks out of the bedroom.

A sixteen-year-old.

I walk naked into the living room, pick up his dressing gown and put it on, then find my bag where I'd dropped it by the door. I look at my phone—there's a message from Lindell. A video. I push Play.

"What do you want to say to Aunty Nono?" Lindell says from behind the camera. Audre and Julius are in the frame, sitting on the couch.

"We're changing your name." They giggle.

"What are we changing her name to?" Lindell prompts.

"Aunty Yes-Yes!" Audre screeches gleefully. They dance on the couch, jumping up and down. Audre is wearing a hard hat with a tool belt wrapped around her waist and Julius has a long lilac cape that he swishes as he jumps.

Lindell comes into the frame. "I had nothing to do with this. This is all her doing but it made me happy. I fucking—"

"Papa!" Audre bellows, sounding shocked.

"Sorry." He raises his eyebrows at me and it feels like he's right here in the room in front of me. "I freaking miss you, my best. And I love you. And I'm proud of you." He kisses the screen. "What do we say?" He sits between the kids and they clamber all over him. "We love you, Aunty Yes-Yes," he says.

"We love you, Aunty Yes-Yes," they bellow. "Aunty Yes-Yes. Aunty Yes-Yes!"

And I laugh as familiar, happy, homesick tears fill my eyes.

"What's that face?" I look up to see a shirtless Beau striding toward me, looking concerned.

"Love," I say.

He wraps his arms around my waist and burrows into my neck. I push Play again and he watches, laughing gently as the kids squeal in delight.

"They're all beautiful."

"I know, right."

"Aunty Yes-Yes?" he asks.

"Aunty No-No. No-*ni*. No*no*." I sound it out.

"Excellent." He kisses my neck. "You never told me about your new job."

"It's helping a photographer friend of mine. I met her at that retreat I went on. She's amazing. She's shooting this naked-in-nature series."

"Sounds awesome." He nuzzles my shoulder. "Seeing as you're sticking around for a bit, will you let me take you out on a proper date?"

"Yes," I say quickly.

Aunty Yes-Yes indeed.

24

My mum has been an emergency room nurse forever. My favorite stories of hers are the ones about the weird shit that people do to require a trip to the ER. Mostly these stories involve people lighting things on fire that shouldn't be lit on fire or jumping off things that they shouldn't have jumped off—like the lady who jumped off a too-high fence, landed strangely, and broke both her ankles and both her wrists. Now that's a bad day. There are also the people who come in with things stuck up, and/or in, their private parts. These are my absolute favorite because the stories that people tell to explain why they're in the emergency room are the best. Like the man who had a whole mackerel stuck in his anus, who told my mother that he'd been hosing out the cold room in the fish shop he works in and slipped—which, similarly, is how another lady got a Coke can stuck up her clacker, and another man a vacuum rod. Just a vigorous naked Saturday-morning clean and *whoops*. I've never cleaned anything that deeply.

What I've always found fascinating about these stories is thinking about the moment when the person finally admitted defeat and headed to the emergency room—because you assume by that stage they would have tried *everything* to get that foreign object out of their body.

This is no longer theoretical for me, however. I know for certain it's the case, because I have tried every single possible yoga position, squat, lunge, dance, and pelvic-floor wiggle I can muster. I have prayed, cried, tried to relax, and convinced myself I am surely going to die from some kind of plastic poisoning, or toxic shock, or embarrassment—because my Moon Cup is very much stuck.

I message Lindell. **Bear down, sweet cheeks** is all he replies, along with four baby emojis.

I lie helpless on the floor of my tiny Scottish unit realizing, quite poetically, that I am well and truly alone. Well, not completely alone—I am meant to be going on a date with Beau today. I sent him a text telling him I was feeling poorly, that I'd call him later, and that I was most definitely not blowing him off. I thought about making a joke about actually blowing him off but decided to refrain. I refrain, too, from explaining exactly what my affliction is. I don't think he needs to know just yet about the capacity of my vagina to both swallow and lose objects. The word *lose* in this sense is not quite right, I know, because the Moon Cup isn't lost, I know roughly where it is, I just don't know exactly where. Kind of like telling someone you'll meet them at the botanical gardens.

I have a day off tomorrow. I want to see you, he'd texted the afternoon after the booty call.

I'd exclaimed "*Yessss!*" so loudly that everyone in the coffee shop stopped and looked at me. I'd smiled politely, but I felt like jumping up onto my chair and making a speech that would've gone something like; *I've met a Viking. He's good at conversation. And he told me he likes me. And then we had great sex. And he's good at it. Like, really good. And he just texted me. A very excellent text. No games. No bullshit. Straight to the point. Vikings don't fuck around, do they?*

We'd agreed that he'd pick me up at eleven. There's a twelve-hour limit of Moon Cup insertion. I'd already gone over this as I'd slept in. I'd then spent about two hours trying to get the damn thing out, which meant I was verging on the sixteenth hour. I finally admitted defeat, decided I needed help and headed to the emergency room. There was no way I could go out on my date knowing there was a foreign object stuck inside me.

The first nurse I spoke to didn't know what a Moon Cup was, so I had to google it and show her.

"Blimey, love, that's a smart idea, isn't it? Economical." She smiled. "If I was still getting the bleed, I might've given it a go." *She called it the bleed!*

I nodded, horrified. The very young, very blond doctor similarly had no idea, so the nurse explained it to him like he was a fucking idiot while winking at me. Knowing what it was didn't help him, though, because he just fumbled about in my vagina for a bit before admitting he wasn't feeling too confident about this specialist gynecological assignment and called in a second doctor. *Great.*

Now a spotlight is shone into my vagina and there's a fair bit of standing about and musing before the crabby nurse calls both of the young doctors blathering idiots, tells them to get out of the way and shuts the curtains. She gives me a wink as she reaches inside me with a giant fucking dildo-looking tool, explaining that she thinks the Moon Cup has suctioned itself very securely onto my cervix. She cheers when she finally pulls it out, and I die from embarrassment. She leaves the room while I get dressed.

My phone rings. It's Beau.

"Hello," I mutter.

"Just wanted to see how you were feeling?" He sounds concerned, as a message blares loudly over the hospital PA system. "Where are you?" he asks.

"At the hospital."

"Shit, Noni, are you okay?"

"Yeah, fine, just needed a hand with—"

The nurse reappears and throws me a pad and my now clean Moon Cup in a plastic ziplock bag. "It's been a pleasure, Noni," she says, and I laugh, unable to believe I'm going to be one of this woman's vagina stories tomorrow. Serves me right.

"Noni? Are you okay?" Beau asks again.

"Shit. Sorry. Yes. I'm fine. I'm leaving now."

"Wait there. I'll come and get you. Like ten minutes, okay?"

"You don't need to do that. Seriously, it's—"

"I'm coming. Just wait."

I find a bathroom and stare in the mirror. I look like a fucking wreck. I'm wearing a tracksuit and no bra. I had let my hair dry on its own after getting out of the shower, being too distracted trying to reach my hand into my own vagina to worry about the perfect blow-dry, so I look like an adolescent boy trying to be Eminem circa 2002. I wet my hands, dampen my hair and try to take back some control. I look in my handbag, where I've got a roll-on perfume, some pink lipstick and an old crumpled compact. I work with what I've got. This master absolutely, 100 percent blames her tools.

I'm sitting in a plastic emergency room chair as the Viking busts in through the doors. If the nurse hadn't found my Moon

Cup, the flood of feeling in the pit of my stomach at seeing him surely would've popped it right out.

"Fuck, Noni, you okay? You good?" He grabs my shoulders and looks at my face, worried.

I grab his hands with both of mine. "Yes, all good," I say with as much positivity as I can muster.

"What happened?"

I smile. "Can you take me home?"

"Of course."

When I accepted the job with Lil, I decided to rent a one-bedroom flat that belongs to a lovely woman named Pam, who has a penchant for floral decoration and lives in Spain for half the year.

We pull up outside and Beau leans over the back seat, pulling out a bunch of what look like flowers.

"Here, I got you these," he says.

I take the cellophaned bundle and look at the blooms, but I realize very quickly that they're not blooms at all. They're fabric. I look at Beau suspiciously and he nods, suggesting I unravel one. So I do and I instantly start laughing when I realize what they are. They're tights. Six pairs of different-colored tights rolled up to look like flowers.

"Apparently this brand is the best for bodies like yours."

I laugh loudly from a deep, glorious place. "This is the best thing that anyone has ever...oh my god." I laugh again. "Thank you. This is brilliant. Thank you."

"That's okay. I asked for some help at work and, well, yeah, I didn't realize what an ordeal getting dressed was for women. He smirks.

"This is truly amazing. The best present ever." He looks coy, he's blushing, and I reach out and squeeze his arm. "Beau, really, I love this."

"Good. I'm glad." He looks me in the eye and there's a silence that feels like it's purposely built for smiling at each other.

"So, you coming in?" I finally ask, undoing my seat belt.

"I thought you might need some—"

"I need to get changed, but come in. I wanted to see you today, just not in a tracksuit, without a bra, you know."

"You're making that a bit of a habit."

"What?"

"Me seeing you without a bra."

My cheeks flush. "Come up." I pause. "You know, if you want."

"Oh, I want."

We trudge up the stairs and I try to mentally assess the level of disarray that I left the flat in before I marched out the door to the emergency room. I do a quick scan as I open the door and realize it's okay.

"This is nice." He smirks, pointing at the palm-leaf wallpaper, which clashes with the floral couch.

"It's good, isn't it? Do you want a drink? I have green juice and that's it. I'm not obsessed with tea like the rest of you lot, if that's what you were hoping for, but there may be some in the cupboard."

"I'll make it." He comes into the kitchen and starts poking around. He's close to me but he doesn't touch me. I watch him delicately rip open a small paper packet with some fancy tea bag in it. My mind flashes back to his grin as he'd done the same with the condom the other night. He rips open a second tea bag and my face feels hot. The kettle pops and whirs and I look at it, grinning. *I know how you feel, kettle.*

He hands me a cup. "Here. You'll find that tea makes everything better."

"Thanks."

"Are you sure you're okay?" He looks so worried. His big eyes are looking at me with real concern.

"I'm fine, really."

"But the hospital? Noni—"

"My vagina swallowed my Moon Cup," I blurt without thinking, or rather I was thinking I should tell him some version of the truth because I didn't think he was going to let up with his concern, but before I could put a cool and planned response together, my overzealous mouth was like the drunk teenager at a party, all "Don't worry guys, I've got this," before they set their eyebrows ablaze by getting too close to the fire.

"Your what?" he asks.

Oh, god. Here we go again. I pull it out of my handbag, still in its plastic bag, and throw it at him. "This. Was stuck."

I tell him about the grouchy nurse and the two young blushing doctors and about my mum and the guy with a mackerel up his ass. Beau laughs. A lot. With tears streaming down his face, he leans back into the counter, the hem of his jumper lifting slightly above his belt, showing his bare skin. I want to reach out and place my hand there, my mouth there, but I refrain.

He wipes his eyes, pulling it together, and looks at me. "I could've helped you—"

I cut him off. "Absolutely not. There are stages of intimacy, I think, and you reaching into my cavernous vagina to find a plastic cup is not the stage we are at right now." He howls with laughter, and I join in. I like that I make him laugh. "Just give me ten minutes, okay?"

"Take as long as you need."

I shower quickly, imagining the Viking striding in here naked and joining me, but I have to shut that thought out to be as productive as I need to be to get ready as quickly as I'd promised. The door to the bedroom is open just a crack, and as I dress, I can see Beau standing near the bookshelf, reading. He puts the book back and undoes his hair, which had been tied in a messy low-slung bun. He throws his head back, shakes it out and loops it up in a bun on the top of his head with a band from his wrist in one fluid movement. The stretch of his shoulders, the pull of his jaw, the hair cascading down his neck, the flex of his biceps—it all pulsates something primal deep in me. My desire escapes my mouth in a breathy noise, and if I didn't have my period right now, I'd be sure he'd just impregnated me from across the room.

"All right?" I say, hoping he hasn't heard the mouth orgasm I just had. I step into the living room. "If you could replace your image of me from this morning with this one, I'd be deeply appreciative."

He turns and smiles and looks at me for longer than the agreed social contract. He looks at me so long that I start to feel self-conscious. "I wish—" I stop myself. *I wish I could read your mind* feels entirely too naive.

"What?" he asks.

"Nothing."

"So," he says, taking slow steps toward me. "Can I ask you a really important—"

"Yes." I cut him off and he laughs. He's standing right in front of me. I glance up at his lips.

"Can I kiss you?" he asks from his throat. His closeness means that words don't formulate and instead I make a weird throaty adolescent rasp, nodding. He kisses me, lips soft against mine. Pulling back, he smiles slightly, and I breathe him in. He pushes against me, his hands wrapping around my waist, his tongue in my mouth, and my stomach at my knees. I grab at his shoulders, trying to pull him in as close as possible.

He looks at me, staying close to my face, and it's too intense, so I look away. "Okay, I concede, Ginger Spice is the best," I mumble.

He laughs loudly, and his chest muscles tense under my hands. He kisses me lightly under my ear. "So," he says, whispering in a way that travels right into my pelvis and explodes. I tense my legs. "You need to go and put on the warmest things you own."

"So I should just put all of my clothes on?" I ask.

"It's kind of the opposite of what I actually want you to do, but yeah."

I'm not used to this kind of unabashed flirting. This direct level of dreamy-wants being spoken loudly. I'm used to ambiguity, confusion and long hours spent pondering whether the emphasis on particular words was in fact a clue signaling desire. I'm used to weeks, or even years, of not being sure how they feel and plotting ways to talk to gather more evidence. But this? I don't know what to do with this. So I say nothing.

"I want to take you somewhere," he says and I draw on every inch of my willpower to not utter the words, *You can take me anywhere.*

25

Beau takes me for a walk up Calton Hill and I marvel at monuments to philosophers and sprawling city views. "I can't believe this is just in the middle of the city," I say repeatedly.

We talk as we walk up the winding gravel path.

"Do you have brothers or sisters?" he asks. It's windy so our hands are stuffed into our pockets and we walk close together.

"Nope. Just me. And my dysfunctional parents." I stop and explain. "Like, a normal level of dysfunction. A manageable dysfunction."

"Oh yeah? Tell me more."

"We're talking parents who hate each other and couldn't bear to be in the same room since I was eleven. A messy divorce and a father whose life kind of halted around that time, and has never started up again. Who absolutely blames my now happily remarried mother for every misfortune in his seemingly fine life," I say, raising my eyebrows to provide a real-life exclamation mark.

Beau takes my gloved hand and kisses it. "I worry about my kid. He was five when we split up." He pauses. "His mum, Sabine, and I were young, just in our early twenties, when we had him." He pulls his phone out of his pocket and shows me a recent photo of Zeppelin. He's gorgeous. *His mum must be gorgeous.*

"He looks like you."

"Sometimes." He smiles, looking at the photo with a kind of longing in his eyes. "Sabine got a job in London. That's why they moved. She's a TV producer. Some bigwig job. Apparently she's a big deal."

She's beautiful and smart. Great. Be cool, Noni. Be cool.

"And it fucking sucks not seeing him every day." Beau looks sad.

"I bet."

"He comes up whenever he can. I go down whenever I can. They've only been down there for six months or so." He flicks through his photos and shows me one of the two of them. Zeppelin has tight ringlets sprung into a bouncing Afro circled around his soft features. He's broad like Beau. They have the same beaming smile.

"We FaceTime—but yeah, it's not the same. He's like the coolest person I know."

His mouth is closed in a sweet, pained, love-filled smile, and I swoon. Like I'm a blob of paint and a brush has come in and swirled me in a perfect circle.

"We need to talk about the fact that you named your kid Zeppelin," I tease.

He chuckles. "We thought it was the most badass fucking name in the world at the time. But it suits him."

"I like it. So many names are ruined when you work in schools." The view has changed to another part of the city where the ocean is in the distance, smashing into the clouds. This incredible collision of nature and concrete all at once.

"Yeah, I'm sure." Beau stands behind me as I stop and take it in. He puts his arm around my shoulder, and I lean my head into his chest. "We were together for six years—we weren't right for each other. But we're close. I mean, we have to be. Our relationship is solid now, because we've done the work on it." He seems so together. It makes me feel so untogether.

"That's good. That's good for him. I know so many kids whose parents really fuck it up. Exhibit A." I point to myself. "So that's good."

We keep walking, and I put my arm around his waist.

"She's married to a nice Brazilian guy. He's a great step-dad to Zep. Which makes me equally love him and hate him at the same time."

"What's he like?"

"He's a cameraman," he says.

I shake my head. "No, Zeppelin, not the Brazilian stepdad."

"Yeah, right." He laughs. "He's so much more confident than I ever was at sixteen. He loves music and politics and he's emotionally sound. He talks a lot. Writes wild rhymes. He's funny. He's into clothes and that's what he wants to do. Fashion. Tailoring. He makes his own stuff. Screen prints. That T-shirt you liked the other day, he made that."

"Amazing." Of course this human has created a whole other brilliant young man. Of course. I smile at Beau.

"What?"

"I like watching your face when you talk about him. You smile in a way that I haven't seen."

He blushes. "He's my kryptonite. Completely. I can't talk about him too much because I get emotional. Wanna cry."

It takes all of my willpower to not "aww" audibly.

We walk up concrete steps set amid a kind of parkland next to a giant structure that looks akin to the Parthenon.

"It's called Edinburgh's Disgrace," Beau says. "It was meant to honor the dead, but it's basically just a concrete monument to bad financial planning, because it was never finished."

I laugh as we follow a path around the structure.

"What about your parents?" I ask.

"Like, the actual opposite of yours. Stupidly happy, have been married for forty years, ridiculously supportive of my younger sister and me."

"So, the disgruntled-artist fuck-you-mum-and-dad stereotype is not even close?" I tease.

"Not even in the same stratosphere. *We just want you to be happy, Beau,*" he says, changing his voice to mimic his parents.

"Ah, for my parents, that sentence always comes with a *but. I want you to be happy, but…*" I mimic my dad's dubious tone perfectly.

We sit on a park bench facing Arthur's Seat, an extinct volcano. And he opens his backpack and pulls out a thermos full of a whiskey-flavored hot chocolate concoction that makes my eyes widen with glorious surprise when I first taste it.

"My dad's special recipe," he says.

"Good work, Dad." I sip slowly and feel warm from the inside out. We sit in silence for a moment before Beau looks at me.

"Do you think your parents are to blame for distorting your idea of happiness?" He draws circles on my knee with his finger.

I laugh, insecurely. "I've never thought of it like that. Maybe. I don't know. When my ex, Joan, and I broke up, it was big, yeah, some big shit went down." He raises his eyebrows and I nod. "And I kind of didn't know myself anymore."

"Of course," he says.

"And I realized that I had gotten happy being unhappy, you know? Or not even unhappy. Ambivalent, maybe? Or numb. Indifferent. Yeah. I was indifferent about my life."

"I like how you do that."

"What?"

"Search for the right word. Try it out. Find the right one."

"Do I?"

"Yeah. It's cute."

"Cute?" I ask, whacking his leg.

"Intelligent? Disarming? Hot as hell?" he says, putting his arm around my shoulder again.

I laugh. "The last one, please."

"It's hot as hell." I lean into him and kiss his neck lightly and lay my head on his shoulder. I wish there was a word to describe this thing that happens when you meet someone new. The way they look at you through a new lens and notice things about you that you didn't even realize about yourself. The delivery of this information is like these little explosions of recognition. Feeling seen and surprised all at once.

"How long were you and your ex together?" he asks.

"Nine years," I say. He makes a throaty sound in acknowledgment. "Dog. Mortgage. Joint bank accounts. The lot," I say.

"And why did it end?"

I pause. "It just did."

"I think endings like that are sadder than the big dramatic ones."

I raise my eyebrows and look at him. "Ooh, big dramatic ones, I want to hear about those." I start tracing patterns on this thigh.

"When I was twenty and at art school, my girlfriend cheated on me during an installation piece while I was in the audience."

"Shut up."

"Yeah. I told her she was fucked, she yelled about my lack of vulnerability, all in front of an audience. People thought it was staged."

"Oh my god."

"That's kind of an isolated fuckery. But I've been in situations where I've messed up, or they've messed up, and in those moments you can at least rest the blame somewhere. Or you have a reason for the end. But I had my heart completely shattered by a relationship a few years ago that just sailed its course. It's tough."

"Yeah. I mean, it's been two years now. So I've totally exited that crying-lady chrysalis, but yeah." We sit silent for a moment; he puts his hand on top of mine, squeezing it, and I squeeze his back.

"So, what started all of this? Like what was the final ass-kick?" he asks.

"A firefighter."

"Oh, really?"

I tell him about Ruby the firefighter, about the months of flirting, the one-night stand after the sex drought, and about reading of her tragic death in the newspaper. I tell him about the disaster that was Ben. And Niko.

He laughs. "And the girl here?"

"All fantasy and missed opportunities. Our timing was always off. But this time closed that book. She has a girlfriend. And she didn't tell me. And I found out after we'd... So, that is very much done."

"Oh, god, Noni, that's rough."

"Yeah. And then I decided that I was going to focus on myself, and my own pleasure, and I got a tattoo to commemorate that fact, and then I met this handsome tattoo artist who I like making out with." I look at him.

"Cool," he says. And I can't help but think that he is. Cool. So cool. Probably too cool for me.

"What does your sister do?" I ask.

"She's an optometrist."

"So, the favorite?" I smirk. He's so handsome that I need to really expend energy focusing on what he's saying instead of drifting into jawbones and squinting green-blue eyes and plump lips.

"Yeah, something like that." He moves so he's facing me. "I like talking to you."

"I like talking to *you*," I tell him. He stares at me and smiles. "What?" I ask.

"Just waiting."

"What for?"

He smirks, staring at my lips.

"Oh." I laugh, leaning into him so our lips are close, but they don't touch. "Something like this?"

"Something like this," he says and he kisses me.

Later he drops me home and we sit out in front of my unit. "Hypothetically, if I were to ask you to come in, what would you think about that?"

"I would love to. Really. But I have got a huge day tomorrow, which means I have a huge drawing night tonight. And if I come in, well, there'd be no drawing. Something else entirely would be happening. You know. Hypothetically."

"Thank you for a lovely day," I say, and he kisses me softly on the mouth. I get out of the car and walk inside, up the stairs to my unit.

My phone buzzes.

Hypothetically. If I'd
come up, what would
we be doing now?

I take a photo of the barrel of monkeys on the bookshelf
and hit Send.

                                        Sexy, he replies.
                                        Tomorrow night?

Please, I reply.

26

I love working with Lil. For starters, her studio is gorgeous. Tall white walls, high ceilings, a whole wall of big windows flooding the room with natural light. There's a tiny kitchenette with bright-colored appliances and every surface and corner of the room is filled with plants. They hang from beams and a hat stand, sit on plinths and tiny tables in every corner. They flood out of a pastel-blue painted set of drawers in the center of the wall. There's an air diffuser sending the loveliest-smelling puffs of air into the space. I feel instantly calm.

"Are you nervous?" Lil asks, playing music through a speaker. A grounded male voice sings along to sweet melodies. I'd already been on two shoots with Lil, but today was my turn, to shoot the promised Amsterdam lingerie photos.

"Weirdly, no."

"Good. Do you want a cup of tea?"

We drink tea and sit on the plush dark pink couch and I

make her laugh with tales of my cavernous vagina and tell her about my dates with the Viking. Three now. Officially.

One night he took me to a barbershop that was actually a bar, right near his house. We had to walk down a quaint winding staircase before opening a door set secretly into a bookcase, prohibition-style, and ended up in a funky little cocktail bar. It was all dim lighting and bearded bartenders with the same haircut. We drank cocktails, ate hot chips and made each other laugh before tipsily stumbling the short distance back to his flat, where we barely made it inside to have pants-around-our-ankles, jackets-still-on sex in his living room. And then again in his shower. And bed.

The day before, I'd met him for lunch at the studio and all the other artists had given him shit when he kissed me.

"Such a smitten kitten," one of them shouted, and they all oohed and aahed.

"Fuck off. Everyone, this is Noni. Noni these are the assholes I work with."

"You're right, Bojangles, she's well lush," one of the girls with a whole arm blacked out and a thick Welsh accent said, smiling.

"Let's go, Noni, before they destroy all my cred."

"What cred?" one of the older artists chuckled.

"They seem lovely," I'd said as we walked toward a pub.

"They're great. It's a great shop to be in. I've worked in some shit places in the past. If the people are wrong, or arrogant, or whatever, it just ruins everything. You can't be creative in a place like that."

"Would you ever want your own shop?"

"No way. I like being able to rent a space and go away when I want. I think I'd hate the pressure."

Later over lunch he'd looked at me and asked, "What else

do you want to do while you're here, Noni? Is there stuff you want to see or do?"

"You mean apart from you?" He'd nodded, smiling. "I don't know. I kind of like making my mind up a few days at a time. That feels very liberating," I said.

"I get that."

"I'm so used to only having weekends, or school holidays, it's nice to not really be beholden or bound to anything."

"Or anyone?" he asked.

Oh, fuck, I thought. *What on earth do I say to that?*

"I mean, you can tie me up if you want," I'd joked. It was the best I could think of in the moment.

"And what did he say?" Lil smiles sympathetically. Her tiny tanned nose crinkles with an almost cautious wince.

"He laughed and said he'd love that, then we had lunch and we didn't talk about our feelings and it was lovely. He's lovely. But if this was the real world, if this was where I lived, if this encounter wasn't directly linked to the pleasure-quest version of myself, then surely around now is when we would be having a chat about whether this thing was an actual thing, you know?"

"You want boundaries?"

"Sure. I just want to make sure we're on the same page that this is a fling, and that's it."

"That's what you want?" she asks.

"Yeah." I nod. "I wouldn't mind a bit of insight too. Like, what is he thinking about me?" I lean my head back onto the edge of the couch with a smile.

"Tell him and ask him. This anxiety about what he wants can quite easily be avoided by talking to him," she says very calmly, the beaded wood bangles on her wrist spinning as she rests her head on her hand, looking at me with nothing but compassion.

"Oh, Lil, stop being so practical."

"This is how the old you would've navigated this, yes? Pleasure-quest Noni only wants to feel pleasure." She pokes me in the ribs. "Are you feeling pleasure?"

I swat her away, shaking my head. "No."

"Exactly. Then just ask. Talk about it. Find out if you're on the same page. If he's seeing other people, if shagging gorgeous travelers is his thing," she says casually.

Is he seeing other people? Should I be seeing other people? Do I even want to see other people right now? Between dates with Beau, working with Lil and spending time on my own, I hadn't really thought about seeing anyone else. I suppose I could, if I wanted to. But I don't think I do. I like things how they are. But now I have to know, I have to ask. I also feel naive—as if this gorgeous human is seeing only me. He's probably got a whole harem of beautiful women he's making feel like this. *You idiot, Noni.*

I smile at Lil, pretending everything is fine, as my mind conjures images of Beau with other women.

She stands up and offers me her hand. "Now, let's take your photo before our shoot this afternoon."

It turns out I love having my photo taken. Eventually. At first I feel weird and awkward, and I don't know what to do with my hands. But Lil is magic, and excellent at her job. I've already assisted her on a few shoots by this stage, so I know her tricks, but they work tremendously. She plays loud music and tells funny stories and makes herself vulnerable, and eventually I feel comfortable, I feel powerful, I feel fucking hot. She shoots me in my clothes to start with, and then piece by piece I undress to reveal the Amsterdam lingerie. Nothing is too posed or over-the-top.

"These photos are just a celebration of your body on this day. In this moment," she says. And I like that. In this moment, on this day, this woman feels fucking happy in this body.

Later, I carry this energy into Beau's local bar, which has ample fairy lights and cozy lounge chairs. I see a woman staring at us. Staring at me. She's tall and thin, with a sharp, asymmetrical haircut. Her hands, knuckles and neck are tattooed in bright colors, peeking from her tight top, which is showing off perfect perky boobs. Her posture is so impeccable it forces me to roll my own shoulders back and sit up straight.

"She's beautiful." I nod in her direction and pick up my drink for distraction. I want to see what he does. I want to bring up the us situation. I want to see if he's shagging other people and try to feel out what I want to be doing too. He turns his head and looks quickly at the woman and then looks back at me.

"Yeah," he says. "So I was thinking we could get a take-away—"

I try to say it nonchalantly. "You should go and call her Sassenach." I smile so he knows I'm not being weird.

"I don't want to fuck her, Noni," he says, his forehead pinched as he tries to read me.

"That's not what I said."

"No, but it's what you meant. Didn't you?"

"Yes."

"So just say that," he says so pointedly that I scoff, shaking my head.

"What?"

"You're so sorted—"

"Sorted? Noni! We barely know each other. Don't you see? I'm playing my best cards right now. I'm doing everything in my power to make sure you think that I'm—"

"What?"

"A total fucking dreamboat!" He squeezes my knee. "Aren't you?"

"Of course, although I don't think I have quite as many dreamboat cards as you," I say, sipping from my glass. This conversation is not going at all like I thought it would.

"Oh no, Miss Fuck-me-against-this-wall-when-I-booty-call-you-at-one-o'clock-in-the-morning?"

I think about what this means. "What are your other cards?" I ask.

Beau smirks, bites the corner of his lip and breathes in deep. "You wanna see my deck, babe?"

"Yes."

"I'll show you mine if you show me yours."

"My deck is pretty straightforward, like—" I say, but he cuts me off.

"Are you a human?" I look at him confused. He continues, "This shit is never straightforward."

"So—"

"What do you want to know? Ask me anything."

"Anything?"

"Yes."

The dossier of curiosity labeled The Viking flies open in my mind and my heart beats as I think about what I want to know. Who was the woman who broke his heart? Why does he seem so together? Is it because he's incapable of commitment? Does he like me? Am I good in bed? Does he want to be with me? Does he think I'm good enough for him? What did his ex-girlfriends look like? Were they skinnier than me? Could he fall in love with me? Why is he with me? Is he still in love with Zeppelin's mum? Does he believe in monogamy?

"I want to know—" I stop myself.

"I want to know what's going on in your brain right now. That's what I want to know," he says.

"I want to know…everything," I say, and feel silly. I try to make it sound cooler. "Everything about you, and about what you think…" I fail and stop myself.

"About?"

"Me," I say softly, looking at the floor. He pulls his chair closer toward me so his knee is between my legs.

"Everything about what I think about you?" he leans in closer to me, resting his arms on the arms of my chair.

I don't look up. "Yeah."

"What do you think I think about you?" he asks.

I shrug. "Me? Oh, god. I'm trying to not be such a dick to myself. I think I've been a dick to myself for most of my life, really. And I'm having all of these epiphanies lately about why that is. I'm just so worried about what people think about me all the time. And saying that now out loud that feels so adolescent, like I'm still fifteen, you know, looking at the boy I have a crush on, hoping desperately that he thinks I'm pretty enough to kiss me." I stop, looking at him. He's smirking, "I don't know what I'm trying to say."

"You care what I think."

"Yes." I nod. "Everyone. What everyone thinks."

"Why do you think you're so hard on yourself?" His hands sit flat and high on my thighs.

"I don't know. Why do you think you're not?" I look at him.

He shrugs. "I don't know, practice. I've done some big fucking work on myself. I have walked into the woods and sat with my pain."

"Metaphorically?" I ask.

"No, actually. I've been on retreats and done my version of your pleasure quest. I guess the difference between us, though, is that finding things that gave me pleasure was never my issue. The opposite stuff was my problem. I got very good at numbing shit out with pleasure. But there's an expiry date to all of that. The one benefit of getting older is that you stop tolerating your own bullshit," he says. He grabs his drink with one hand, taking a mouthful, then putting his hand back on my thigh, like that's where it belongs.

"Yes. Absolutely. You get over it, maybe," I say, but the next thought that crosses my mind makes what I've just said a lie. Some thoughts you don't get over. Some insecurities never fade. *He's too good for you, Noni*, I think, and I wince.

"Like that—I want to know what that thought was," he says, brushing the side of my face with his fingers. I open my mouth but he speaks before I do. "And if you say *nothing*, I swear to all that is holy that I will throw you over my shoulder and carry you out of this pub."

"You wouldn't."

"What was that thought?"

"Nothing," I say, raising my eyebrows at him, and in one swift move he lifts me up out of my chair and flings me over his shoulder. I squeal as he pats my butt and walks me outside, up the alleyway next to the pub where it is cold and dark. He puts me down and leans me against the brick wall.

"My coat's inside."

He presses his body against mine and kisses me. When he pulls away, he whispers in my ear. "I want to kiss you, Noni. I want to kiss you all the time. I want to kiss you, and I don't want to stop kissing you."

My insides flutter and I feel adored, turned on. I wrap my hands around his neck and kiss him back. I feel his hand fiddling with the top button of my jeans and undoing the zip, then slipping his hand inside. I don't care that we're in public. I don't care that it's freezing. I don't care that anyone could walk up this alley in any moment. In fact that adds electricity to how urgent my need feels. I want more. Now. I grab at his jeans.

"God, woman!" he moans and I laugh, looking at him. "So fucking sexy," he says, before leading my hands away from him. "This is all about you." I kiss him and lean into his hand, rocking my hips.

"You're very good at that." I gasp with every breath, the closer I get. We kiss and he reads my body and breath. *Close. Close. Close.* I orgasm softly.

"I like making you feel good." He kisses my forehead. "Now, let's go back in before we freeze."

People look at us as we enter the bar again. The beautiful tattooed woman and her equally angular friend smile at me, and I smile back. I sit down and Beau pulls his chair close into mine, so his thigh is back between my legs, his shoulders square with mine, face-to-face. There's a skinny tattooed guy with a floppy haircut playing guitar in the corner. But it doesn't matter. Fuck meditation apps and mindfulness practice—what they should tell you to do is have a Viking make you cum in an alley, because I've never been more present in my life. In my body. In this moment. With this human.

A guy with a small orange beanie perched on the crown of his head comes over. "Quite the barbaric display," he says with a brilliant Australian accent. He raises his eyebrows, his thin black mustache twitching. "We all get it, she's yours. Did you leave your club at home tonight, Beau?"

"Noni, this is Archer. Archer, this is Noni."

"G'day," he says.

"Hello." I pause. "Can I ask you something?" Archer nods. "Did you ever say g'day at home? Or only now that you live here? Because I've never dreamed of saying it, but now I'm only ever half a beer away from sounding like Alf Stewart."

"Fuckin' strewth. I know, right?" He laughs. "Wine? Whiskey?"

"Both," Beau says and Archer nods and leaves.

"He's very handsome. Why don't you go," Beau says, mocking me, "and fuck him?"

"Is that a thing?" I ask, taking the opportunity. "That you are doing? That we are doing?"

"Fucking other people?"

"Yeah. Just want to know what you're—" I wince from the awkward that's encroaching on my insides.

"I'm not fucking anyone else right now, Noni, if that's what you're asking. Are you?"

"No, I'm not."

"Do you want to be able to?" he says. I shrug my shoulders, searching for the words, but he continues. "I don't want to limit your quest or anything, Noni, by placing some unrealistic expectation, or some unnecessary boundary, you know?"

"Yeah, of course, likewise," I say.

"Let's just agree to keep talking about what we want, yeah?" He says, and I nod. Of course, this is a simple conversation to him. *Why must I overthink everything?*

Archer comes back with drinks. "When is Zep back up?" he asks.

"Half term. In a couple of weeks."

"He can do some glassy shifts if he needs the cash."

"I'll let him know." Archer walks off.

"Zeppelin is coming up?" I ask.

"Yeah. I am pumped."

"Brilliant." I squeeze his leg.

"I can't wait." He sips from his glass. "What about you? Is kids something you've thought about?"

I can tell by the way he asks that he thinks this is a light topic. He's expecting a yes or no answer. He's expecting this to be easy. But nothing about my response to this question is easy. I could lie. Or say ambiguous things, or just say "I don't know" and then change the subject. But that doesn't feel right. I want to be honest with him. I want to tell him things. I want to show him my deck. I exhale loudly. *Here we go.*

"Joan and I, well, we tried," I say. "IVF. We did a few cycles." Beau slowly puts his glass down and looks me in the eye. *Just talk, Noni. Just talk.* "It's really fucking brutal. Fertility bullshit is…" I make a disgusted groan. "Needles and hormones and disappointment." I swallow and feel every muscle required to make the action possible. "And then we fell pregnant." I slug wine into my mouth in a big gulp. "Got to fifteen weeks and—" I stop.

"Oh, Noni, I'm so sorry."

"Yeah," I nod. It's a grief that is wild, angry and always present, and it's right there in my gut at the mention of it. "And we weren't right before we started trying, but then we were trying and we were in too deep, you know?"

"Yeah. Of course."

"Then you can't be the asshole who pulls the pin amid the worst thing that you've ever had to deal with." My voice cracks. "So we persevered with our relationship for a whole extra year." Beau is nodding, his face pained, but he stays silent. "Look, Joan is a good person, she's amazing, an amazing person, she's just not my person. But she was. I really legitimately thought that she was. For a long time. And yeah."

Beau nods. "That's really, really shit."

"That's the perfect summation of it all," I say, and I try to stay on top of these feelings. I breathe in deep and look at him. "Daisy."

"What?"

"That's her name. My daughter."

Realization floods his face. "Ah, the daisies." And he touches my stomach, my tattoo.

I nod and tears spring. I grit my teeth to try to stop them, scrunching my nose, not because I feel uncomfortable crying in front of Beau, but because tears like this tend not to stop once they start. "It took me a really long time to feel okay calling her that. It felt wrong. I felt like a bit of a parental fraud." The tears keep coming, and the downlights in my peripheral vision cast bright gold patterns in the corners of my eyes. "Like, somehow I hadn't earned the right to call her that, because she wasn't full-term."

"Oh, that's so wrong," he says quietly, wrapping his hands around mine.

"Yeah. I know. I know that now. I spent a lot of money with a very funny therapist, Dr. Lalit, who helped me work that out."

"Good."

"But it smashed me. Completely. Like, heartbreak and rejection on crack. Not that I've ever tried crack, but I assume it's intense," I try to joke, and Beau smiles slightly. "It's really fucking difficult to feel those things about your own body. Normally you can tell the wanker that makes you feel those things to fuck off, but—"

"It's really hard to get away from yourself," he says.

"Yeah, and now I'm trying really hard to work out who I am. Because so many of the bits pre-her seem so pointless, or useless, but there's so much shit that's just ingrained, you know?"

"Yeah. Absolutely. It's all patterns," he says and I wipe my eyes. "A lot of the self-work I've done these last few years has been about owning my shit and leaning into my vulnerability," he says, looking at me, and I nod, so in awe of this man who talks so openly about himself. "We really fuck men over, and believe me, I'm fully aware of the epic proportion of fuckery that women have endured since, well, the beginning of time." He stops smiling and I laugh, nodding. "Fuck the patriarchy, et cetera." He says matter-of-fact, swigging his drink. "And because of this, and a few other things, I had so many dumb ideas about what I deserved, and I was a real dickhead in my twenties."

"I think that's a prerequisite to being in your twenties," I say.

Beau smiles. "Yeah. I was jealous and angry. I'd drink too much and never talk about my feelings. Use sex and drugs as really good avoidance strategies."

"Oh, at least you got the fun ones. I picked carbohydrates, so you win."

Beau laughs. "This thing between us, Noni, it's not what I thought it was going to be."

"Yeah, I know."

"We might be in a spot of trouble, hey?"

"Potentially."

"Well, can we agree to just enjoy it, enjoy each other, till you go? Yeah?"

"Yeah," I say.

And that's all he says about it, so that's all I say about it.

Enjoy it, Noni.

27

"Your butt looks amazing amid the flowers, darling," Lil tells Stef, the woman we're shooting today in a bright field of yellow flowers.

"That's something I don't normally hear when I'm at work," I say, and Lil chuckles. I'm absolutely loving working with Lil, and watching as she praises and compliments the people she's shooting. I love the way she sees and acknowledges their insecurities but gently cajoles them to step out of their comfort zones.

"Stef, what's the best compliment you've ever received?" she asks.

Stef, a woman in her fifties with a silver-gray quiff and a single mastectomy scar, bites her lip and ponders.

"Come on, what was it?" Lil asks.

"Ironically, it used to always be 'great rack,'" Stef says with a smirk.

"Not a physical compliment, something about you, who you are," Lil says.

Stef pauses and then she smiles with her whole face and Lil snaps away. "Someone once said I was like living glitter."

"That's a fucking brilliant compliment," I say.

"Sparkling. Radiant. Golden. Bold. Fearless," Lil says and there it is, that special moment that happens in every one of Lil's shoots. It's like you can actually see when something physiologically shifts inside her subjects, even just for a moment, and they believe her, they believe in their power and their beauty. It has made me tear up every time, and today is no different. Stef looks like a goddess, standing naked in the fields with her glittering soul and scarred body.

"You're stunning, Stef," I say without thinking.

"Thank you," she says with an ease and comfort that makes me smile wide and take a big deep breath.

The photos Lil takes are magnificent, and spending time with her is having a really profound impact on me. I'm enamored by making beautiful things in beautiful spaces with beautiful people, and Lil loves her job. Like, *love* loves her job. It makes me envious and reflective, because I don't think I've felt that way about my job in a long time. I took the behavior support promotion a few years ago because I wanted the challenge, but it's not what I thought it would be. I hate dealing with teachers who aren't willing to try new strategies and meet kids where they're at. I hate working in a system that fails to actually meet the needs of kids, and I absolutely hate that I have to pretend that I care about uniform policies and mobile phone policies, and standardized testing data, because I just don't. I feel like I've lost my mojo. I've started to realize that in my work, like most things in my life before now, I was just going through the motions. I haven't missed it at all while I've been away.

For as long as I can remember, I thought I'd work my way

up to one day be a principal, but I've come to understand that's not what I want at all. It's scary when you realize that you don't really have a backup plan, that you've been striving for one thing for so long you haven't considered any alternatives. I've been pushing that niggling feeling that things weren't right further and further back, and telling myself that everything was fine. But now, thanks to the pleasure quest, I have the bar set way, way above "fine." Hanging around people like Lil and Beau, and even Naz and Tom, people who love their jobs, has reminded me that "fine" isn't good enough anymore.

I've realized the people I've welcomed into my life lately are this supremely self-motivated group who are so committed to going deep with the self-work. And I want to be one of them too. Truly.

"I'm really loving working with you, Lil," I tell her when we get back to her studio.

"Oh, darling, thank you, that's lovely. I'm loving working with you too," she says.

"I think you've made me realize I hate my job," I tell her.

Lil laughs loudly and from her belly. "Is that a good or bad realization?"

"Good."

"Well, what are you going to do?"

"I don't know yet." I pause. "And for the first time ever that thought doesn't freak me out."

"And so what does that mean?" Lindell ponders on the phone as I walk through the supermarket, popping precut vegetables into my basket.

"It means we're enjoying each other until I leave," I tell him.

"So, are you together?"

I bite my lip and catch my reflection in the mirror above the produce. "I don't know. Yes. No. I guess. It's a fling. That's what it is. I'm trying my best to not overthink it and just be in the moment."

"Is he seeing other people?"

"No, he's not. He would tell me. He says what he thinks. And he's all about communication."

Lindell scoffs through the phone. "God. How are you coping with this?"

"Because I have to. Pleasure-quest Noni has flings and is fine with it, Lindell," I tell him, throwing chocolate biscuits into my basket. I hear him laugh loudly. "I'm trying to be as cool as he is."

"You shouldn't have to *try* to be anything, my darling." I can hear the ice machine in his fridge rumbling loudly. I picture him in his kitchen, fixing a drink.

"No, that's not what I mean. I'm going with the flow and I'm not forcing anything."

"Yeah, but you know what else goes with the flow? Sewage. Dead fish. Lost balloons."

"Fucking hell, Lindell." I laugh as I walk mindlessly up the aisles, not really paying attention.

"I'm sorry, not what you want to hear?"

"No. What I'm saying is, I'm happy with what's happening, it's exactly what I want, it's all on my terms, my pleasure, it's good. This self-indulgent moment in my life is good, Lindell. I promise. I'm happy, and that's all that matters, isn't it?"

"Yes. That is all that matters, but I also don't want you to think you can't tell him what you want under some illusion of cool."

I sense some underlying tension in his voice. "What's wrong?" I ask.

"I got into another fight with sour-face at work and it's really rattled me. She's so lazy and it drives me insane and I said to her today, I said, 'Merilyn, if you make one more fucking passive-aggressive comment about queer studies, I will choke you with a fucking rainbow flag.' And apparently that was threatening, so it's now a whole thing."

I start laughing loudly, and an old woman with a walker stares at me. "Oh my god, Lindell."

"She's actually void of all pleasure in her life, I think, and I'm trying to be Zen, I'm trying to think—what if being an underhanded, lazy piece of shit is her doing her best? But it's not working." He pauses. "They want me to apologize. And I will. And I will hate every second of it. But I wish I was on a pleasure quest with you and not stuck in stupid HR meetings. So I'm thrilled everything is going so well for you. Lil sounds amazing. The Viking sounds amazing. You sound amazing."

"Oh, babe, you do not sound amazing," I tell him, a pang of worry stopping me still in the cereal aisle.

"I'm fine, darling. It's fine. I'm just maybe living vicariously through you right now, so can you please just go all in on all of the pleasure, please? Because this isn't just about you now."

"I miss you."

"I know. I miss *you*." Neither of us says anything for a moment; we just sit in our longing for each other. "What about fuck-face, have you heard from her?"

Fuck-face is what we're calling Molly now. "I blocked her number and I deleted her from my socials. I don't want to know. I don't want to know anything."

"Fuck Face Molly and Sour Tits Merilyn should date. They deserve each other."

I laugh loudly. "I wonder if she and her girlfriend sorted it out?" I say, before I realize I have.

"Do you care?" Lindell asks.

"No."

"Liar."

"I just still can't believe she did it, you know? It just makes me feel so gross when I think about it."

"Fuck Molly. Fuck Merilyn. Fuck these pleasure-sapping assholes. That's my new motto," he says.

"I love you," I tell him. We hang up, and I tell myself to not give Molly another thought.

28

I look across the room at Lil, who smiles wide, touching her heart with her hand and nodding at me. Then she drops her robe off her shoulders and swings it around enthusiastically, laughing. She is the first in the room to get naked, and the fifteen or so other women cheer.

I feel my stomach twist with nerves and excitement. I agreed to come to nude yoga because Lil had sold it to me as a revolution in vulnerability and bravery.

"You will let go of all the bullshit, Noni. It's amazing. Please come with me," she'd asked. As if I wasn't going to agree to that.

We're told to get naked and wear a robe or sarong into the candlelit room. I'm relieved by the fact that the other women are a complete mix of different ages and sizes. We stand in a circle—which I'm grateful for, because no one needs to see me in three-legged downward-facing dog, except maybe my gynecologist. Our instructor, a magnetic woman with powerful brows, speaks to us with a calm, sensual lisp. After listening to her for a moment, I'm completely smitten, but it's not so much that I want to sleep with her, it's that I want to be her, or have whatever energy she naturally emanates rub off on me. She takes up space. She wears whatever she wants. She is the living embodiment of the pleasure quest. She tells us to close our eyes and breathe while we do some very simple stretches, and then she tells us to slowly, and only when we're ready, take off our robes. We stand with our hands by our sides, and she asks us to cast our eyes around the circle.

"No one is looking around this circle right now and thinking about any of the things you are insecure about. No one is glancing around this circle and thinking anything other than loving thoughts about your body. No one in this circle is thinking anything negative about your body, apart from you." She pauses. "Smile if you have had a beautiful thought about someone else's body in this circle." We all smile. "See!"

For the next hour I hang on every word she says. When she tells me to breathe, I do. When she tells me to soften, I do. When she tells me to surrender, I do. I let tears spring in the corner of my eyes. When she asks me to picture my body at its most joyous, I'm struck with an image of me ecstatic in a field of wildflowers, arms wide and high, open, bold, joy filling every cell in me to the brim.

We stand back in our circle, acknowledge one another and clap, and then the most magical thing of all happens, we drink tea and eat cake and chat—in the nude. No one gets dressed. No one hides. It feels as if I always eat carrot cake in the nude in a room full of other people, like it's the most natural thing in the world. I look over at Lil and mouth "thank you," touching my heart and gesturing toward her. She places both hands on hers, like she's receiving my thanks, and I laugh wholeheartedly, with my whole body, maybe for the first time ever.

★ ★ ★

Beau and I sit facing each other on the couch, our limbs interwoven, reading. I watch him biting his lip as he concentrates, his hair plopped on top of his head in a bun, gold frames sitting perfectly on his nose. He's shirtless, his muscles strong but relaxed. He's fucking sublime. He strokes my leg up and down without even realizing he's doing it.

"How many flings like this have you had?" I ask.

He puts his book on his chest. "Like this? None."

"Bullshit." I smile, trying to keep it light.

"Are you asking me how many women I've slept with?"

"No."

"Really?"

"No. I don't want to know. It doesn't matter," I say, looking back at my book and pretending to read.

"Damn it." He laughs and I look back up at him.

"What?"

"I was hoping you'd say yes. I want to know how many men—"

I cut him off. "People."

"People you've slept with," he says, folding the corner of his page over and closing the book.

"Why?" I ask, feeling insecure.

"I dunno." He puts his book on the coffee table, looking at me. "Noni?"

"Yes?"

"Do I not make you feel special?"

"What?"

"I mean, do you feel like this is all moves? Like this isn't just for you?" He lifts my feet so they sit either side of his body.

"You make me feel too special," I say.

"What do you mean?"

I breathe in and decide to speak the truth. "This can't possibly be just for me."

"That's awful." He rubs his hands up my shins. "Who hurt you?"

"A few people. Have you ever had your heart broken?" I ask.

"Of course," he says. "Twice. Three times if you count Delilah MacGregor."

"Who is Delilah MacGregor?"

"She was my first girlfriend. She broke up with me at a dance in front of all my friends because she told me my breath stank like grass."

"What a bitch," I say and he laughs. He continues tracing patterns with his fingertips. I like that he does this whenever he's thinking, like his hands are programmed to draw.

"What do you want, Noni?" he asks eventually.

"I want to believe this is all for me, and that I deserve it." I pause. "'Cause I do," I say, watching his hand. "What do *you* want?" His patterns circle higher and higher up my thighs.

"I want to watch you."

"What?"

"I want to watch you make yourself..." He looks at me and I know what he means instantly.

"Really?"

"Yes, really."

He's looking at me expectantly, eagerly, and I breathe deeply and slowly. I feel hot. I stand up in front of him. Staring at him, I untie the knot in my dressing gown, lightly thumbing the fabric so it falls open. I run my fingers up the lapel, lightly skimming my nipples, as I pull the gown off of my shoulders, and it falls to the ground. I bite my lip, looking at Beau, and run fingertips up my thighs.

"Show me," he whispers.

I move slowly, giving myself over to the pleasure. I watch

him watching me. I close my eyes, my finger gently moving. I glance through my eyelashes watching him as he moves, placing his butt on the floor. He doesn't take his eyes off me. I feel incredibly exposed, but so turned on. I slowly kneel to the ground, so I'm sitting on my haunches. I keep my eyes tightly closed.

"Don't hide," he says.

I open them. He grins this sexy half smile and I stare at him, taking a deep breath, running one hand over my stomach up to my nipple and running my palm over it. Sighing slightly. I touch my face and bite my knuckle as the feeling begins to build and I get close. Beau bites his lip. I flip my head to one shoulder and move my hips forward into my hand, moving up and down as my breath gets quicker in my chest. I keep my eyes open and locked on Beau as my body shudders with joy. But I don't stop. I keep going. Breathing heavy through my nose, hips rocking, building a second orgasm. And I feel like a powerhouse woman writhing around on the hardwood floor, staring at the handsome man who I know is turned on. Turned on by me. I feel a kind of freedom, a kind of power that I don't think I've ever felt. I've never done this, like this, in front of someone else. This is what it's like on my own. I moan. I can see his breath quicken. All for the wanting.

"Oh, fuck." Beau shakes his head. "You are—" He stops and stares. "Fuck me," he says, and I smile and keep touching myself. "Please." I shake my head and cum again. "Fuck me, Noni," he says.

So I do, and it is incredible.

We lie on the floor wrapped up in each other.

"Maybe I should go to naked yoga," Beau says.

"You don't need to go to naked yoga," I say as he poses, showing off his body, and I laugh loudly.

"I want you to meet my kid," he says suddenly.

"Really?"

"Yeah. It feels weird that you haven't. Me and Zep, we kinda share everything, and I've told him about you and I want you to hang out with us."

"Your time together is sacred, though," I say, knowing how much he misses Zeppelin and how much he loves spending time with him when he gets to see him.

"The fact that you get that is just one of the reasons I want you to meet each other." He pauses and tucks my hair behind my ear. "Don't for a second think this is some test or something, Noni. This is one hundred percent bragging by default on my part because I think my kid is awesome, and I think you will think he's awesome, and the next obvious step in this line of thinking is—"

"Is that I will think you are awesome? I see. Well, that plan is flawed because I can't stand you," I say.

"I thought as much." He shuffles up so his body is hovering above me, his hair falling in my face. I have to push it back with my forearm to see him.

"I can't bear to be around you," I say. He kisses my neck. "You're infuriating." He nuzzles in closer so his beard tickles me and I giggle, throwing my head back and grabbing his shoulders. Beau laughs loudly, too, and falls on his side so we're facing each other.

"I'd love to meet him, of course."

He kisses my forehead. "Good."

29

Zeppelin, Beau and I are sitting in a booth in the middle of a giant games arcade.

"So the most important question of them all, Noni," Zeppelin says, pointing a pinch full of fries at me.

"Oh, god, I don't know if I'm ready." I bite into a cheeseburger.

Zep looks at Beau, grinning conspiratorially. "I don't know what you're gonna ask," Beau says, laughing. Zep eats more fries out of a centrally placed red plastic basket like they're about to disappear, wiping grease from his chin with his sleeve and smiling so wide his Afro moves from side to side.

"Okay." He pauses for effect, smirking. "How do you feel about Disney?"

Beau laughs loudly. "Oh! Good one!" I look at him, hoping he'll catch me up, but he just nods.

"Specifically," Zeppelin adds, "musicals. Disney musicals."

I sip my milkshake. "I feel an immense amount of pressure right now."

"You should," Zeppelin says.

"Like if I get this wrong I won't be allowed to win *Mario Kart* again," I say. I'd won two rounds in a row earlier. It was a total fluke, but a victory all the same, and I have been proudly brandishing my triumph over them all afternoon.

Zeppelin and Beau groan. "See that? See how she keeps bringing it up?" Beau says, nudging Zeppelin with his shoulder.

"That I beat you both? Twice?" I ask.

"Yeah, on easy rounds. Which we only did for you," Zeppelin says.

"Try me."

"Answer the question."

"I think Disney musicals are…" I pause for effect and they both watch me with the exact same beaming smile. Zeppelin clutches at Beau's forearm in anticipation. "Fine. I think they're fine," I say.

"Explain more, please," Beau says.

"I don't lose my mind over a Disney musical," I say, wiping my face with my napkin and pushing my basket away. "I think it depends on your childhood connection to them. They were never embedded in my childhood. My mum watched romantic comedies and didn't care about age limits and my dad watched action movies. So my sense of nostalgia is for Patrick Swayze and Sylvester Stallone over Timon and Pumbaa." They nod like detectives and I can't read their faces. "So?" I ask.

They stare at each other and Zeppelin stands up on the booth seat using his milkshake as a microphone. "Yes! Yes! Yes! That is well safe, Noni." Beau pulls at his leg and he sits down with a bounce.

"Well safe? What?" Beau asks.

"It means good, Dad, god." Zeppelin shakes his head, looking at me with a "Can you believe this guy?" face and I crack up.

"Yeah, god," I mimic him.

"Disney women is a theory Dad and I have," Zep says.

"Disney women?" I ask.

"Dude, don't expose our secrets. We don't know if she's worthy of this information," says Beau out of the corner of his mouth.

Zeppelin nods and says quickly, "It's patented."

"Okay, tell me more."

"Women who have an affinity for Disney are more, like, hard work. It's a red flag."

"Fairy tales over reality, hey, mate?" Beau says.

"Shit politics," Zeppelin says seriously. "Disney kind of fucks with your idea about who you should be and how you should behave. Mum and Dad were weird about me watching them because there are no badass girls, and Walt Disney was hella racist." He's looking at me, so I nod. "Except *Toy Story*," he adds. "*Toy Story* is fucking awesome."

I'm blown away by how articulate and funny and confident Zep is, but I'm not that surprised, because Beau is all of these things too. "So what did you watch instead?" I ask.

"My favorite movie as a kid was *Point Break*."

"I love *Point Break*," I say.

"It's the best film ever," Beau adds.

"Did you watch the new one?" I ask.

"No!" They both say in unison, clearly repulsed by the suggestion.

"Neither did I!" I say with both my hands up in the air.

We play three rounds of basketball, working hard for tickets. I'm better at it than I think I'll be, but against Beau and Zeppelin, who are ridiculously tall and have probably actually played basketball in real life before, I am pathetic. I bow out, and they compete in a best-of-three competition. Beau wins the first round and Zeppelin the second. In the decider they're neck and neck, matching basket for basket and giving each other shit. Zeppelin gets ahead and Beau pushes him with his arm, trying to throw him off his game.

"Noni! Help me! He's cheating," Zeppelin says.

I leap at Beau and duck under his arm and sit with my butt against the machine, moving the balls away with my hands. Beau tries to get around me.

Zeppelin cracks up and swishes in four balls, one after the other. The buzzer sounds and he wins.

"Unfair!" Beau says.

"I just needed a rest," I say innocently.

"You two—" he points at us, faking rage "—such bullshit." Zeppelin and I high-five and he shakes his head. "I'm going to the bathroom to sulk," he says as he leaves.

After a moment Zeppelin looks at me. "You're a teacher, yeah?"

"Yeah."

"You'd be a good teacher."

"Thank you. D'you like school?"

"Bits."

"Same," I say as we walk away from the basketball machine.

"Why did you want to be a teacher?"

"Because I had a really awesome English teacher when I was in high school. I loved the way she made classes relevant, and she was nice. She encouraged me. My parents got divorced when I was young and they fucking hated each other." I look at him. "They still do. Things were really shit. And she was just an adult that made things less shit, you know?"

"Yeah," he says.

"I loved the idea of being that for someone else." I smile

and he nods, thinking. "Do you know what you wanna do when you leave school? Or are you sick of people asking you that question?"

He snickers. "So sick of it. I wanna do lots of things."

"Cool."

"You wanna know what things?" he says, and I realize he was expecting me to ask, but I always like to let kids take the lead.

"Of course," I say.

"Like, fashion is probably number one. But I want to run a cause, you know? Help people. Raise money for something. Run a business that isn't just about profits but people too."

"I love that."

"This one," he points at a game that's a small enclosed room with a giant angry zombie on the side. "Wanna?" he asks and I nod.

We slide onto a single bench seat in front of two crossbows and a giant screen. Zeppelin swipes our card and pushes buttons, getting it set up. He does mine for me.

"We're a team and we have to shoot all the zombies in the head. You're green. To reload pull that thing back and then forward," he says, pointing at the plastic crossbow in front of me.

"Okay," I say.

It's one of those point-of-view games where zombies lunge at us and we have shoot them as quickly as we can. It's loud and the seat shudders and the zombies are quick. I squeal a lot. And swear, which Zeppelin thinks is hilarious. I eventually work the game out and we get into a rhythm, switching sides, covering for each other. It is stressful. We are supposedly in a prison and we've done pretty well, getting out of one building, across a packed yard, over a wall and in through a door to a dark ledge, where we're suddenly surrounded by a swarm of growling zombies. Zeppelin dies.

"I'm dead. Noni, look out." He points and instructs me what to do, but I quickly descend into squeaking, flailing and wildly shooting arrows hoping they'll land. This plan doesn't hold up and soon I'm eaten too. My heart is pounding. My palms are sweaty.

"That was too stressful," I yell at Zeppelin.

"Yeah, that was full-on."

There's suddenly a loud bang on the side of the machine and we both jump and I scream. Beau appears, laughing.

"Dad!" Zeppelin yells.

"You asshole," I say, whacking him hard. "We were just murdered by zombies, do you know how stressed we already are?" I get out of the machine with Zeppelin right behind me. He jumps on Beau's back, a hand around his neck. Beau heaves, trying to break free.

"I couldn't find you. And then I heard you screaming."

"That was wild, Dad."

We head toward the front of the arcade, handing all of our tickets to Zeppelin, who counts them and starts perusing a counter of shit plastic prizes and lollies.

"He is brilliant," I say quietly, so Zeppelin can't hear.

"I know, right?"

"His mum must be brilliant." I grin.

Beau nods. "She is."

"You're brilliant," I say, knocking into him playfully with my shoulder.

"Noni, you are—" Beau stops as Zeppelin walks over with three lollipops and hands one to each of us.

"Is that all we got?" Beau asks. "Bullshit"

Zeppelin reaches into his pocket and pulls out three pairs

of ridiculous brightly colored sunglasses. He hands me a pair shaped like yellow stars and I put them on. Beau has purple love hearts and Zeppelin blue squares. We laugh at each other. Beau pulls out his phone and we take selfies. Zep puts his finger up Beau's nose and his arm around my shoulder as we pull stupid faces.

"I'm gonna head off," I say as we start the walk back out to the street.

"Really?" Beau asks.

"Yeah, I'll let you two watch *Point Break* on your own."

Zeppelin gives me a hug. "See you soon, yeah?"

Beau raises his eyebrows with a pleased nod.

"I'd love that," I tell him. I watch the two of them walk off in the opposite direction, Beau with his arm around Zeppelin's shoulders and Zeppelin with his arm around Beau's waist, gesturing wildly with his other hand.

I message Lindell.

I met his kid.
He's amazing.

I love it. I love you,
he replies and
it makes me smile.

Another message appears.

Nons, is this
really just a fling?

Fuck.

30

"You look happy," Beau says when he greets me outside his studio. He kisses my cheek and takes my hand as we start walking.

"I am happy," I say.

"Good." He tells me about his day, and I tell him about mine and then we don't talk for a while, content holding hands and walking, but then he stops suddenly, standing directly in front of me.

"Noni, I have a question to ask you."

My heart pumps with the suddenness of the energy shift. "Okay," I say with trepidation. I try to read his face, to see how worried I should be.

"I think you should move in with me until you leave. You're there all the time anyway and you could save money, and, I mean, it's a suitcase." He pauses and I suddenly become very conscious of my eyelashes and the speed at which they're blinking. "Don't you think that makes sense? I mean, you head back in a month, yeah?"

He's asking me to move in with him. For a month. I go home in a month. I'm meant to go back to work in a month.

"I just—" I start, not really knowing how I'm going to finish the sentence.

"I feel like you might need a boundary chat, Noni?"

I am startled by this but I try not to let it read on my face. "What makes you say that?"

"A feeling." He puts his arm around my shoulder and we keep walking. "I like you. A lot."

"I like you. A lot," I tell him.

"And I like spending time with you. This fling is excellent, yeah? You are excellent."

A fling. It's a fling. Of course it's a fling. Why does it sting, him saying that, though? *Don't be ridiculous, Noni.*

"Yeah, I feel exactly the same way."

"You do? Great. I thought you would." He squeezes my hand with his, to punctuate his enthusiasm. "Because there's no future beyond you getting on that plane, is there?" He looks at me. *What do I say?* I pause for too long, so he keeps talking. "I mean, you're going home. And this is my home. So we know what's gonna happen. So, it's easy, yeah, Nons? Easy and brilliant."

Easy and brilliant. No future. This isn't my home. He doesn't want a future. Got it.

"So move in with me. It makes sense."

It does make sense, financially. Emotionally, it makes sense, too, because all I want to do is be with Beau. But logically? It doesn't make any sense at all because the closer we get to me leaving, and the bigger my feelings feel about him, the harder it's going to be to get on a plane and fly away from this little life I've built for myself here.

"Will you?" he asks.

I take a deep breath. "Yes."

"Fucking hell, Nons. What did you say?" Lindell says on the phone as I flick the shower on.

"I said yes, and then we went to my place, called Pam and told her I was leaving a bit early, packed up my stuff, and brought it around here. And now I'm here. I've moved in."

"Just like that?"

"Just like that."

"Why are you whispering?" Lindell asks.

"Because I'm hiding in the bathroom." I open the door slightly to make sure Beau isn't in earshot, but he's in the kitchen making dinner. "Is this crazy?"

"No. Yes. I don't know. Does it feel right?"

"Yes," I tell him. It does feel right.

"Then that's your answer." Lindell yawns and I wonder if he's still in bed. It's early in the morning for him.

"But it also feels incredibly reckless in the grand scheme of future Noni's feelings."

"Babe, let future Noni deal with her feelings, okay? Not you. Not your job right now."

"Okay. How are you? I miss you. How are the kids? What's happening in your life?"

Lindell takes a deep breath. "Well, Graham's been head-hunted and he thinks he's gonna take the new gig."

"Why are you whispering?" I ask.

"Because he's in the shower and we're not talking."

"What?"

"It'll mean more travel, which means he'll be away more. He suggested we get a nanny with the extra cash to support me and I called him an asshole and things are at about a two out of ten right now. But, onward." He exhales forcefully and I feel a pulse of concern.

"Shit, darling, I'm sorry."

"Nons, what first-world fucking concerns to have. My husband will be earning so much money he can afford to pay someone to take care of our children. I feel irrational being angry about it. But also, I'm fucking furious."

"Why, do you think?"

"I dunno. What about *my* career? But then what else do I even want with my career? Maybe I'm just bored. Or jealous. Maybe I just miss you," he says and my heart hurts wishing that I was there with him, having this conversation in real life, not in hushed tones locked in the bathroom.

"I miss you," I tell him. "I think it's completely rational to feel all of those things. You are a brilliant human who is more than just a parent, and it's okay to want more, and resent Graham's success a little, and feel like you're missing out. Because you are."

"Fucking hell."

"I mean, you're always going to be missing out on something, we all are, that's life, that's making choices, I guess. We can't actually have it all."

"Yes. I know. And we've been sold a fucking ridiculous tale that has led us to believe we can have it all. Fuck Instagram."

This makes me laugh. "Yes. Fuck Instagram."

"I love you," he says now at full voice. Graham must be in the room.

"I love you, darling. Tell Graham how you feel. Sort it out, please. You're my relationship hope."

"Great. No pressure." He pauses. "Graham and I always work it out."

"Hi, Noni!" I hear Graham bellow in the background.

"Enjoy your new house. Hear me, Noni? Enjoy. It."

"I hear you."

Enjoy it.

31

The buzzer on the door to Beau's flat sounds loudly and startles me. I'm mindlessly watching TV, waiting for him to get back from work.

"Hello?" I say into the intercom.

"Hey. It's Zep. I don't have my key," he says.

"Oh, hi." I buzz him in and then wait for him with the front door open. "Hey, your dad isn't—"

"Yeah, I just messaged him. Told him I was here." He walks in and dumps his bag on the floor, flopping on the couch.

I stare at him. "You all right?" I ask. He turns and looks at me, and sighs loudly. "Does your mum know you're here? It's a school day. Did you catch the train?"

"Yeah. Yeah. Are you kidding? She'd fucking murder me if I left without telling her. I mean, she's still pissed, but I rang her on the train."

"Good." I watch as he covers his eyes with his hands and

rests his head on the back of the couch. "Do you want to talk about it? Or do you want me to—"

"I had sex with my girlfriend."

"Okay." I pause. "Are you okay?"

"Yeah. Just—it's a bit—"

Fuck, Noni. This is a foundational moment.

I sit on the very corner of the other side of the couch, so I'm not just standing in limbo like a piece of shocked furniture. He rubs his face with both his hands.

"It's a bit full-on, yeah?" he says.

I nod. "Yeah."

"And there's this huge party this weekend and everyone knows that we did it and I don't—" He stops.

"You don't…?" I ask.

"I don't want to do it again." He looks at me. "I mean, like, not right now. Eventually, I probably will, just—" He groans loudly, covering his eyes again.

"That's okay. You don't have to."

"Yeah. I know. But—"

"But high school is a fucking nightmare." I laugh, and he laughs a little, too, which makes me feel better.

"Yeah. So I made up this lie about needing to come to Dad's and I was just gonna stay at home, but then it became a thing so I got on the train and—"

"Here you are."

"Yeah."

We sit silently for a moment. "This is going to sound like the most obvious and adult thing to say, but you don't have to do anything you don't want to do. Ever," I tell him, trying to read if he'll let me go on. He stares expectantly, so I keep going. "You have complete autonomy over your body and your choices," I ramble. "And I know that there is, like, an astronomical amount of pressure on you right now, because being a teenager is just about the worst thing ever. You know, besides war and genocide and melting ice caps and that weird fashion moment we're having right now where people other than speed dealers are wearing bum bags across their chests." Zeppelin laughs so loudly he starts coughing. "But you need to choose what's right for you. That's part of all of this. That's what sex is—choices. Choosing what you want and what feels right. Does that make sense?" My own advice hits me hard in my own chest.

"Yeah. Just—" He folds his knees under his body and looks at me. "She's like…my girlfriend, Amy. She's been freaking out and I don't know what to say. And she's just like, I can't wait for the party, and I'm like, yeah. And I know I'm making it weird. And it's all changed between us now. Before it was cool but now it's not."

"I bet."

"And now she is properly freaking out. Totally. And so she just keeps trying to talk about it and then I freak out and don't say anything and—"

"You're in this vicious freak-out cycle."

"Yeah."

"Have you told her what you're thinking, or how you're feeling?" I say.

"No way." He looks at me like I've just asked him to shit on the table.

"Okay. Have you asked her how she's feeling?"

"Nup."

"Well, she's probably coming up with a million reasons in her head as to why it's all changed, yeah?"

"Yeah."

"And I am willing to put money on the fact that she thinks it's all her fault."

"Fuck. I didn't think of that. I don't want her to think

that." He lies back into the couch and groans in frustration. He looks like Beau. "What do I do?"

"You gotta talk to her."

"But she's just gonna think that I'm—"

"I know that's how it feels, but what she thinks about you is actually none of your business," I tell him.

He looks confused. "What?"

"It's got nothing to do with you. That's her choice. All you can do is give her the correct information. Be honest with her. And then she gets to choose what she thinks."

"What if she hates me?"

"Then that's gonna suck," I say and he scoffs and I smile. "But wouldn't you rather she know than having to keep coming to Scotland every time you two are gonna be alone together. I mean, I know your Dad will fucking love this plan, but—"

He laughs. "Yeah. Ugh. It's really shit."

"You know what the worst bit is?"

"What?"

"It doesn't get any easier."

"Why would you say that?" He throws a cushion at me. "Why would you smash the unrealistic expectations of a sixteen-year-old like that?"

"It's best you know now. I don't want you to get your hopes up."

"Heaven forbid." His phone starts buzzing. "It's Dad." He answers. "Hey. Yeah. Yeah, I'm at your place. Yeah, she's here. We're just talking. Yeah. We're fine. Okay." He hangs up and looks at me. "He's leaving now."

"Okay," I say.

"Can you not tell him about…" He trails off.

"You should tell him."

"He'll just be—"

"He'll be great. He'll say weird dad things, because that's his job, and you'll feel weird and he'll feel weird, but I think he'll have good advice. He was sixteen once. And he's had sex," I say, throwing the cushion back at him.

"That's disgusting, Noni."

"Just the once. Just for your sake. You should be grateful," I say.

He laughs. "So what do I do? Just message her?"

"Maybe this is an in-person thing. I know you young people don't know how to do that, but this is an actual conversation."

"Yeah."

"Do you like her?"

"Yeah. A lot. I just freaked out about the sex bit. I think we rushed it, you know? But I don't want to break up with her."

"Well, maybe just send her a nice message. Tell her that you're thinking about her. That she's pretty, or something else that you like about her that isn't her looks. And then wait till it's the two of you and tell her what you're thinking."

"You make it sound easy."

"It is easy. In theory. Talking in theory is always easy. But it's the hardest thing ever. We're just scared of looking like we're dumb. Or that people won't like us. But your opinion and your feelings, they're important. You shouldn't ignore them. It's just practice."

"Okay." He thinks for a moment and then he stands up. "I'm done."

"You cooked, mate? Too much vulnerability?"

"Yup."

"Good. Go and slam your bedroom door or something. Call me a bitch. I don't know, how do we right the balance between us now?"

He walks toward his bedroom. "Your students are lucky, Noni. I don't have any teachers like you."

"Thanks," I say, feeling it right in my heart. "Talk to your dad." He groans loudly and slams the door. I laugh.

He quickly opens it again. "That was so much louder than I thought it would be."

"You nailed it and then you ruined it again." We both laugh and he shuts the door quietly. I lean my head back on the couch and close my eyes. The front door opens and a very puffed Beau comes in.

"Is he okay?"

"Yeah."

"He in his room?" I nod, then he asks, "Did he tell you what's up?"

"Yes."

He sits on the couch next me, his face furrowed and worried. "What's going on?"

"I told him I wouldn't tell you. But he's okay. He just needs to chat to you about it."

"Okay." Beau looks at Zeppelin's closed door.

"But be cool."

"Be cool? What's he done?" he whispers.

"A girl."

"A girl?" he whispers, his face all startled eyebrows.

"Stop it." I push him. "Just go and talk to him. I'm not saying anything else." I cover my mouth.

"Has he had sex? Fuck. What do I say?" Beau looks terrified.

"Just don't be weird," I say as Beau rubs his face with both his hands exactly as Zeppelin had done. "He's a really cool kid."

"Noni, I'm freaking out."

"I know, you should see your face."

"Stop. This is full-on."

I laugh. He leans in and kisses me, then pulls back and stays just inches away from my face, looking at me. I put my hand up to his forehead. "That one."

"What?"

"I want to know what that one was. That thought," I say.

He bites his lip. "Just—" he stops himself and instead kisses me slowly. I grab his cheeks with both my hands and kiss him back. He pulls away, sitting on the opposite side of the couch.

"What are you doing?"

"I can't talk to my kid about sex with a giant semi."

"Giant? That's very generous."

Beau laughs loudly. The bedroom door opens and Zep comes out. Beau grabs a cushion and places it over his lap.

"You orright?" Beau asks.

"Yeah. Did you tell him?" Zep asks and I shake my head.

"Tell me what?" Beau feigns ignorance.

Zeppelin looks at me. "I messaged her."

"Good."

"She said she thought I hated her."

"Yeah."

"So, you were right," he says.

Beau looks at me and I nod. "Wanna go out? You and me?" Beau asks him and Zep nods. He removes the cushion and stands up and I stare at his crotch.

"Pervert," he mouths, grabbing his coat and keys.

"Thank you," Zep mouths as he walks toward the door. I'm glad I've been able to help him speak honestly about his feelings.

Maybe it's time to take your own advice, Noni.

32

"Don't forget I can't work this weekend," I tell Lil as we stand staring at a maze of black-and-white prints scattered all over the floorboards of her studio.

"Shit. Yes. I remember. Why, again?" she says without looking up. She's looking critically at the photographs, her thin blond hair tied up in a too-high ponytail with a metallic blue scrunchie, a look that somehow she pulls off.

"We're going to London."

She looks at me. "What for again?"

"He won't tell me."

"Ooh. Romantic." She smiles with both her mouth and her shoulders.

"I guess," I say. I'm unsure of what to expect from our weekend away.

"Come to London with me this weekend," Beau had said earlier in the week, wrapping both his arms around my waist as we stood waiting for battered cod. Our new cohabitation plan was in full swing, and going well. Maybe it's the impermanence of the situation that has taken the pressure off, but it's like we can't bear not being together. Even when we're in the same house.

"Of course," I'd replied. "Where are we going?"

"It's a surprise," he'd said excitedly, and I was intrigued. "You'll have to wear something nice," he'd added, kissing my neck lightly.

I spun around, looking at him. "How nice?"

"Just something you feel brilliant in."

"Do you know how much anxiety these instructions will cause me all week?"

Beau laughed. "I knew it as soon as I said it."

"Just give me a gauge of how nice, like fancy nice, or like lovely nice."

"What's the difference?"

"Constrictive underwear."

Beau shook his head as though what I was proposing was ridiculous. "Yeah, don't wear that stuff. Wear something you've already got. You'll look great in anything."

"Okay." I'd said suspiciously, but smirking. *What is he up to?*

"This is what the fucking brilliant jumpsuit on the back of the bathroom door over there is for, yes?" Lil asks, tucking a pencil into her ponytail and nodding at my new purchase.

"Yes. What do you think?"

"*Lush*," she says. "Tea?" I nod, then I head to the kitchen to make it for us.

I, of course, went and bought something new to wear for the weekend, something that very much fit in the proviso of the pleasure quest. Something nice, very nice, with a touch of sexy. A lilac caped wide-leg jumpsuit with a plunging neck-line. Think Solange Knowles's wedding jumpsuit, but in a pale springtime purple. I figured that I had only two weeks left with this glorious man, in this glorious part of the world, on this glorious quest, and if everything wasn't set with glorious pleasure-centered intention, then what would be the point?

I hand Lil her favorite tea in her favorite mug, and she nods in appreciation. "Noni, have either of you talked about life beyond you leaving?"

"No more than I'm leaving and he's staying and that's where this will end," I say, sipping.

"Do you want to talk about it, though?"

"Yes. No. Of course." I exhale loudly, shrugging my shoulders. "I'm waiting to see if it comes up." I want to know what Lil thinks, but I also do not want to know in case I don't like what she has to say. Because more often than not she's right.

"And he hasn't brought it up?" Lil asks.

"Nope. Do you think he will?"

"Do you want him to is the question you should be asking."

Beau thinks we have talked about it. He thinks we're on the same page, and we are. But I'm starting to wonder whether I'd like there to be more pages. Or at least the possibility of more pages. I don't know what he thinks will happen once I leave. Will we stay in touch? Will we not talk anymore? Will we be done-done? Do we just get on with our lives and pretend it never happened? Will we be friends? What does he want? And more important, what do I want? Well, I want him to go first. Tell me what he wants. I want our so-called "easy" fling to be easy on me. My thoughts are spiraling, so I take a deep breath and look back at Lil. It helps that she's not concentrating on me; she's still assessing the photographs. "I'm very much in denial about leaving," I say. "It doesn't feel real."

She turns to me, grinning, and throws up her arms at the whole beautiful mess. "You're telling me, babe. We've got to get this whole fucking exhibition done before then." She softens. "Plenty of time." Her eyes scanning the images on the floor. Beautiful images. They match landscapes with bodies with such beautiful subtlety that I don't get sick of them, no matter how often I look at them. "Something is missing." She squints.

"No, they're all here." I'm instantly worried. I'd hate for her to think I wasn't competent at my job. "I counted. Three times."

Lil smiles. "Of course you did. No, it's—" She picks up some of the photos and mumbles under her breath. "The balance is off."

I find it hard to believe that anything could be wrong with the photos. "They're all so beautiful, Lil."

"Oh, I know that, darling. I mean the balance of subjects. I think we need to do another shoot."

"Okay," I say immediately, thrilled. I love going on shoots with Lil.

"I think it needs to be a couple." She pauses, glancing over at me. "Maybe a couple where one of the people is incredibly tattooed." She looks at me with expectant and hopeful brows.

"Lil, no."

"What? You loved our shoot."

"I did love our shoot, but those photos were for me. And people will see these." I shake my head.

"If the fucking Mailchimp invite worked, then yes, yes that is the hope of a public exhibition, that people will come and see these photos, yes." She smiles, and it makes me laugh.

"I'll ask Beau," I tell her, hoping this will be the end of it, and then that she'll be so distracted by exhibition-related jobs that she'll forget she asked.

"You know he'll be up for it," she says with a smirk.

"I do."

"So, this is all about you," she says, kindly mocking me.

"Yeah."

"Look, it's your call, but I'd love to shoot the two of you together. For this." She looks around the room. "But also for you."

"Let me think about it," I tell her.

And I will. I will think about it. Could I pose naked knowing other people will see it? Well, yes, technically I could. I can do anything. But do I want to? Would it spark pleasure?

33

Beau has been noticeably edgy all morning. He was weird yesterday on the train down too. Himself but highly strung, tense. I kept trying to crack jokes and lighten the mood, but none of my tricks landed. It's making me nervous. He won't tell me anything about what we're doing today; he just keeps telling me it's a surprise.

In the hotel, I get dressed while Beau is in the bathroom and look at myself in the mirror. I feel fucking incredible. It's one of those joyous moments where the outfit you plan in your head looks as good in real life.

"Thank you," I say out loud to whoever the gods are that willed today to be one of those rare days. And then I very purposely place myself on a chair to do up my shoes. It's a position that makes it look like I am nonchalant and oblivious to my own majesty, when Beau comes out of the bathroom, he'll see me in my full regal glory, and I'll just look up and blink my eyelashes a few times and say, "What?"

"Wow," he says. "You look amazing."

"Oh, really?" I say with a grin. *Yes!*

He gets dressed and I watch him. He'd brought a suit bag with him, which surprised me as I'd never seen him in a suit. But now that I'm seeing him a suit, I wish it was all I'd ever seen him in. The man looks ridiculously good. He sits on the bed, putting on his shoes. I put in my earrings and then turn to him.

"Is this too sexy for whatever we're doing?" I ask, pointing to my cleavage and stepping closer. Beau shakes his head, takes my hand and pulls me toward him, so my chest meets directly with his face. "I'd say this is the perfect amount of sexy." He kisses my chest. I run my fingers through his hair, which is neater than normal.

"You look very handsome."

"This old thing," he says.

"I think you should wear a suit every day."

He smiles. "Come on. We're gonna be late."

Wherever we're going is only a short walk from our hotel. Beau holds my hand as we walk, but he doesn't say much. He's focused, on a mission, and I get a giddy kind of anticipation, because we're in the middle of nowhere.

"Where the hell are we going?" I giggle after a couple of minutes of silence.

"Here." He points to an old gray-and-orange brick building with a clock tower. The building is beautiful. But I still don't know what we're doing here.

"What is this place?" I ask as we walk inside.

"The registry office," Beau says, but he doesn't stop walking, or look at me, when he says this. *A REGISTRY OFFICE? Holy fucking shit. He wants to marry me.*

I am stunned. He squeezes my hand and I squeeze it back.

I can't talk. *This is wild. What do I do?* I feel giddy. Lindell will fucking kill me. Surely this is something we should have a conversation about? I mean, I guess it's romantic. Maybe. Beau lets go of my hand as a flurry of limbs and squealing white tulle leaps into his arms. He clings tightly as legs are wrapped around his waist, arms tight around his neck.

"You ready?" the woman asks and he beams, not putting her down, just squeezing her in an enormous hug.

"Fuck yes!" he yells.

I think I'm smiling as I'm wildly trying to process. First, I notice her dress. Her white dress. Her wedding dress. He doesn't want to marry me. He wants me to watch him get married to squealing legs? The sadistic fuck. He puts her down and she launches at me. "You must be Noni." She hugs me tight. "Thank you for being here today."

"She doesn't know why she's here," Beau says.

"What?" The bride lets me go and stares at him.

"You told me not to tell anyone."

"You could tell *her*," she says, annoyed, and she looks at me, shaking her head with an expression that reads as a massive apology as she squeezes my shoulders with her hands.

"Oh my god." Beau says grabbing another human into a big hug. A striking woman wearing jeans and a waistcoat. Her blue-black hair is short against her androgynous features. The woman in the tulle turns to her and takes her hand. "He didn't fucking tell Noni anything."

The second woman whacks him hard. "You idiot."

"What?"

"She probably thinks you've brought her here to get married," she says, her voice deep, raspy with a thick cockney accent.

Beau looks surprised and turns to me. "Oh, fuck, Noni—"

I cut him off. "What?" I laugh hard. "Oh, god, hadn't even

crossed my mind." I think I say it with enough conviction to be believable.

"I'm Ray. And this is Meg. And my brother is an idiot." The woman in the tulle smiles. *Ray? Oh, Ray!* Beau's little sister, Ray.

"And you're gonna be a witness at our wedding today," Meg says.

"Oh my god. Really?" I stare at Beau. "Wow. Congratulations. This is—it is so nice to meet you both. I've heard a lot about you." I say as the girls look at each other and the only thing that feels like it makes any sense is to just hug them both as I would hug anyone I was meeting for the first time.

"That's Gregor." Ray points to a skinny guy hiding behind a camera, snapping the whole interaction in the distance. We all turn and look at him and he nods discreetly. Meg heads toward him as Ray whispers something to Beau and he laughs with his whole body. I finally look around and take in the building. It's beautiful in here. Pale pink and forest-green walls, white balustrades, a grand staircase and checkerboard tiles, ornate architraves and marble. *Why didn't he tell me this is what we were doing today?*

"Are you okay?" he asks coyly as he steps closer to me.

"Yeah. Of course." I say, trying to hide a million thoughts and feelings. "Are you sure this is—"

He takes my hand. *Okay* is what I want to say. *Are you sure this is okay? That I'm here. That I'll be in your sister's wedding photos.* But instead all I say is "Why didn't you tell me?"

"It all happened pretty quickly, the girls telling me, I didn't want you to overthink it."

"Overthink what?" I ask.

"You'll see."

"Beau—what? This is—" I'm reeling with what this all means.

"Just be in the moment with me, yeah?"

And that sentence cuts through all the crazy building in my mind. I take a deep breath and nod, smiling.

We move into a small room with wooden floors and white walls. A plump, red-nosed man cheerfully officiates the ceremony. I stand to the side with Beau and watch. Ray beams the same way that Beau does. With her whole face. She's radiant. Like she might actually defy gravity and shoot happiness beams right out of her feet that lift her from the ground. I wonder if I've ever looked, let alone felt, that happy. Beau slides a hand around my waist, pulling me in as close as he can. He squeezes my hip tenderly, and when I look up at him, he kisses my forehead as a single tear glides down his cheek. I wilt.

Ray tears up, but she smiles wide. Through smiley, happy sobs she says, "You are everything I want and everything I need. You are my every thought. My every happiness. Every action from now will be made to make our home the happiest it can be. This is my home. You are my home."

Meg says the same thing. I cry. Beau cries more. Gregor wipes his eyes with a hanky. The officiant laughs at us all as he lovingly says, "I now pronounce you married." We all whoop and holler and hug tightly, smiling and jumping up and down. We sign the necessary paperwork and I push down any feelings that suggest that this is weird and just try to lean into all of it. The privilege of being here, of witnessing this kind of love, and feeling these feelings, overwhelms me.

We head out of the room and down the grand staircase, where Gregor snaps wildly, and then outside into the afternoon sun. Beau pops champagne and we all swig from the bottle and throw confetti at Ray and Meg, and my heart can't take any more of this.

"I'm just so happy to have been here," I gush. "That was... you both are..." I start crying again and they sweep in and wrap me in a hug.

We walk up to a park and Gregor takes more photos of the girls as we laugh and drink and eat crisps straight from the bag and recount the day to one another. Meg gets out her phone and hits Play on a song, and she and Ray entwine around each other with such ease that they seem like they're one entity.

"May I?" Beau asks, holding out his hand.

"You may," I tell him. "That was glorious."

"You are glorious," he says as I push against him, and he wraps his arms around my waist and I link my arms around his neck.

"You're beautiful," I tell him. "Sneaky, but beautiful."

"I'm so glad you are here with me today for this, and no matter what happens, I will always remember how I felt watching that, with you."

"How did you feel?"

"I felt—" Beau is cut off by Ray.

"Oi! Love birds. We better get going." Meg hands me the rest of the third bottle we'd opened. "Noni, you finish this off, you're going to need it." She smirks.

"Where are we going?" I ask.

"Just the pub." Beau smiles and Meg and Ray laugh knowingly.

Fuck. What next?

"You two head in. We'll follow in a sec," Ray says when we get to the pub.

Beau and I walk inside hand in hand. As we step through the doorway, a beautiful woman stands up from her seat and grins at us in the same way Ray and Beau do. She's like a human firework, and I half expect joyous colors to burst from the top of her perfectly blow-dried head as we walk toward her. Beau sweeps her into a hug, lifting her off the ground.

A gray-haired man puts his hand out to shake mine. "Noni. Call me Paul."

"Hi, Paul," I say, assuming this is Beau's dad.

The joyous woman grabs me in a tight hug. "I'm Jackie."

"Hi. Hello."

"Where's Nan?" Beau asks, hugging Zeppelin hard. Zep waves at me as they sit down on a bench seat next to each other.

"In the bathroom," Paul says, pulling a chair out for me across from Beau.

An old woman approaches the table and Beau stands up and hugs her. "My boy. My boy." She touches his face lovingly, and then she looks at me. "Oh, Noni, you're beautiful. He said you were beautiful but you're beeeaaauuutifuuulll."

"Nan." Zeppelin laughs. "He's trying to play it cool. You've blown his cover."

"Oh, he's never been cool, love," she says, sitting next to me and holding my hands.

"This is my nan," Beau says. "Dorris."

"Call me Nan."

"Okay. Hello, Nan," I say, trying to take all of this in. I'm meeting his family. He's told his entire family about me.

"We're so happy to meet you, Noni," Jackie says. "When Beau said you two were coming down and asked if we wanted to meet you, I said to Paul—didn't I?—I said, I don't care what our plans are, change them all." Jackie laughs. I suddenly realize they have no idea about the girls and I look at Beau, my eyes wide. He just raises his eyebrows, smiling.

"So what are you two doing down here?" Paul asks.

"We've got a friend's show to go to later," Beau says.

"How lovely," Jackie says.

"That's why you both look so nice." Dorris smiles. "I feel underdressed."

"You look lovely," I tell her. She's still holding my hand in hers.

"Is that Deirdre?" Paul asks, looking over at a woman with long gray hair in a braid running down the middle of her back.

The others turn. "Yeah, it is!" Jackie looks stunned.

"What a bloody coincidence," Paul says, getting up from his chair and waving to Deirdre, who looks surprised and starts to head over.

"Deirdre is our daughter's partner's mother," Jackie says to me, filling me in.

"What are you all doing here?" Deirdre says.

"Beau and his girlfriend are down from Edinburgh, so we're having dinner."

His girlfriend.

"I'm meeting the girls." Deirdre seems happily shocked.

"You are?" Jackie glows. "I called and asked if they were coming but they said they were busy, and so that's what they must've been—well, this is just—Paul, isn't it? Quick, let's pull another table over, we can all eat together. Let's grab some more—"

At that moment, the girls enter through the doors of the pub holding hands and radiating joy. Ray smiles at us and laughs, swishing her skirt. Meg spots her mum and is instantly emotional. They look so happy that it catches my breath and makes me clutch my chest and laugh. As they approach our table, time goes into slow motion as Jackie starts squealing and jumping up and down. The girls stand in front of the table, holding up their ring fingers. Deidre bursts into tears. Jackie has already swept the girls into her arms.

Paul looks absolutely stunned. "You're bloody kidding," he says to Beau, who nods at him reassuringly.

"Dad, did they get married?" Zep asks.

"Yeah, dude."

"So cool," Zep says. He gets teary and that makes me start again, but I look around and everyone is crying.

I head to the bar with Beau and he kisses the side of my head.

"This outfit is entirely too fucking sexy for the activities you had planned for today," I say, nodding at my cleavage, and he laughs.

"No way."

"Yes way." I roll my eyes. "Your entire family?"

"Surprise!" He grins cheekily.

"Yeah, you seem to be full of them today."

"I knew if I told you, we'd have to have numerous conversations about it and you'd get all worked up and I just wanted you to be here, Nons. It was really simple," he says, paying for the drinks. "Was it a bit of a dick move to give you no warning? Probably." He waits for my answer.

"Yes," I say, meaning it, but also feeling fine.

"Okay, yes. But I wanted you here. As yourself. Cleavage out. Pleasure-quest babe face on, not giving two fucks. And you would've given so many fucks if I told you, yes?" he asks. And he's right.

"Yes. Of course. Because it's—"

"It's what?"

"It's a big deal," I say.

"I care about you, and I care about them, and I wanted you to meet them. That's all. This doesn't change anything about the next week-and-a-bit of our lives," he says.

And I wish he hadn't said that, because I'm starting to think

I want this to change everything. I want this all to mean something has changed for him, that he hates our plan, that he wants more, that he wants me to stay. But if he felt that way, he would say it. I know him well enough now to know that. He still thinks the plan is good. He's happy with this being a fling. He's happy with our expiration date. And I have to be happy with it too. I should be chuffed that he cares enough about me to introduce me to his family. He cares about me and this thing, expiration date and all, enough to bring me to his sister's wedding. And he's entirely right, I would've overthought it all and we would've had to talk about it a lot, and I probably wouldn't have come. I wouldn't have listened to the fact that he wanted me here, because I would've been thinking too much about what it meant. The bigger picture. But there is no bigger picture. There's just this picture. And this picture looks like hanging out with his family in a pub and celebrating his sister's wedding. That's it.

Wine is drunk. Food is eaten. The merry is immense. I enjoy delightful conversations with everyone and I like them all. Beau's Nan was a teacher for fifty years, and we bond over teaching, Mills and Boon red-label novels and adoration of her grandson.

"He's a good egg, love," she tells me.

"He is," I agree.

Zeppelin and I compete for top score on an old arcade game in the corner. He is positively overcome when I beat him three times in a row.

"One more game, Noni."

"You will never beat me, I'm a child of the eighties, babe."

"Let me try," he wails, pulling on my arm as I walk away.

Paul does an incredible toast about how he already feels like Meg is his daughter. He says that their marriage makes him so proud and happy and I tear up again, because my dad would never say things like that. I excuse myself and head to the bathroom to have a moment. Undoing a jumpsuit in a cubicle on your own when you are drunk and emotional is a test of both physical dexterity and mental strength. When I finally get it off, I take a big, half-naked breath. *Today has been positively lovely.*

When I step out of the stall, I am stunned by what I see. Who I see.

"Of all the gin joints," Molly says, smiling. She is leaning on the basin, dressed in a floral-print shirt unbuttoned to just below her boobs. Her hair is slicked to the side.

"What the fuck?" I say, my heart suddenly pounding.

"You look gorgeous."

"What are you doing here?" I walk to the basin and wash my hands. She doesn't move. I can smell her perfume.

"A coincidence." She smiles, pulling a paper towel out of the dispenser and handing it to me.

"But you don't live here," I say, looking at her in the mirror, and she turns to look at me, the real me, not the reflection of me.

"I guess the universe just needed us to see each other one more time."

I scoff loudly, facing her. "It did. And we did." She touches my hand. "And the universe decided we were done." I pull my hand away.

"Are you with that guy?" she asks.

"Yes."

"Is it serious?"

"It's none of your business."

"Look, Nons, I just wanted to—sorry, okay. I saw you'd tagged this place online, and I was in town. I needed to see you."

"Is your girlfriend here?" I spit. *How dare she come here.*

"No."

"Molly, what do you want?"

"I hated the way we left things. I hate that I hurt you. And you wouldn't answer any of my texts and calls and I—"

"Can you blame me?" I say, exasperated. "Oh, god. Why now? Why tonight? No. We've been going around in circles forever. And it's okay." My voice is louder than I want it to be. "We got our answer."

"But did we? How do we know it's the right answer?" she says. There's no room in this bathroom. She's too close.

"I need to get back out there," I say, trying to move past her toward the door.

"I've been freaking out since I saw you," she says, blocking my way. "Because I felt the same way as I've always felt and it scared the hell out of me. I'm not bold like you—I could never just pack up my shit and seek pleasure halfway around the world."

She makes a move as if to hold my hand, but I recoil.

"You weren't real, you didn't feel real when we didn't see each other, you were just a girl in my phone. But when I saw you, the thing between us felt very real. So I've been thinking maybe I can…maybe I can pack up my shit and follow my heart. Because I can't stop thinking about you, and about what could be." She touches my arm and I don't like any of this. I'm struggling to comprehend it all.

"No," I say. "No. There is no *could be*. Our *could be* was months ago and—no. It's done. Finished."

She doesn't say anything, but she starts to tear up. And something in me softens. "I was really sure when I was coming on this trip that we would be together. And that night was everything I thought it would be until you—" I stop.

"It was fucked," she says.

"Yes. But we got an answer."

"I'm sorry, oh, god, I'm so sorry. I've just always been, like, four steps behind you." She looks at me, her eyes pleading.

"Our timing has always been really shit." I half laugh through my anger and confusion, "Like tonight. Your timing actually couldn't be any worse."

"I'm sorry. But don't you think we should—that we owe it to ourselves to just see what this is?"

"I did. I don't think so anymore."

"Because of man-bun?"

"Yeah. And because of me. Me, mostly."

"That breaks my heart," she says.

"Yeah, well, we've been doing that for years," I tell her. I'm tired. I want this conversation to be over. I push her hand off my arm. "I've got to go."

"Let's say goodbye, then," she says, standing up taller.

"What?"

"Let's say goodbye properly and promise we won't contact each other again, and agree it's done. But let's not leave it how we left it last time. I care about you, Noni, I really do. And I hate the idea that you're just going to be out there in the world hating me."

"What do you mean?"

"Just hug me, you idiot."

I pause, staring at her. I feel so different from the woman I was when I met up with Molly. I've worked hard to feel the way I do about myself now. But nostalgia is powerful, and I want to believe her. That this will be goodbye. The resolution that should've come much earlier than now. The closing of this chapter, officially, to make space for all of these new, amazing things.

I put my arms around her loosely but she holds me tight, so I give over to it, to all the fantasies and could've-beens. We hug for a long time. I'm the first to let go, and as I pull back, she holds my face with both her hands.

"Goodbye, Noni," she says.

"Goodbye," I say. And she kisses me soft on the lips as the bathroom door opens and Ray looks at us, then heads straight back out the door again. *Fuck.*

"Fuck!" I yell. "Molly, you've got to go. Fuck." I open the door and call after Ray. "Wait. It's not what it—she kissed me and—Beau knows—"

She spins on her heel and whisper-shouts, "He knows that you're kissing women in bathrooms?" Molly walks past and Ray points at her as she heads back into the bar. She is furious.

"No. No. He knows about her. Please, can I explain? It really wasn't what it looked like. You only saw one tiny moment."

"It looked pretty fucking clear to me."

"She kissed me. I didn't want her to kiss me. We have a long history and I tagged a photo and she showed up. She thinks there's unfinished business between us. But it's done." Ray looks completely repulsed by me and I start to panic. "I am so wildly in love with your brother," I say all at once, emotion springing quickly, because I'm unprepared for this level of honesty. Feelings I've been trying to push aside and hide rush out.

Her expression softens slightly. "Does he know that?"

"No. Yes. I don't know. We haven't said it. I don't think we will, with me leaving in like a week. But I think he knows. I hope he knows. Do you think he knows?" I'm nervous and rambling and sweating; I can feel it prickling my temples. "I just—please—" I grab her wrists and hold on to her, I can't let her leave, I need her to hear me, but I know I'm not making any sense. "The idea that you would use that thing that you just saw—" I stop, correcting myself. "That entirely fucked thing that you just saw, to make some kind of judgment about me is—I feel sick." It's not a lie. I do. I feel nauseated. I grip my own forehead. "And I don't want to ruin today. This. I am so overjoyed to be here." My breath is quick. I'm speaking so fast I've puffed myself out.

"Noni?" she says, but I don't stop.

"And I'm so confused about how that thing you saw even happened, because I didn't want it to happen. I mean, I did when I first came to Europe. I wanted to know, you know? I wanted an answer, but I got an answer. Months ago. I haven't spoken to her in months because, well, the way we left it was shit, but then I met your brother and I'm just, like, kind of obsessed with him, really, if I'm honest." Tears spring to the corners of my eyes but I keep them balanced there.

"Noni?"

"And I will tell him. I will tell Beau everything about what just happened and what you saw, I will. I feel like we have that kind of relationship, you know? There are things I've told him that I've never really told anyone. And I think he will understand. He will be okay with what just happened. Because I feel like I can tell him anything."

"Except that you're in love with him?" She is smiling ever so slightly.

"Well, yeah. I'm going, and that just feels—"

"Noni. Can I be really honest with you?" she asks.

"Please," I say.

"I think he's a bit obsessed with you too."

I sigh, relieved. "Really?" And then the tear topples over the edge and down my cheek.

"Yeah. I wish you could hear the way he talks about you when you're not around. I always think that's the real measure, you know? I think he's pretty enamored, Noni."

More tears. "I just don't know what's going to happen."

She smiles sweetly and rubs my arm.

"What are you two doing?" Beau is suddenly behind me. I quickly wipe my face.

"We're just talking about you," Ray says.

"Oh, really?" He puts his hands on my shoulders.

"I'll let you tell him all about it," she says, touching his hand and my shoulder with a gentle squeeze as she walks away.

"Tell me what?"

"Later. I'll tell you later," I say, turning to look at him.

"Have you been crying?" he asks, touching my face.

"All day."

"Who knew you were such a big sook. Want to dance?" He grabs my hand and marches me onto the dance floor, where he wraps his hands around my waist and I wrap my arms around his neck and happily breathe him in, trying to process everything that has just happened.

"You okay?" he asks, looking at me. I nod, because I'm worried if I talk, I'll cry, and I don't want to do that. Not now. Not here. "Good." Beau kisses me and I kiss him back because he is precisely who I want to be kissing.

Fucking Molly. How dare she. I'm so angry. And confused.

And in love. I am so in love with this human. He keeps kissing me.

"Can you two not be gross, please?" Zep nudges Beau and we both laugh. Beau lets me go and grabs him in a bear hug, which moves quickly into a proper dance hold and they laugh their way around the dance floor. I stand watching them, smiling and laughing and swaying to the music, willing the tears to fuck off because it feels like I fit here. But I have no idea if this version of my life is even possible. And there's a pang, because I don't think it is. I don't think this is possible.

34

The realization on the dance floor acts like a snap freeze, icing out my feelings and holding them in place, trying to stall everything so I can't feel it anymore. Because if I can't feel it anymore, it can't hurt me.

I'm acting cold. I know I am. And Beau knows it too. He's trying every trick he has to melt the ice: inventing wild dance moves, cracking jokes, keeping his hands permanently attached to some part of my body at all times, kissing me against the wall of the elevator back at the hotel. But none of it works. It just makes me sad, and then angry that I'm sad. Angry at myself for ruining it.

When we get inside our hotel room, Beau sits on the edge of the bed, undoing his shoes. He looks up at me and sighs loudly. "So, Ray said she saw you kissing someone in the toilet. It was London girl, wasn't it?"

I swallow hard. "She told you? Of course. Of course she

told you." I look at him, trying to read what he's feeling. "I was going to tell you."

"I know," he says. I stay silent. "You gonna tell me what happened, then?" he says, leaning back on his hands, watching me.

"You're being very calm," I say, groaning. Always so fucking calm. And together. And not at all messy or emotional. "I tagged a photo. She saw it and came there. She cornered me in the toilet. She had this monologue about missed opportunities and I told her no. So she said fine and we hugged goodbye. And she kissed me at the precise moment Ray walked in." I know I'm talking in robotically short sentences. But I can't help it.

"So, that's it?"

"Yeah," I say. *Don't be an asshole, Noni.* "It's entirely fucked. And I've probably ruined your perfect day, and Ray's day, and I'm shit and really sorry."

"Noni." Beau sits forward, leaning his elbows on his knees. He looks disappointed, which makes me feel even more awful and embarrassed.

"I basically had a fucking panic attack when I was telling your sister. I was freaking out."

"Yeah, she said." He stops, waiting for me. Always waiting for me.

"I just—fuck. Today was a lot. There was a lot. I'm feeling a lot. Forget it, okay? Can we forget it, please?" I ask, pulling my earrings out of my ears and getting undressed. I feel trapped by fabric and feelings.

"I don't know why *you're* angry," he says.

"I'm angry because you're not listening," I say, and wish I hadn't because it's a lie.

"I am listening, but you're not communicating."

"Forget it." I shake my head and start thrusting my shit into my bag.

"Noni, what are you doing?" He stands up. I don't reply, I just pack. "Don't leave, let's sort this out. Now. We can talk about this." He tries to run interference and touch me but I move around him.

"I don't want to talk."

"Fine. Don't talk. Just don't go." He is pissed off but calm; I've never seen anything like it. "Nothing is solved if you leave."

I scoff loudly. "That's just it."

"What?"

"I *am* leaving!" I yell, frustrated.

"That's why you're angry? Because you're leaving?"

I pause as the sting of vulnerability whacks my whole body. "Yes."

"So why didn't you just say that?" He smirks and it's a look that derails my frustrated energy instantly.

"Because I don't like thinking about it. The idea of this being done. Of you being happy to see the back of me. It's just awful, no, unpleasant, shit, no—" I shake my head and throw a T-shirt onto the ground in frustration. "Un-fucking-bearable." Beau smiles. "Don't smile at me. This has always had an expiry date and ten thousand miles of space between it. It's easy to persevere for the short term, but in the long term? You don't want to do the long term, not with me, and that is abundantly clear."

He looks stunned and shakes his head. "You've just made this whole thing up," he says.

"What?"

"This whole narrative you're spinning in your head to make yourself feel better, it's made up. What do you want to know,

Noni? Have I ever lied to you?" I stare at the floor and he raises his voice slightly. "Have I?"

"No."

"Have I always told you the truth?" He is irritated and his voice is strained.

"Yes."

"So what do you want to know?" he asks and I look up at him. "Don't insult me by making up some bullshit story where I am the villain." He sighs loudly and rubs his temples. "Or act like you know exactly what's going on in my head when you've never fucking asked."

So I ask. "What do you want?"

"You."

"But why? I don't get it. I don't get why—"

"Do you know how insulting that is to me? You're basically saying that something I love is not worth wanting."

"I'm not," I say, feeling like a toddler throwing a tantrum. *Wait.* "Something you love?"

"Yes!" he exclaims like it's the most obvious thing ever. "You dickhead."

"Don't call me a dickhead." I can't help but smile a little.

"Well, stop acting like a dickhead." He speaks slowly, punctuating each word. "I am in love with you, Noni Blake." He steps toward me. "And I'm not afraid of that. But you are."

My throat feels tight. "Well, yes."

"Because you're going?"

"Yes. And because I don't get why someone like you would want—"

"I want you because I want you. Because at a base level my chemicals are infatuated by your chemicals and every time I see you I want to do outrageously sexy things to you."

I smile. But I suddenly feel underwhelmed. He's attracted to me, sure, but love? This doesn't sound like love. Beau shakes his head and groans.

"Nope. Shit. That's a cop-out." He's flustered. He paces. "The idea of you kissing someone else, it really hurts," he says and I nod. "And the idea of you leaving, well, that really fucking hurts too."

"Yeah, I know—I'm sorry. You've got to know—"

He cuts me off. "Noni, I want you because I am enamored by you." He steps toward me, looking me in the eye. "I want to know what you think about…well, everything. I want to be with you when I'm not. I love how you think. I love how I feel when I'm with you. You talk about *your* pleasure quest, and you are the most pleasing thing ever to me. In *every* way."

I want to cry, dropping my bag with a heavy thud to the floor. "This is too much."

"Come here," he says and I shake my head. "Please?" he asks.

I exhale loudly and walk the two paces to get to his chest. His forefinger lifts my chin to look up at him as his thumb traces my bottom lip, kissing it sweetly. "I love you. And I love that I love you. And I'm not scared of loving you." He pauses. "You might be leaving, but you haven't left yet. Have you?"

"Nope," I sigh. "I love you too," I whisper.

"I know," he says. "Now, kiss me like you just saw me after being away from me for a year." He smiles and I laugh. "Go on. That's what it felt like tonight, you all the way over there, pouting with your bag in your hand. A whole year."

I wrap my arms around his shoulders and plant my lips on his, and I kiss him like I've missed him with my whole heart. Because I will.

Miss him.

With my whole heart.

35

We meet Lil just before sunrise at an old inn. She tells us there's a walk of about four miles that is a divine mix of lake and woodland and castle in the background that she thinks will provide stunning locations. She makes us get naked in the car but wear our coats. She gets naked, too, in solidarity, which makes me laugh. I feel like a naughty teenager as the three of us set off on our naked exploration. When she finds a spot she thinks is perfect, she sets up her camera and makes us stand with our coats on until she's ready, and then we drop them out of frame, run in and wrap ourselves up in each other.

"Perfect!" Lil yells, and we put our coats back on and keep walking.

The first few times I'm desperately self-conscious and try with all my might to hide behind Beau. But by the third or fourth time you'd think I'd always been larking naked through the Scottish woods.

When I told Beau about Lil's idea, he knew instantly it was

something he wanted to do. After the wedding debacle I've been alternating between feeling guilty and sad, but equally happy and amazed by everything. I am a swirling contradiction of feelings, pummeling me moment to moment. "It'll be brilliant," he'd said, and I'd thought: he's right. Why is he always right?

We're standing on a sandy lakeshore with a fucking castle in the background and the sun filling the sky in perfect shades of pinks and yellows and oranges, and all of the feelings rise up in me at the same time. Beau puts his coat down and we sit on it, me between his legs, his arms wrapped around my shoulders. I lean my head on his bicep, kissing it slightly.

"How do you feel?" he whispers.

"Well safe," I say, and he laughs loudly. "But actually, that's true."

"I'm glad." He kisses my neck, and we sit and watch the sky and breathe each other in.

"Holy shit, you two. These are going to be fucking beautiful." Lil is ecstatic.

Suddenly a dog appears out of nowhere, running right up to us. It sniffs and licks us as we laugh loudly, We're unable to move our naked bodies. Lil keeps snapping photos as an older man in a flat cap appears, looking mortified.

"We're doing a—I'm a professional, I swear," Lil says, walking over to him as Beau and I stay exactly where we are.

"Orright!" Beau says with a nod.

"I'm so sorry," flat-cap says, not looking at us. "Roger! Roger! Here! Now." He grabs the dog and apologizes over and over again as we all fall about laughing hysterically.

"There's one more spot I want to shoot," Lil says. "Quick sticks, let's catch this light."

We follow a path to some woodlands. Tall moss-covered trees line a winding walkway and the effect is so stunning my breath catches. Lil sets up a shot so we're standing on the path with the trees in the background.

"Face each other," she says, so we do.

"You're fucking beautiful, do you know that?" Beau says to me softly.

"You're fucking beautiful, do you know that?" I reply, and he kisses me, both hands on my cheeks.

"Okay, now, Noni, you face me, and Beau, face away." We do as she says. "Hold hands," she shouts. Lil comes in close around us. "Close your eyes. And breathe," she says, and I am grateful for the reminder.

I breathe in and out, and smile with the mindful recognition of what exactly is happening right now. I'm naked. Next to a very naked man who thinks I'm beautiful. In public. I'm getting my photo taken. Photos that people are going to see. I don't feel as self-conscious as I thought I would, not really. I don't feel any hatred. I don't really feel anything, other than a kind of peace. This is my body today. These will be photos of my body today, and that's okay. I feel fine. I feel better than fine. And I kind of hate that there's the possibility that I might mar these big, glorious, contented, cared-for, wild, brave feelings I'm having with any negative thoughts. It genuinely feels like a waste of energy, and of the goodwill of Beau and Lil. So I decide not to. I whisper under my breath to myself, "You did good, kid."

"And now open your eyes," Lil says, and I do and I smile with my whole body, from the tips of my toes to the top of my head.

Beau and I sit in a café after our shoot, drinking coffee, eating eggs and toasting to our morning. The city is only just waking up, with normal-looking people heading to work and school, and I feel like I want to grab them and yell, "I just had an epiphany in the woods while I was naked. And not on drugs. And see this Viking here? He thinks I'm beautiful and isn't that brilliant? Life is brilliant!" But I don't, of course; I just smile and sip from my mug and picture the scene playing out in my mind.

"This morning was one of those perfect moments," Beau says, and I nod, agreeing. We both sit silently for a moment. "Anything you want to do in your last week?" he asks.

"Not think about the fact that it's my last week."

"Okay. We can do that." He bites his lip. He's not saying something, I can tell, but I don't ask what.

I'm not saying something, too, so I get how he feels.

36

We're sitting in a fancy restaurant and Beau is smiling wide. "What are you thinking?" he asks.

"This is nice," I say. I indicate the restaurant, but I really mean Beau and me. This thing between us. It's been nicer than nice. It's been bloody amazing. Since London, we've spent days wrapped up in each other, saying *I love you* and having the kind of sex that is an extension of those words. It has been all eye contact and closeness. But neither of us has said anything about the future. And now that I'm leaving tomorrow, I don't want to be the one to bring it up. I want him to. Desperately.

"What are you thinking?" I ask.

He stands up, walks around the table, grabs my face in his hands and gives me the slowest, sweetest kiss. He pulls away and smiles at me before sitting back down. I laugh giddily.

"I'm bummed this day has arrived," he says.

I sigh, relieved. "Me too."

"You're—I've never met anyone like you."

"Oh, that's because I've lulled you into this false idea of me. You've only met nomad, holiday, pleasure-quest, fun Noni. You haven't met boring, overworked, awkward Noni. She's not nearly as cool."

"I never said cool."

And that's it. That's all we say about it. I don't ask him if he wants something more, and he doesn't ask me. We eat and talk and drink expensive champagne and have sex in the bathroom of the fancy restaurant because I made some comment about them being bigger than my last unit back home. And then we start the walk back along the cobbled streets to Lil's exhibition, him walking behind with his arms tightly around my waist. I tell myself it's because he doesn't want to let me go. My heart is thudding too hard and fast. *I go home tomorrow. I go back to my real life tomorrow.* I don't want things to go back to the way they were. Before the could've-been list, before Beau, before this wild quest to try to land somewhere in the sphere of happy. The pleasure quest can't continue at home, at least not this version of it, because there are work and bills and real life, and the challenge ahead of me now will be to maintain some kind of pleasure-reality balance.

I look up at Beau and he kisses me, but we don't say anything. We just walk. The voice in my head tells me not to leave. To stay right here in this city with him. But I can't work out if that voice is intuition, or just fear. It's unclear. *What would happen if I didn't leave? What would happen if I stayed?* I let the thoughts and images creep in and fill me up a little before I block them out. It's too much to think about, because that's too much change, too much unknown. Too much of a risk. And I don't think that's what he wants. We agreed. The perfect fling.

I exhale loudly. I know I can be happy at home. I can be happy anywhere, I realize. Because I now know that I am the common denominator in my own happiness. Not things, or clothes, or Vikings, but me.

We walk into the gallery and there is already a throng of cool-looking people schmoozing inside, lit beautifully by tiny downlights. My hands are clammy, but Beau doesn't let go. There's a table of drinks and I pick up a glass of champagne and down it in one hit, then pick up another. Beau shakes his head, laughing. There's a girl with cropped pink hair playing acoustic covers. She's very good.

Lil kisses us both. "I'm shitting my pants," she says.

"Well, you look great, considering," Beau says. "I think Noni has shit herself in solidarity."

"I don't know how you do this," I tell her. "Look at my hands." I hold them up so she can see the sweat on my palms.

"This part is the whole point. Making people take just a second to marvel at beautiful things, to feel something other than ambivalence about their lives. What a fucking privilege." She squeezes my hand as she waves to someone across the room, and then she's gone.

The place is pretty full already and we wander around the exhibition. I cling to Beau with one hand, my champagne flute in the other.

"These photos are stunning," Beau says calmly, taking them all in. He's stopping and doing just as Lil had hoped, marveling. I'm pretending I am, but all I want to see is our photos. Beau and I agreed to let Lil choose because everyone, me included, figured I'd chicken out.

It turns out our photos are impossible to miss because the second you move past the first front-facing wall, there we are, three huge black-and-white shots of us. One is just of our faces, side profile, from when we were sitting on the beach. One is of us entwined in each other's arms in the foreground of the field of flowers. And the central one, the biggest, is me front facing in all my naked glory, next to Beau, who has his back turned but his face looking at me, beaming. My head is lolled back and I am laughing, ecstatic, one hand holding Beau's, the other holding my heart as I laugh. The extremeness of it all takes my breath away. The size contrast, us compared to the trees, the size of my joy. Tears spring in the corners of my eyes and I look at Beau, mouth agape. His face mirrors mine.

"Are you teary? I'm teary," he says and I nod. "They're really beautiful," he says. "You're so beautiful." He bites his lip, breathes in deep and exhales fast, sniffing and clenching his teeth together. He smiles too hard, trying to contain his feelings. I wrap my arm around his waist.

"Hey. You good?" I say and he nods. He's trying to hold it together. "It's okay," I tell him.

"Fuck, Noni," is all he gets out. He pushes his hair back and turns to face me. "I don't want you to go." His eyes are full of wanting and relief, apology and concern and tears that haven't fallen yet. I smile and my tears come fully now too. "But you've got to. I know. We agreed. That's the plan. But just, fuck—" He points at the photos. "Look at us."

"Fucking real life," I sob.

"Fucking real life," he repeats.

He kisses me gently. But I don't want gentle. I want him. I want to press our lips and bodies together so close. We kiss like everything depends on it.

"Babes! You look fucking stunning!" Naz is staring at the photos with slicked-back hair and a red lip. Tom smiles and waves, looking a little flushed with embarrassment at seeing me in the nude. Naz hugs me.

"These are incredible. Lil is incredible. Tom googled her, she's a big deal. This is a big deal. Hi, you must be Beau." Naz hugs him and it looks comical, her tiny frame against his. Beau shakes hands with Tom and then excuses himself. I watch him go.

"You guys good? That was a pretty intense kiss we interrupted," Naz asks, holding my hand.

"I just don't want tomorrow to come."

"Are you sure you can't stay?" Tom asks.

"Work and life and—"

"Fuck all of that," says Naz. "What do you want, babes?" She points at me with a toothpick, the olive from her canapé in her mouth. Lil approaches and we both squeal and tell her she's amazing.

What do I want? I want to him to come with me. I want to stay. I want to go home. I want it all.

"You happy?" Tom asks Lil.

"Absolutely. Are you?" she asks me.

She's asking about the photos, but I can't help taking her question more literally. "Too happy," I say. "That's the problem. I don't know what this next bit looks like."

"You don't have to know—you just let pleasure lead. Look." She points at someone from the gallery with two long black plaits down their back placing a red dot on the central photo of the two us. Someone bought it.

"Who bought…"

"I dunno," Lil says.

Beau rejoins us. He's been crying, I can tell, but he smiles and pretends he's okay. We all drink and talk, but I'm not in the mood, and neither is he.

"Do you want to go?" I ask him an hour later and he looks relieved and nods.

"I'll fucking miss you, babes." Naz squeezes me tight as we say our farewells.

"You know what to do, darling. Don't overthink it." Lil kisses me boozily on both cheeks.

★ ★ ★

"I can't believe someone bought our photo," I tell Beau as we wait for a cab.

He smiles at me. "I did. For you," he says. "Whatever happens next, I wanted you to know that this thing, these feelings, are real."

I don't say anything. Because I don't know what to say.

I set my alarm to give myself enough time to orgasm twice more with my beautiful Viking. We'd promised we'd stay awake all night, but he fell asleep as soon as his head hit the pillow. Emotionally exhausted. I lay awake, running through possibilities. Should I stay, not go back, just pretend my life back home doesn't exist and this is my life now? I'd have to quit my job. That would be a dick move on such short notice. I'm meant to start back in a week. Or do I go home temporarily? Get organized. Move here for real. Live with Beau. What about work? I guess I could teach here. Do I even want to live in Edinburgh? What about Lindell and Graham and the kids? *What do I want? What do I want? What do I want?*

I'm no closer to an answer when the alarm sounds, so I don't tell Beau what I'm thinking. I go along with the plan. I wake him up by straddling his waist, kissing him all over. Trying to savor each moment. To end this chapter of the pleasure quest trying to drink up this beautiful human.

"Are you sure you don't want me to drive you?" he asks, as we lug my things toward the door.

"Nope. We say goodbye here. On our terms, like we agreed," I say, trying to clear the awkwardness in the air. We're both being too delicate and it feels weird. Claustrophobic.

"I've had the most brilliant time with you, Noni."

"Me too. Thank you for—" I stop. I'd planned a whole

speech but none of it feels right now. It all feels weird. "For being glorious. You are glorious."

"It's been a fucking pleasure, Noni Blake." He smiles cheekily and I laugh.

"It absolutely has." We hug for the longest time, but eventually I break it. "So what if I get drunk and want to message you?"

"Then message me. Don't overthink this next bit, Nons. You'll be there. I'll be here. I'm sure the universe will put us on a dance floor together again." I swoon and instantly feel sad.

"Okay. Yup. You're right." He seems calm, really calm. I'm pretending to be calm, but I'm like a duck on a pond with a quick-moving current; false grace on top and flailing erratically under the water. He kisses me lightly on the mouth, and then on my forehead, and I lean into his chest. There is a toot of a car horn outside.

We drag my suitcase to the front of the building and hand it to the taxi driver, and then we stare at each other.

"See you when I see you, then," I say, looking up at him.

"Exactly. Bye, Nons." He squeezes my hand and holds it as I get into the car.

I stare at Beau, Shaquille leaning into his leg, standing on the street, and tell myself to take a mental snapshot of this moment, so I'll never forget it. A mental capture of a perfect goodbye, a celebration of how grown-up we're both being. He smiles at me and I smile back and we drive off. I thought I'd cry. I thought he'd at least get teary. I thought there'd be grand confessions, maybe more talk of how much this sucks, a mention of other options. But it was so calm. I felt so calm. And now I feel sad and nervous, but also okay.

★ ★ ★

At the airport, I don't cry through check-in, or customs, or while drinking my coffee. I just feel cool. For the first fucking time in my entire life, I feel genuinely cool. Because I did it. I did this whole thing for myself and it wasn't a disaster. Quite the opposite, in fact. Letting pleasure lead in my life has manifested in some magnificent ways. I've worn less makeup and gone on more walks. I've said what I thought. I've said yes more. I've said no more. I've listened to, and trusted, that voice in my head. I bought lingerie. And wore pleather. Because I wanted to. I got naked in a fucking forest and had my photo taken and then watched other people look at those photos and tell me I was beautiful. I said thank you when they complimented me, and meant it. I didn't listen to the part of my brain that told me that I shouldn't dare do any of those things. That people might think I looked ridiculous. That I was too fat or ugly or plain or beige or boring or flabby or whatever shit thing I've led myself to believe. I've danced. And drunk too much wine. And had great sex and terrible sex. And great conversations and terrible conversations. I've backed myself. And let shit go. I fell in love. I've honored my baby. And myself. I've realized it's no longer acceptable to be unhappy or, worse still, to be ambivalent. The pleasure quest has taught me that I'm ready, and worthy, of happiness. Not if, not when, but now. I feel so proud of myself and these revelations, and then I think of Beau, and wonder when the thought of leaving him behind will stop making me feel so unhappy.

37

Lindell flings himself back onto the huge hotel mattress in a flurry, like a snow angel amid the crisp white linen. I get teary, again, from jetlag and heartache and the joy of seeing my beautiful friend, who has made me laugh since the second we saw each other at the arrivals gate this morning.

Lindell has booked us into a lush hotel, the kind where there's a lavender-spray turndown service and chocolates with your name embossed on them. We pretend like we totally belong here but giggle loudly at every lavish detail.

"Now what?" he says, rolling onto his side.

I lie down on the bed facing him. "Now I go back to school on Monday and work out what the fuck my life looks like."

"Are you sure you don't want to stay with me?"

"No, no. I'll stay with Dad until I work out where I want to live. I'm going to go slow for a little bit, I think."

He rubs my shoulder. "You look different."

"I am different." I place my hand on his.

"And Beau?" he asks. We haven't talked about it yet, but I've known it was coming.

"And Beau is in Edinburgh and I am here and that means we're not together."

"How do you feel about that?"

I breathe in deep. *How do I feel about that?* "Heartbroken, but not. Heart-hurt. Heart-bruised, maybe." I roll onto my back. "It was never going to work out any other way, so it feels exactly as I expected it to." I turn my face to Lindell so he can see I'm serious. "It was a fling, a lovely fling, the perfect fling. But it wasn't real life, Lindell. It would never work in real life."

"How do you know?" he says with conspiratorial eyebrows that I don't like at all.

"Because I was different there. I wasn't working, I was being frivolous and self-indulgent, and that's not how life works."

"Isn't it?"

"Lindell, you know it isn't. I need to work, and figure out what's next. I need to be a grown-up."

"And what? Undo all of this gorgeousness you've discovered?"

"Of course not. Joy in my real life, that's the mission now." I pause. "And I'm excited."

"I am too." He rolls onto his back and intertwines his pinkie finger with mine. "So this means you're single?"

"I guess. Yes. God. I don't want to think about that yet." I'm not ready to think about that yet. "So Graham took the job?" I ask, tired of talking about me.

"Yes. Negotiated a no-travel weekend clause into his contract and some other things to replicate balance and a shared parenting load, but let's fucking see how it unravels." Lindell breathes deep. "I'm happy for him. He's happy."

"And you?" I ask.

"I'm happy, too, Nons. Work is good. My babies are great and beautiful. My best friend is back, in every sense of the word." I smile at this, understanding his meaning. "Thank you," he says.

"What for?"

"You know your list hasn't just changed your life, my girl— it's changed mine too."

"Why? Because you've had to endure months of my antics? I must be so exhausting, I'm sorry."

"No. I'm being serious. I'm grateful. You inspired me. I wrote my own list of shit I want to do. I've been wading in parent-brain for so long that I forgot that I even had a list. So did Graham. And us collectively, too, we have a list now. A sex list. Of things we want to try and do. It was the most vulnerable we've been in front of each other in ages."

"Really?" I roll over to face him, feeling better.

"Yes. Who'd have guessed Graham would be mad into role play," he says. "We now have a whole section of the closet dedicated to costumes," he whispers.

"What costumes?" I ask, elated.

"A whole assortment. He has all of these very specific fantasies he's never told me anything about. And it's fucking awesome. So thank you."

"You're welcome." I smile, and then we laugh, and we don't stop for a very long time.

"And a big welcome back to Ms. Blake, who is finally back after her long service leave. I know you'll all agree that we've missed her around here." Niko addresses the assembly and adolescent faces spin to look at me as I wave awkwardly. Nothing has changed at school, but there's still so much I've missed. My head is spinning with new information.

"How you feeling?" Niko pops his head around the door of my office later in the day.

"Overwhelmed. But fine," I say.

"Good. Just yell out if you need anything." We stare at each other for a moment. The energy between us has shifted. It's not awkward, but it's not comfortable either. It's heightened. "Okay." Niko nods. And he leaves.

I feel weird. I feel like I want to debrief with Beau. He'd messaged, checking I got to the airport okay, and home, but nothing major. I'd sent him a photo of the bottle of duty-free whiskey I'd bought. Very safe. Very friendly. Very few feelings, but maintaining some kind of connection. I'd missed a call from him and he'd left me a very short, sweet voice mail. "Nons, just wanted to hear your voice. I'm about to go to bed...you must be at work, I guess."

I'd called back and left a voice mail for him. "It's my night, your morning. You'll still be asleep. Just wanted to say have a good day."

And that's how our interactions happen now. Text messages with long delays. Missed calls. Trying to find the right balance between staying in touch and giving each other space. I begin to realize just how far away Scotland, and the pleasure quest, really are. So I keep calling, and leaving messages, and he sends me photos of his work, and we talk a little bit every day in some capacity, until we finally agree on a time to chat.

I'm nervous when I wait for the phone to ring at 6:00 a.m., which is his 9:00 p.m. I feel adolescent and nervy. It's early and I've barely slept as I'm too excited. I pick up the phone the second it lights up. "Hi," I say and I hear him laugh and I feel my whole body relax and the sound of his voice.

"Sexy morning voice," he says.

"Yeah, six o'clock on a Saturday, that's love," I say and wish I hadn't. "How are you?" I add to cover it.

"I'm okay, Nons. It's been a weird ten days, yeah?"

"The weirdest," I say.

"I need to say something. Otherwise I'm going to chicken out," he says, and my whole body tenses. "I need to lay a boundary, I think." He pauses, and my heart races. "I don't think we can talk for a while. Okay?" I take a sharp intake of breath and hope he doesn't hear. "Just till we're through the other side of this bit. And I know I said let's just see what happens, but basically I'm such a miserable fuck right now—"

"Without me and my witty repartee?" I cut him off, trying to keep it light, trying in vain to change his mind. I don't want to not talk to him. I don't want that to be how this unfolds.

"Exactly." I hear him smile, but he continues. "So in the interest of pushing ahead, I just need to ignore that you exist for a bit."

Ignore me? Fuck. "Okay" is all I get out. Tears well.

"Shit. Not ignore you. That's not what I wanted to say. Nons, tell me you know what I mean?"

"Yeah. Of course. It's hard."

"Harder than I thought." He pauses. "So, do you agree?"

"How's Zep?" I ask instead. *No. I don't agree. I don't want to not talk to you.*

"He's good. He and his girlfriend broke up."

"Oh no. Is he okay?"

"Yeah. He's fine. He's being so mature about the whole fucking thing. They wanted different things and didn't want to hurt each other. He inspired me to have this conversation with you, actually."

"If the sixteen-year-old can do it?" I say. I tug on a thread on the blanket and watch it unravel in my hands. I know exactly how it feels. "So, now what? We just go cold turkey?" I ask.

"Yeah. Total detox from each other." He sighs. "For a bit."

The tears plop on my cheeks and I try not let him hear that I'm crying, but I can't help it. Neither of us speaks for the longest time.

"I really miss you, Noni," he says.

"I miss you too," I blub.

38

"You're a very good kisser." Niko pulls back, his hand on the back of my neck, me straddling his lap on his expensive couch.

"You're a very good kisser," I slur. I'm drunk. I'm so drunk the room spins a little, but I don't care, because in the interest of detoxing from the Viking I am leaning into pleasure in my new life back home. Because I've changed. And pleasure is at my center now, and I can do whatever I want. I can make bold sexual choices and not get freaked out by other people's rubber sheets, because I am powerful, and fuck Beau and fuck my feelings. I can still have a good time.

I'd already drunk a whole bottle of wine by myself by the time I'd messaged Niko telling him we should get a drink, and he'd replied straightaway. *I am desirable. I am wanted. People want me. Even if Beau doesn't.* Niko had suggested a bar. I suggested his place. I am not fucking around. Or I am. That is precisely what I want to do. Fuck this man. I am a woman on a mission, and he accepted my mission immediately. Kissing me against his front door, his knee between my legs the second he opened it.

"So—" I ask him.

"Yes?" He kisses down my neck, to my chest.

"What's this thing with no penetration?" I push back from his kisses, even though it feels good. "Like, ever?" I ask. I know I sound drunk; my voice is high and floaty.

"It just doesn't really float my boat all that much. I mean, it's fine. It's good, sometimes. Just doesn't make me cum." He says it so matter-of-factly that hearing the word *cum* come out of his mouth makes my nipples hard, because of the deeply embedded fucking-the-principal fantasies that have lingered for years.

"I get that," I tell him, because I do. The percentage of times I've cum from penetration alone is fucking low.

"I bet you do." He smiles, pulling my bra to one side and pulling my nipple into his mouth. *Jesus.* "But I like being penetrated." He looks up at me and I grab his shoulders to steady myself.

"You do?"

"Yeah." He kisses and sucks and nibbles and I breathe in deep. "You up for it?" He smirks.

"Me? To you?" I ask.

"Yes."

"With?" I ask, nervous. What on earth does he like to be penetrated by?

"A strap-on, Noni." He laughs. "What did you think I was going to say?"

"I don't know...an eggplant," I say. It's the first thing that comes to mind, and Niko laughs again.

"No thanks, it's more like a Lebanese cucumber."

"Right."

"You'd wear it. It's all very straightforward. I'll show you."

"I was in a lesbian relationship for nine years, so you don't need to mansplain strap-ons to me." I take a bold, sassy breath, poking him in the chest. "I think I can totally do that." I try to be sexy, but I oversell it and it's messy. But I'm curious, and I'm turned on by the idea. I'm ready to fuck a man. Literally.

I stare at my reflection in the mirror. I look vaguely like myself. Wobbly. But myself. Bra still on, wearing a brown leather harness with a small, thin green dildo attached. Part of me thinks I look ridiculous. Part of me thinks I look hot. The logistical maneuvering that the harnesses required meant that I had sexily slinked to the bathroom to put it on instead of awkwardly jumping about in front of Niko. I grab my phone and I take a selfie, meant for Lindell's eyes only, and notice a text message from a UK number.

No Noni. Don't. Just leave it.
But I open it.

Noni, it's Zeppelin. Just wanted to say I hope you're okay and to tell you your advice is still well safe. We all miss you. But hope you're happy.

Fuck. Fucking fuck.
I take the harness off quickly and then I vomit hard and fast into the toilet. There's a knock on the door.
"Noni, you okay?"
"No" is all I get out before I vomit again.

"Welcome," Joan says as she opens the door to her apartment. I hand her a bottle of tequila and kiss her on the cheek, as Carson leaps at my leg with such excited enthusiasm I think he might actually explode. And then I think I might explode, too, with joy. I pick him up, breathing him in, squishing him, kissing his neck. My voice is all shrill glee.

When we've both calmed down, I actually look at Joan. She's tanned and she's got a trendy new haircut. She looks hot. She looks back at me suspiciously.

"What?" I ask, self-conscious, instinctively touching my face to check I don't have crusty toothpaste in the corners of my mouth.

"You look different," she says.

"Do I? Why?"

"I don't know." She shrugs, sitting down on the couch.

"I like your new hair," I tell her and she smiles.

"So," she says, "what's going on?"

I wince a little, feeling embarrassed. I'd left Niko's and drunkenly messaged her last night, telling her I missed her, telling her everything was shit, telling her I wasn't sure if I was allowed to message her these things. She'd called, told me to go to bed, which I did. And it's where I stayed all day today, hungover, feeling embarrassed and sad, reading Zeppelin's message over and over again. The last bit, "But hope you're happy," made me sob into my pillow. When Joan messaged this afternoon to see how I was feeling and to invite me over for dinner, I said yes. Partly because I owe her an apology, and partly because I know she'll make me feel better. "It's fine, I was drunk and emotional and old habits die hard."

"I'm an old habit?"

"Looking to you to make me feel better is an old habit," I tell her, and she nods slowly.

She asks me about my trip and I tell her everything, except the bit about Molly, and the bit about Beau. I don't want to tell her those things. And I tell her a watered-down version of the pleasure quest. I scan her apartment looking for signs of cannellini-beans, but nothing really stands out.

We very quickly fall into our normal, easy rhythm. We order food, we eat, we chat, we get drunk, we giggle and sit on the couch catching up. She chooses music she knows I'll like and my heart pangs with a loud melancholic strum. Everything about this is so comfortable, and yet it all feels so different. I'm different.

"These are amazing," she says, staring at one of the photos Lil took of me. She'd asked to see them.

"Thanks," I tell her, pulling my phone away.

"You look amazing." She pauses. "Happy."

"I was."

"Was?" she asks, eyebrows raised.

"Am," I correct, pouring another shot and handing it to her, clinking glasses.

"Fuck, Nons, I miss you," she says, shaking her head.

"Me too. Of course," I tell her, and I do, that's not a lie, but I'm looking at her and I'm thinking about Beau. I'm thinking about Scotland. I'm thinking about how nothing about being home, or here, feels right anymore.

"So did you get laid while you were away?" she asks.

"You have no idea." I swallow hard and laugh, avoiding the question.

"Are you seeing someone?" Joan asks, surprised.

"I was," I say, and it pangs hard in my chest. I don't want that to be the answer. *But it is the answer, Noni. So suck it up. You made the right choice. This is the right choice. Get on with it.* I smile at her, so she knows everything is fine. *It's not fine.* "How's cannellini-beans?"

"That's over," Joan says. "We were on very different pages." Joan doesn't move. She keeps looking at me.

"Oh, I'm sorry."

"Don't be. We were fundamentally different."

"Yeah, but breakups are shit," I say, pouring another shot and drinking it quickly. I offer her one but she declines.

"They are."

"Yeah."

"Thank you," she says, patting my hand. "For, I don't know, for being you."

I blush a little, embarrassed. "Thank you," I say, meaning it. I turn my head and look at her. She rolls her head across her shoulder, looks me in the eye, and I know instantly what that look is. She is going to kiss me. And I'm going to let her.

She does and immediately it feels wrong, but I ignore the feeling. Because I'm sad that Beau doesn't want me. And Joan does. Any idea that new Noni could prevail, that the stupid pleasure quest could continue to be my life here, was immature and idealistic. That's not how life works. Because life is tricky and choices are based on more than just joy. Like comfort.

And so I have sex with Joan.

Joan and I know each other so well that the sex itself is good. Great even. It feels different from how it used to, though. Because we're different, I guess. I'm more dominant and I think she likes that. We both orgasm easily. The sex is easy. We know each other's bodies so well. But it's sad. Sad sex that speaks of what we used to be and confirms that we'll never actually be again. That's it. We're done. And we both know it. It's just like we had to come back together one last time to really be sure. She kisses me lightly as we face each other. It's too much staring at her face, so I roll over and we spoon as we sleep and neither of us says anything.

In the morning I lie in bed and I mentally update my sexual conquests list.

PEOPLE NONI HAS HAD SEX WITH: A LIST

1. Jakob
2. Randall
3. Felicity
4. Noel
5. The British bartender
6. Othello
7. Debbie
8. Rachel
9. Charles
10. Joan
11. Ruby, the firefighter
12. Ben
13. Niko
14. The trumpeter
15. The magician
16. Molly
17. Beau
18. Gideon
19. Beau. Beau. Beau.
20. Joan

The addition of Joan on the list after Beau shoots pangs of guilt and regret into my chest. *You're so stupid, Noni. What were you thinking?* I get up and get dressed as quietly as possible. It feels weird as I look at her and Carson asleep, like nothing has changed. Except everything has changed. The image is so familiar to me, yet it feels completely foreign. Everything feels completely foreign. Nothing feels right. Nothing has felt right since I got home. *So, what do you want, Noni?* I sigh loudly, not because I don't know what I want, but because I do.

★ ★ ★

I sit on the edge of the bed and touch Joan's arm. "I'm gonna go," I tell her as she rubs her eyes and wakes up.

"Okay." She sits up and looks at me, and she knows. "Are you okay?" she asks.

"Yeah. Sad. But okay," I tell her.

"Me too." She smiles softly. "Last night shouldn't have—"

I cut her off. We do not need to have this conversation. "Yeah."

"Bye, Nons," she says, and we hug hard.

"Bye, Joan," I say. She holds my hand and squeezes it and I leave.

39

The voice in my head repeats the same loop it has for the last six months. *How dare you be so self-indulgent? Who do you think you are? Other people have lives like this, not you.* But my life was like that. For six whole months. And I loved it. And I was happy. I leaned into the pleasure quest because I could justify it as an irresponsible six months, a pleasure-filled blip before the return to normal programming, and I'd stuck to that because I'm a woman of her word, and I'd promised to come back. But to who was I promising? No one. Only to the unshakeable idea I have in my head of who I am supposed to be.

I'd done everything right. I'd ticked every box. I studied. I got a good job. I worked hard. I bought a house and a dog. I committed to someone with my whole heart. I got pregnant. I kept my mouth shut. I stayed in my lane. And I was miserable.

And then I tricked myself into believing that a six-month interlude of being led by joy could somehow alleviate the burden of being myself, because the person I was being, I realize now, was fucking exhausting. I didn't want any responsibilities. I wanted to escape my life. I wanted to escape myself. I wanted to play at being frivolous, and sexy, and passionate. I wanted to pretend. But what I understand now is that I felt more myself when I was being led by pleasure than I have ever felt being led by what I thought was right. I wasn't pretending at all. I was being real. I was trying my real self on for size, and I fell in love. And now that I've seen what life can look like, what it can feel like, I can't go back to what my life was like before. It would be so desperately unfair. And stupid. And I'm not stupid. I know that now. *I know. I know. I know.*

I know that the voice in my head telling me I'm stupid and fat and reckless and wrong isn't my own, not really. When I get still and really pay attention to what I want, to what will make me happy, to what I know, the voice is entirely different. It knows I need to be kinder to myself. It knows my body is perfectly fine the way it is on any given day. It knows that I don't like my job. Not anymore, and that I don't want to spend any more time pretending that I care about it, because I don't. It knows that I don't even like my city anymore. That the only thing I like about being home is being close to Lindell, Graham and the kids. That's it. And that's not enough for me to stay.

I thought that the pleasure quest had to end, that coming home and injecting more joy into my life here is what would bring me joy, because I wanted to do the right thing. The responsible thing. But I realize now that coming home was the wrong thing, because, once again, I've forgotten to follow my heart.

So, what do you want, Noni?

I want to go back to Scotland. I want to be with Beau. I want to work with Lil. And I want to work out what I want next from there. I want to be led entirely by what feels good. I don't want a pleasure quest, I just want to live my life on my own terms. Simple.

"I don't fucking know why you came home in the first place." Lindell clutches the steering wheel tight and drives faster than he should, but I'm okay with that, as he's been tasked with getting me to the airport in time.

"Now you tell me. I'm sorry for leaving you with all the shit to sort out."

"It's some boxes. It's fine."

Lindell yells as he beeps his horn at a black BMW that nearly cut us off. "You piece of shit dickhead wanker, you are not fucking with me tonight. Do you hear me?" He stares into the window of the car as we speed past. "We are on a mission." He beeps the horn again for good measure, as he weaves in and out of other cars.

"Thank you for not telling me you think I'm crazy."

"I don't think you're crazy. I think you're amazing. I think you're brave. I think you are the coolest fucking person I know."

I tear up. "It just feels…right." I hear the words come out of my mouth and they stun me a little bit, so I say them again to be sure. "Lindell, it feels right. I'm doing what feels right."

Lindell whoops and then he starts to cry a little bit too. "Yes. You. Are. Baby! Yes, you are. I fucking love you."

The tears keep falling. "I'm gonna miss you so much. You're the only thing I care about leaving." I sob hard, and we both cry for a while. Lindell signals and cuts in and out of lanes with such focused precision I can't help but cheer when we pull in to the drop-off bay exactly like we had seven months ago, only everything is different now. I am different now. I am myself now.

I kiss him on the cheek and he squeezes me quick and tight. I jump out of the car and grab the one haphazardly packed bag I put together after I booked my ticket. I don't even know what I packed, I was in such a daze. I booked the ticket. Called Lindell. Packed a bag. And now we're here.

"Go! I love you. Update me when you get there."

"I love you. I will. Wish me luck," I tell him, slamming the door.

"You don't need it, baby," he yells as I sprint into Departures and scan the board for my check-in desk.

"Have you got luggage to check?" A blonde woman with bright red lipstick looks me up and down and I shake my head, indicating my carry-on. "You're lucky, you had one minute before this closed." I smile so ferociously I can no longer see out of my eyes, and tears pummel my cheeks. "It's okay, you made it," she says, looking at me with a sympathetic smile. "You're gonna make it. Everything is going to be fine," she says, which makes me smile and cry more.

"It is. It absolutely is." I nod as I take my boarding pass out of her hand.

40

Everything is not fine. Everything is far from fine, because I'm a giant fucking idiot. I've made a terrible mistake. Another one.

"Fuuuck!" I scream, staring at the locked door.

The thing about the core of your joy being an over twenty-four-hour plane ride away is that you have a lot of time to think, and to plan.

I had a two-hour stopover at Changi airport, from where I sent an email to Niko officially resigning, which made me feel equal parts sick and exhilarated. I then emailed Pam and booked my old unit for two nights, because as excited as I was about declaring my love for Beau, my vanity would not allow me to do it without first taking a shower and changing into a pair of knickers that I hadn't been wearing for a full spin around the sun.

I'd meticulously created a three-part plan. Part One of the plan was to get to Pam's apartment, shower, eat some food and breathe. Part Two was Operation Declare Love and True Pleasurable Intentions to Beau. Part Three, of course, was Live Happily Ever After. *Easy.*

Except I hadn't counted on the food-delivery man not coming inside and upstairs, despite my buzzing him in repeatedly. I hadn't counted on my mindlessly opening the front door to run down and grab a bacon fucking sandwich of all things, and letting it close behind me. My gut plummeted to the ground the second I heard the automatically locking door click shut. *You fucking idiot, Noni.* I didn't have my phone. Or keys. Or shoes. I didn't even have underwear on.

"Noni?" I spin on my heel. A young delivery driver holds up a brown paper bag and looks at me.

"You asshole," I scream, and swipe the bag from him.

He winces slightly, like I'm going to hit him. "I'm sorry, I couldn't get the door to—"

"Oh, god, I'm sorry, not you. Me. I've locked myself out—I can't get back into my—"

"Whatever, lady," he storms back out the front door.

"Shit! Shit! Shit!" I scream into the hallway, quickly banging on the three other unit doors, but there's no answer. Of course there's no answer, because it is 9:00 a.m. and everyone is at work, or living their lives, not standing in a hallway without any underwear on trying not to panic. I have no idea how to contact Pam. I don't know anyone's phone number except Lindell's house phone from when we were kids.

I could go to Lil's. *Yes. Go to Lil's and she will…be in South Africa visiting her family. Shit.* I grit my teeth and groan loudly, pacing up and down the hallway. *What do I do? What do I do? What do I do?*

Beau will be at work in an hour.

This is not the plan. The plan included a dress and flowers and perfect winged eyeliner. The plan was not damp hair, saggy boobs and untrimmed bush on full display through the faded oversize "Cowboy Butts Drive Me Nuts" T-shirt that Joan bought me when we first started dating. It's the most comfortable thing I own, threadbare and holey. I should throw it away, but it is sacred to me. I stare down at it and shake my head, tugging at the shirt, willing a solution to appear. I sit with my back leaned against my locked door, eat the sand- wich, flatten my hair with my palm, and realize that there's only one choice, and that is to move directly to part two of the plan. I have to tell Beau how I feel and what I really want. Exactly as I am.

My head is foggy, my heart is pounding and every insecu- rity is firing, but I decide to fake it till I make it, and make my current predicament look as intentional as I possibly can. I power walk up the street, willing a better plan to formulate in my mind. Some boys in a car honk at me and I give them the finger, which makes them crack up laughing. Slowing down, they yell "Nice legs!" and whoop as they drive by, and I shake my head, trying to assert some kind of authority, but I know it's pointless.

As I get closer to the tattoo shop, I try to find that feeling, that knowing, which makes all of this right. And even if he doesn't feel the same, it'll be okay, because then I'll just do the next right thing.

I take a deep breath before opening the door to the shop. The same Australian girl who was there the first time I walked in smiles at me. "Noni! I thought you'd gone home?" She looks flustered.

"I did. But, I'm back. Can I— I need to talk to Beau."

"He's not here. He's got a day off today…he's sorting out all—" she stops.

I sigh. "Right. Shit." I crumble a little bit and sit hard on the bench seat in front of the desk, carefully pulling my shirt under me.

"Noni, you okay?" the girl asks, coming around the desk. I start to cry-laugh at how ridiculous this whole situation is, so I tell her everything, and within seconds an entire shop of tattoo artists and people being tattooed are listening. They find the unit listing online and message Pam, but she doesn't reply.

"We can just try breaking into your fuckin' unit, Noni," bearded Rob, the owner, says seriously, and a few others nod.

"I think I just need to see Beau, like now, before I lose my nerve," I tell them, standing up. Lip gloss and perfume are thrust in my direction, one of the guys gives me his denim jacket, another gives me a clean pair of socks out of his bag, and one of the girls asks me what size foot I have and is handing me the ankle boots that she's wearing. I cry harder. "You're all being very lovely to me."

"Of course, we love Beau, and he…" The girl who gave me her shoes pauses. "Is gonna fucking lose his mind when he sees you."

I assess myself in the mirror and I look kind of punk, cool even.

"It doesn't matter what you're wearing, Noni," Rob adds. "Trust me. He won't care."

I get out of the taxi, take a deep breath and buzz Beau's apartment.

"Hello?" he says.

"Hi. It's me. I'm back. I'm here and I'm all in—"

"Noni—"

I cut him off. "Don't say anything, just listen. I've had a lot of time to think, and I got scared, I got scared about following my heart, about being in love with you, about going all in, about doing what I've been taught to believe was reckless and wrong. But I haven't followed my heart, pretty much my whole life, and I did with you, and it was the best decision, and you are so fucking amazing. I love how you just go all in, even if you're scared, and I want to be like that, I want to be with you, 'cause, Beau, I am so in love with you, so I'm here and this morning has been—"

Then my heart plummets to the floor. I hear him before I see him. His laugh fires a sensation up the back of my spine, tingling in my neck, which makes me turn, and I see him. With his arm around a woman. A beautiful woman. She is holding Shaquille's leash in her hand. They are laughing as they walk across the street. They are happy.

"Noni? Noni?" I stare at the speaker. "Noni, Dad's not here."

He didn't hear the speech. He doesn't know I'm here. "Zep, don't say anything. Don't say a thing, okay?" And then I start to run. Away. Away from Beau and the beautiful woman he's with.

I run down the hill, scooting around people going about their day. I run and I panic. I run and I wince from the breeze, from the stupidity, from the shock. I run and I pant and then all of a sudden I'm no longer running, because I'm tripping and tumbling and skidding down centuries-old Scottish cobblestones, slipping and hitting the ground hard. Skin tearing as my hands scrape along the ground, and my knees follow, the jacket and my T-shirt flying high as I kneel like a bare-assed bleeding sprinter squatting awkwardly about to start a race. Two women gasp as I grunt in pain, trying to get my bearings, feeling the breeze on my backside and sitting back, wincing at the sight of my hands.

"You okay, love?" An old man wearing an entire outfit of beige stares at me, startled.

I shake my head, staring at my bloody hands and my gravel-rash knees.

"Noni?" Beau yells.

I look up the hill and there he is, striding fast, hair billowing behind him, the wind embracing the fabric of his shirt and pasting it to his chest, and the image makes me laugh because I think he might actually be the most beautiful thing I've ever seen. I shake my head. No. There's no way. Not like this. I'm not having this conversation with him like this. I stand up.

"Love, are you sure you're okay?" the old man asks, helping me up, as I start to quickly hobble down the street.

"Noni!" Beau calls.

"Love, do you know this man?" the old man says, taking a step between me and Beau, who is close now. So close that I could touch him if I wanted to. "Is this man trying to hurt you?"

"What? No! Noni—" Beau says.

I don't look at him; I keep hobbling away. "It's fine. It's all good. I'm fine." Tears sting my eyes.

"Stop. Stop." He's standing in front of me, holding my shoulders, staring at me. "Are you hurt? Are you okay? What are you doing here?" I lean into his chest and I sob, because I don't know what else to do. He wraps his arms around my shoulders and folds me into his body.

Eventually I pull back and look up at him. "I'm fine, really, I'm going to go, though, okay?" I go to step around him, but he blocks me, shaking his head.

"What the fuck, Noni?"

"You're with someone and that is good. You're busy. And happy. You look happy and I don't want to ruin—"

Beau is confused. His mouth gapes, staring at me, trying to compute all of my crazy.

"I locked myself out of my apartment. I'm gonna find a locksmith and go now." I try to push past him again.

"He loves you, too, Noni." I spin on my heel and it's Zeppelin, smiling, with the beautiful woman beside him. "He's been fucking miserable without you."

"Zep." Beau shakes his head at him.

"What? You have." Zeppelin pulls a face at Beau. "Mum, this is Noni. I told you she was awesome."

It's his mum. Sabine. The beautiful woman is Sabine.

"Hi, Noni," she says.

"Hello. You're really very attractive," I tell her. "That's Sabine," I tell Beau.

"Yeah." He looks confused.

"Not your new girlfriend?"

"No." Sabine shakes her head.

"That's why you ran?" Beau asks. "I saw you just as you started sprinting away. What is Zep talking about?"

"My plan. My grand plan. That has gone so wrong. I locked myself out of my unit and I don't even have clothes on. I went to the shop." Beau looks at my outfit, and I open the jacket so he can read the shirt. "So then I got to your place and I told, who I thought was you, how I felt through the speaker so I didn't chicken out, but then I saw you with her, and you were happy, and I didn't want to ruin it—so I ran. I ran away." I watch his face trying to process it all. "I ran away and I just ran away again. And I'm sorry."

"Noni, you were pretty clear about what you wanted. About what this was," Beau says, taking a step back from me.

"I was wrong."

Beau stares at me and I stare at him, willing him to say something.

"She said she wants to go all in with you," Zeppelin says, his voice sounding desperate.

"Zeppelin," Sabine whispers.

"Dad? Tell her."

"Did you say that?" Beau looks at me.

"Yes. I did. I do."

"Are you sure?" he asks.

"More sure than I've ever been about anything."

He smiles. "That's pretty sure."

I nod, smiling back, and he grabs my face in both hands and kisses me, and kisses me, and kisses me.

"Noni?" Zeppelin's voice makes us stop and I turn and look at him. He takes a step toward me and says in a low, concerned voice, "Everyone can see your butt." I crack up laughing, and Beau shakes his head.

"Let's get you home." Beau holds my hands up, looking at their puffy, bloody state.

"We're gonna stay and get a coffee, aren't we, Zep?" Sabine says.

"But *Mum*," he says, but she lifts her eyebrows with expert motherly precision, and he nods. She smiles at me and I try to make my face express a million embarrassed apologies and thank-yous all at once.

I sit on the edge of the bath as Beau silently cleans my hands and my knees and I wince as it stings. I make sure I'm always touching some part of him as he works away at my wounds, both of us behaving like these tasks are the most important jobs we'll ever have. He finishes his first-aid duties with a kiss to my now bandaged knee. He's kneeling on the floor in front of me and I put my hands on his shoulders as he looks up at me.

"Are you really all in, Nons? Because I can't be some item on a list anymore." He sits next to me on the edge of the bath. "This has to be legit, 'cause this is my life, this is my kid's life." He stops, searching my face, and I nod. "Zep is moving here, full-time, that's what he wants. So, if you're not sure, then I can't do that to him. Have you leave. Or be unsure." I start to speak, but he takes my hand and cuts me off. "And I need to know now. So, it's okay if you're not sure."

"I wouldn't be here if I wasn't sure."

"Okay."

"I should never have left."

"Why did you?"

"I was scared."

"Of what?"

"Of everything. Of what people would think if I just packed up my whole life and moved to Scotland to be with a Viking."

Beau smiles.

"I was scared of being happy," I say.

"You deserve to be happy, Noni. It's simple."

"It is and that scared me. I'm so used to everything being difficult, or hard work." I pause. "And I'm scared of you."

"What? Why?"

I put my throbbing palm on his cheek. "Because you're so sure of yourself. Of what you want. And who you are. And that's like the sexiest thing about you." He softly takes my hand, so he's holding both. "I'm not there yet, though. I'm working on it. But I'm not where you are."

"I'm sorry if I ever made you feel pressure to be where I'm at."

"No. No. You didn't. I did that. I might only be beginning

to work out the me stuff, but I do know what I want, and what I want is you." He kisses me slowly, sweetly. "I had this whole plan worked out, there was a dress and flowers and a speech."

"Let me hear your speech," he says and I laugh and hobble to stand up in front of him.

"Okay." I gesture down my body. "Pretend this is a cute dress."

"This is much better." He flicks the T-shirt up, pretending to be shocked by my naked body underneath.

"And you have a bunch of flowers I've just given you." He nods. "I want you," I say. "I do. And I want to live here, and I want my life back, the one I made here that I didn't think was permanent, because I didn't know it was possible to actually be that happy. I thought it wasn't real. This. All of it. But it's the realest I've ever felt, and the most me, the most in love. I am so in love with you. And I'm sorry. I'm so sorry that I did that to you, that I left, that I pretended I didn't want to keep the life we'd made. It's because I didn't think I deserved it. But I do."

He stands up and wraps his arms around my waist. "You do. We do."

"What do you want?" I ask him with a smile.

"You, Noni. All of you." He hugs me tight and I throw my arms around his neck and squeeze.

"I have been so fucking miserable," he says.

"Me too. I hated being home. None of it felt right. Other than Lindell's family, nothing there brings me any joy at all."

"I can't believe you're here." He holds my face, staring at me. "And I can't believe you traipsed all through the city wearing this."

"That part did not bring me any pleasure," I say.

"So, what now?"

"Well, first, I want you to kiss me."

"Oh, really? Well, I'd hate for you to not get what you want," he says. And he kisses me, and I kiss him.

We kiss, and kiss, and kiss. The joy and relief in my body escape with a laugh. I pull back, holding his face in my hands, taking him in, his beautiful smile beaming as he looks at me, squeezing me tight as if to check it's really happening. It is. This is real.

"What do we do now, Nons?"

I shrug and smile. "Whatever we want."

★ ★ ★ ★ ★

ACKNOWLEDGMENTS

Firstly, I'd like to acknowledge the significance of getting to live and work on Aboriginal land, over which sovereignty has never been ceded. The majority of this book was written in Meanjin, on the traditional land of the Yuggera and Turrbal people. I pay my deepest and most heartfelt respects to their Elders—past, present and emerging. This was and always will be Aboriginal land.

My heart is so tremendously full for the encouragement, assistance, championing, hard work and love that has taken this book out of the Notes section in my phone and into real life.

I am so immensely grateful to the following people:

My dreamboat of an agent, Candice Thom, and my RGM team, thank you for backing me, giggling with me and telling me when my ideas are good (and bad).

Thank you to the glorious Texters—Mandy Brett, Michael Heyward and everyone at Text Publishing—it's a JOY to be part of the Text family. To my lovely editor—*it really has been a pleasure, Sam Forge*. Thank you.

To Emily Ohanjanians and MIRA Books—thank you for your unwavering belief in me and in Noni Blake.

Rebecca Starford and Bri Lee—you backed this story in the very beginning, your encouragement helped me to keep writing.

To Khadija Caffoor, Leah Napier, Jane Hultgren, Gabrielle Tozer, Jools Purchase—thank you for your help and/or encouragement. Much appreciated. Mega babes the lot of you.

To my dear friend Michelle Law—you, me, Paul and Beau—double date? Yes. Love you.

Rose Thrupp—you're a dead-set fucking glorious creature in every sense. So much love and gratitude.

To my TRACTION babes, my Mama's Boys, and my Con kids—dream big, dears. Telling stories is a joy, and a privilege, and how grateful I am that I get to do that with you all.

To my friends—thank you for being big, glorious, brilliant nerds who make me giggle. I love you.

To the women who contributed their ideas and thoughts about pleasure in the survey that inspired huge parts in this book—thank you.

To the Claire and Pearl community—you big babes. Thanks for supporting my shit.

To Sanja Simic, Dave Burton, Heidi Irvine and Sam Holmes—thank you for backing me, telling me I can, and should. I love you.

Jacq Horvat, my brave best—thank you for championing my pleasure always. I love you.

Toby Madonna—I just think you're kind of very…good. *Thank you. Thank you. Thank you.*

To Nan (you'll like this one—it's sexy), Grandad, Liam, Anne, Felix, Uncle Steve, and Aunty Theresa—I love you all. My glorious family. So grateful for your belief in me always. And to Chris, Cathy and Carla—thank you for your love and support.

Dad, you taught me to dream big and then work hard to get it...the best lessons of them all. I love you, moo.

Mum, my love, my witch, my shadow. You have made, and make, everything possible for me. The woman I am is because of the woman you are.

Steve and Midge—It's a pleasure doing life with you. I love you. And I like you. A lot.

And you, you glorious bloody book-reading human, my goodness, thank you. I really hope you find ways to center pleasure in your life. As Beau would say... *What do you want?* Because you should totally do / eat / dye / buy / get / kiss / fuck / tattoo / leave / say that thing. Yeah. You really should. If you think it'll feel good—well, I'm happy to take the blame for that.

All my love. And gratitude.
Claire

IT'S BEEN
A PLEASURE,
NONI BLAKE

CLAIRE CHRISTIAN

Reader's Guide

1. What do you think of the overall concept of Noni's story—putting oneself first and the singular pursuit of pleasure?

2. Does the idea of Noni's trip to Europe, and her wish to simply pursue pleasure, appeal to you? Which part of it appeals to you most?

3. Would you ever consider going on your own pleasure quest? What would your pleasure quest look like?

4. Noni, Lindell and Graham write their "*should-have-could-have-would-have*" lists about people they never slept with but wish they had. Do you have such a list, not necessarily for sexual dalliances but for any paths not taken in your life?

5. Do you agree with Lindell's assertion that we get used to ourselves as we age, and that's what makes us more comfortable with ourselves in general? How have you found you've changed and grown as you've gotten older?

6. Noni has to work hard to speak nicely to herself, versus saying damaging things to herself, which comes more

naturally to her. Do you think women are harder on themselves than men are on themselves? If so, why do you think that is? What feeds the narrative that runs through women's minds?

7. Before she commits to embarking on her pleasure quest, Noni makes a decision she regrets—to sleep with Ben. She feels no but says yes. What did you think of her decision to go home with him when so much of her didn't want to? Why do you think she went against her better judgment?

8. When Noni meets Lil at the yoga retreat in Scotland, Lil tells her: "There were already so many things in the world, even people, that were inevitably going to make me unhappy, and I didn't know why I'd been letting myself be the main culprit for so long." What did you think of this statement? Do you think we are often the culprits of our own unhappiness? If so, how can we overcome this?

9. Noni makes a list under the header "What Pleasure Looks Like to Me" that includes points like being the first on the dance floor, or wearing whatever you want. What would your list look like? What would ultimate pleasure look like to you?

10. Despite her growing confidence, Noni doesn't understand why Beau could want someone like her. Why do you think that is? Can you identify with her feelings within their relationship?

11. Did you have a favorite scene in the novel? What was it? Why was it your favorite?

12. If you were to cast the movie version of It's Been a Pleasure, Noni Blake, who would you cast in the various roles?

What inspired you to write *It's Been a Pleasure, Noni Blake*?

I read, or listened to, Elizabeth Gilbert say something along the lines of pay attention to the conversations you keep having, because there could be energy in that...it could be your muse trying to tell you something. So, I paid attention and realized I kept having conversations with predominantly women who would reflect back on their lives and says things like "If I knew then what I know now..." Or "If I felt the way I do about myself now, then, well, lots of things in my life would be different." And I found that concept fascinating—woman feeling more confident in herself trying to go back and do things differently. That's what book I thought I was writing when I began... Noni having sex with the people she wished she had. But then it became about more, it became about Noni and valuing the pleasure in her life. The more I read and wrote about women and pleasure, the more I realized it had to be about more than just sex. I did an anonymous survey very early on, asking women what they thought about pleasure, about fantasies, about what in their lives would be different if they prioritized pleasure...a lot of the moments in the book came from those insights.

Could you identify with Noni's character? How?

Absolutely. I love the woman I'm becoming the older I get. I feel far more confident in myself now than ever before, and I care far less about what people think about me. I feel like I'm finally at a moment where I'm really valuing my intuition and what I want. Believing that voice, or impulse, and then acting on it— it takes practice, but I'm getting better. I really, truly believe that you can't go wrong if you value your own internal knowing more than anything else.

Have you ever considered embarking on your own pleasure quest?

I'd love to go on a Noni-shaped pleasure quest, absolutely. But I think my version of the pleasure quest is much more of a slow burn. Small things, every day, feel big and important. Doing things differently than I may have done in the past. Speaking up. Following my gut. Making choices that really reflect what I want and how I want to feel. Being clear about boundaries. Valuing what makes me feel good in any given moment. I want my whole life to be a pleasure quest.

Do you have a favorite secondary character in the book? Who is it, and why?

If I had to choose, I think I'd have to say Lindell. He's such an important ally for Noni. He helps her be brave. I feel very fortunate to have a few Lindell's in my life.

What was the most challenging part of writing this book? What was the most enjoyable?

It wasn't necessarily challenging, but perhaps the bit I feel most vulnerable about, especially as this is my first contemporary romance novel, is that sex scenes I've written will be read by others. I have been amused by the idea of people I know reading them and having quite an intimate insight into my mind. The most enjoyable part, hands down, was anything to do with Beau. Dreaming up this emotionally savvy, sexy, present, Viking-like dreamboat was a joy. I wanted to create an authentic character, a real-life complicated character that would also make readers swoon.

Can you describe your writing process? Do you tend to outline first or dive right in and figure out the details as you go along?

I am a pantser through and through. Yup. I happily fly by the seat of my pants and then see what unravels. I tend to not write sequentially either. I think it's my theater background. I think about moments as scenes, what's being said, and how it feels, first. I write the scenes that have the most energy first. Usually I'm pretty clear about the beginning, middle and end, and then I spend a lot of time filling in the blanks. I've realized this isn't an entirely time-savvy way to create, as I end up deleting a lot of words, and having to hone logistical things I've missed at the back end, so I'm now trying to find a process that helps me plan more but still allows me the freedom to be surprised.

Can you tell us anything about what you're working on next?

I'm currently writing a novel that I'm calling a love letter to female friendship. It's about two single mums who are best friends, who, after the devastating collapse of both their long-term relationships, decide to move in together to make their lives easier. Their new week-on, week-off custody arrangements line up, and they're both ready to dive back into the dating pool and be wingwoman for each other...one week at a time. I want the book to be a reminder that people have the power to dictate the terms of their lives and relationships... which seems to be a reoccurring theme for me lately.